No
Rings
~~Attached~~

Come Away with Me

"Rachel Lacey has become a go-to author for heartwarming books."

—Jude in the Stars

"*Come Away with Me* is beautifully written."

—Rainbow Moose's Reviews

"Utterly delightful!"

—Thoughts of a Blonde

"Looking for a well-crafted, heartfelt lesfic romance? Rachel Lacey's *Come Away with Me* is a lovely one."

—The Lesbian Book Blog

Risking It All Series

Love to the Rescue Series

No Rings Attached

a novel

RACHEL LACEY

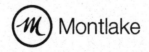

Published by Montlake, Seattle

www.apub.com

Amazon, the Amazon logo, and Montlake are trademarks of Amazon.com, Inc., or its affiliates.

ISBN-13: 9781542037419
ISBN-10: 1542037417

Cover design by Caroline Teagle Johnson

Printed in the United States of America

No
Rings
~~Attached~~

CHAPTER ONE

"I can't believe I have to fly to London alone." Lia Harris carefully folded the garment bag containing her bridesmaid dress into her luggage, feeling her mood fold along with it. She zipped her suitcase and set it on the floor with a thump. She'd planned this trip down to the last detail, and yet somehow, she'd failed to prepare for this moment.

"It's such a bummer," Rosie agreed, sitting cross-legged on Lia's bed with her little dog, Brinkley, in her lap. "I wish I could go with you."

"So do I," Lia said, trying not to sound as wistful as she felt. Rosie was her best friend, but since she owned Between the Pages Bookstore and Café and Lia managed the store, they had to alternate their days off.

When Lia had first learned that her brother was getting married, she'd dearly hoped she would have a partner to bring with her on the big day, because her family had been insufferable lately in their quest to see her happily paired off. The problem was, despite many, *many* dates, Lia remained frustratingly single. One by one, her friends had fallen in love. In less than a week, both her siblings would be married, and Lia would still stand alone.

Worse, her ex would be at the wedding, and her mother was on a mission to get them back together. Lia hated that she was preoccupied with her dating woes ahead of such an important weekend. She loved weddings, and she was especially excited to see her brother tie the knot. If only she had someone special to bring with her . . .

At the other end of the apartment, the front door swung open with a distinctive squeak, followed by a thump as it bumped the stopper.

"Dinner's here!" a voice called.

"Yay." Rosie set Brinkley down and stood, brushing a hand through her blonde curls. Brinkley trotted out of the room, and Lia and Rosie followed him down the hall, where the rest of their roommates had gathered around several large white paper bags on the kitchen table.

"The containers marked with a *C* are chicken piccata," Paige said as she began to unpack the bags of food. "The rest are portobello wellington."

"Mm," Rosie said appreciatively as she took one of the wellingtons. "You're spoiling us tonight."

Paige worked at her girlfriend Nikki's catering company, and occasionally, they were able to bring home leftovers. The food was extremely well timed for Lia tonight, because she needed to leave for the airport in about fifteen minutes and now she wouldn't have to eat there.

"Thank you," Lia told Paige as she took a container of chicken piccata.

"You bet. All packed?" Paige asked.

"Yes." She smiled, feeling a spark of excitement about her trip, even though she'd be making it alone. The UK was lovely in June. Too often, she only went home at Christmastime, when the weather was cold and dreary. And because tomorrow was Wednesday, she'd have a whole day to herself in London before she drove to her parents' house for the wedding.

"Don't forget lip balm," Paige said. "Airplanes always dry me out."

"And earbuds so you can listen to music . . . or an audiobook," Jane said as she walked into the kitchen. She paused to kiss Rosie before selecting a meal for herself. "This smells amazing."

Paige beamed at her. "Thanks."

Nikki brought plates and utensils to the table, and they all moved around each other, preparing their plates.

Lia took her usual seat at the end of the table as Brinkley nosed around her feet, already looking for any morsels she might have dropped. "I've got lip balm and earbuds."

"They've been in your bag for days," Rosie teased as she sat beside her. "Your suitcase has basically been packed since last weekend."

"You're so much more organized than I am," Nikki said. "I'm a total last-minute packer."

Lia shrugged as she bit into her chicken. Yes, she was organized. She planned ahead. And yet, she couldn't seem to plan her love life, no matter how hard she tried. She imagined her mother's reaction when she arrived for the wedding weekend alone: the disapproving look she'd receive, followed by a lecture about her age, and then the matchmaking would begin. Dread soured her stomach.

"Do your parents still think you're bringing your girlfriend this weekend?" Paige asked, giving her a sympathetic look.

"Unfortunately, yes." A few months ago, Lia had dated a woman for several weeks, long enough that she'd become hopeful. Long enough that she'd told her mother about her. Lia got ahead of herself and planned too far into the future with the wrong person, an unfortunate habit she was trying to break. But when the relationship ended, she'd never set the record straight with her parents. It had been so easy to let a nonexistent girlfriend keep her mother from obsessing about finding someone suitable for Lia to date.

"So you're not going to tell them until you get there?" Rosie asked.

"Would it be awful if I just tell them she couldn't make it?" Lia asked as she looked at her friends. Rosie and Jane sat beside her, and Paige and Nikki were across from them. Two couples. Even in her own apartment, Lia was the odd one out these days.

"If it would make the weekend easier for you, I say go for it," Nikki offered.

"I'm never going to hear the end of it if they find out I'm single again, especially with Asher there," Lia lamented. Her ex was a big part of the reason Lia had left the UK and moved to New York in the first place.

"Well, here's an idea . . . what if I call Grace?" Rosie suggested. "If she's not busy, maybe she could pretend to be your girlfriend for the weekend."

Lia rolled her eyes. "Your imaginary friend? Forgive me for being skeptical that she'd show up." Grace was Rosie's best friend from high school, and she was notorious for backing out of things at the last minute, so unreliable that Lia had never even met the woman. After Grace bailed on one of her planned visits a few years ago, Lia had jokingly called her Rosie's imaginary friend, because it was ludicrous that none of Rosie's friends had met her, and the name had stuck.

"It's hard for her to make it to New York," Rosie said, sounding pensive. "But she's not flaky otherwise, and as you know, she moved to London a few months ago. It's late over there now, but I'll call her in the morning, okay? Worst case, she says no. Best case, you get a date to the wedding after all, and my two best friends will finally meet."

Grace Poston sipped her coffee as she walked home from lunch, her gaze drifting from the ornately carved buildings before her to the gray-tinted sky above, and if it was possible, she fell a little bit more in love with London. Okay, the weather wasn't her favorite, but she would happily put up with it to be here in the city. After she'd spent over a decade in the Spanish countryside, London's hustle and bustle felt like a homecoming. It reminded her of growing up in Manhattan, and as she strolled through her new neighborhood, she felt alive in a way she hadn't in years.

She'd needed a change, and so far, this seemed to be a good one. Humming along with the Spanish pop tune playing through her ear-buds, she turned the corner and let herself into the building where she lived. She climbed the steps to her third-floor flat and shoved the key in the door, jiggling it until the lock caught and turned.

"Honey, I'm home," she announced as she stepped through the door, tugging the earbuds from her ears.

"You have *got* to stop that," Oliver said, looking up from his spot on the couch, but his eyes twinkled with amusement despite his stern tone.

"Oh, humor me. I've always wanted to say it," she said, because it was fun to needle him, but she'd lived alone for a long time, and it was surprisingly fun to have a roommate. Maybe she'd get sick of it, but for now, she was loving everything about her new life in the city.

"London brings out an odd side of you, Gracie."

"A fun side, I think you mean."

He leaned forward to grab the remote control and silenced the TV. "Speaking of fun, the crew is going out for drinks tonight after the show. They've been asking after you. Say you'll come?"

"Of course I'll come." She'd enjoyed herself the last time she'd gone out with Ollie's friends from the theater, even though Violet had persistently hit on Grace despite her multiple attempts to tell her she wasn't interested.

She sipped her coffee as she headed to her bedroom to work for the rest of the afternoon. An office was a luxury she no longer had, although the small desk she'd set up in the corner of her room was working well so far. She'd known returning to the city would mean sacrificing some of the comforts of her country life, including her home office, but her job as a translator for *Modern Style* magazine meant she could work anywhere, so when Ollie had dangled the bait that he was looking for a new roommate here in London, she'd jumped at the chance.

After her grandmother died last year, there was no longer any reason for her to stay in Spain. On the contrary, she felt as if she'd outstayed her welcome. Grace couldn't seem to stay in places where she'd lost someone, so she did what she did best—she left.

With a sigh, she set her insulated cup on the desk and turned on her laptop, stretching her arms over her head as she waited for it to boot up.

The tinny notes of Miley Cyrus's "Party in the U.S.A." played from the bed, the ringtone she'd assigned Rosie many years ago, and Grace smiled as she spun in her seat to grab the phone.

There wasn't much about America that appealed to Grace these days, but Rosie was the exception to that rule. They'd met in eighth grade and had been inseparable all the way through high school. At this point, she felt almost like family. Grace connected the call. "Hello, beautiful."

"Hello yourself," Rosie said with a smile in her voice. "How's London?"

"Gloomy and gray and just perfect," Grace answered. "I love it."

"I'm glad. As soon as things are more settled at the store, I want to visit."

"I'm going to hold you to that," Grace told her. "And bring Jane with you, because I'm dying to meet her."

"That feeling is mutual. You're something of a mythical creature to my friends at this point," Rosie joked.

Grace flinched. Yes, she knew she had a bad habit of backing out of her planned trips to the States. As much as she missed Rosie and as much as it made her sick to acknowledge how long it had been since she'd seen her paternal grandparents, every time she tried to board a flight to New York City, she just . . . couldn't do it. There were certain ghosts from her past that she wasn't ready to face, and they all resided in New York. "I'm sorry. I want to see your new store so much. This year, I promise."

"I hope so," Rosie said. "It's been entirely too long since I've seen you. But listen, I have a favor to ask . . . kind of a big favor, but hear me out."

"Sure," Grace agreed.

"Lia's brother is getting married just outside London this weekend, and she needs a date to the wedding."

Grace could feel her face scrunching up as Rosie spoke. She rubbed a hand over her forehead, because she hated weddings. She hated everything about them. And Lia . . . well, it wasn't her fault that Grace resented her for her importance in Rosie's life, but Grace couldn't help the way she felt.

Once upon a time, Grace had been Rosie's best friend, and now Lia held that honor. They'd gone to college together in Manhattan, and now Lia was Rosie's manager at Between the Pages. They were always together, while Grace had fled New York after high school and never looked back. But despite the ocean between them, Grace still thought of Rosie as her best friend. No one else had ever come close to being as important to her as Rosie.

She knew she was one of Rosie's closest friends, but Rosie had a lot of close friends, while Grace only had one. It was an awkward thing when your best friend considered someone else *their* best friend. And Grace dealt with it by . . . avoidance. If running from your problems were an Olympic sport, Grace would be a gold medalist. She'd have a whole shelf full of gold medals.

"Grace?" Rosie said in her ear, reminding her that she hadn't yet responded.

"I hate weddings," she said on a sigh. She hated weddings almost as much as she hated the idea of attending one with Lia. *Ugh, Lia.* But Rosie never asked for favors, even though she must know that Grace would do pretty much anything for her.

"I know you do," Rosie said. "And this would involve spending the whole weekend at Lia's parents' house in Sevenoaks, so if it's too much or if you already have plans, feel free to say no."

"Well, I'm meeting a few friends for dinner on Saturday night, but I guess I could cancel. Why can't she just go alone?" Grace asked.

"She can, and she will, but you know how her family is." Now Rosie sighed, and yes, Grace had heard stories of Lia's uptight family and how relentlessly they hounded her to settle down. If there was anything in this situation Grace could relate to, it was the discomfort that came from being pressured to fall in love when it wasn't what she wanted. "Lia told her family she'd be bringing her girlfriend this weekend, to get them off her back, and now she needs to either find someone to fill that role or be hassled about it all weekend."

"So I'd have to pretend to be her girlfriend?" Grace asked, pressing a hand against her forehead. Pretending to be Lia's girlfriend was a much bigger deal than just being her date to the wedding.

"Yes," Rosie confirmed. "I mean, you don't have to kiss her or anything; just hang out with her all weekend. Anyway, I know it's a huge favor, but maybe you and Lia could at least grab a drink together and talk it through? She's staying in London tonight."

"Fair enough," Grace conceded. "I guess the day has finally come when Lia and I meet in person."

Lia's eyes were gritty behind her glasses as she made her way down the jet bridge into Heathrow Airport. Her flight had been delayed out of New York, and consequently it was already past noon here in London. Lia never slept well on overnight flights. She'd watched two movies and dozed a bit here and there, and now, she was exhausted.

Still, she was excited to be back in the UK, and she had the rest of the day to herself in London before she drove to her parents' house in Sevenoaks tomorrow. She'd hoped to spend the afternoon at the British Museum. Lia's love of museums—and this one in particular—was legendary among her friends, but with her delayed arrival, there probably wasn't time. Maybe she'd nap instead.

Lia yawned as she inched through the customs line, scrolling through notifications on her phone as it pulled in everything she'd missed while she'd been over the Atlantic. There were several texts from Rosie, an email from her mother, and a text from an unknown number. Lia clicked on that one first.

Unknown:
At long last we meet! Dinner tonight to get introductions out of the way? ~ Grace

Lia Harris:
That sounds perfect. Just name the time and place, and I'll be there.

Lia stored Grace's number in her contacts, too tired to work out how she felt about seeing Grace tonight. While she was undeniably curious and even a little bit excited to finally meet Rosie's elusive friend, she wasn't sure she wanted to spend several days with her at her parents' house, pretending Grace was her girlfriend. She had serious doubts that Grace would even agree to the plan, but at least they'd finally meet.

Lia sent off a quick message to Rosie and one to her mom, letting them know she'd arrived safely. What felt like a million hours later, she finally left the airport and made her way to the underground. From there, she rode the train downtown and checked into her hotel. Her room was small but clean, and right now, that bed was calling her name. She freshened up in the bathroom and climbed right in, then set an alarm to wake herself in an hour so she wouldn't sleep through dinner with Grace.

When the alarm jolted her awake at four o'clock, she grumbled into her pillow, reaching blindly for her phone to shut it off. She felt groggy and out of sorts, with a dull headache from her disjointed sleep and probably some dehydration from the flight. She got up, drank a glass of water from the sink, and took a shower.

Grace had texted her the name of a pub in Covent Garden and asked if Lia wanted to go with her to a show afterward. Apparently, Grace's roommate was one of the performers. Lia sent her a quick confirmation, and then she finished getting ready and headed out. She hopped on the Tube and rode across town, taking a quick detour to walk through the gardens along the Thames for some much-needed fresh air before she made her way to the Flying Pig.

The pub was loud and crowded, and *God*, she'd missed this. She did love an English pub. There was nothing quite like it in the States. She'd arrived right on time, but there was no sign of Grace, so Lia made her way to the bar and ordered an amber ale. She and Grace were Facebook friends, so Lia was confident she'd recognize her when she saw her . . . *if* she saw her.

Because it wouldn't surprise Lia a bit if Grace bailed on her, and this time, she could hardly even blame her. It couldn't be Grace's idea of a good time to spend the weekend with Lia and her family, pretending to be her girlfriend. She sipped her beer, relaxing on the stool as the noise of the bar swallowed her up.

She was halfway through her beer before she saw a familiar figure slip through the door, and . . . wow. Grace was a striking woman. Her hair was dark brown, hanging almost to her waist in loose, shiny waves. Her complexion was several shades darker than Lia's, and her lips were painted a vivacious red. She wore a black knit dress that clung to her figure, and as she scanned the bar, her gaze settled on Lia.

Grace's smile brightened, and she crossed the bar as Lia stood from her stool to greet her. She was significantly taller than Grace, who leaned in for a quick hug and an air-kiss on each cheek, reminding Lia of how long she'd lived in Europe.

"So you do exist," Lia said as they faced each other.

Grace's expression hardened, just slightly, just enough for Lia to realize she'd offended her, which was not at all the first impression she'd wanted to make. "I sure do," Grace said lightly. "And you—as I had apparently forgotten—are British."

Lia nodded with a smile. "We make an interesting pair, a Brit from New York and an American living in London."

"Yes, we do," Grace agreed. "Should we get a table, or do you want to stay at the bar?"

"A table," Lia said. "I'm starved. I haven't eaten since my flight."

Grace led the way to the hostess desk, where they were shown to a small table against the back wall. Grace settled across from her, and for a moment, they regarded each other in silence. Lia wasn't shy, and she didn't get the impression that Grace was, either, but something seemed to be making this awkward. Maybe it was the way they'd known each other peripherally for so many years through Rosie without ever meeting in person, or maybe it was the fact that Grace had come here tonight because Lia needed a wedding date.

Grace lowered her gaze to the drink menu in front of her. "You must be tired after your flight."

"Exhausted," Lia confirmed. "But I had a nap at the hotel, so I'm hoping it will fuel me through the evening."

"That's good," Grace said, toying with a strand of her hair as she studied the menu, and well, this conversation was off to a stilted start.

"How do you like London so far?" Lia asked.

Grace immediately brightened, looking up with a smile. "It was love at first sight. I'd forgotten how much I love city life. So yeah, I think this was a good move."

"I'm glad," Lia said. "I'm a city girl as well. Do you know many people here yet?"

"Mostly just my roommate, Oliver, so far. We met through a mutual friend in Spain. He's a dancer, so he's introduced me to plenty of his theater friends, and they're a lot of fun."

"Is Oliver just your roommate?" Lia asked, because a boyfriend would make her request even more awkward, and she wasn't sure of Grace's sexuality. She'd always had the impression that Grace was queer—and Rosie probably wouldn't have suggested this if Grace were straight—but Lia couldn't actually remember her mentioning Grace's dating anyone.

"Roommate only," Grace confirmed. "He's gay. I'm gay. My ideal roommate situation. No potential for awkward attraction."

"That's good," Lia said with a laugh. "Somehow, I share an apartment with several other queer women, and we've managed to avoid any uncomfortable attraction between friends."

"I'm super intimidated by your roommate situation," Grace admitted. "Ollie's actually my first roommate since college. I lived alone in Spain, but I think I prefer rooming with a man for that very reason."

"Luckily, I'm not prone to crushes on my friends," Lia said.

"Never?" Grace asked, eyebrows raised.

Lia spun her beer glass, thinking. "No, actually. Never."

"That's impressive," Grace said. "I thought it was, like, a lesbian requirement to fall for at least one of your friends."

"Well, I'm not a lesbian," Lia told her.

"Bi?" Grace asked.

"Yes. So you have, then? Fallen for a friend?"

"Once," Grace told her, dropping her gaze to the menu again.

"Hello, ladies," their waiter said, interrupting their conversation before Lia could ask more. "Can I start you off with another pint? Or are you ready to order?"

Grace ordered a lager and a chicken salad, while Lia got another ale and the steak pie, because she was famished, and it was an indulgence she missed in New York.

"So," Grace said after he'd left, propping her elbows on the table as she stared at Lia. "Let's talk about this wedding."

"Please feel free to say no," Lia told her. "I'm really glad I got to meet you tonight, but the wedding involves a whole weekend with my family and letting them think you're my girlfriend, so it's kind of a huge ask."

"It is," Grace agreed, looking none too thrilled at the prospect. "And for the record, I hate weddings."

"Then let's just have dinner and leave it at that," Lia told her. It was one thing to bring an actual girlfriend with her to London. It would be another thing entirely to pretend with Grace, who was essentially a stranger. There was a lingering awkwardness between them that made Lia think she might prefer to spend the weekend on her own, even though her mother would be insufferable if she showed up alone.

"Rosie was awfully persuasive on the phone on your behalf," Grace said, sounding skeptical. "Aren't you even going to try to convince me?"

CHAPTER TWO

"Give me your best pitch," Grace told Lia. "Maybe I'll say yes." She didn't want to go to this wedding with Lia, not even a little bit, but she was curious why it was so important to her that she'd even consider taking Grace.

Lia sat back in her chair, giving Grace a long look as she drank her beer. She was an attractive woman, with wavy, light-brown hair and glasses that gave her a bit of a studious look. In fact, Grace had always gotten a serious vibe from Lia's Facebook posts, but she didn't come across that way in person. There was humor lurking behind Lia's words, and her clothing suggested she was more of a free spirit. She wore a blue skirt with an off-the-shoulder white top that flattered her figure, and her accent was sexy as hell. Grace had always been a sucker for a British accent.

"Here's the thing," Lia said finally. "I'm the middle child in a very traditional, career-oriented family. My younger sister, Audrey, is married and working as a psychologist. My older brother, Colin, is getting married this weekend. He and his wife-to-be work in the financial sector. My parents are both doctors. And I, as my mother so eloquently puts it, moved an ocean away to work in retail while sharing an apartment with four other women. Perhaps, if I put my degree to better use, I'd be a museum curator by now. Maybe then I'd be able to find a man willing to settle down with me."

Grace flinched. "I'm sorry. I've known families like that. Are they not supportive of your sexuality?"

Lia shrugged, pushing at her glasses. "On the surface, they're very supportive. But while they've welcomed my girlfriends, they've also dropped some not-so-subtle hints that they're hoping I'll marry a man."

Grace sighed. "And that just makes me want to flaunt my very gay self all over that wedding this weekend."

Lia's lips twitched with a smile. "Earlier this year, I dated a woman for a few weeks. I thought it might be the start of something serious, and when my mum started needling me, I just blurted out that I was seeing someone. I usually don't tell her unless things are serious, but *God*, it was so nice to have a reprieve from her constant inquiries into my relationship status."

"But you and this woman broke up?" Grace asked.

Lia nodded. "We broke up, but somehow . . . I never told my mother."

"Oh jeez," Grace said.

Lia sighed. "Right. So she thinks I'm bringing this girlfriend to the wedding. I never gave her any specifics, so she has no idea who my girlfriend is. It could easily be you."

"Hmm," Grace said. She could totally understand how that had happened, and while she balked at anything resembling an actual relationship, maybe she could handle a fake one.

"The real kicker is that my ex will be there, as well as his parents," Lia told her. "Both of our mothers are still convinced we'd be the perfect couple, and I have a feeling that he agrees with them."

"He's still into you?" Grace asked.

Lia's lips pressed into a thin line. "According to my mother, he's still interested, but I don't know for sure. It's been a long time."

"How long?"

"Secondary school. We dated for three years in our teens, and I did love him, but I didn't feel like he was the one, you know? Our families were talking about sending us to the same university and planning our eventual marriage. I felt suffocated, to the point that I broke up with him and enrolled in college in New York."

"He's the reason you moved to New York?" Grace's eyebrows rose. "Wow."

"He's a big part of the reason," Lia said. "I had a very sheltered upbringing, and I wanted to see the world. I wanted to have an adventure. Plus, I'd just realized I was bi, and I wanted the chance to date girls."

"Well, good for you. Was the adventure worth it?"

"It was." Lia stared into her beer, lips pursed, looking suddenly less confident.

"You sure about that?" Grace asked.

Lia lifted one shoulder in a halfhearted shrug. "I guess the adventure didn't play out exactly how I'd envisioned it, but I have no regrets."

"What part didn't go to plan?"

"Traveling," Lia said. "I wanted to go places. I wanted to explore museums in every city I could find."

"Interesting," Grace said, and she meant it. She sipped her beer, picturing young Lia exploring museums around the world. The image made her smile. "So why didn't you?"

"Rosie's mum got sick right after we graduated, and then she and I took over the bookstore together. That store keeps us busy."

"Yes, it does," Grace agreed. She hadn't visited in a long time, but it seemed like Rosie was always at the store, and she assumed Lia was too. And this was the thing she and Lia had in common . . . their love for Rosie.

"So my grand adventure began and ended in Manhattan, but like I said . . . no regrets."

"Because of Rosie?" Grace asked.

Lia nodded as she lifted her beer. "I'd do anything for her."

That made two of them, and it was the reason Grace was going to say yes. She was deeply uncomfortable with the idea of spending an entire weekend with Lia's family, pretending to be her girlfriend, but she owed Rosie for all the times she'd bailed on her over the years. At least Lia was better company than Grace had expected. Under different circumstances, she might actually enjoy hanging out with her. "All right. I'll do it. I'll be your wedding date."

Lia and Grace arrived at the theater just before seven. Lia paused for a moment to study the posters on the building. Grace's roommate was part of an ensemble musical called *Inside Out* that Lia wasn't familiar with. She enjoyed going to the theater, though, so she was looking forward to the evening ahead.

Actually, she was so relieved that Grace had agreed to be her fake girlfriend for the weekend that nothing could spoil her mood tonight. This musical was just the icing on her London-themed wedding cake.

"Ready?" Grace asked. The light from the marquee cast a golden glow over her face and highlighted the way that dress clung to her curves. *Stunning.*

"Yeah." Lia pushed her hands into the pockets of her skirt and gave her head a quick shake, because while there was no denying Grace was a beautiful woman, she was also one of Rosie's best friends, so a real relationship between her and Lia would be extremely complicated, to say the least. She followed Grace to the door, where an usher scanned the tickets on Grace's phone. "Have you seen the show yet?" Lia asked.

"Yes," Grace told her. "This'll be my third time. I'm kind of a theater buff, or at least I used to be, before I moved to Spain."

"Don't they have much theater?" Lia asked as they stepped inside. She took a moment to look around, because she loved old theaters, although the lobby of this one was fairly small and crowded, preventing her from soaking up the ambiance.

"They do," Grace told her, "but I lived too far outside the city to take advantage of it."

"So you went to a lot of Broadway shows before you left New York?"

A funny expression crossed Grace's face, one Lia couldn't quite read. She knew Grace's parents had died in a car crash when she was a teenager and that she'd lived with Rosie and her mom for a while afterward before moving to Spain to be near her grandmother, and suddenly, Lia felt inconsiderate for bringing it up. Rosie had lost her mom at a young age, too, but she loved to talk about her and reminisce on fond memories, to the point where perhaps Lia had forgotten that not everyone handled grief in a similar way.

"I love Broadway," Grace said, casual smile back in place. "In fact, when I was a little girl, I wanted to be one of those glamorous people onstage, singing and dancing in fancy costumes. I was pretty smitten with the idea."

"Did you ever give it a try?"

Grace laughed quietly as she led the way into the seating area. "No. I took dance lessons for a few years, but alas, I'm not very good at it. I do love watching, though."

Lia paused in the doorway as she swept her gaze around the theater. It was oval shaped with a high ceiling, intricately painted in a baroque style with sculpted molding that was brightly gilded. The seats were a plush rose-colored velvet, and the stage loomed before them, currently cloaked in a white curtain. "Wow."

"Beautiful, isn't it?" Grace looked around with appreciation. "It took my breath away the first time I stepped inside."

"It's taking mine right now." Lia stood there another moment while she soaked it all in, loving the rush she got in a building like this, an architectural high. When she glanced beside her, Grace was watching her quietly. "Sorry. Just geeking out a little bit."

"Well, don't apologize for that," Grace said. "Too many people go through life without taking time to appreciate the little things that bring them joy."

"Deep thoughts," Lia said as they walked to their seats, about midway back in the stalls. "These are great seats."

"A few weeks ago, I downloaded an app that has daily lotteries for last-minute free and reduced-price seats to most shows. I've been putting my name into as many drawings as I can, and I've gotten to see so many shows."

"Ah, yes. I do that in New York as well."

"So what's the plan for tomorrow?" Grace asked as they took their seats.

"I've rented a car for the weekend, so I could pick you up at your place around three? My parents are expecting us for dinner."

Grace rolled her lips inward, then nodded. "All right."

"Is that okay for you, work-wise? I'm sorry for disrupting your week." Lia wasn't sure if she was imagining the awkwardness between them now that the wedding had come up.

"I'll need to work at least a few hours on Friday, as long as you don't mind me hiding away somewhere with my laptop."

"Oh, that's totally fine. Take as much time as you need. What do you do exactly as a translator?"

"I work for *Modern Style* magazine. Essentially, I translate their issues into Spanish for the international market."

"You translate the entire magazine?" Lia asked.

Grace shook her head with a smile. "There's a team of us."

"Did you grow up bilingual, or did you learn Spanish after you moved to Spain?"

"A little of both," Grace told her, and there was something wistful, almost sad, in her expression. "My mom was born and raised there, so she often spoke Spanish with me, and we visited a lot while I was growing up, but I wasn't fully bilingual until I moved there. English is definitely my first and strongest language."

"I'm fascinated with languages," Lia told her. "But despite many years of French and Latin classes, I am completely inept at learning anything but English."

Grace's lips curved in amusement. "That's a shame, but I suppose I can overlook your shortcoming since you speak with such a beautiful accent."

It wasn't the first time someone had told Lia they loved her accent. Americans seemed to have an odd fascination with accents, which she didn't entirely understand. She didn't mind the way Americans spoke, but she'd never found a certain accent more appealing than another. She'd be curious to hear Grace speak Spanish, though.

The lights dimmed, indicating that the show was about to begin. Around them, people began to move toward their seats.

"Oliver is part of the dance ensemble?" she asked.

"Yes," Grace told her. "He'll be out during the first musical number, about ten minutes into the show. He's the one in the red pants. You can't miss him."

"Got it," Lia said with a nod.

She and Grace fell quiet while they waited for the show to start, and Lia took the opportunity to look around again, absorbing the atmosphere in the theater. It really was beautiful, and the buzz of the crowd was exciting. Even though she didn't know anything about this show or its actors—other than Grace's roommate—she was looking forward to it. There was nothing like the energy of a live performance.

Her gaze drifted to Grace, who had leaned back in her seat and was reading something on her phone. No matter what happened this weekend, Lia was glad for the chance to have met her. Grace was important to Rosie, and that made her important to Lia as well. Besides that, Grace was an interesting person to talk to, and she certainly seemed to be a loyal friend, since she was willing to do this enormous favor for Lia basically because Rosie had asked her to.

Lia didn't take something like that lightly. She was loyal to her core, and it seemed that was something she and Grace had in common, although it also made her wonder why Grace didn't visit Rosie more often. Why hadn't she come to see the new store or to meet Jane? Grace worked remotely, which would allow her to attend Colin's wedding with Lia, so why didn't she just bring her laptop with her to New York for a visit?

Lia felt somewhat guilty for all the times she'd called Grace "Rosie's imaginary friend" now that she'd met her, but still . . . she did wonder why Grace was so elusive at times. She certainly seemed steady and reliable in her everyday life.

But then again, that remained to be seen. She might ghost Lia tomorrow when it came time to drive to Sevenoaks. She'd certainly backed out of enough events in Rosie's life at the last minute. Lia wouldn't count on Grace's attendance until they were in the car together.

Grace tossed back the shot in front of her as Oliver's hands settled on her shoulders. Liquor warmed her belly, and the bass of the dance floor thumped in her chest. She beamed at Ollie, glad she and Lia had joined him and some of the other dancers from *Inside Out* at the bar where they often congregated after the show.

She'd needed a night out, a chance to cut loose before she spent the next few days at Lia's parents' house for the wedding. She wasn't looking forward to it, but she had to reluctantly admit that she liked Lia more than she'd expected to. She was straightforward and had a good sense of humor, and her devotion to Rosie was evident, which earned her big points with Grace.

She was the kind of woman Grace would be glad to have as a friend—if not for her poisoned feelings over being replaced as Rosie's best friend—the kind of woman Grace might have even wanted to date, back when she was interested in such a thing. Currently, Lia was deep in conversation with one of the other dancers.

"Your fake girlfriend is hot," Ollie stage-whispered in her ear.

Grace spun to face him, giving him a playful punch on his biceps. "She is, but I'm not interested. However, I *am* interested in dancing with you."

"It would be my pleasure." He extended a hand.

She took it and followed him to the little dance floor at the back of the bar. It was already packed with other patrons, including several dancers from the show. Ollie started grooving to the beat, keeping one hand on her hip. She didn't have any professional dance moves, but she loved moving to the music, especially once she'd had a few drinks to loosen her up.

She and Ollie danced to several upbeat tunes, and when a slower song began to play, she settled in his arms. She didn't let many people get this close these days, and she was surprised by how good it felt to be held, the warmth of his hand on her back and the comfort of the connection between them.

"I can't believe you're going through with this wedding-date thing," he said, dipping her during a dramatic beat in the song. "I've become used to having you around, and now I'm going to miss you."

"I'm mostly doing it as a favor to Rosie," she told him. "But don't lie. You're going to love walking around naked this weekend and being as loud as you want with Raj."

He laughed. "Okay, I will enjoy both of those things, but you're good company too."

"Well, I'm certainly glad you think so." She gave him her most charming smile. Truly, she loved sharing an apartment with Ollie and hoped things between him and Raj didn't get so serious that he'd want to move in with his boyfriend, at least not anytime soon.

"How is being Lia's wedding date a favor to Rosie, though?"

"Because Rosie's the one who asked me," she told him. "And I certainly sympathize with Lia not wanting to fend off matchmaking attempts all weekend."

"But you hate weddings," he said as he spun her.

She clutched his hand to keep herself upright, giggling as he pulled her back in. "I do, and yet, I'm confident I'll survive attending one. Maybe it'll even be a good reminder of why I never want to get married."

He winked playfully. "Or maybe it'll change your mind about marriage?"

"Not a chance." On that, she was firm. She was happy for her friends when they got married, but it didn't change the fact that Grace didn't believe two people could truly promise to love and cherish each other for life. She'd seen it go wrong too many times, for others and for herself. She'd already had enough pain in her life, already lost too much.

"Mind if I cut in?"

She turned to find Raj standing there, and she stepped automatically out of Ollie's arms. "He's all yours."

As they began to dance, she made her way back to the bar. She found Lia on a barstool, sipping her beer. Grace was tipsy and in a good mood, and she almost invited Lia to dance, but something held her back. Maybe she didn't want to know what it felt like to be held in Lia's arms, the way she had with Ollie, although she'd probably find out before the end of the weekend. "Ready to head out?" she asked instead.

Lia nodded, finishing off her beer.

Grace led the way outside, grateful as the cool London air met her overheated face. She didn't even mind the misting rain, at least not until she saw the way Lia's glasses had fogged from the moisture. Lia took them off, swiping at them with a cloth from her purse, and she looked somehow softer without them, less serious. Grace liked it.

Lia slipped her glasses back into place. "So I'll see you tomorrow at three?"

Grace sucked in a fortifying breath, nodding. "See you then."

Lia stepped into her hotel room at just past eleven London time, but her internal clock was out of sorts from jet lag and her afternoon nap, so she wasn't even remotely tired. Rosie had texted earlier, asking how her meeting with Grace had gone, and since it was only six in New York, Lia called her while she walked to the sink to pour herself a glass of water.

"Hi," Rosie answered, sounding breathless.

"Hi, yourself," Lia responded. "Got a minute?"

"Yeah, I just dashed to my office so I can chat while Jane handles the counter, because I want to hear all about your dinner with Grace."

"She's not at all what I expected," Lia admitted. "She's . . . well, she's gorgeous, for one thing."

Rosie laughed into the phone. "Oh my God, Lia. Do you *like* her?"

"What?" Lia rubbed the bridge of her nose. Why had she said Grace was gorgeous? An image of Grace twirling on the dance floor flitted through her mind, and she blinked it away. "Don't be silly. She's not even remotely my type. She's more your type, to be honest." Rosie was the one who liked dressy, feminine women like Grace. Lia had always preferred a grungier look in the people she dated. She had a weakness for ripped jeans and tattoos.

"That's true," Rosie agreed. "I did think she was my type, once upon a time."

"You did?" Lia asked, surprised, because she'd never had the impression that Rosie and Grace had been anything more than friends. She filled a glass and took several gulps.

"We went out for, like . . . five minutes," Rosie said. "If you could even call it that. We were the only queer girls in our grade, or at least the only girls who'd come out yet, so of course we tried dating each other, but there was no spark. We became best friends instead."

"Wait a minute." Lia sat heavily on the bed. "Are you telling me Grace was your *first*? And I've never heard about it before now?"

"Lia, it was a couple of awkward kisses when we were sixteen. That's all."

"Well, now you've made this wedding-date idea weird." Lia flopped backward in bed. How had she not known that Grace was Rosie's ex?

"It's not weird. I don't think of her as my ex, and even if I did, it still wouldn't be weird. In case you forgot, I'm head over heels in love with Jane, so gorgeous Grace is all yours."

Lia sighed, rubbing a hand over her face. "This is so complicated."

"She agreed to go to the wedding, then?"

"Yes, she did," Lia said. "But now I'm wondering if I should just go by myself."

"Oh, come on," Rosie said in her ear. "Grace is a lot of fun. Let her go with you."

"I guess," Lia said. "At the very least, I'll finally get to know your mysterious friend, right?"

"She's not mysterious," Rosie said with a laugh. "She's not flighty at all in real life. It's just hard for her to make the trip to New York."

"I suppose," Lia said. "And how are things at the store?"

"All good here," Rosie told her. "Jane got recognized at the counter this morning. She turned so red you wouldn't believe it."

"Oh, I believe it," Lia said. "Your girlfriend embarrasses easily. That's great, though."

"It is," Rosie said, sounding absolutely lovestruck. "She had posted on Twitter that she'd be helping out in the store this week, and one of her readers stopped by just to meet her."

"I love that," Lia told her. Rosie's girlfriend, Jane Breslin, was a successful author, writing lesbian romance as Brie. She'd recently quit her day job to write full time, and this week she was helping Rosie at the store while Lia was out of town.

"So . . . you and gorgeous Grace, girlfriends for the weekend," Rosie said with laughter in her voice. "I can't wait to hear *all* about it."

CHAPTER THREE

As Lia pulled her rental car into the driveway of her parents' house in Sevenoaks late Thursday afternoon, a jittery sensation filled her stomach. She didn't get nervous very easily, but apparently bringing a near stranger to pose as her girlfriend for the weekend had done the trick. Beside her, Grace gazed at the house in open curiosity, not looking the least bit nervous. Either she hid it well, or this was easier for her since the personal stakes were lower.

"Ready?" Lia asked.

"Sure," Grace said.

"I know I've already said it, but I really appreciate you doing this for me."

"Of course." Grace gave her one of the breezy smiles Lia had come to expect, and she wondered if Grace was truly as carefree as she acted. There were moments when Lia thought she glimpsed something darker behind her casual veneer, but she might be imagining it. She barely knew Grace, after all.

Lia shut off the car, surprised by the number of other vehicles in the driveway. She'd hoped she and Grace could get quietly settled into their rooms before they had to play "meet the family," but it looked like most of her relatives—and who knew who else—were already here.

She and Grace gathered their bags and made their way toward the front door. It opened before they reached it, revealing Lia's mother standing there in linen trousers and a matching blazer, smiling widely.

"Hello, darling," she called, pulling Lia in for a quick hug and a kiss before turning to Grace. "And you must be Grace. It's lovely to meet you."

"You too, Mrs. Harris," Grace told her politely.

"Please, call me Catherine." She took Grace's elbow and guided her into the house. "We're delighted you could make it. It's been ages since Amelia's brought someone home to meet the family."

Grace glanced over her shoulder, mouthing, "Amelia?" with a confused smile.

Lia shrugged, fighting her own smile. She'd given up on trying to get her parents to call her by her nickname, and it wasn't as if she disliked Amelia. It was just a mouthful and tended to lead to her having to spell out her name for people.

"You girls will be staying in the upstairs guest room," her mother said, and Lia stumbled over her feet.

"Both of us?" She heard the incredulity in her voice, but her mother never let unmarried couples share a room under her roof.

"Yes, dear," Catherine said. "Audrey and Mark are in the other guest room, and several of your cousins are staying with us as well. I've put an inflatable mattress in my office for Sarah and James, and Ryan is sleeping in the den."

"Okay," Lia said, not wanting to make a scene while she sent silent apologies in Grace's direction, because she'd definitely thought Grace would have her own room.

But Grace seemed as unruffled as ever as she turned toward Lia. "Lead the way. I'd like to freshen up before dinner."

"Sure." Lia took her upstairs to the room her mother had indicated, motioning Grace in ahead of her. At least it had a full-size bed, but . . . "I'm so sorry about this."

"It's fine," Grace said. "I've taken plenty of trips where my friends and I had to share a bed, haven't you?"

"Well, yes." And it wouldn't have bothered her to share the bed with Rosie, but for some reason, sharing it with Grace felt awkward, maybe because they didn't know each other as well.

"So, Amelia, hmm?" Grace said as she set her bag on the bed and unzipped it.

"All my friends call me Lia," she said, still inexplicably flustered. Why did Grace have this effect on her?

"Lia suits you," Grace said as she pulled a red dress out of her bag and moved to hang it in the closet. "But Amelia's a beautiful name too."

"Thank you." She followed Grace's example and started hanging up the clothes she'd brought to wear to the various wedding events this weekend, trying not to look too hard at that red dress. Lia never swooned over dresses, but the thought of Grace in this one . . . *phew.*

"Your mom seems nice." Grace had moved to the bureau and was touching up her makeup.

"She is, when she's not meddling in my love life, at least," Lia confirmed. "My parents are great—just a bit old fashioned at times."

"But not too old fashioned to let us sleep in sin tonight," Grace said with a wicked smile, meeting Lia's eyes in the mirror.

Lia dropped her gaze to the suitcase in front of her, her cheeks uncomfortably warm. "I'm pretty shocked about that. It's a first."

"Anything I should know before dinner?" Grace asked.

"No. I'll make introductions, but tonight's just family. Olivia and Colin will be here—the bride and groom."

Grace tipped her head toward the door on the other side of the room. "Is that a bathroom?"

"Yes. We've got the only room with its own bath, so that's a plus."

"That is nice," Grace agreed before she went into the bathroom, closing the door behind her.

Lia sat on the bed to wait for her so they could walk downstairs together. So far, Grace had taken everything Lia had thrown at her perfectly in stride. She was easygoing and polite, not to mention interesting company, and Lia could certainly see why she and Rosie had become friends back in high school. She scrolled through notifications on her phone and soon found a text from Shanice, who—other than Grace— might have been Lia's only remaining single friend.

In fact, at one point, Lia had considered asking Shanice to be her wedding date, but her sister's first baby was due this month, so Lia hadn't asked, knowing Shanice wouldn't want to miss her nephew's birth. And *oh*, Lia gasped as she saw the photo attached to the text. Shanice beamed as she held a tiny baby wrapped in a pink-and-blue-striped blanket.

Shanice Banks:

Nathaniel Mason Lamarre, 7 lbs 12 oz. Mom and baby are both doing great

I'm officially an aunt!

Oh and I met a super cute nurse while I was visiting baby Nate, and we're going out tomorrow. Her name's Riley. Cross your fingers for me!

Shanice followed the texts with a whole row of emojis, everything from hearts to a stethoscope, and Lia grinned. She was so happy for her friend, especially after all the nights she and Shanice had texted back and forth, commiserating over dating woes. If things worked out for Shanice and Riley, Lia would be the last single in their group of friends, which was slightly depressing.

Lia tried so hard. She dated endlessly, and she'd fallen in love twice . . . or at least she thought she had. She'd been in two relationships where she felt devastated when they ended, but after watching Rosie and Jane fall for each other last year, Lia wasn't sure she'd ever experienced anything as intense and *wonderful* as what they'd found together. And she wanted it. She was *so* ready.

The bathroom door opened, and Grace stepped out. "Ready?"

Lia nodded, suddenly glad for her presence. Grace was a kindred spirit, a fellow single watching as all her friends settled down. Just last night, Lia had met Oliver's boyfriend, and she wondered if that had put a damper on her new status as his roommate.

She and Grace walked downstairs, following the sound of voices to the back patio, where she found Audrey and Mark and her dad, all with drinks in hand. They turned as she opened the door, their gazes collectively tracking to Grace, and Lia really was going to owe her one for putting up with her family all weekend.

"Hello," Audrey said brightly. "I'm Audrey, Lia's younger sister, and this is my husband, Mark."

"I'm Grace," she said. "It's nice to meet you."

"Walter Harris, Amelia's father," her dad said, extending a hand. "We're so glad to have you here this weekend, Grace."

Grace turned on the charm, effortlessly winning over Lia's family without any help needed from Lia herself. She'd always felt like a bit of an outlier with her family. Not an outcast, because there was no bad blood between them, but they were all straitlaced and traditional, while she was, well . . . Lia.

She shared an apartment with four other women, wore offbeat clothes, dated offbeat people, worked in a bookshop after earning a degree in museum studies, and lived in New York, the only member of her family to have left the UK.

"What do you do for work, Grace?" her father asked as he poured glasses of wine for her and Lia.

"I'm a translator," she told him.

"What language?" Audrey asked, and the conversation went from there.

Lia sipped her wine, standing close to Grace to give the appearance of a relationship, close enough to smell the vanilla scent she'd noticed earlier in the car, shampoo or lotion, something warm and sweet she was starting to associate with Grace.

"Well, if it isn't the couple of the hour," Audrey said, and Lia turned to see Colin and Olivia joining them on the patio.

There were more introductions, and Grace continued to hold her own, smiling politely and saying all the right things. Lia found herself remembering the last person she'd brought home to meet the family. Shawn had been constantly outside smoking, earning the disapproval of her father the cardiologist, and he'd worn ripped jeans to dinner, earning the disapproval of her mother. And Lia had loved him to bits . . . until he cheated on her.

Grace, in her gray knit dress with her perfect manners, was probably the most appropriate person she'd ever brought home, at least since Asher in secondary school. Already, she could see her family swooning over her, no doubt wondering how Lia had fallen for someone so posh. By the time they'd sat for dinner, Lia was half waiting for someone to call her on it, to say, "There's no way someone like you could fall for someone like Grace," but no one did.

Instead, she watched her whole family fawn over Grace, and she wasn't sure how she felt about it. Surely she should be glad to see them approve of her date, but why hadn't they ever been so accepting of the people she was actually interested in? What did that say about Lia's taste in partners, or about her family's judgment on who was right for her?

She leaned in to whisper in Grace's ear. "My family adores you."

They exchanged a smile, and Lia wondered briefly what it would be like if Grace were actually her girlfriend. Her gaze dropped to Grace's mouth, and she wondered what it would be like to kiss her.

Grace's lips twisted in a smirk. "They're going to be so sad to learn of our demise."

Grace slid into bed beside Lia that night, exhausted, out of sorts, and wishing she were at home in her own space. Lia's family was nice, and dinner had been fine, but this wasn't her thing. There was a heaviness pressing over her from all the forced cheer she'd had to exude tonight. She sighed as she pulled the covers over herself, annoyed by Lia's closeness.

"You okay?" Lia asked quietly.

"Yep, just tired." Grace peered at her in the semidarkness. Lia was barefaced against the pillow, and Grace found herself disarmed by the image. She couldn't put her finger on what it was, but every time Lia took off her glasses, she seemed somehow . . . naked, like Grace was seeing her without her clothes, which was ridiculous. Lia had dressed for bed in a Taylor Swift T-shirt and pink-striped boxers.

Grace was the one who should be feeling exposed in her flimsy tank top and super-short sleep shorts, but she tended to get hot while she slept and hadn't had any idea she'd be sharing a bed this weekend. She tucked the sheet under her chin and closed her eyes, hoping Lia didn't feel like they needed to talk before they fell asleep, because Grace was all out of conversation.

"Do you . . . ," Lia said quietly, and Grace opened her eyes, because *of course* she wanted to talk. "Do you ever feel like everyone else is coupled up except us?"

"Sometimes, but I don't mind it."

"Really?" Lia asked, pushing back a wavy lock of hair. "I feel so lonely sometimes, like I'm never going to find the right person."

"It's only lonely if you let it be," Grace told her. "And really, how can you feel lonely when you're surrounded by your friends?"

"That's different," Lia said. "I want a partner, someone to share everything with, someone I love and who loves me . . . I want what Rosie and Jane have."

"That's where we differ," Grace told her, resisting the urge to roll away.

"Really?" Lia sounded surprised. "You aren't looking for love?" She said it like she couldn't imagine such a thing, like it was ludicrous for Grace not to buy into the notion that she needed a life partner to be happy. She was perfectly happy on her own, thank you very much.

"No," she told Lia. "I don't want any of that. It's not for me."

Lia hummed under her breath, as if she was contemplating what that would be like. "So you're more of a casual dater, then? One-night stands?"

Grace sighed again, because she already knew Lia wasn't going to understand anything she told her, but she also knew Lia wouldn't let it go until she'd explained herself. "I don't enjoy one-night stands. I need to get to know someone before I feel attracted to them, so bringing home a stranger holds no appeal."

"So . . ."

"So I stopped dating about five years ago," Grace told her. "I refuse to accept this societal notion that I need another person in my life to be happy, because I don't. I'm very happy on my own. There's nothing missing from my life."

"Sex?" Lia asked, one eyebrow lifted questioningly.

"I'm perfectly capable of giving myself orgasms," Grace said, suddenly aware of how close Lia was, that if she slid a few inches to her left, she could press herself into Lia's body. And for the first time in years, she was aware of how long it had been since she'd felt that kind of touch and that maybe she did miss it, just a little bit. But not enough to want any of the baggage that came with a relationship. She was done with that forever.

"Masturbation is wonderful," Lia said, her voice soft and contemplative, "but it doesn't compare to sex with another person, at least not for me. You really don't miss it?"

"Nope," she said, putting as much force into the word as she could, because she knew where Lia's mind would go next. It was where everyone went after she told them she'd sworn off relationships. *Is this because of what happened to your parents?* or *Did someone break your heart?* The honest answer to both questions was yes, but it didn't matter. Her reasons were hers, and they were valid, and she was tired of talking about it. She was happy. Why couldn't people just accept that?

But Lia didn't ask either of those questions. Instead, she reached out and took Grace's hand beneath the covers, her fingers warm and soft. This might have been the first time they'd touched, and it felt unsettlingly intimate here in bed. "I admire you for being so sure of yourself," Lia said, "and I fully support the idea that a woman doesn't need anyone else to define her or to make her happy. Good for you."

"Thank you," Grace said, trying not to sound as surprised as she felt. Not even Rosie, hopeless romantic that she was, had understood Grace's decision. Lia's words were surprisingly validating.

"Sleep well," Lia murmured as she released Grace's fingers and rolled to face the window.

Grace stared at her back, oddly unsettled by Lia's insight into her psyche. "You too."

Lia woke in the middle of the night, disoriented. Her body clock was still annoyingly out of whack from jet lag. Without her glasses, she couldn't read the time, but the sky was black outside the window. The room around her was out of focus, but not so blurry that she couldn't see Grace lying beside her. Her tank top had twisted around her torso, and her face was relaxed and peaceful in sleep.

It was for the best that Lia couldn't see her clearly, because she didn't need this image of Grace burned into her mind in high definition. She didn't need to know the curve of her breasts or the sweep of her dark eyelashes against her cheeks. Lia closed her eyes and drifted back to sleep.

The next time she woke, soft sunlight filtered into the room, and Grace lay facing the opposite wall, leaving Lia with a view of her back and the strip of tanned skin visible between her tank top and her sleep shorts. Lia turned her gaze toward the ceiling, because she had no right to ogle Grace in her pajamas. If she hadn't already been off limits because of her history with Rosie, she was 100 percent off limits after her confession last night.

Grace didn't date, and Lia respected that. She just needed to be careful to keep her hormones in check, because there was definitely an attraction brewing on her end. Lia needed a distraction. Maybe later she'd look through her online dating app and see if anyone caught her eye. Obviously, she couldn't go on a date this week, but a little online flirting might help to divert her attention before her attraction to Grace got out of hand.

Lia reached for her glasses and put them on, discovering that it was only six o'clock. No wonder Grace was still asleep. They didn't need to be up for hours, but Lia didn't think she'd be able to get back to sleep, so she slipped quietly out of bed, gathered her things, and went into the bathroom for a shower.

When she came back out, Grace stirred, rolling to face her. "Morning," she mumbled sleepily.

"Morning," Lia said. "Sorry if I woke you."

"It's okay." Grace tucked the sheet more securely around her, because yeah, that tank top seemed to have a habit of shifting, not that Lia was looking at her breasts.

"There's no rush," Lia told her. "I just woke up early."

Grace nodded. "What's the plan for today?"

"Nothing much until later," Lia told her. "I'm going to see what my mother needs help with this morning, and you said you needed to work, right?"

Grace nodded again.

"This afternoon, my parents are hosting a gathering for friends and family who've come into town for the wedding, and afterward, the women are going out for a little informal bachelorette for Olivia. We call it a 'hen do' here in the UK."

Grace smiled. "Okay. I'll work until you need me this afternoon, and then I'll be free the rest of the weekend."

"Perfect," Lia said. "Do you want to come down with me to get some tea and breakfast, or would you like me to let you sleep?"

"No, I'm awake." Grace sat up, then straightened her tank top and ran a hand through her hair. "Just give me a minute to freshen up, and I'll come down with you." She slid out of bed, pulled a few things out of her bag, and went into the bathroom.

While she waited, Lia responded to a text from Rosie, and to her surprise, Rosie texted right back. It was almost two in the morning in New York, and Rosie was usually in bed well before midnight.

Lia Harris:
What are you doing up?

Rosie Taft:
We went out for drinks for Jane's sister's birthday and stayed out WAY too late!

Lia Harris:
Ah, that sounds fun.

Rosie Taft:
Super fun, but I'll pay for it in the morning lol.

Lia smiled, amused that Rosie hadn't gone to bed yet when it was already Friday morning here in London. A moment later, her phone rang with an incoming FaceTime call from Rosie. She connected it, and Rosie and Jane appeared on her screen.

"There you are!" Rosie exclaimed, sounding a bit tipsy. "I missed your face."

"Same," Lia said. "Glad you called."

"How's London?" Jane asked.

"I'm at my parents' now," Lia told her. "Getting ready for the wedding tomorrow."

"And Grace?" Jane asked, her lips quirking with a smile. She'd heard Lia tease Rosie about her "imaginary friend" enough times that it had become something of a joke between them.

"She's here," Lia told her, mindful that Grace was just on the other side of the bathroom door. "She's been great."

"And gorgeous," Rosie said with a giggle.

Lia rolled her eyes. "Everything okay at the store?"

"We're doing fine," Rosie told her. "Jane's having so much fun you might have to kick her out of the store when you get home."

"Oh, really?" In the back of Lia's mind, she'd worried this might happen, that Rosie and Jane would decide they loved working together as much as they loved living together. Lia was the odd one out in so many areas of her life lately, but the bookstore was hers and Rosie's, and she selfishly hoped that wouldn't change.

"Don't worry," Jane said. "I do enjoy working at the store, but my next book is suffering for it. Consider me your official backup any time you want to take a vacation, though."

Lia exhaled, nodding. "It would be nice to have a backup," she told Jane gratefully. Lia and Rosie hadn't had much time off since they'd taken over the store together eight years ago. Lia remembered what she'd told Grace, how she'd left home looking for adventure. Well, she hadn't really done that, and . . . maybe she wanted to.

The bathroom door opened behind her, and then Rosie called out, "Hi, Grace!"

Lia turned to see Grace approaching the bed, wrapped in a pink robe. She'd traded her sleep shorts for a pair of gray lounge pants.

"Hey, Rosie," she said, sitting next to Lia. "Hi, Jane."

Rosie's eyes widened, and she and Jane exchanged a quick look. Lia felt herself flush as she realized what this looked like . . . she and Grace sitting in bed together first thing in the morning.

"My parents put us in the same room," she said, hoping she wasn't making it even more awkward by trying to explain. "There are more guests in the house this weekend than there are beds."

"Ah," Rosie said, but the delighted look on her face said she hoped it was more than that. Being a hopeless romantic, Rosie would probably love for her two best friends to fall in love, even if that was the last thing either Lia or Grace wanted.

Lia's cheeks were burning, but when she glanced at Grace, she looked as cool and unruffled as ever. "I should let you two get to bed," Lia said, changing the subject.

On the screen, Rosie nodded, resting her head on Jane's shoulder. "You kids have fun at the wedding and send us lots of pictures."

"Will do," Lia said before she ended the call and turned to Grace. "So, breakfast?" She could only hope the rest of the day would go more smoothly, because her nerves were already beginning to fray.

CHAPTER FOUR

Grace leaned back in her chair to stretch her shoulders. With so many guests currently staying at the house, she'd ended up working at the small desk in her and Lia's room, although the wooden chair wasn't very comfortable. Her butt was sore and her back was stiff, but she'd finished her translation work, which meant she should be a good guest and join Lia's family downstairs.

She shut down her laptop and stood, wishing she had time for a jog or at least some yoga. She got restless when she didn't exercise, and this weekend was already making her restless for other reasons. She missed her apartment and Ollie and even London itself. Pretending to be Lia's girlfriend took more energy than she'd anticipated, and she'd barely even started.

With a sigh, she went to the closet and pulled out the blue dress she'd brought to wear tonight. She went into the bathroom to change and do her makeup, and then she walked downstairs. There were several people she didn't recognize in the living room, but Lia and her parents were nowhere in sight.

Great.

Grace could hold her own in most social situations, but this . . . well, she didn't want to be here, and that made it harder to mingle. She forced a casual smile as two women Lia's mother's age turned toward her.

"Hello," one of them said, extending a hand. "I'm Candace Walters. Are you Peter's new girlfriend?"

Grace had no idea who Peter was. She shook her head as she took Candace's hand. "Grace Poston. I'm with Lia—Amelia—actually."

"Oh," Candace said, eyebrows rising slightly. "Well, isn't that lovely."

Grace nodded, still smiling as she greeted the woman beside Candace, who introduced herself as Tilly Markham.

"So you and Amelia are friends?" Tilly asked, and Grace was so done with this conversation already, but Lia had brought her here to serve as a buffer with her meddling family, so she might as well do her best.

"I'm her girlfriend," she told Tilly, who pressed her fingers against her lips, exchanging a loaded glance with Candace.

Grace wasn't sure if their reaction was because Lia had brought a woman to the wedding or because they'd thought she would be attending with Asher, but either way, she didn't like it. "If you'll excuse me . . ." She waved in the general direction of the kitchen, eager to make her escape. She slipped through the doorway, exhaling deeply.

"Hello there."

She jumped, whirling to face a man about her grandfather's age who stood by the window. His white hair was neatly combed, and he wore a tailored gray suit, giving him a distinguished look. "Hi," she said, walking toward the refrigerator to pour herself a glass of water.

"Alistair Harris," he said, smiling in her direction, and she was deeply regretting her decision to come downstairs without making sure Lia was here first.

"Grace Poston," she told him as she reached for a glass and began to fill it.

"I don't think we've met before, Grace," he said. "Who are you here with?"

41

She steeled herself, hoping he reacted better than the women in the living room, because her patience was running extremely thin. "I'm with Amelia."

"Ah," he said, nodding. "Amelia is my granddaughter. It's a pleasure to meet you."

"You too," she said, forcing another smile. She gulped from her glass of water, debating if she could sneak back upstairs and hide until Lia got home.

"I was about to step outside for some fresh air. Would you care to accompany me?" Alistair asked.

Ugh was her gut reaction, but then again, Alistair seemed friendly, and some fresh air would be nice after being cooped up inside this house all day. "Sure," she agreed.

She set her glass in the sink and followed him out the front door. The afternoon was pleasantly warm and sunny, and she tipped her face toward the sky, sucking in a grateful breath.

"Beautiful day, isn't it?" Alistair said.

"Yes," she said, eyeing the colorful flower beds along the front of the house. She'd barely noticed them yesterday when she and Lia arrived, having been so preoccupied with making a good first impression on the family.

"Did you know that the church where Colin and Olivia will be married tomorrow is just down the street?"

"I didn't," Grace said, clasping her hands in front of herself.

"Would you like to see it?" he asked.

She would, actually. Not the church, necessarily, but she'd love to go for a walk and see a little bit of Sevenoaks, although she wasn't sure if it was the best idea to do it with Alistair. He had to be in his eighties, although he seemed to be in good shape for his age. "If it's not too far," she said, keeping her tone neutral.

"It's not far at all, and I could use the exercise," Alistair said. His crisp accent and poised demeanor made Grace think of British royalty, and she smiled as she fell into step beside him. "How long have you and my granddaughter been together?"

"Oh, not very long, but we've known each other for years," she told him, repeating the story she and Lia had decided on during the car ride from London. "We were introduced through a mutual friend, Rosie."

"The Rosie who owns the bookstore where Amelia works?" he asked.

"Yes," she said, and this time her smile was genuine. She was getting a good vibe from Lia's grandfather, and she was impressed that he remembered the name of her best friend, a woman he'd probably never met.

"The church is just up here on the corner," he said as they made their way slowly down the sidewalk. His gait was stiff, but he walked with purpose, and while maybe she should've been concerned that a seemingly straitlaced old man was leading her to church, he didn't seem like he meant to lecture her on her sins when they got there.

"Oh, it's beautiful," she said when she caught sight of the church. It stood out from the surrounding brick buildings with its bright-white paneling and stained glass windows, with a slender steeple pointing toward the blue sky overhead.

Alistair nodded. "I married Amelia's grandmother in that church."

Grace gave him a quick smile. She knew better than most when not to ask prying questions. Alistair appeared to be here alone, which likely meant his wife was no longer around, and she didn't want to cause him any undue pain by asking about her.

"Florence passed on a few years ago," he said, confirming her suspicion.

"I'm sorry to hear that," she murmured.

Alistair led the way across the street and gestured for her to sit beside him on a bench in front of the church. Grace wondered again what they were doing here, but he'd been good company so far, so she wasn't complaining. "I loved another once," he said quietly, and now she really had no idea what to say. Was Lia's grandfather about to confess an affair? She shifted subtly away from him.

"His name was Charles," Alistair said.

"Oh." The word slipped past her lips, and she blinked, looking at him in surprise.

"We were just mad for each other," Alistair said, a wistful smile on his face. "The love of my life, you might say, but times were different then. It was very hard for us to be together, and we were so young. In the end, we went our separate ways."

"I'm sorry," Grace told him. Here she'd been worried he had brought her to church to judge her, and instead she'd found an ally.

"Don't be sorry," Alistair said, resting a hand on hers. "I've had a wonderful life, and I loved Florence very much. But I'm glad things are easier now, that you and Amelia have opportunities Charles and I didn't."

Grace swallowed, both touched and saddened by his story. And while she was fairly sure it hadn't been his intent, she saw this as yet more evidence that she'd made the right decision in remaining single, because love hurt. For Alistair's sake, she forced a smile. "Me too."

"There you are."

Grace turned at the sound of Lia's voice, glad to have finally found her. While she'd been outside with Alistair, the house had filled with yet more people. "Hi."

"Thought I'd lost you," Lia said, stepping in close to take Grace's hand.

"I went for a walk with your grandfather," Grace said, glancing over her shoulder, but Alistair was nowhere in sight.

"You did?" Lia asked, and when Grace turned back, her eyebrows were raised.

She nodded. "He's very nice, maybe my favorite person I've met here so far."

Lia broke into a wide smile. "He's pretty great. I'm glad you two hit it off. Mind if I introduce you to a few more people?"

Grace shook her head, even though meeting more of Lia's relatives was the last thing she wanted right now. But she'd agreed to this, and she would see it through. "Sure."

Lia kept her hand in Grace's as she led her through the room, introducing her to various family members. Grace smiled and said all the right things while wishing she was still upstairs working or, better yet, back in London. It was going to be a long weekend.

Lia stepped closer and leaned in. "Asher is here."

"Asher as in . . . your ex?"

Lia nodded, pressing her lips together.

"Oh." Grace definitely hadn't expected to meet *him* tonight. "Why is he here?"

"His mum is my mum's best friend," Lia told her, keeping her voice low. "It's a whole . . . thing."

"An unfortunate thing, it sounds like." Grace looked around the room. "Which one is he?"

"You're about to find out," Lia murmured as a tall man with sandy-brown hair and fair skin approached, and maybe her judgment was skewed based on what Lia had already told her, but Grace immediately picked up on a cocky air about him.

"Amelia," he said before resting a hand on her shoulder as he air-kissed her cheeks. Any man who didn't appreciate her enough to call her by her chosen nickname got an automatic thumbs-down from Grace. Not to mention, he held on to her a little longer than he should have, especially in front of the woman he believed to be her girlfriend.

"Hello, Asher," Lia said.

His gaze shifted to Grace. "And who's your . . . friend?"

Oh, this asshole. Grace narrowed her eyes at him. "I'm her girl-friend, Grace."

Asher's lips twisted into a slight frown, but he recovered quickly, smiling at Grace as he extended a hand. "Asher Frommel. I didn't know Amelia was bringing a date."

"Because we don't keep in touch," Lia said pointedly. "Although I'm surprised my mother didn't pass along the information."

"Hmm," Asher said, and by the look on his face, Grace got the feeling he *had* received the news but had chosen to ignore it.

It made Grace feel irrationally pissy and possessive. She had little patience for people like Asher who disregarded the boundaries of the people who were supposed to matter to them. She stepped closer to Lia, close enough that their shoulders were pressed together, their hands still intertwined. She gave Lia's fingers a reassuring squeeze as she stared him down. After several long seconds of uncomfortable silence, he cleared his throat.

"What do you do for work, Grace?"

"I'm a translator for *Modern Style* magazine," she told him.

"Is that so?" Asher asked. "What language?"

"Spanish."

"*¿Hablas español?*" he said, looking stupidly proud of himself.

Grace resisted the urge to roll her eyes, because of course she spoke Spanish. How else would she work as a translator? *"Por supuesto, pero no me di cuenta de que tú también lo sabías."*

"How nice for you," he said, and she smirked, having successfully called his bluff. If he knew any Spanish at all, it was what he'd learned in school.

Lia, however, was staring at Grace with unabashed admiration. "I love it when you do that," she said, as if she'd heard Grace speak Spanish hundreds of times.

Grace was surprised by the smile she felt on her face. She liked the way Lia was looking at her right now. It made her feel light on her feet. Impulsively, she leaned in and pressed a quick kiss against Lia's cheek. Lia blushed, giving Grace a look that seemed almost shy, and she belatedly realized they hadn't discussed kissing . . . even on the cheek.

"El gusto es mío," she told Lia to cover the moment. And it was true. The pleasure was hers, except she was just messing with both of them now, because neither of them had any idea what she was saying. That power made her want to impress Lia and fuck with Asher, a potentially dangerous combination.

"There you are," Lia's mother said, sweeping in to join them. "The elusive Grace."

Her smile hardened. Catherine had no ulterior motive in calling her "elusive," other than that she'd been upstairs working most of the day, but Grace was painfully aware that it was one of the things Lia and the rest of Rosie's friends called her, and therefore, the word made her cagey. "Here I am."

"Did you finish your work?" Catherine asked.

"Yes," Grace told her. "Thank you for not minding."

"Of course," Catherine said. "I'm just sorry I didn't have a proper office for you to use."

"Oh, it was totally fine," Grace told her. "I work at the desk in my bedroom at home too."

"Asher," Catherine said, transferring her attention to him, and Grace watched as they air-kissed each other's cheeks. It annoyed her, because Grace hadn't received the same honor when she met Catherine yesterday. Catherine was showing more affection for Lia's ex than for her girlfriend. No wonder Lia had wanted a date this weekend.

"Grace, would you like a drink?" Lia asked, and Grace turned to her, realizing she'd been giving Asher a rather intense look.

"Sure," she said, smiling gratefully at Lia. She followed her to a table set up against the wall with a variety of open bottles of liquor and wine.

"You meant a drink-drink, right?" Lia asked as she gestured to the table. "There's Perrier if you prefer."

"Wine would be great," Grace told her, because she was definitely going to need alcohol to make it through this evening. Glancing over her shoulder to make sure no one was within earshot, she leaned in to whisper, "Your ex is an ass."

Lia's lips twitched. "Don't I know it. Thank you for . . . all of that."

"You're welcome," Grace said, and she meant it. She'd probably enjoyed messing with Asher more than she should have, given the circumstances.

"Chardonnay?" Lia asked, gesturing to an open bottle, and Grace nodded. "I really did love hearing you speak Spanish," Lia said as she poured two glasses.

"Thank you," Grace told her, accepting the glass Lia held toward her.

They sipped their wine, standing close to each other. Lia looked beautiful in her off-the-shoulder blue top and loose, flowery skirt. It was colorful and unusual, like Lia herself. Her style made her stand out from everyone else in the room, and Grace admired her uniqueness as much as she appreciated her beauty.

She had just started to relax when she looked up to see Asher headed their way . . . again.

Lia stood with her back against the bar, drink in hand, waiting for the tension in her shoulders to ease. The club where they'd come for Olivia's hen party was loud and flashy, the perfect place for Lia to unwind. That scene with Asher was exactly what she had been expecting, and yet it still bothered her. He was just so obnoxious, and her mother still thought he'd hung the moon. It was infuriating.

She gulped from her drink as Audrey slid in beside her. "You okay?" her sister asked. "You've been kind of quiet tonight."

Lia nodded. Her sister was the one member of her family who knew exactly how she felt about Asher. "Just wish a certain someone hadn't been at the house earlier."

Audrey grinned. "He was so jealous of Grace."

"Good," she said.

"I think he feels emasculated to see you with a woman," Audrey said. "He definitely reacted more dismissively to Grace than Shawn."

"He didn't like Shawn either," Lia said. "But there's probably some truth in that."

"Well, fuck him," Audrey said, tapping her glass against Lia's. "I think Grace is fantastic."

"She's pretty great," Lia agreed. She liked Grace a lot and hoped to call her a friend after this weekend was over. It was probably for the best that they lived on different continents, though, because her feelings for Grace were starting to go beyond friendship, and Grace wasn't interested in a relationship.

Currently, she was on the dance floor with Olivia and several of Olivia's friends, grooving to the beat while Lia brooded at the bar. This was her future sister-in-law's bachelorette party, and she needed to ditch her mood and celebrate with the rest of the group. She finished her drink, feeling the alcohol start to do its job.

As if she'd felt Lia watching her, Grace turned and smiled at her, and then she headed toward Lia and Audrey. "Come dance with me, Lia," she said when she reached them, taking Lia's hand and giving her a tug toward the dance floor. "You too, Audrey."

Audrey held her hands up in front of herself. "Oh, I don't dance. But you two have fun."

"All right," Lia agreed, turning to set her empty glass on the bar, and then she let Grace lead her onto the dance floor. "Having fun?"

"I am now," Grace said pointedly. "I'm not wild about your ex, but I do enjoy dancing. Olivia seems really sweet. Your brother has good taste."

"He does," Lia agreed. They were standing close to be able to talk like this, and consequently, it was hard to dance without bumping into her.

Grace didn't seem bothered by this fact as she let her hip collide with Lia's. "I needed this to finish off the day."

And now that she was out here on the dance floor, Lia was glad for it too. This was a chance to blow off some steam after a long and sometimes frustrating day. As Grace threw her hands in the air, bumping her hip against Lia's again, she let herself admire the way Grace looked in that powder-blue dress. Under the guise of their fake relationship, surely she could appreciate Grace's curves and . . . well, her *grace* as she moved on the dance floor.

Grace seemed lost in the music, her body moving to the beat, face tipped toward the lights overhead, and Lia couldn't deny—at least not to herself—that she was affected by the sight, that she was attracted to this woman. Grace's long, dark hair swung behind her as she danced, and it only added to the overall effect.

And then Grace stepped toward her, taking Lia's hands in hers as their bodies came together. Lia was exquisitely aware of the press of Grace's breasts against hers and the way her brown eyes sparkled with the reflection of the lights swirling overhead.

They grinned at each other, hands clasped, and since Grace was the stronger dancer, Lia followed her lead. The song changed, picking up the pace, and Grace spun her. Lia laughed as she twirled before Grace hauled her back in against the warmth of her body.

Someone bumped into Lia from behind, knocking her into Grace, who stumbled backward with a laugh. She placed her hands on Grace's shoulders, and they kept dancing. The alcohol had kicked in now, and Lia felt loose and relaxed.

Out of the corner of her eye, she saw Olivia dancing nearby. She wore a short veil on her head, an homage to this being her hen party. She looked happy and carefree, as she should the night before her wedding. Lia truly was glad that Olivia was joining her family, no matter her feelings about the wedding itself. Lia loved weddings. She was just tired of attending them alone.

She was tired of *being* alone.

Grace spun her again, and Lia held on to her hand with a laugh. A strand of Grace's hair slid over her shoulder, silky soft against Lia's exposed skin, and her pulse jumped. Their eyes met, their faces only inches apart, and Lia couldn't catch her breath. Her gaze dropped to Grace's lips, pink and glossy, and *God*, her lips were gorgeous.

It would be so easy to lean in and kiss her, but that hadn't been part of their arrangement. Grace had sworn off dating and didn't even truly want to be here this weekend. So Lia gazed longingly at her lips, wishing the circumstances were different, and when Grace spun her again, Lia almost fell over backward she'd been so distracted.

Grace tugged her hand to compensate, and they crashed into each other, the warmth of Grace's body again pressed against Lia's. They stayed like that for several long seconds. Grace's hands rested on Lia's hips to steady her, and Lia's heart was pounding, her skin flushed. She was completely intoxicated by the woman in front of her.

Grace leaned in, and Lia's breath caught in her throat, because as smitten as she was right now, she hadn't actually expected it to happen. She should step back, because this would be a mistake. If she and Grace ever kissed, Lia needed to know that it was because Grace wanted to kiss her, not because she was putting on a show for the people around them. But Grace bypassed Lia's lips to whisper in her ear, "Want to get a drink? I'm thirsty."

"Yeah," Lia managed, trying to reel herself back in, because her thoughts were completely out of line right now. It must have been all the wedding talk that had her seeing hearts every time she looked at Grace all of a sudden.

Grace kept one of her hands entwined with Lia's as she led the way toward the bar. They each got a glass of water and one of the pink sparkling drinks that were being made especially for the wedding party, something with cranberry, seltzer, and vodka.

Grace leaned her elbows on the bar as she sipped, her face glistening with a sheen of sweat from dancing. Lia stood beside her, back to the bar, watching the other women still dancing, because the last thing she needed right now was to watch Grace sip her drink, to admire her gray-painted nails against the pink glass or the way her throat worked when she swallowed. Lia seriously needed to get a grip.

Olivia made her way over and threw her arms around Lia. "Tomorrow this time, we'll be sisters," she exclaimed, and Lia laughed, because Olivia was drunk, and maybe she should rein her future sister-in-law in before she started her wedding day with a hangover.

"I can't wait," Lia told her. "But in the meantime, you should drink some water."

Olivia giggled as she leaned heavily against the bar. "Yes. Probably a good idea."

Grace leaned forward to say something to the bartender, who nodded and began to fill a glass of water.

"Your girlfriend is hot," Olivia whispered in Lia's ear with another giggle.

"She is, and you're drunk," Lia whispered back.

"You seem happy together," Olivia said. "I like her." And then she gave Lia the most ridiculously overdone thumbs-up.

Grace lifted an eyebrow, probably having guessed they were talking about her. Olivia wasn't exactly being subtle, but it was all in good fun, right? Lia gave Grace what she hoped was a reassuring smile, receiving an unreadable look in return. Lia sobered. Sometimes, she felt like she understood Grace, that they'd bonded this week and might even remain friends after the wedding. Sometimes, Lia wanted to kiss her and wished they could be more than friends.

And then, in moments like this, she felt like she didn't know Grace at all. She had no idea what she was thinking or if she even wanted to be at this bar tonight, helping Olivia celebrate. That was the danger of an arrangement like theirs. Grace wasn't exactly free to speak her mind this weekend, and Lia felt suddenly guilty for roping her into any of it. She should have held her head high and been proud of her single status, the way Grace was.

The bartender pushed Olivia's water toward her, and she thanked him. "I should call it a night soon," she said pensively, staring into the water.

"You need your beauty sleep," Lia agreed.

Olivia nodded, lifting her glass for a drink.

Lia turned to ask Grace if she wanted to leave soon, too, but the words died on her lips as she got a look at her. Grace was staring at her phone, lips pressed tightly together and a dazed look in her eyes. She stood so still Lia wasn't even sure if she was breathing, her posture tense and rigid.

Lia stepped around Olivia and touched Grace's arm. She jumped, locking her screen as she looked at Lia. There were no tears, but she was visibly distracted and unfocused, as off center as Lia had ever seen her.

"Are you all right?" Lia asked tentatively.

Grace nodded, looking down at the darkened phone in her hand. "Fine."

"Did something happen?" Lia pressed, because if Grace needed to leave, Lia didn't want her feeling any sort of obligation to stay at this bachelorette party.

"No," Grace said firmly. She pushed her phone into her purse, and when she looked at Lia this time, she did look fine. Whatever it was, she obviously didn't want to talk about it, or maybe Lia was reading too much into things. Maybe she'd just seen an offensive post on Facebook. That had certainly been known to put a frown on Lia's face from time to time.

It was a reminder that they didn't really know each other, though, because Lia was used to her friends confiding in her, and confiding in them in return. She was a good listener and a good problem-solver, a person her friends often sought advice from. She wasn't used to being shut out, and she didn't quite like it, or maybe that was just her emotions talking, because she liked Grace more than she ought to.

"Olivia's going to leave with Mia soon to get some sleep before the big day," Lia told her, and as she looked over, she saw Olivia with her arms around her sister, a dreamy smile on her face. "Are you ready to leave too?"

Grace nodded, and Lia hoped she wasn't imagining the relief on her face. "Sure. Let's go."

CHAPTER FIVE

Grace couldn't sleep. She and Lia had gotten into bed hours ago, but her body refused to settle. Every time she closed her eyes, she saw that email from Your-Gene. "Good news! We've found a match!" And she was lost in the shock and horror of that night all over again. She'd been at Rosie's apartment when she got the call, a stern but sympathetic police officer informing her that her parents had been in a car accident and that she should get to the hospital immediately.

She didn't cry, not then. She felt oddly numb, like this wasn't really happening. Rosie's mother called a cab, and she and Rosie went with Grace to the hospital, holding her hand and assuring her that everything would be fine.

It wasn't fine.

Her mother was already dead by the time Grace walked into the ER, gone without a goodbye. That didn't feel real, either, maybe because she hadn't yet seen her body. Grace was quiet until she saw her father on a gurney, blood soaking his shirt and a frantic, haunted look in his eyes. She took one look at him and dissolved in tears.

"It's just a scalp wound, Gracie," he told her, gripping her hand so tightly it hurt. "I'm going to be fine."

But he wasn't fine.

The machines beside his bed began to wail, and she was hauled out of the room before she could say another word, before she could even tell him that she loved him. He was rushed into emergency surgery to repair a ruptured spleen. He needed a blood transfusion, and Grace desperately insisted that they should take hers.

There was a fuss about her age, because she was only seventeen. She needed a parent's permission to donate, and suddenly, horribly, she didn't have a parent to sign the form.

While they attempted to get her grandparents on the phone, Grace was rushed into a cubicle, where a nurse pricked her finger to see if she was a suitable donor. And she tried not to cry, to scream, to absolutely fall apart because her mother was dead, and her father was dying, and this was not the time for her to give in to her fear of needles.

The apologetic nurse later told Grace her blood type wasn't a match with her father's. Despite receiving a transfusion from the hospital's blood bank, he succumbed to his injuries, and just like that, Grace was an orphan.

It wasn't until weeks later, after the funeral and the chaos of moving in with Rosie and her mom so that Grace could graduate with her class, that she realized what the nurse had told her that night. She'd sat through a biology lesson on blood types and gone home to look at the paperwork from the hospital. Her mom was A negative, and her dad was O negative. Grace was AB positive, an impossibility.

The man she'd grown up with—the man she'd called "Dad"—wasn't her biological father, a fact she'd been running from . . . until tonight.

Grace rolled to her back, trying not to wake Lia but aware that she'd been fidgeting under the covers for hours now. Her body twitched with restless energy, and not for the first time, she wished she were at home. She wished she could go for a walk around her neighborhood or even sit on her couch and watch TV to clear her mind.

"Want to talk about it?" Lia asked quietly, her voice unsettlingly close in the darkness.

"No," Grace said. "Sorry if I woke you."

"I don't mind," Lia said, "but I can practically hear your thoughts racing over there. It might help to talk it through with someone."

Grace sighed, annoyed by how perceptive Lia had been tonight. Grace hadn't said a word when she received the email and still wasn't sure how Lia had realized anything was wrong. She wasn't used to having people in her life who could read her so easily. She preferred to keep private things private, but maybe it *would* help to talk this through with someone. And Lia might be a good person to confide in, since she was going back to America in a few days. They never had to mention it again.

Grace stared at the faint glow of the window. "I don't even know where to start."

"Start wherever feels easiest," Lia said.

"You know my parents died in a car crash when I was seventeen."

"Yes," Lia said, and her hand found Grace's beneath the blanket, giving it a reassuring squeeze.

"What you don't know is that my dad needed a blood transfusion that night, and I . . . I wasn't a match. Our blood types are incompatible. He wasn't my biological father."

Lia inhaled sharply. "Oh, Grace, what a horrible way to find out."

"Yeah." She blew out a breath, surprised to realize she *did* feel calmer. It had been a long time since she'd talked about any of this out loud, so long that maybe she'd forgotten talking could be a good thing. "Rosie and her mom were the only people who knew, because they were at the hospital with me when I found out, and they helped me sort through it afterward."

"I'm glad they were there for you," Lia said quietly.

"Me too," Grace admitted, her voice embarrassingly small in that dark room. "I didn't know what to do. My parents were gone, so I couldn't ask them about it. I didn't want to tell my grandparents on my dad's side, because . . . my mom cheated on him. It would have broken their hearts, and to what purpose?"

"Are you sure she cheated?" Lia asked calmly, her hand still gripping Grace's. "What if you were adopted?"

"Rosie's mom wondered that, too, so she helped me send off all our DNA to be tested, which confirmed what I had learned from our blood types. My mom was my mom, but he wasn't my dad. Anyway, I look just like my mom. Everyone always commented on it."

"Okay," Lia said. "So you never asked any of your relatives if they could shed any light?"

"No. I felt so awkward around my dad's family after he died, like I knew this awful thing they didn't know, and I just felt so *betrayed* by my mom. I was mad at the world, so I did the mature teenage thing and ran off to live with my grandma in Spain."

"Ah," Lia said. "Interesting that you went to your mom's family and not your dad's."

"I know, right?" Grace said with a bitter laugh. "I never said I made good decisions. But my *abuela*'s house had always been a refuge for me, and she was the only person left who I was biologically related to. I was afraid my dad's family would turn their backs on me if they knew, and I hated lying to them, so I went to Spain."

"I can't speak for people I've never met," Lia said, "but blood doesn't make a family. I hope their love for you wouldn't change, regardless of what's in your DNA."

"One would hope," Grace said, "but in my experience, people are endlessly disappointing."

"That's often true," Lia agreed quietly. She'd been steady and supportive without pushing or judging Grace for her actions, and maybe she'd been right in saying she was a good person to talk to. Suddenly, Grace couldn't get the words out fast enough.

"Around the time I graduated from college, those DNA kits were becoming popular. You know, the ones that tell you about your ancestry?"

"Yes," Lia said. "So you got curious and submitted your DNA?"

"I did," Grace said. "I thought it might help me figure things out, like maybe it could tell me I was fifty percent German, and I'd be able to track down some German man my mother had known, but it didn't. It confirmed that I'm half Spanish, but the rest was a crapshoot. I'm a little of this, a little of that—nothing that would help me narrow down who my biological father is."

"That's too bad," Lia said.

"Do you know how many nights I lay awake thinking about all the men in my life, wondering if they could be the one? The doorman, the guy across the hall, that man she shared an office with at work. I've run through all their faces in my head, trying to imagine if I look anything like them."

"I'm so sorry," Lia said. "I can't even imagine what that's like."

"Anyway, after a while, I quit thinking about it. I'd built a new life for myself in Spain. I was happy. It just didn't matter anymore. I can't spend my whole life wondering."

"That sounds understandable," Lia said.

"Well, apparently I checked a box when I submitted my DNA that allowed them to match me if a relative entered their database, and . . ." She choked on her words then, squeezing her eyes shut as everything she'd been suppressing all evening surged up inside her.

"They found a match," Lia guessed. "Someone from your biological father's side of the family."

"Yes," Grace whispered. "A half sister, and I . . . I don't know what to do or how to feel about it. I just . . . I don't know if I want this."

"Well, you certainly don't have to decide anything tonight," Lia said. "Decisions like this generally take time to weigh the pros and cons."

"Why now?" Grace asked quietly. "Why did she submit her DNA now? What if she needs a kidney or something?"

"I doubt she wants your kidney," Lia said with laughter in her voice. "Most likely, she just got around to it for whatever reason. Maybe someone gave her a kit as a gift."

"Maybe," Grace said. "What if her parents are happily married, and finding out about me breaks up her family because now they know that her dad has an illegitimate child?"

"That's a risk she took when she submitted her DNA, and she already knows about you at this point, right? You both received the email about the match?"

"I guess, yeah."

"The first thing you need to do is decide if *you* want to meet. And if you do, then you can find out if that's what she wants too," Lia said. "And if she doesn't want to meet, maybe she could still give you answers. She could potentially give you all the answers you've been looking for, even if she does it via email."

Grace blew out a breath as a hot, prickly sensation crawled over her skin. "I didn't think that was a possibility, and now it feels . . . terrifying."

"Which is why you shouldn't decide tonight. It's late, and you're emotional. Sleep on it. Take all the time you need."

"You're really easy to talk to," Grace whispered.

"Thank you," Lia said. "I'm happy to help, and I'm a pretty good problem-solver."

Grace glanced at the clock and sighed. "Lia, it's the middle of the night. Your brother is getting married in the morning, and I'm keeping you up. I'm so sorry."

"Oh, don't you dare apologize. I'm glad for the chance to get to know you better and to maybe offer something helpful in return after all you've done for me this week. I'd love to talk more about this with you once you've had a chance to process."

"I think . . . I think I'd like that," Grace said, gulping another breath. "I don't usually talk about this with anyone. Sometimes Rosie, but not even always with her."

"I know," Lia murmured. "I appreciate your confidence, and I don't take it lightly."

"Thank you." Grace rolled toward her, wrapping her arms around Lia for a hug, but in her impulsiveness, she'd forgotten that they were in bed together and that she was only wearing skimpy pajamas. Suddenly, her body was pressed against Lia's, her hands fisted in the back of that Taylor Swift T-shirt, her nose buried in the rose-scented depths of Lia's hair.

The first thing she felt was warmth. Lia was so warm against her, their bare legs threaded in a way that was entirely too intimate for the situation. Grace's heart was pounding, and not just that . . . Lia's was beating just as hard against Grace's breast. Arousal licked through her, hot and fast, something she hadn't felt for another person in *years*.

Her friends had teased her relentlessly when she'd given up dating, but it truly hadn't been a hardship. Grace needed to know someone and feel comfortable with them before she developed any sort of attraction. She'd tried a few one-night stands, but they'd left her cold. They were awkward and uncomfortable, but she didn't want the emotional baggage that came with a relationship.

It had been easy to keep herself clear of entanglements this way. She hadn't been tempted to break her rules since she'd quit dating almost five years ago. Until tonight, this moment, right now, with Lia's hands in her hair, Lia's breasts pressed against hers, Lia's knee resting against her bare thigh.

Grace felt a dizzying swoop in her stomach, like sparklers were going off inside her, turning her warm and tingly, and *oh*, she'd forgotten this feeling. Her skin flushed, and her heart sped, and an insistent ache built between her thighs. And this hug had gotten really long.

She pulled back, breathing hard, her mind spinning in a hundred directions, because that wasn't all her. Lia felt it, too, or at least Grace was pretty sure she did. There'd been a moment on the dance floor earlier when Grace had thought Lia wanted to kiss her, but there was just no way it would be a good idea. Grace was the very definition of commitment-phobic, and Lia wanted to settle down and get married.

"Still thinking so hard over there I can hear it," Lia said softly into the darkness.

"Sorry," Grace breathed. Everything about this moment felt too intimate now—the darkened bedroom, the late hour, her skimpy attire, and the shared bed. Her pulse was out of control, and she was still just as uncomfortably aroused.

"You have nothing to apologize for." Lia slid closer, taking Grace's hands in hers. "We both feel it, but nothing has to happen unless we both want it to."

"Oh," Grace whispered, not having expected Lia to address it so directly. But then again, wasn't that perfectly Lia? She was breathtakingly, refreshingly earnest.

"Right now, we need to sleep," Lia said. "Everything else will wait until morning. All right?"

"Mm-hmm," Grace murmured.

Lia's fingers traced up and down her arm, and it felt so good. Grace had forgotten the intimacy of moments like this, simple touches that went beyond a platonic hug between friends. And right now, she'd never felt anything better than Lia's fingertips on her skin, tracing tender patterns as Grace's heart slowed and her eyes grew heavy.

"Good night, Grace."

Lia's hushed whisper was the last thing Grace heard before she drifted into sleep.

For the second morning in a row, Lia woke to the blurry image of Grace asleep in bed beside her. This morning, her vision was bleary not only from her lack of glasses but also her late-night conversation with Grace. Lia didn't mind, though. On the contrary, she was so glad Grace had opened up to her and for the connection that seemed to be growing between them.

She wished she could spend more of today with Grace to nurture that connection, but the day ahead was extremely busy with Colin and Olivia's wedding in a few hours. Lia's bridesmaid duties meant she wouldn't get to spend as much time with Grace as she would have liked.

She slid out of bed and went into the bathroom to freshen up, then tiptoed downstairs for tea before the day got away from her. Her mother had set out a spread of fresh fruit, yogurt, and granola in the kitchen for guests to help themselves, so she fixed two bowls, grabbed a tray, and brought everything up to their bedroom.

Grace blinked at her from the bed as she entered the room.

"Good morning," Lia said as she set the tray on the desk where Grace had worked yesterday. "I brought up some tea and breakfast so we could have a few minutes to ourselves before the day gets hectic."

"That sounds good. Thanks." Grace got up and went into the bathroom.

Lia sat with her tea and checked her messages. She hadn't heard from Rosie, which hopefully meant everything was running smoothly at the store. Shanice had texted a photo of her and Riley in Central Park, which made Lia smile. Apparently, their first date had gone well.

Grace came out of the bathroom wearing her pink robe over her pajamas. She took her tea and her yogurt with a murmured thank-you and sat on the edge of the bed with her back to Lia. Everything about her body language this morning read closed off and defensive.

Lia sipped her tea, considering how to handle this. Generally, she addressed difficult things head on, but she didn't want to press too hard and push Grace away. Perhaps a gentle approach was best.

"How are you feeling about things this morning?" Lia asked. She had meant the DNA match, but when she saw the way Grace's shoulders hunched, she wondered if Grace was thinking about that hug that had almost been more than a hug. "Do you think you'll try to get in touch?" Lia asked to clarify her original question.

"I don't know," Grace said, still with her back to Lia.

"I'm here if you want to talk it through."

"Thanks." Grace turned to give Lia a hesitant smile, sitting cross-legged in bed with her tea. "You have a busy day, then?"

"Super busy," Lia confirmed. "Sorry I'll have to leave you on your own for a while. I have to go to Olivia's parents' house to get ready with the rest of the bridal party. You'll have most of the morning to yourself if you want to stay in here, although there will be lots of family in and out of the house if you're looking for company."

"I'll hang out here if no one needs me," Grace said. "I might spend some time researching this woman, my half sister."

"What do you know about her so far?" Lia asked, glad Grace had brought her up.

"Her name is Laurel Byrne, and she lives in Virginia. I thought I might try to stalk her on social media and see—I don't know—if she looks like me." Grace's gaze fell to her teacup, and she sucked her bottom lip between her teeth.

"Did they give you contact information?" Lia asked.

"No, but they said it could be provided if we both agree to it."

"You have a big decision to make," Lia said.

Grace nodded. "There was a time when I would have jumped at this chance, but now I just don't know. I'm happy with my life the way it is, and part of me thinks I should just let sleeping dogs lie."

"Well, you've got time to think about it."

"Yes, I do."

Lia finished her breakfast and gathered her things to shower. Afterward, she blow-dried her hair and left it down, since she would have it styled with the rest of the bridal party later that morning. She put on a simple cotton dress and went back into the bedroom, where she found Grace asleep in bed.

She'd had a long, restless night worrying about this new half sister, and Lia was glad she was getting some rest now, although she didn't like that she'd have to leave without saying goodbye. Grace was nestled under the covers, looking peaceful . . . and beautiful.

Lia had never expected to develop feelings for this woman, and she certainly hadn't expected Grace to be attracted to her in return. Realistically, nothing could come of it with Lia flying back to New York the day after tomorrow.

But what if it did?

CHAPTER SIX

Grace sat at her laptop as the house bustled around her, feeling a bit like the eye at the center of a hurricane. Of course, she could go downstairs, but she was afraid she'd be in the way, that Lia's mother would feel the need to babysit her when she had more important things to do today. Grace was used to being the odd person out at these things. She'd been on her own for so long now that sometimes she forgot what it felt like to be part of a family.

And anyway, the only thing she could concentrate on right now was finding out whatever she could about Laurel Byrne. Her half sister. Nope, it didn't sound right. Even if the same man had knocked up both their mothers, did that really make them sisters? Did Grace want it to? As a little girl, she'd wished for a sister, someone to play with and share all her secrets, but this was something else entirely.

Had Grace's mother known Laurel was out there all along and not told her? Not for the first time, rage boiled inside her for the things her mother had done . . . and for the fact that Grace would never get to confront her about any of it. Hot, angry tears spilled over her cheeks, and she swiped them away.

Exhaling slowly, she typed Laurel's name into the search bar on Facebook and waited for the results to populate. There were more Laurel Byrnes than she'd anticipated. She clicked on the first profile and saw a blonde woman in a graduation cap and gown, but this Laurel lived in Michigan, so Grace backed out and clicked on the next.

Laurel Byrne Number Two looked to be in her midthirties, with brown hair and eyes, a husband, and two kids. There was no location listed. Grace studied her, looking for anything familiar, but . . . nothing.

She made her way through profile after profile until she'd reached the end of the list. There were several Laurels who didn't list their location and several more whose profiles were set to private. Any of them could have been Grace's half sister, or Laurel might not even use Facebook. She ran a few searches on other sites, but she didn't find anyone she felt confident was the right Laurel.

With a sigh, Grace accepted that she'd have to contact Laurel through Your-Gene's site if she wanted to know anything more about her. And she was surprised by the tug in her gut that said she *did* want to know. She wanted answers, however many Laurel could provide. Just because they shared DNA didn't mean they had to maintain any sort of relationship afterward. Grace had grown up an only child, and that wouldn't change.

Whew. Had she just decided to do this? Her finger hovered over the keypad on her laptop. She clicked the "Yes, Connect Me!" button as a tingly feeling gripped her stomach.

Please don't let me regret this.

Someone knocked on the bedroom door, and Grace jumped, closing her laptop like whoever it was could somehow see what she'd just done.

"Grace, are you in there?"

It was Lia's mother, and Grace's stomach tightened for a different reason, guilt gripping her that she'd hid in the guest room all morning while the rest of the family prepared for the wedding. She stood and walked to the door, pulling it open with an apologetic smile. "Hi, Catherine."

"Hello," Lia's mother said. "I just wanted to check in, since we hadn't seen you yet today. You missed lunch."

"I'm so sorry," Grace told her. "I was just finishing up some work."

"It's quite all right," Catherine said, but her eyes held a hint of disapproval, or maybe Grace was projecting her own guilt. "Come downstairs whenever you're ready."

"I'll be down as soon as I get dressed."

With a nod, Catherine headed for the stairs, and Grace closed the door with a sigh. She ought to get ready as quickly as possible and head downstairs, but . . . the thought made her want to scream. Her emotions were in chaos, and she would be terrible company right now. Instead, she sat on the bed and picked up her phone to check her messages.

Rosie Taft:

How's it going as Lia's girlfriend for the weekend? I need updates! Call me!

Grace pressed her lips together in frustration, because she'd inadvertently been ignoring Rosie since she got here. She'd been busy and preoccupied, but that was no excuse. She clicked on the phone icon next to Rosie's name, and it began to ring.

"Hey, stranger," Rosie said in her ear.

"Hi," Grace said, twirling a strand of hair around her finger.

"How's everything?" Rosie asked. "Are you and Lia getting along?"

Too well, perhaps. She held in a sigh. "Yeah, she's great, although the wedding stuff has been kind of crazy and her family probably thinks I'm antisocial because I keep hiding in the guest room."

Rosie laughed. "I would never call you antisocial, but I don't blame you for staying out of the way when you can. So you and Lia are sharing a bedroom?"

"We are," Grace told her, glad Rosie couldn't see her face right now, because she'd surely read Grace's conflicted feelings about this particular topic. "Too many people in the house this weekend. It's fine, though. You and I have shared a bed plenty of times."

"True." Rosie sounded thoughtful, and Grace could only hope she would let the subject drop, because she was still feeling out of sorts about that hug last night and had no desire to talk about it, least of all with Rosie. Grace was out of sorts on every front today.

"You still there?" Rosie said, dragging Grace from her thoughts.

"Yeah, sorry." Grace rubbed at her brow. "I just realized it's later than I thought. I need to start getting ready for the ceremony."

"Okay, I'll let you go, but . . . are you okay?" Rosie asked. "You don't sound quite like yourself."

Grace huffed under her breath, because of course Rosie would notice, but she didn't have time to get into the whole Laurel mess right now. "I'm fine, just a little overwhelmed with all the wedding stuff. I'll call you tomorrow when I get home, okay?"

"Definitely," Rosie said. "Well, have fun . . . or try to, anyway."

"I will," Grace told her. "Bye, Rosie."

She ended the call and sat on the bed, staring at her hands. She needed to shake herself out of this funk *now*. This wasn't the time to obsess about whether or not Laurel would get in touch . . . or her inconvenient feelings for Lia. She needed to shower and get dressed for the wedding.

But her body wouldn't move. She closed her eyes, recognizing that all-too-familiar heaviness in her chest, that sinking pit of grief and loneliness and anger that used to overwhelm her so often in the early days after her parents' death. She'd reopened a lot of old wounds last night, so she probably should have expected to pay the emotional toll today.

She pressed a hand against her diaphragm and sucked in several slow, deep breaths, a technique a therapist had once taught her. She focused on her breathing until the pressure in her chest had eased, and then, she went into the bathroom to get ready.

Thirty minutes later, she stepped into the hallway to find the house suspiciously quiet. Had she gotten the time for the ceremony wrong? A bolt of alarm raced through her that she might have messed around and missed the event she'd come here for. But no, the ceremony wasn't for another forty-five minutes, and the church was only just down the street.

She walked through the empty house, irrationally annoyed that Lia's family had left without her. Of course, she should have come downstairs sooner, but somehow, she had a feeling Catherine would have made more of an effort for Asher.

She poured herself a glass of water in the kitchen, remembering how she'd met Alistair here yesterday. It brought a smile to her face, maybe the first time she'd smiled today. She drank her water and went out the front door, glad she could walk to the church. The day was unusually sunny and warm, beautiful weather for a wedding. Briefly, she tipped her face toward the sun and soaked it in. As much as she loved the UK, its endlessly gray skies were terrible for her tan.

She walked down the street to the church, which was bustling with people, most of whom she didn't recognize. Inside, she found an available seat about halfway back and sat, smiling politely at the couple beside her.

"How do you know Colin and Olivia?" the woman asked with a friendly smile.

"I'm with Lia," Grace told her, and at the woman's blank look, she clarified. "Colin's sister, Amelia? I'm her girlfriend. Grace." She offered her hand.

"Oh," the woman said, accepting Grace's hand after a brief pause. "I didn't realize Amelia . . ." She gave her head a slight shake. "It's lovely to meet you, Grace. I'm Mary, and this is my husband, Richard."

"Nice to meet you," Grace told her, hoping she hadn't just outed Lia to a family friend, but Lia had been out since college, and she'd invited Grace to the wedding, after all. This woman had probably just turned a blind eye to Lia's bisexuality because of the way her family fixated on her relationship with Asher. Birasure was a real thing, and Grace had no patience for it.

She left her purse on the pew and walked to greet Lia's parents at the front of the church, where she was introduced to several more family members and friends. Almost all the women except Grace were wearing hats, everything from feather-adorned fascinators to more elaborate hats with floppy brims. Grace made a mental note to get one for herself if she was ever invited to another British wedding. She might look good in a fascinator. It would certainly be fun to pick one out for herself.

She made it back to her seat just before the ceremony started. Soft music began to play, a tune that Grace associated with weddings but couldn't name, and a young girl with bouncy brown curls made her way down the aisle, tossing rose petals.

To Grace's surprise, the bride came next. Obviously, she had a lot to learn about British weddings. Olivia walked down the aisle, looking radiant in a white, lacy dress, but Grace's gaze was drawn to the bridesmaids walking behind her, or rather . . . one bridesmaid in particular. Lia wore a copper-colored dress, her hair swept into an elegant updo, smiling brightly as she made her way down the aisle. Her dress was strapless, snug through the bodice with a loose, flowing skirt.

Their eyes met, and Grace felt a funny zing in the pit of her stomach. Dammit, this attraction hadn't gone away like she'd hoped. On the contrary, it seemed to be growing.

Lia felt like a terrible friend. She'd barely seen Grace all day, had been forced to leave Grace to mingle with Lia's friends and family—people she didn't know—without her. But at last, after what felt like hours of photographs following the ceremony, Lia made her way into the dining room for the reception with the rest of the bridal party.

She walked behind Audrey, her eyes scanning the room for Grace. Lia hadn't gotten a good look at her in that red dress yet, and suddenly, it was all she could think about. Luckily, it also made Grace easy to spot. That splash of red drew Lia's attention to a table near the front of the room where Grace sat with Mark and several other spouses and partners of the bridal party.

Lia and Audrey headed in that direction together, and Lia was surprised how eager she was to see Grace. As they approached the table, Grace looked up with a bright smile. This was the unflappable woman Lia had first met three days ago, but Lia knew another side to her now, too, the vulnerability she'd shown last night when talking about her family.

"Hi," Lia said as she reached her chair.

"Hi yourself." Grace had pulled back the front of her hair, which seemed to accentuate her cheekbones and the column of her neck. How had Lia not noticed before what an elegant neck she had? And that dress . . .

Lia's gaze dropped to the spaghetti straps on Grace's shoulders, following them down to the bodice of the dress, which perfectly hugged the swell of her breasts. This was the first time Lia had seen her in a bold color like red, and *phew*, what was happening to her hormones this week? Lia didn't drool over pretty, feminine dresses. She lusted over fitted tees and ripped jeans . . . until she'd met Grace. "That dress is stunning on you," she said, aware that her voice sounded lower and more husky than usual.

"I could say the same about yours," Grace responded, standing from the table to give Lia a quick kiss on the cheek. "Do you want a drink? I waited for you because I didn't know what you'd want."

"I'd love a drink," Lia said, taking Grace's hand. "This day has been a whirlwind . . . a wonderful whirlwind, but I'm so ready to relax."

Grace smiled softly. "The ceremony was beautiful, and I say that as a woman who hates weddings."

"High praise indeed, then," Lia said as she led the way toward the bar.

"They seem happy together," Grace said.

"They're very happy together."

"I believed that about my parents too," Grace said, her voice gone quiet. "And look how wrong I was."

Ah. Lia frowned as the pieces came together in her mind. So this was why Grace had sworn off relationships. She'd believed her parents were happily married, and it hadn't been true. Surely there was more to Grace's decision than her mother's indiscretion, but this was part of it. "It's true what they say, I guess," Lia said. "No matter how happy someone seems in public, you never truly know what's going on behind closed doors."

"Even if you live in the same house with them, apparently," Grace murmured.

Lia gave her hand a squeeze. "Maybe they *were* as happy as they seemed, Grace. Maybe they'd worked through whatever issues they had in the past."

"I'll never know, will I?"

"Maybe you'll get some of your questions answered by Laurel Byrne," Lia said as they waited their turn at the bar.

"I gave my permission to get in touch," Grace said. "If she did, too, we should receive each other's contact information."

"Wow, that's a big step. I'm glad you decided to go for it."

"Yeah, I guess." Grace's lips pressed together.

"If you really want to know the truth, maybe you should come back to the States for a visit. Talk to your dad's parents, talk to your mom's friends, meet Laurel, if she's up for it."

"I had made my peace with it." Grace looked down at her shoes, black strappy heels that revealed her red-painted toes. "But now . . . I don't know. Maybe."

The bartender approached them, and Lia ordered a negroni while Grace got a glass of chardonnay. As they made their way back to the table, Grace glanced at Lia, and a soft smile touched her lips. Lia wasn't sure what she was thinking, but whatever it was, Lia liked it. She liked *Grace.*

If they didn't live on different continents, if Grace hadn't sworn off relationships, if there wasn't the added complication of their mutual friendship with Rosie . . . well, Lia might feel like this could be the start of something wonderful. Maybe she should say something before she left the UK. Lia didn't tend to keep her thoughts to herself. If she liked someone, she generally told them so, but this was a potentially sticky situation for so many reasons.

The last thing Lia wanted to do was put Grace in an uncomfortable position. She'd been clear that she didn't want a relationship. Lia was pretty sure she was feeling this attraction, too, but that didn't mean they had to act on it. Certainly, it meant that if they did, they needed to have an important conversation first.

Lia sat beside her at their table, with Audrey on her other side. Olivia's sister, Mia, and her husband, Bilal, were across from them. The rest of the seats were currently empty as people socialized and got cocktails while they waited for the bride and groom to arrive.

"What are you two up to tomorrow?" Audrey asked, turning to Lia.

"We're leaving midday to drive back to London to return our car and get ready for the flight home," Lia told her. In fact, she and Grace would part ways when they arrived in London, but she'd let her family think they would be flying to New York together.

"I know Mum's got a family breakfast planned," Audrey said. "But what if we do lunch together, Mark and me, and you and Grace? I feel like your whole visit so far has been swallowed up in wedding mayhem."

Lia glanced at Grace for approval. She was smiling as if she liked the idea, or at least she was going along with her role as Lia's girlfriend. Lia didn't like not knowing the distinction. She loved the idea of lunch with Audrey tomorrow. She wanted to spend more time with her sister and for her sister to get to know Grace better, but she hated not knowing if

Grace wanted the same or if she was just playing along. "I'd love that," she told Audrey.

"Perfect," Audrey said brightly.

They chatted for a few more minutes, and then Colin and Olivia arrived to rousing applause and took their first dance together as a married couple. After that, food was served, and conversation flowed easily around the table while they ate.

Once the plates had been cleared, Lia turned to Grace. "Care to dance?"

"I'd love to," Grace said, extending her hand.

Lia took it as she rose, taking another moment to admire that red dress. It was long and silky and clung to Grace's curves in all the right places. Truly a shame that Lia wouldn't get to touch it, other than a few well-placed hands on the dance floor.

"Having fun?" Lia asked as they made their way onto the floor. She'd been hoping to hold Grace in her arms, but just as they reached an empty spot to dance, the ballad ended, and an upbeat tune began to play.

"I am now," Grace told her, seemingly undeterred by the change of music as she started to move to the beat.

Lia didn't dance often, but she enjoyed these moments with Grace. "This weekend has been a lot. I don't think I fully realized what I was asking of you until we were here."

Grace bumped her hips against Lia's with a smile. "I'm sure you would have had more fun if you'd had a real girlfriend to bring with you."

"Well, of course," Lia said. "But I'd say you and I have had a lot of fun too. At least, I know I have."

She looked at Grace, almost afraid of what she'd see in her eyes, that this weekend had been nothing but an obligation to her, a favor in return for whatever debt she felt she owed Rosie. But Grace's expression was unreadable. She twirled, her dark hair fanning out behind her as her dress flared around her legs.

They danced together through two fast songs before Lia heard the opening beats of "Electric Slide." It was met with a variety of groans and cheers from the other people on the dance floor, depending on their opinions of the song. Grace laughed as she stepped into line with the people around her, grabbing Lia's hand so that they were next to each other.

"This song is so silly," Lia murmured.

"Oh, come on, don't be a spoilsport," Grace said.

"I'm not." To prove her point, Lia started moving with the group, shuffling from side to side as they followed the synchronized dance. It didn't take her long to step left when she should have stepped right, and she and Grace bumped into each other, giggling as they staggered to the side.

Lia leaned in to whisper in her ear, "Did you know this song is about a vibrator?"

Grace doubled over in laughter, her cheeks blooming an adorable pink. Lia had completely lost the pattern of the dance now, but Grace tugged her into line before the person beside her crashed into them. "It is not," she whispered back, still giggling under her breath.

"It's probably not, but there was a whole thing on social media about it, and once you've heard the lyrics that way, there's no unhearing it," Lia told her, stepping backward as she tried to keep up with the dance.

"You've ruined it for me forever now," Grace said, her cheeks still pink. Her expression alternated between shock and amusement as she danced to the song, probably imagining the lyrics in the context of a vibrator. Her lips were pressed firmly together, and her chest shook with barely restrained laughter.

The song seemed to go on forever, while Lia and Grace stepped and jumped and clapped, but *finally* it came to an end. "All of Me," by John Legend, began to play. Thank goodness, a slow song at last.

Lia turned toward Grace, who stepped forward, settling her hands on Lia's waist.

Grace smiled as they began to sway to the music, and while the "Electric Slide" had been fun, Lia could dance with her like this for hours. Actually, she didn't want to do anything else tonight but hold Grace in her arms as they danced together to romantic songs. Grace's dress was satiny beneath her fingers, and Lia could feel the warmth of her skin through the thin fabric.

Lia was taller than Grace, especially in her heels, and she liked the way Grace had to tilt her face slightly upward to meet her eyes. This was something she liked about being with a woman. Sometimes, it was nice when she dated a man who was bigger and taller than she was. It could be romantic to be literally swept off her feet.

But sometimes, she really fucking loved being the taller person, and right now, she was absolutely intoxicated by Grace's petite stature, by the knowledge that Lia would be the one to sweep Grace off her feet in this scenario, if there was to be any sweeping. She could lift her so easily. She would *love* to do it.

Grace leaned forward until her cheek rested against Lia's. Their breasts pressed together, and Lia's thoughts scattered. "Don't look now, but we have an admirer," Grace whispered, her breath fanning over Lia's cheek.

"We do?" she said, resisting the urge to look.

"Mm-hmm," Grace said. "And he's not very happy about what he sees."

"Asher?" Lia guessed.

"Of course."

"He came alone tonight," Lia told her. "Perhaps he was still hoping you were just a friend."

"Rude of him," Grace whispered. "But also . . . his loss."

Lia grinned, holding Grace a little closer in her arms. "I hope he's jealous as hell."

"Oh, he is, if the scowl on his face is any indication. But . . ." Grace pulled back to meet Lia's eyes, clasping her hands behind Lia's neck. "I think we could make him even more jealous."

"We could?"

In answer, Grace smiled wickedly before she leaned in and pressed her lips against Lia's.

CHAPTER SEVEN

Grace's breath left her in a rush as her lips met Lia's. A delightfully tingly sensation swept through her system, her body coming alive in a way she hadn't felt in years. Her eyes slid shut as Lia's lips pressed more firmly against hers. She'd meant for this kiss to be quick and chaste, a performative kiss for Asher's benefit.

But now that she was here, she didn't want it to end. She wanted to kiss Lia for real, a kiss made safe by the roomful of people around them and the guise of their fake relationship. She'd given up dating in large part because it took her too long to develop this kind of chemistry with someone to get any real pleasure out of a one-night stand, but it didn't mean she'd forgotten how to feel.

Right now, she was exquisitely aware of everything she'd given up. Her lips parted, seeking more. Lia's breath hitched. Her hands pressed firmly against Grace's lower back, but she made no move to deepen the kiss, and Grace understood that Lia was respecting her boundaries. Grace had seen the lust in her eyes. She knew Lia wanted her, and it only made her want Lia more to see her being so polite about it.

Grace wasn't feeling very polite at the moment. Later, she could pretend this was all for Asher's benefit, but right now, this kiss was absolutely benefiting Grace. She was remembering exactly how it felt to be so aroused from the simple press of someone's lips that she could hardly control herself. She sucked Lia's bottom lip between her own, tracing it with her tongue.

Lia groaned, seeming to surrender to the kiss as her hands slid a few inches lower, stopping just above Grace's ass. Her tongue swept into Grace's mouth, and it was her turn to groan, a guttural sound she couldn't have held back if she tried. Lia's tongue stroked hers, and Grace felt it in her core.

Vaguely, she was aware that they were still swaying to the music. Her body followed the song on autopilot as she melted in Lia's arms, absolutely lost in their kiss. Had a first kiss ever been this wonderful? This powerful? This intoxicating? Maybe it was because it had been *so very long* since Grace had been kissed, or maybe it was just Lia.

Maybe their chemistry was just that powerful. It had certainly scrambled Grace's brain. Right now, she couldn't remember why she'd ever given up dating in the first place, why she shouldn't get naked with Lia tonight and let her remind Grace just how amazing sex could be. Because if this kiss was any indication, sex with Lia would almost certainly be amazing.

Lia's lips left hers, moving to press a kiss against her cheek. Grace opened her eyes, and the room slowly came back into focus around her. She saw the dance floor full of other couples moving to the music and Asher still watching from his spot on the wall, drink in hand and an ugly scowl on his lips. Lia watched her with a slightly dazed expression on her face.

Impulsively, Grace turned her head, bringing their lips together for one more kiss, just a quick one now that Lia had reminded her of their surroundings, but *God*, Grace wanted so much more. Her mind was spinning, and her body buzzed with arousal.

"That was nice," Lia said, her lips curving in a smile.

"Very nice," Grace croaked, and whoa, her throat was dry. Her heart was racing out of control, and there was a restless ache deep inside her, like a hungry beast that had just come out of hibernation.

"Want to get some air?" Lia asked, and if that was code for a more private kiss, Grace was all for it. Actually, fresh air in any context sounded like a great idea, because she was flushed from head to foot.

"Definitely."

Lia nodded toward the bar. "Drinks to take with us?"

"Yes, please," she managed, because Lia was full of good ideas right now, while Grace still wasn't forming coherent thoughts.

Lia took Grace's hand in hers as she led the way off the dance floor. They ordered fresh drinks at the bar, and Grace gulped a glass of water while they waited for the bartender to pour them. Then they went through the double doors that opened into the gardens behind the wedding venue.

Outside, it was late afternoon, startlingly bright, and Grace blinked as she adjusted to the sunshine. After the dancing, a glass of wine, and that kiss, she felt like it should be midnight, dark and romantic. But this was a glaring reminder that after the event ended here, there would be a private reception back at Lia's parents' house for the immediate family, a dinner that suddenly sounded way less fun than sneaking Lia upstairs to their bedroom.

They were quiet as they crossed the lawn toward an empty bench next to some flowering bushes. Here and there, other wedding guests wandered through the garden, talking and admiring the greenery. Grace sank gratefully onto the bench. She sipped her wine and looked at Lia, unsure what to say. She'd changed the rules of their agreement with that kiss, but did she really want to take it any further?

Lia sipped her drink, staring across the garden. There was a smudge on the lens of her glasses, and Grace had a feeling she'd been the one to put it there. "That was more than a performance for Asher," Lia said finally, turning her gaze to Grace, straightforward as ever.

Grace was starting to find that she liked it, even though Lia was continually catching her off guard, because Grace tended to keep her feelings to herself. Hell, she tended to keep *everything* to herself, but somehow Lia made her feel safe every time she let go just a little bit. "It was more," she agreed.

"We should talk about it," Lia said, eyes crinkling behind her glasses as she smiled. "A good kind of talk, Grace, because I can already see you starting to freak out over there."

Grace pressed a hand over her eyes, surprised to find herself laughing. "I don't even know what I'm feeling right now. A lot of things."

"We're attracted to each other," Lia said. "And that wasn't part of the plan."

Grace nodded, watching her closely.

"What do you want?" Lia asked, catching Grace off guard all over again with the question. "A few kisses under the guise of putting on a show for Asher? More? Less?"

"I don't know," Grace admitted. "I like you a lot, more than I probably should, given my relationship hang-ups."

"That's what I was worried about," Lia said. "I like you, too, more than I've liked anyone in a long while, if I'm being perfectly honest, but I don't want to put you in an uncomfortable situation, because you were very clear about not wanting a relationship."

"I still don't," Grace whispered, feeling less sure about her decision than she had in the five years since she'd made it.

"You said you didn't do one-night stands because you usually don't feel attracted to anyone that quickly, but I sense that wouldn't be a problem in our case," Lia said with a wry smile.

"Definitely not," Grace agreed.

"But if we had sex tonight, it wouldn't be a one-night stand. We already know each other too well for that. And we respect each other too much to just rip each other's clothes off without talking through the ramifications first. We have to be clear on what this is, and what this isn't."

Grace huffed a laugh. "Lia . . ."

"Yes?"

"Do you always talk this much after someone kisses you?"

Lia's eyes went wide behind her glasses. "Well, I just . . ."

Grace leaned in and pressed their lips together, just for a moment. "I know, and I appreciate it."

Lia took off her glasses and rubbed the bridge of her nose. "I'm so confused."

"Same." Grace plucked the glasses from her hand and used the hem of her dress to wipe away the smudge she'd noticed before. "But I *do* appreciate the way you put everything out there. Sometimes, you ask questions before I know the answers, but I'm still glad you ask."

She handed the glasses back, and Lia put them on, regarding her quietly. Grace loved the chance to look directly into her eyes, but honestly, Lia looked more like Lia when she wore her glasses. They were a part of her aesthetic, and Grace found them incredibly charming on her.

"One thing I didn't anticipate about our arrangement is not knowing what's real," Lia said finally. "Every time you smile at me or agree to dance with me or . . . kiss me, I'm wondering if it's because you agreed to be my fake girlfriend for the weekend or because it's something you genuinely want."

"Oh." Grace looked down at her hands, which were folded in her lap, as a smile tugged at her lips. Of course Lia would be wondering these things. It aligned perfectly with her directness and was part of the reason Grace was so charmed by her. "You really like to know where you stand with people, don't you?"

"I do," Lia said.

"There's not a simple answer to your question," Grace said. "Obviously, I wouldn't be here at all if not for our agreement. Sometimes, I might be smiling at you because I think it's what your girlfriend would do, and I did initially kiss you for Asher's benefit, but I was also partially using it as an excuse to kiss you because I wanted to."

"And how do you feel now?"

Grace sighed. "Well, from a purely practical standpoint, when I spent the day working in the guest room, I noticed I could hear a *lot* of what was going on in the house around me, which makes me hesitate to do anything we don't want an audience for."

Lia's lips twitched, and then she burst out laughing. "Not what I expected you to say, Grace, but you have a habit of doing that."

"So do you," Grace countered playfully, and then she sobered. Lia had been direct with her, and Grace ought to at least try to return the favor. "The truth is, as much as I enjoyed kissing you—and *God*, I really enjoyed it—we should probably stop here. Like you said, we're in too deep for a one-night stand at this point, and I'm not in a place to offer you anything more than that. We'd probably both end up getting hurt if we tried."

"You're right," Lia said as her laughter faded away. "We should keep our hands to ourselves tonight."

Grace pressed her lips together as regret swept through her. She hadn't truly wanted to have sex with Lia tonight, but she hadn't *not* wanted it either. Physically, she wanted it more than anything, but emotionally . . . well, that was another story. "Right."

"And besides, you're celibate anyway." Lia nudged her shoulder into Grace's.

She wrinkled her nose. "I hate that word. You make me sound like a nun."

"Oh, you're definitely not a nun." Lia's gaze slid appreciatively over Grace's dress, making her flush.

God, Lia made her feel so many things. Grace's life had been so much easier before she remembered how this felt, the way her whole body sizzled with awareness every time Lia looked at her, the way arousal rose inside her until she craved the feel of Lia's fingers on her skin more than her next breath.

At that moment, she wished she'd said no to this whole thing, because then she'd still be at home in her blissfully temptation-free bubble. But then again, it had probably been inevitable that sooner or later, someone would come along and shake her up like this. "Maybe we can just kiss some more, though," she whispered.

"I like that plan." Lia leaned in, pressing her lips against Grace's.

She tried to absorb absolutely everything about the kiss so she could draw on the memory of it when she needed fuel for her fantasies alone in bed at home. She memorized the soft slide of Lia's lips, the hard stroke of her tongue, and the sharp taste of liquor from her drink. Her hands slid lightly up and down Grace's arms, and *oh*, that felt nice. Goose bumps pricked her skin as pleasure rolled through her body.

She slid closer to Lia on the bench, resting a hand on her thigh. Lia's dress was soft and silky, and Grace traced her fingers idly over it as her lips explored Lia's. There was that hunger again, rising insistently inside her. The warmth of arousal spread through her, centered in the ache between her thighs. It was heady and surreal to feel like this, especially because she was with Lia.

This was Grace's best friend's best friend, a woman who—until a few days ago—she'd resented, a woman she'd purposefully avoided meeting because Grace didn't like the petty things she felt whenever Lia's name was mentioned. And now here she was, kissing her, and this wasn't just any kiss. It was the kind of kiss that lit Grace on fire, and she had no idea what to do about it. Thank goodness she was going home tomorrow so she could get her head back on straight.

Lia shifted to press feather-light kisses over Grace's cheek to her earlobe, and she shivered at the sensation. After a moment, Lia sat back, smiling. Her nipples had tightened beneath the bodice of her dress, and her chest heaved, and Grace felt absurdly pleased that Lia was as affected by their kiss as she was.

"Glad the wedding's almost over?" Lia asked, reaching out to brush back a strand of Grace's hair.

"Yes, but I've had more fun than I was expecting."

Lia smiled. "You're not what I expected, that's for sure."

They were still leaned in close, and Grace couldn't bring herself to pull away. "No?"

"Well, I guess you're not Rosie's imaginary friend after all."

And just like that, the spell was broken. Grace sat back, her hands clenched into fists against her dress. "I can't believe you ruined the moment by bringing that up."

"What?" Lia gave her a puzzled look.

"Oh, please. You honestly have no idea how much I hate that stupid nickname?"

Lia's lips parted, eyes widening behind her glasses. "No, I . . . you hate it?"

"I do. Thanks for reminding me." She could hear the bitterness in her voice.

"It was just a joke," Lia said. "Rosie was always saying you were going to be at some event or another, and at the last minute, you'd back out, and I . . . well, it was funny. She talks about you all the time, but none of us had ever met you. I meant it to tease Rosie, not you."

"Yeah?" Grace gave her a harsh look. "So, you just decided to call me 'imaginary'? She's the most important person in my life, and you decided I was flighty and insignificant because I didn't cross an ocean to meet you?"

Lia blinked. "Grace, I'm sorry."

Grace looked away. Her cheeks burned with anger and embarrassment, and she just wanted to go home.

"If she's the most important person in your life, why don't you visit?" Lia asked softly.

"Because it's hard, okay?" Grace's voice cracked, and she flinched. "I buried my parents in New York, and I left because I couldn't bear to be there anymore without them. And the next time I went back, it was to bury the woman who'd taken me in after my parents died."

"Rosie's mum," Lia murmured.

"After that, every time I tried to get on that plane, it just made me feel so helpless and sad that I couldn't do it. So I stood Rosie up, and you turned me into a joke."

"Oh, Grace." Lia flung her arms around her, hugging her fiercely.

Grace tensed to resist, but somehow she ended up hugging her back, clinging to her as she battled the tears burning her eyes. She was *not* going to cry at Lia's brother's wedding in front of all these people.

"I'm so sorry," Lia whispered into her hair. "I'm such an asshole. I thought I was being funny, but I never considered how that silly nickname made you feel."

"It's okay," Grace murmured. All the fight had gone out of her in the warmth of Lia's embrace, because deep down, she suspected she was being overly sensitive about the whole thing. Lia had had no way of knowing her words had hurt Grace. It wasn't her fault Grace was such an emotional mess.

When she pulled back, there were tears on Lia's cheeks. "I'm truly sorry."

"Apology accepted," she whispered, leaning in for another kiss, because she needed to blot out the ugliness of the last few minutes, and *phew*, it worked like a charm. Within moments, she was swamped with pleasure.

"I'll come up with a new nickname for you," Lia murmured against her lips, her hands cupping Grace's face. "'Rosie's most lovely friend' or something along those lines."

She turned her face to kiss Lia's palm. "You can just call me Grace, you know?"

Lia's smile was tender. "I'll do that."

Grace sat back, blowing out a breath as she composed herself.

"Why didn't we meet at Rosie's mother's funeral?" Lia asked, looking pensive.

Grace dropped her gaze to her hands, ashamed of the truth—that she'd seen Lia with her arms around Rosie and felt left out, that she'd been so overwhelmed with memories of her own parents' funeral that she'd been a bad friend. She'd avoided Lia that day and cried quietly at the back of the church by herself. "There were a lot of people there," she said instead. "Maybe we met and don't even remember."

Lia reached out to touch Grace's cheek as she shook her head. "Impossible. There's no way I could forget meeting you."

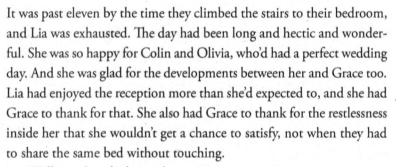

It was past eleven by the time they climbed the stairs to their bedroom, and Lia was exhausted. The day had been long and hectic and wonderful. She was so happy for Colin and Olivia, who'd had a perfect wedding day. And she was glad for the developments between her and Grace too. Lia had enjoyed the reception more than she'd expected to, and she had Grace to thank for that. She also had Grace to thank for the restlessness inside her that she wouldn't get a chance to satisfy, not when they had to share the same bed without touching.

Well, maybe a little touching.

Lia sank onto the bed with a sigh, gratefully kicking off her heels. While Grace went into the bathroom to change, Lia rubbed the arches of her feet and tried not to feel disappointed that she wouldn't get to take her out of that red dress. A damn shame, really.

She set an alarm on her phone to wake them in time for breakfast tomorrow, and then she slipped into her pajamas while Grace was in the bathroom. Okay, maybe she was daring Grace to catch her in her underwear . . . just a little bit. But she didn't. Lia was comfortably dressed when Grace came out, hair down, face scrubbed free of makeup, and wearing the tank top and shorts she'd slept in the last few nights.

"All yours," Grace said as she sat on the bed and picked up her phone.

"Thank you." On one hand, their routine had started to feel familiar and comfortable. This was the third night they'd shared this room, but tonight it was different, because they'd kissed. They'd admitted their attraction but decided not to act on it, and now it seemed to fill the room. Lia couldn't look at Grace in her pajamas—or even at the bed—without thinking about it, and she wondered if Grace was feeling the same thing.

Based on the way Grace was studying her phone without a single glance in Lia's direction, she suspected she might be. Lia went into the bathroom, gratefully releasing her hair from its updo. Her scalp felt tight and sore, and she rubbed at it absently, wishing this wasn't her last night with Grace.

Tomorrow, they'd return to London, and Lia doubted that Grace would keep in touch after they said goodbye. Most likely, Grace would retreat into her life in London, and Lia might not ever see or hear from her again, except through Rosie. The thought made her indescribably sad.

When she went back into the bedroom, the atmosphere had changed. Grace sat cross-legged in the middle of the bed with her phone clasped in her lap, her eyes wide and unfocused. Had there been a development with Laurel? Because Lia wasn't sure how to read the somewhat wild look on Grace's face.

"News?" Lia asked, sliding onto the bed beside her.

Grace nodded jerkily, staring at her phone. "Your-Gene sent out mine and Laurel's contact information, and . . . she emailed me. She asked if I lived nearby and, if so, if I'd like to meet in person."

"Wow," Lia said. "That's huge."

Grace looked at her, eyes bright and panicked. "I don't know what to do."

"Well, you *don't* live nearby, so you could ask if she'd like to talk on the phone or do a video call instead."

Grace nodded, lips pressed together as she stared at the message on her phone.

"Or—and I'm just putting this out there without any expectations attached—the flight to America might be less intimidating with a friend. In fact, I'd be happy to go with you to Virginia to meet her."

Grace gave her a skeptical look. "Why would you want to do that? And don't you need to get back to work?"

Lia laughed. "To be honest, I think Rosie and Jane are having entirely too much fun at the store without me. Rosie's given me several not-so-subtle hints that I should take more time off now that she has Jane to stand in for me."

"Oh," Grace said.

"And to answer your other question, remember how I told you I moved to New York to have an adventure? Then I ended up managing a bookstore right out of college, and I've barely left the city since. I've never been to Virginia. It's near DC, though, and possibly you're aware of my love for museums."

Grace's lips curved into a soft smile. "I may have heard a thing or two, and DC has some of the most amazing museums. You'd love it."

"So what do you say . . . will you fly to New York with me?"

CHAPTER EIGHT

Grace swallowed hard, looking down at the message gleaming on her screen. Should she take this chance to fly to New York with Lia? She was ridiculously overdue to visit Rosie's store in its new location and meet Jane. And it might be easier to face her half sister with Lia beside her. "Um . . . yeah. Okay."

"Oh, this is exciting." Lia beamed at her. "Let's book it right now, before we go to bed."

Grace exhaled. She was exhausted. The last thing she wanted to do right now was book a flight, but Lia was right. If she didn't do it now, she wouldn't do it at all. She'd talk herself out of going and continue to blow off her best friend, continue to be Rosie's imaginary friend, and she'd put off meeting Laurel and learning the truth about their biological father.

"What flight are you on?" Grace asked.

Lia pulled up the flight information on her phone, and Grace spent the next few minutes booking herself onto the same flight. It was ridiculously expensive, but she had savings she rarely dipped into, money she'd gotten from her parents' estate, money that she'd never known quite what to do with—but surely some of it should fund this trip to help solve the mystery of her DNA.

She booked a return flight two weeks later, giving herself time to stay with Rosie in New York for a few days. Then there would be the trip to Virginia to meet Laurel. And she really ought to visit her grandparents while she was in town. She rarely got the chance to see them in person, although they video chatted often. Luckily, her job was flexible this way. She could work from anywhere. As long as she met her deadlines, it didn't matter what continent she was on.

As she completed the transaction, a cold finger of panic slid down her spine, because this trip had the potential to be awful. She might hate everything she learned from Laurel. She might feel like an outsider in Rosie's apartment among the women who knew her so much better than Grace did at this point. And then there was Lia.

"I'll hold your hand anytime it gets scary," she said quietly, as if she'd read Grace's mind.

"I don't need a hand holder," Grace grumbled, which was silly, because she definitely did, and she was glad it would be Lia. How much things could change in three days.

"Should we tell Rosie, or should you just show up and surprise her?" Lia asked, tapping her lips thoughtfully.

"We land really late in New York. If we don't tell her I'm coming, she'll probably go to bed, and waking up to find me on her couch might be a weird surprise."

"Good point, and yeah . . . the couch. I suppose we'd never hear the end of it if I let you sleep in my bed."

"Definitely not," Grace agreed. "She's already going to give us hell, just knowing we shared *this* bed."

"We'll call her tomorrow," Lia said. "In the meantime, we should get some sleep."

"Yep." Grace put her phone on do not disturb, plugged it into the charger, and set it on the table beside the bed. Behind her, Lia shut off the light, plunging the room into darkness. Grace rolled to face her, disarmed by the image of Lia snuggled beside her.

Impulsively, Grace reached out to trace the contours of Lia's face without her glasses to get in the way. Her skin was soft and smooth beneath Grace's fingers. She trailed her fingers through Lia's hair, which was stiff in places from the hairspray that had held her wedding-day updo in place.

Lia slid closer, one of her hands coming to rest on Grace's hip as she leaned in for a kiss. Grace kissed her back, tasting toothpaste in Lia's mouth. Funny how that cool mint flavor warmed Grace from head to toe. This was a dangerous kiss, because they were alone in bed with only mental barriers—and thin walls—to keep them from going too far.

Lia's hand was firm on Grace's hip, her fingers warm where they touched Grace's skin above her pajama shorts. As much as Grace loved the feel of Lia's fingers on her skin, she also realized Lia was using that hand to literally hold Grace at arm's length. If their bodies came together under the covers, it would be all over.

"We have to stop kissing once we get to New York," Lia murmured against her lips.

"Yes," Grace agreed.

"But I just wanted you to aknow that if you *did* want to try a relationship—however casual or long distance it would need to be, given the circumstances—I'm definitely interested, but I'll leave it to you to make that call, because I don't want to pressure you to break your no-dating rule," Lia said quietly, her hand still on Grace's hip.

"You really are one of a kind," Grace said. Lia never failed to catch her off guard with her directness, and this time, it was undeniably turning her on. "What kind of relationship could we even have, though? I mean, assuming I wanted to break my rule."

"We could have a road trip fling while we explore museums and meet your half sister," Lia said. "And if that went well, we could try things long distance after you go home."

"I don't see how that could ever work," Grace deflected, although a road trip fling sounded oddly enticing right now.

"All I'm saying is that anything's possible," Lia said. "Either way, I'm glad we've become friends this week, and I hope that doesn't change."

"I'm glad too," Grace said, and she meant it.

"Good night, Grace."

"Night."

Lia gave her another quick kiss, and then she rolled over, leaving Grace blinking into the darkness, buzzing with the electricity of their kisses and pondering all sorts of things she had no business even considering.

It was past two by the time Lia and Grace arrived for lunch with Audrey and Mark at the pub down the street. Grace sat next to Lia, wearing skinny jeans and a black top, and Lia could hardly take her eyes off her. As much as she knew a road trip fling was probably a terrible idea, she couldn't help hoping Grace would take her up on her offer.

"Look," Audrey said, holding her phone across the table to show Lia and Grace a photo she'd taken at the wedding yesterday. "They look so happy."

"They do," Lia agreed, smiling as she saw the way Colin and Olivia gazed adoringly at each other in the picture.

"You two looked pretty cozy yesterday too," Audrey commented, looking between her and Grace.

"We had a good time," Lia said.

"Well, I hope you both come to visit again soon," Audrey said. "Stay with us so you don't have to deal with Mum inviting Asher to dinner."

"Oh, we'll definitely stay with you next time," Lia told her. "And you and Mark should come visit me in New York sometime. It's been ages."

"I know," Audrey said with a regretful look on her face. "Work's been so busy."

"I'm sure," Lia agreed. Her sister was a child psychologist, and she kept a full calendar. In fact, she generally had a wait list of prospective clients seeking her services.

"And, um . . ." Audrey glanced at Mark, who placed his hand on hers and gave her a reassuring smile. "There's another reason I might not be able to travel soon."

"Oh?" Lia's stomach dipped, hoping her sister was about to share happy news, but she couldn't quite read the look on Audrey's face.

Audrey sucked in a breath and nodded. "I'm pregnant."

"Audrey!" Lia exclaimed, bouncing out of her chair to wrap her sister in a hug. "Oh my God, this is the best news. I can't believe you waited so long to tell me. Congratulations."

"Thank you," Audrey said breathlessly as she hugged her back. "We didn't want to distract from Colin's wedding, and besides, it's still quite early. You're the first to know, actually."

"Mum and Dad don't know yet?" Lia asked as she released Audrey, her gaze automatically falling to her sister's stomach, which looked as flat as ever.

"No," Audrey said. "We aren't sharing the news just yet, but we couldn't resist telling you in person while you were here."

"Congratulations," Grace said politely. "That's wonderful news."

"Thank you," Audrey told her, cheeks flushed a happy pink.

"She's been bursting to tell you all weekend," Mark said, nudging his wife playfully. "I kept telling her to just go ahead and do it already."

"I'm going to be an auntie!" Lia could hardly sit still she was so excited. "I've always wanted to be an auntie. When are you due?"

"February third," Audrey told her.

"And how are you feeling?" Lia asked.

"Not bad," Audrey said. "Tired, mostly. I get a little nauseous sometimes, but I really can't complain."

"I'm so glad," Lia told her. "Well, if you were looking for a way to convince me to visit more often, I'd say you've found it."

"That would be wonderful," Audrey told her. "I miss you, you know?"

"I know," Lia said. "God, Colin and I are never going to hear the end of this from Mum and Dad, are we? The baby having the first baby."

Audrey rolled her eyes. "Well, I've been married the longest."

Lia couldn't stop smiling, and when she glanced at Grace, she was watching Lia with a quietly amused expression on her face. Audrey showed them sonogram pictures, and Lia badgered her with silly name suggestions while they ate, with Mark and Grace occasionally jumping in with ideas of their own. It was all so fun and happy, and as they were saying their goodbyes outside the pub, Lia felt a bittersweet tug of regret.

She missed her sister already, and she felt guilty for letting Audrey believe Grace was her girlfriend. Maybe she would call her and tell her the truth after she was home. She ignored the voice in the back of her mind reminding her just how badly she wanted the kind of love and happiness that both of her siblings had found. She'd let herself get too attached to Grace this weekend, and it was going to hurt when the time came to say goodbye.

"Remember not to say anything to Mum and Dad yet," Audrey reminded her as they parted ways. "We'll tell them in a few weeks."

"My lips are sealed," Lia said, giving Audrey another hug. "Keep me posted, okay? I want to know everything, and I'm going to need regular pictures once you start showing."

"We'll see about that part," Audrey said, but she was smiling.

They said goodbye, and Lia and Grace got into their rental car to drive back to London. Grace had been fairly quiet during lunch, but she didn't seem uncomfortable.

"You're a very excited auntie-to-be," she commented as Lia guided them down the road that led out of Sevenoaks.

"So excited," Lia confirmed.

"Do you want kids of your own?" Grace asked.

"I'd love kids," Lia told her. "But I don't feel like I *have* to have them, if that makes sense. I think I could be happy spoiling my nieces and nephews and my friends' kids if I'm not in the right situation to have my own."

"That sounds like a healthy outlook."

"Do you?" Lia asked. "Want kids, that is?" She assumed the answer was no, but Grace had been known to surprise her.

"Not particularly," Grace said with a shrug. "It's not really something I've thought about, especially since I don't want to get married. Being a single parent sounds hard. I think I'm happy on my own."

"Fair enough," Lia said.

"You'll be a great auntie," Grace told her. "That kid will be so spoiled."

"*So* spoiled," Lia agreed.

They drove for a few minutes in silence, but it felt like the comfortable kind. Grace gazed out the window at the English countryside, her posture loose and relaxed.

"Where are you staying tonight?" she asked out of the blue.

"Shit," Lia muttered. "I meant to book a hotel before we left, but I got distracted with the baby news."

"You can stay with me and Ollie if you like," Grace offered. "Our couch pulls out, although I've never slept there, so I don't know if it's comfortable."

"Oh," Lia said, surprised by her offer. "Actually, that would be perfect, if you don't mind. Then we can just head to the airport together tomorrow."

"That's what I was thinking," Grace said. "No sense in you paying for a hotel room."

"You're sure Ollie won't mind?"

Grace grinned at her. "You met him. He's a social butterfly. He'll be thrilled."

"Then yes, I'd love to sleep on your sofa. Thank you."

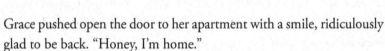

Grace pushed open the door to her apartment with a smile, ridiculously glad to be back. "Honey, I'm home."

"Still not your honey," Ollie called from the direction of the kitchen. "How was your long weekend with your not-girlfriend? Any hanky-panky? Please tell me there was hanky-panky."

"Um." She glanced apologetically at Lia. "Actually, Lia's here with me."

"Oh my God." Ollie came around the corner, dressed in cutoff shorts and a sleeveless top. "Well, if it isn't the not-girlfriend in person. Hello, Lia."

"Hi, Ollie," she said, seemingly unruffled. "Grace offered to let me crash on your sofa tonight before our flight tomorrow. You don't mind, do you?"

"I don't mind a bit," Ollie said. "But what's this about 'our flight'? Are you leaving me, my dear?" He raised his eyebrows at Grace.

"I was overdue to visit my friends in New York and decided it would be fun to fly over with Lia," Grace said, because while Ollie knew her pretty well, he didn't know about her mother's infidelity, so she couldn't tell him about Laurel without having to start from the beginning, and she just didn't have the energy for that tonight.

His eyebrows went even higher. "Really? That seems so . . . out of character for you."

"I'm trying to be impulsive for a change," she said with a shrug.

"Okay." He glanced at Lia, as if she might say something to explain Grace's odd behavior.

And now that Grace had left the surreal bubble of the wedding weekend, she realized that this would be Rosie's reaction too. Of course, she could tell Rosie the real reason for her visit, but this *was* out of character for her, and she hated having to explain herself. She held in a sigh.

"Could you point me toward your restroom?" Lia asked.

Ollie gestured over his shoulder. "End of the hall."

"Thank you."

As soon as she was gone, Ollie turned to Grace with a delighted expression on his face. "Oh my God, I was totally joking about the hanky-panky, but look at you! Did you fall off the wagon?"

"What wagon?" she asked, exasperated, even though she knew exactly what he meant.

"The 'no women' wagon," he clarified with a shit-eating grin. "You did, didn't you? You have a certain glow about you." He waved his hands dramatically in front of her.

She swatted him away. "I did no such thing."

"Not even a little messing around?" he asked, following her into the living room. "You deserve some romance in your life."

"I don't *want* any romance in my life," she deflected. "But there might have been a little fooling around."

"I knew it!" He tapped his knuckles against hers. "So you fooled around with Lia at the wedding, and now you're flying to America with her. Are you sure you aren't falling for her?"

"Positive," Grace told him. "The kissing was mostly because we were trying to make her ex jealous. We aren't doing that anymore."

"If you say so," Ollie said, and from the look on his face, he had a lot more to say on the topic, but luckily, Lia chose that moment to come back into the living room.

And when Grace looked at her, she knew she was lying to herself if she wanted to believe the attraction wasn't still there. It was there. She still wanted Lia—a *lot*—but she could ignore it. It helped that they wouldn't have any privacy at the apartment in New York, and if things got out of hand, Grace could always make the trip to meet Laurel by herself.

"Tonight's my night off from *Inside Out*," Ollie said. "You ladies want to go out to dinner? I'll call Raj. It'll be like a double date."

"Dinner, yes," Grace said. "But it's not a date."

CHAPTER NINE

Lia tucked her bag under the seat in front of her and fastened her lap belt. She glanced at Grace, who sat beside her, staring out the window. Since their plane was still at the gate, there wasn't much to see yet, just the ground crew loading their baggage. Grace had been quiet all day, and Lia hoped she wasn't regretting her decision to make this trip.

"Really hope this seat stays empty," Lia commented, patting the seat to her left. If no one sat there, she could move over once they were in the air and give her and Grace a little more room to get comfortable, because this was a long flight and these seats were small.

Grace gave her a tight smile, holding up her fingers, which were crossed. Their phones chimed almost in unison. Lia reached for hers and tapped the screen to reveal a text from Rosie, sent to both of them.

Rosie Taft:

Have a safe flight! Can't wait to hug you both tonight! 🤗 ☺

"Oh no, we're in group-text territory now," Lia joked.

Grace smirked. "She's going to lose it when we get there, isn't she?"

"'Enthusiastic' will be an understatement," Lia agreed. Rosie was enthusiastic on any given day, but it had been several years since she'd seen Grace in person, so her excitement was likely to be off the charts. "If you're not careful, she'll be attached to you all week."

"That wouldn't be so bad," Grace said, her expression softening. "I've missed her too."

Lia watched as a grumpy-looking man in a business suit walked toward them, then exhaled in relief as he passed their row. It seemed like the majority of passengers had boarded now, so maybe they'd actually get to keep their extra seat.

Beside her, Grace looked cozy in black leggings and a loose gray-and-white-striped top. She'd dressed comfortably for the flight, but there was a tension in her posture that belied her casual attire. Lia felt terrible for the way she'd teased her over the years, calling her Rosie's imaginary friend without knowing why this flight was so difficult for her. Now that she knew, she just wanted to give her a hug.

Or a kiss. The chemistry between them was as potent as ever, and Lia could only hope Rosie wouldn't pick up on it. Lia would *never* hear the end of it if she found out, but maybe the spell would be broken once they landed in New York. She could hope, anyway. But as Grace glanced at her, those full lips pursed, Lia knew she was screwed.

She was so busy staring at Grace that she didn't even notice their new seatmate until she felt the seat dip beside her. She turned with a polite smile, which was returned by the middle-aged woman sitting there. Well, at least their seatmate seemed friendly.

A few minutes later, the cabin door closed, and the flight attendant at the head of the plane began to run through the safety information for their flight. Grace was unnaturally quiet, and Lia found herself similarly at a loss for words. She was tired. Grace probably was too. It had been a whirlwind of a week. Hopefully they would both get some sleep on the flight, although Lia usually wasn't able to do much more than nap.

"When's the last time you visited?" she asked in an attempt to break Grace out of her window-gazing reverie.

"About four years ago," Grace told her. "I spent Christmas with my grandparents in Albany, but I think you were here in the UK."

"Yes, that's right," Lia said. "I always fly home for Christmas."

"I spent the night at your apartment with Rosie and Paige," Grace said. "In fact, you even lent me your bed, since you weren't home."

"Oh my God. Yes, I did." And now she'd be thinking about Grace in her bed when she slept in it tonight. She'd thought about her last night, too, as she slept on the pull-out sofa in Grace's apartment. It had been a long time since Lia had slept with someone in the literal sense, sharing a bed the way she and Grace had this week. Not since Shawn, and that relationship had ended almost two years ago.

"That was the trip where I found out about your nickname for me," Grace said, returning her gaze to the window.

"It was hilarious to me at the time," Lia told her. "You'd slept in my bed, but I still hadn't met you."

"I get it," Grace murmured.

"And I get it now too," Lia said, reaching over to squeeze Grace's hand.

"You don't really have to go to Virginia with me, you know."

"I know, but I want to," Lia said. "I'm really looking forward to it, actually. I mean, unless you'd rather me not be there."

"I might go alone to meet Laurel," Grace said.

"That's fine. Whatever you feel comfortable with, but if you want me there for moral support, I'm happy to do it, especially after everything you did for me this week. And I can't wait for our road trip. Do you know that I've never taken one?"

Grace turned, giving her a small smile. "No?"

She shook her head. "I mean, not that New York to Virginia is very far, but London to Sevenoaks is as far as I've ever driven."

"In that case, it's too bad it's not a longer drive." Grace's smile looked more natural then.

With a jolt, the plane began to back away from the gate. Outside the window, the sky was nearly dark. Thanks to the time difference, they'd take off from London at eight and land in New York just past ten local time, but it would feel so much later. Grace seemed more relaxed now that she'd started talking, and they kept chatting about their road trip as the plane taxied down the runway, falling silent as it lifted into the air.

"This part always takes my breath away," Grace said softly as they watched the earth fall away beneath them, the blinking lights of the airport growing smaller as they rose into the sky.

"I do enjoy flying," Lia said. "Although these transatlantic flights can be uncomfortable."

"The seats definitely didn't used to be this cramped," Grace agreed.

"If either of you need to get up during the flight, just tap my shoulder," the woman beside Lia said, reminding them of her presence. "I'll probably fall asleep at some point, but don't be shy. I won't mind."

"Thank you," Lia said appreciatively. She looked at Grace. "That goes for me, too, if I fall asleep. I'm not hard to wake."

"Thanks," Grace said. "I don't sleep much on planes, so I'll definitely need to get up."

"I don't sleep much, either, so I'll keep you company."

"And thanks, you know, for distracting me." She dropped her head, a bashful smile on her lips, and Lia must have been rubbing off on her, because Grace didn't usually address her feelings so directly.

"Anytime," Lia told her. "That's what friends are for, right?"

"Right." Grace leaned back in her seat. "I'm not used to my friends being in my head so much, though. You're dangerous that way, Lia Harris."

"Not dangerous," Lia deflected.

Grace opened her mouth and then shut it, giving her head a slight shake, and maybe Lia really was in her head, because she had a feeling she knew what Grace wasn't saying. It probably did feel dangerous to her for someone to understand her this well, after she'd kept everyone at a distance for so long. Lia had the impression that, as well as Grace got on with Ollie, she didn't tell him the darker things in her mind. Rosie knew, but Grace had put an ocean between them.

"You could be dangerous," Grace murmured, so quietly Lia almost wasn't sure she'd heard her speak the words. "If I let you."

Grace blinked several times, but it was no use. Her eyes were so dry she could barely read the words illuminated on the screen of her Kindle. She'd started reading *On the Flip Side*, one of Brie's most popular books, Brie being the pen name of Rosie's girlfriend, Jane. Grace had never read a romance novel before. She'd assumed she wouldn't like it, because she wasn't very impressed with romance in real life, but she was totally invested in the characters, and their chemistry together was hot. She'd planned to read the whole flight, but exhaustion and the dry air were starting to take a toll.

Her gaze fell to Lia, who had dozed off beside her. Her glasses were slightly askew, her lips parted, and honestly, no one should be that cute when they slept. It was just unfair. As she watched, Lia stirred, and her head slipped to the side, landing on Grace's shoulder. Oh, she was dangerous, all right, because Grace felt warm and happy just looking at her.

She'd scoffed earlier at her apartment when Lia had come out of the bathroom wearing a fitted blue top tucked into a flowing, rainbow-striped skirt, thinking it was totally impractical attire for the airplane, but Lia looked perfectly comfortable sleeping in her skirt, and the cozy socks she'd put on before she fell asleep only made her look even cuter. *Oof.*

Hopefully Grace could get her hormones under control once they landed in New York. Being surrounded by Rosie and her friends should help, because Grace and Lia probably wouldn't be alone together again until they left for their road trip next weekend.

Grace turned her gaze to the darkness outside the window punctuated by the red blinking light on the wing. The map on the screen in front of her showed that they were approaching New York. They were expected to touch down in under an hour, and any thought of sleep vanished as adrenaline burst through her veins. Would coming home ever get easier? Would she ever feel anticipation instead of anxiety as she prepared to exit the plane?

Tears pricked her eyes, and she closed them, grateful for the moisture to counteract the dry air. She hadn't replied to Laurel yet. Grace had flown across an entire ocean to meet her half sister without actually making plans to do so. She needed to fix that before she lost her nerve, before she used this trip as an excuse to catch up with Rosie instead of solving the mystery that had haunted her for thirteen years.

What if Laurel blamed Grace for her mother's infidelity? What if this DNA match had resulted in Laurel's parents' divorce? What if Grace's biological father was there with Laurel when they met? Or was Laurel looking for the same information as Grace? Were they going to pump each other for information about a father neither of them knew?

Grace's stomach churned until she felt sick. She'd lived in a form of avoidance that bordered on denial for so many years. Somehow, learning she had a half sister that she'd never met made the whole situation real in a way it hadn't been before.

She and Laurel were half sisters, but they were also total strangers. Did Grace have other siblings she didn't know about? The idea was horrifying. If she'd been in a car instead of an airplane, she would have turned around right then and headed back to London. She didn't want to do this, not any of it.

A tear rolled down her cheek, only to be brushed away by warm fingers. Grace startled in her seat, her eyes blinking open to find Lia watching her.

"It's all going to work out," Lia said quietly.

Grace wanted to bristle at the sympathy in her tone, but she was too tired, too close to crying for real. She shifted away from Lia, leaning against the wall of the airplane. "We'll see."

"Looks like we're almost there," Lia said, transferring her gaze to the map in front of her. The little airplane symbol on the screen was just off the coast.

"Yeah."

"Did you sleep?" Lia asked.

Grace shook her head.

"So what did you do? Watch a movie?"

"Read one of Jane's books, or part of it, anyway."

"Yeah?" Lia smiled. "What did you think?"

"It's good," Grace said. "I liked it more than I was expecting."

"Not a romance reader?" Lia guessed.

"Not at all, but Jane's talented. I wanted to be able to tell her that sincerely when we met."

"You're a good friend, Grace." Lia nudged her shoulder against Grace's.

She wasn't sure how to respond to that, but the pilot saved her by announcing over the intercom that they were about to begin their descent into New York. She exhaled, bracing herself for the reality of what lay ahead. Lia's hand slid over hers and squeezed. If anyone was a good friend in this scenario, it was Lia.

Grace was exhausted and emotional and wishing she'd booked herself a hotel room so she could panic with privacy. Instead, she'd have to wait until Rosie and all her roommates settled for the night before she could sleep on their couch. There would be no privacy, and the excitement of her arrival would probably have everyone up to meet her, especially after Lia had inadvertently elevated her to a curiosity with her "imaginary friend" nickname.

Grace was quiet as the plane circled Manhattan before setting down on the runway at JFK International Airport. Once they were off the plane, she and Lia visited the restroom and then waited in a miserably long line to retrieve their luggage and clear it through customs. By the time they were at the curb waiting for their Uber—neither of them had patience left for the subway at this point—it was almost midnight in New York, which meant it felt like five in the morning to Grace and Lia.

Her eyes burned with fatigue as she got into their car. Lia looked just as tired, despite her nap on the plane. The streets of Queens bustled around them, busy as ever. As they crossed the bridge into Manhattan, Grace took in the familiar skyline twinkling against the night sky.

She'd grown up in this city. It was in her blood, beckoning to her despite her misgivings over what she'd come here to do. This trip would be nostalgic, a chance to revisit some of her favorite places and reconnect with her best friend.

"On a scale of one to ten, how excited do you think Rosie will be when we walk through the door?" Lia asked as the car turned onto Second Avenue.

"Eleven," Grace told her.

"Funny. I was going to say fifteen."

"Probably accurate." Grace gazed at the buildings as they passed, surprised to realize how much this neighborhood still felt like home, even though she'd left when she turned eighteen.

Ten minutes later, the car pulled up in front of Lia's building. Grace had only been here once, that Christmas when she'd slept in Lia's bed. Lia and Rosie lived in a four-story brick apartment building with a metal fire escape running up the front. They thanked the driver and got out to retrieve their suitcases, then rolled them toward the front door.

"This part's going to suck," Lia muttered as she used her key to unlock the door and let them into the lobby.

Grace gave her a weary smile as she lifted her suitcase to haul it up two flights of stairs. They didn't talk much as they climbed the steps, mostly focused on their task. Grace winced when her suitcase banged against a step. The thump echoed through the old building, and it was past midnight. Most people were probably asleep.

Finally, they reached the landing to the third floor, and before Lia could retrieve her keys, the door to apartment three flew open, revealing Rosie's smiling face. She squealed as she bounded into the hall, grabbing Grace in a hug that squeezed the breath right out of her.

"Hi," she managed as she let go of her suitcase to hug Rosie back.

"You're really here." Rosie pulled back to grin at her, happy tears glistening in her eyes.

"I'm here," Grace said, breathless from carrying her suitcase up two flights of stairs and a little bit from Rosie's hug.

"I'm so happy to see you," Rosie said before hugging her again, her blonde curls pressing against Grace's cheek. She squeezed her tight, and then she was gone, moving to fling her arms around Lia. "And you! I can't wait to see all your pictures from the wedding."

"There are a lot of pictures," Lia said, hugging Rosie back before she gave her a good-natured nudge toward the apartment. "But right now, Grace and I are dead on our feet."

"Right, right, come in," Rosie said, motioning toward the open door. "We got pizza in case you wanted to eat before you crash."

Grace followed her into the apartment, overwhelmed by all the faces she saw smiling back at her. She recognized the brunette on the couch as Paige, and the blonde beside her was probably her girlfriend, Nikki. Jane stood near the kitchen table, a slightly apologetic smile on her face, as if she knew all Grace really wanted right now was to sleep. She recognized Jane easily from the many selfies Rosie had sent over the last year.

"Hi, everyone," Grace said, waving with her free hand as she wheeled her suitcase into the living room. Brinkley—Rosie's little brown dog—trotted over, and she bent to rub him behind his ears.

A flurry of introductions followed. Paige greeted Grace with a warm hug before introducing her to Nikki, while Rosie interjected with a million questions about their trip. Lia rolled her suitcase down the hall to her bedroom, and Grace allowed Rosie to lead her toward the kitchen for a late-night snack, suddenly realizing she *was* hungry, despite having eaten on the plane. There was nothing like New York pizza, and her stomach growled in anticipation.

"Hi, Grace," Jane said, stepping in front of her. Rosie had mentioned that she was shy, and indeed, Grace had almost forgotten they hadn't met yet in the chaos of greeting everyone else.

"Jane, it's so good to meet you in person." Grace surprised herself by pulling Jane in for a hug, but this was the woman who'd swept her best friend off her feet, and for that reason alone, Grace knew Jane was someone she was going to like.

"You too," Jane said, hugging her back. "I feel like I already know you from hearing Rosie talk about you this past year."

"Same," Grace said with a laugh. "I can't wait to get to know you for real this week."

In the end, they all sat in the living room with glasses of water and plates of pizza, laughing and talking despite the late hour. Once the food had been eaten, everyone headed for their rooms to get ready for bed. It was past one now, and most of them had to be up for work in the morning.

Rosie brought Grace a pillow and blankets for the couch, Brinkley trotting at her heels. "I have so many questions for you."

"I'm sure you do." Grace couldn't wait to catch up with her, but she desperately hoped Rosie would wait to ask her questions, because right now, Grace was deliriously tired and emotionally overwrought.

"We'll have to go out sometime this week, just the two of us," Rosie said as she helped Grace spread the sheet and blankets over the couch cushions. "Because I want to know all about why you're here and how things went with Lia at the wedding."

"Definitely," Grace agreed.

"Need anything else tonight?" Rosie asked, placing a pillow at the far end of the couch.

"Nope."

"'Kay. Sleep well. I'm so glad you're here." Rosie grabbed her for another hug, and Grace squeezed her back. She had mixed feelings about so many things, but being here with Rosie wasn't one of them.

"Night."

With a wave, Rosie headed down the hall to her room, with Brinkley at her side. Grace went into the bathroom to wash up for bed. The couch was comfortable enough when she finally lay down on it. She was so far past exhausted that she thought she'd fall right to sleep, but now that she was finally alone, her mind spun with all sorts of uncomfortable things, and she found herself missing Lia's calm presence beside her in bed. She tossed and turned until her overtired brain finally succumbed to exhaustion.

It felt like only minutes later when she heard whispered voices and the soft sounds of people tiptoeing around the apartment. Paige and Nikki had warned her last night that they would be up early, headed to work at Nikki's catering company.

Grace ignored them, feigning sleep until the apartment was quiet again. She drifted back to sleep, only to be awakened as Rosie crept through the living room on her way to the bookstore. Lia would be going in later, but Rosie had insisted that she sleep in after her late arrival. Something nudged Grace's leg, and she squinted at Brinkley, who sat staring up at her.

"Brinkley!" Rosie whisper-shouted from the kitchen, and the dog glanced over his shoulder at her, tail wagging. Rosie came and scooped him up. "Sorry."

"'S okay," Grace murmured, closing her eyes again. She had a feeling she was up for the day, despite still being desperately tired, but she wasn't in the mood for conversation just yet.

"See you later," Rosie whispered, touching Grace's ankle.

A few minutes later, she heard the front door close, and then she was alone. She rolled to her back, blinking groggily at the ceiling. She'd had a miserable night, but such was the hazard of sleeping on the couch in an apartment full of women who had to go to work early in the morning.

The next thing she knew, her eyes popped open to find Lia in the kitchen, hair damp and dressed for work. Grace blinked at her in surprise. Apparently, she'd dozed back off after all.

"Hi," Lia said when she saw Grace watching her. "Are you as jet-lagged as I am this morning?"

"Mm," Grace mumbled. Her head was foggy and sore like she'd been out partying last night. "What time is it?"

"Just past ten," Lia told her. "Feel free to nap in my bed if you want more sleep."

Grace shook her head as she pushed herself to a sitting position. "Tempting, but I should probably get up now and reset myself to East Coast time."

"Probably wise," Lia agreed. "We'll both crash early tonight."

"Yes." Grace rubbed her eyes.

"Tea?" Lia offered. "I was about to make myself a cup."

"Sure."

"What are your plans today?" Lia asked. "Want to walk to the store with me to see it?"

"I need to work too," Grace told her. "But that sounds nice. Are you leaving now, or could I take a quick shower first?" Because she felt scummy after her flight, and maybe a shower would help wake her up.

"I'm in no rush," Lia told her. "Go shower. I'll have tea ready for you when you're finished. You can put your suitcase in my room if you'd like."

"Thanks," Grace told her gratefully.

Forty-five minutes later, she and Lia stepped outside together. Manhattan was cheerfully sunny on this June morning, warm enough that she was comfortable in her T-shirt. A bike messenger whizzed by, and a taxi honked at him as he cut across the street. At the end of the block, a café employee was arranging chairs around the tables along the sidewalk.

Grace's sandals echoed as she walked across a metal grate, and she was struck with a wave of nostalgia, remembering the way she used to tap-dance across them as a little girl. She'd loved the metallic clang of her shoes against the corrugated surface. She hadn't expected the city to still feel so familiar, but as she and Lia turned onto Third Avenue, everything around her felt like home.

"Miss it?" Lia asked.

"No." Grace hadn't missed New York in years. "It still feels like home, though."

"England is like that for me," Lia said. "Although I do miss it at times."

"Think you'll ever move back?"

Lia shook her head. "For a long time, I assumed I would, but I feel settled here now. I think I've become a New Yorker through and through."

"I do, and I don't feel like a New Yorker," Grace said. "I felt at home in Spain. London is still new and exciting, but it feels like someplace that will become home. I'm glad to spend some time here this week, though."

"I bet," Lia said.

They rounded the corner onto East Eightieth Street, and Lia pointed out Between the Pages Bookstore and Café near the end of the block. It was located on the ground floor of a three-story brick row house with a warm, homey feel. There was a rainbow-themed display in the front window with the words **HAPPY PRIDE** at the top. As Grace stopped for a closer look, she saw that all the books in the display seemed to be a part of the LGBTQ rainbow, everything from children's books to nonfiction and, of course, a copy of Brie's latest lesbian romance.

"I forgot all about Pride," Grace said. "Am I going to be here for that?"

Lia nodded. "It's the weekend before you go home."

Grace grinned. "Perfect. I haven't done New York City Pride since I was a newly out teenager. I assume you and your roommates are going?"

Lia smiled. "It's one of the few days of the year that we close the shop so Rosie and I can both go. Ready to go inside?"

With a nod, Grace reached for the handle and pulled open the door.

CHAPTER TEN

Lia followed Grace into the store, happy to be back and even happier to see half a dozen customers browsing the shelves and several more people sitting in the café section enjoying a treat while they shopped. Between the Pages had only been open in its new location for three months, but so far things seemed to be going unbelievably well.

All the same, Lia couldn't wait to sit at her computer and run the numbers. She needed to check their inventory and make sure Jane had done a good job of maintaining Lia's spreadsheets in her absence. Rosie was busy helping a customer—although she waved excitedly—so Lia gave Grace a quick tour of the shop.

"I love the new café," Grace commented after Lia had introduced her to the weekday barista, Tomás. "I'm totally going to hang out here and drink coffee while I work this week."

"Jane does that sometimes too," Lia told her. "The café was her brainchild."

"I remember," Grace said with a soft smile as she wandered through the store, trailing her fingers over book spines as she walked. "This space is beautiful. I mean, the old store was pretty perfect, but this one feels nicer somehow, maybe just because it's new."

"The move gave us a chance to reenvision everything, buy new furniture, repolish the shelves, that sort of thing."

"Not all of your furniture is new," Grace said, nodding to the oversize red chair in the café area, and she was right. That chair had been a part of Between the Pages for longer than Lia had. "I used to sit in that chair to do my homework when I was a teenager," Grace told her, reminding Lia just how long she had known Rosie, again longer than Lia.

Rosie interrupted them then, wrapping an arm around Grace with a wide smile. "Hey, stranger. I'm so glad you came in, because I don't think I could have waited until I get off work tonight to see you. Did you sleep okay on the couch?"

Grace gave her a fond look. "Not really, but my internal clock was so screwed up it felt like morning to me before we even went to bed. I think I'll crash tonight. And I was just telling Lia I might have to bring my laptop and do some translation work in your café. It looks so cozy. I could sit in the red chair like old times."

She rested her head on Rosie's shoulder, looking at peace with the world. Lia had noticed the connection between them last night, but she saw it more clearly in the light of day. Grace looked more comfortable with Rosie than Lia had ever seen her. It was a reminder that she and Grace would always be connected through Rosie. If they had a road trip fling next week, it could never truly be a "no strings" arrangement, not when they shared a best friend.

"I would *love* that," Rosie said. "I still can't believe you're here for a whole week. It feels too good to be true."

"Two weeks, sort of," Grace told her. "I have a lot to catch you up on later."

Rosie's gaze darted from Grace to Lia and back. "Yeah, I got the feeling something was going on that you two hadn't told me about yet. Should we grab a late dinner together tonight?"

"I'll close for you," Lia offered. "Then you two can have dinner at a normal hour."

"That sounds perfect," Grace said. "I can't wait to talk more, but right now, I should probably let you ladies get to work, and I need to get back to your apartment and do the same."

"Okay," Rosie said, then held up a finger. "Wait, let me give you my key. I meant to leave a spare for you at the apartment this morning, but I was tiptoeing around and forgot."

"Thank you," Grace told her as she followed Rosie to the counter.

Rosie took her key off the fob in her bag and handed it to Grace. "I'll text you about dinner, okay?"

Grace nodded, gave her another hug, and then, with a wave, she left the store. The bell overhead tinkled to announce her departure.

Rosie turned to Lia with a giddy smile. "She isn't the only person I want to catch up with. Tell me *everything*."

"About what?" Lia deflected as she set her bag behind the counter. As much as she wanted to go to her office and get to work, she did want to chat with her friend first.

"About the wedding, your trip in general, whatever's going on between you and gorgeous Grace." Rosie's eyebrows lifted dramatically.

"Nothing's going on," Lia told her as she pulled out her phone to bring up her photos from the wedding. "Although we bonded a lot more than I expected. I hope we'll stay friends after she goes back to London."

Rosie cocked her head, watching Lia closely. "Not even any kissing?"

"There was some kissing at the wedding, for appearance's sake," Lia said. She'd tell Rosie everything at some point, but not this week, when Grace had more important things to deal with than Rosie's nosiness. "Grace has important boundaries, and I respect them."

Rosie's eyes widened. "Wow, you two really *did* bond. And how did her no-dating decision happen to come up?"

Lia shrugged. "We were at a wedding. I suppose sharing our own thoughts on love and marriage was inevitable."

"She says she's happier alone, but . . ." Rosie sighed, a faraway look in her eyes. "Sooner or later the right woman will come along and change her mind."

"I don't necessarily agree," Lia said. "There's nothing wrong with a person being happily single, if that's what's right for them. Grace shouldn't have to define herself by her relationship status."

Rosie's brow wrinkled. "Why are you getting all defensive about her? You do realize I'm her best friend."

"I do," Lia said, even as she realized Rosie had a point. Lia didn't need to defend Grace to Rosie, and her reasons for doing so were almost certainly rooted in feelings that weren't strictly platonic. "But you're a romantic at heart, so focused on love and romance that maybe you forget it's not what everyone wants."

"Okay, fair point, but—" Rosie cut herself off as a customer approached the counter. She cheerfully rang up the man's purchases before turning to Lia. "I have a feeling you and I have a lot more to catch up on."

Grace stood in front of the apartment building on East Eighty-Second Street where she'd grown up, still not sure why her feet had brought her here. She hadn't walked past this building since she'd first left New York all those years ago. She'd carefully avoided it on her visits since then, afraid she'd be gutted by the memories it held. Standing here now, her chest ached as she remembered the way she and her neighbor Amirah would race each other up the steps to the fifth floor, both of them gasping and giggling by the time they reached the landing.

She remembered curling up in bed with her head on her mom's chest as she read to Grace in Spanish and cooking with her in the kitchen. She remembered her father's boisterous laugh and the way they'd ride their bikes together through Central Park. He'd always buy her an ice cream cone before they rode home, chocolate chip for her, strawberry for him. And when she was stumped on her homework—no matter what subject—he'd sit with her at the kitchen table and help her work through it.

She would make dramatic gagging sounds when her parents kissed in front of her, but when she heard stories of fighting and divorce from her friends at school, she'd secretly felt lucky. Her parents loved each other. They were happy. They adored her. She had the perfect family.

And it had all been a lie.

Hot tears burned her eyes. Her mother had taken her lies to the grave, and Grace would never get the chance to ask the things she needed to know or tell her mother how much her betrayal had hurt her, how many years she'd wasted being *angry*.

But now there was another way to get those answers, and Grace would be foolish not to pursue it. As soon as she got back to Rosie's apartment, she would email Laurel and set up their meeting.

Grace turned on her heel and started toward the apartment, grateful to have a little time to herself, because she was exhausted and emotional. She let herself into Rosie's building and walked upstairs, stifling a yawn and still feeling like she might burst into tears at the slightest provocation. She unlocked the door to the apartment and then stopped in her tracks when she spotted Jane at the kitchen table, typing on her laptop. *Shit.* She'd totally forgotten Jane worked from home.

She smiled at Grace. "Morning. I just made a fresh pot of coffee if you want some."

"I'd love some. Thank you." Grace walked to the kitchen and poured herself a mug. She'd gotten pretty used to drinking tea over the last week with Lia, but nothing beat coffee for a rejuvenating hit of caffeine. And while she was disappointed not to have the apartment to herself, she knew she should seize this opportunity to get to know Jane. "Mind if I join you?" she asked, motioning to the chair across from Jane.

She shook her head with a smile. "What are you up to today while everyone is at work?"

"I need to work too," Grace told her.

"Ah," Jane said with a nod. "We can be work-from-home buddies, then. I have a lot of writing to catch up on after working at the store with Rosie last week."

"I'd like that," Grace said.

"How was the wedding?"

"Good as far as weddings go," Grace told her. "I'm not a big fan in general, but the bride and groom seemed happy, and Lia had a great time."

Jane's lips quirked in amusement. When Rosie had first started texting Grace about her last year, she'd described Jane as this corporate bitch in glamorous suits who was out to destroy her bookstore. She hadn't known at the time that Jane was also her favorite author or that she'd longed to quit her day job to write full time.

Grace couldn't quite imagine the woman before her as Rosie had first described her. Jane wore a pink hoodie, lounge pants, and no makeup, and it was hard to mistake her demeanor as anything other than content. Clearly, her new life suited her.

"I read one of your books on the flight here, by the way," Grace told her. "It was really good."

"Thank you," Jane said, ducking her head with a shy smile. "I appreciate that."

Grace put down her coffee and went to get her laptop, and then she set up across from Jane. Before she lost her nerve, she sent a quick email to Laurel, asking when she wanted to meet. Then she got started on her translation work. She and Jane worked in comfortable silence until lunchtime, then made sandwiches together in the kitchen, getting to know each other while they ate. Jane was quiet but friendly, and Grace liked her a lot. She could see why Rosie had fallen for her and was glad they'd found each other.

After lunch, Jane and Grace worked through the afternoon. Grace hadn't been sure how much she'd get accomplished today, because her brain was bleary with jet lag, but she got more done than she'd expected. Occasionally, she'd look over to find Jane staring into space, which she explained she did when she was working out the next scene of her book in her head. Grace found herself fighting a smile every time Jane zoned out. It was fun to watch her work.

Before she was expecting it, the door opened, and Rosie and Brinkley came in.

"Aw, look at you two working so hard," Rosie said as she unclipped Brinkley's leash and crossed the room to plant a kiss on Jane.

"She's good company," Jane said, nodding toward Grace.

"I was going to say the same thing," Grace told her with a smile.

"You're warming my heart," Rosie said, pressing a hand against her chest. "Two of my favorite people hitting it off. You still want to do dinner tonight?" she asked Grace.

"Definitely," Grace told her. "Bring Jane, too, and anyone else who's around."

"I could, but I got the impression there was something we needed to talk about without an audience." Rosie lifted her eyebrows.

Grace sighed, dropping her head. "It can wait. I'm pretty tired tonight anyway."

"Nope." Rosie patted Grace's shoulder. "I want to hear everything, and besides, I get to have dinner with her every night," she said, nodding toward Jane with an affectionate smile.

"It's true." Jane made a shooing motion with her hand. "Go on, you two. We'll have dinner together later in the week."

"Deal." Rosie turned to Grace. "Want to go to Jason's for old times' sake?" Rosie's mom had taken her and Grace for weekly dinners at Jason's during the year Grace lived with them.

"It's still here?" Grace asked.

"Sure is," Rosie told her.

"Then I think we have to," Grace said as she saved her file and shut down her laptop. "Just give me a few minutes to get ready."

"Take your time," Rosie said as she sat in Jane's lap, leaning in for a kiss.

"You two are disgusting," Grace called over her shoulder as she went down the hall to Lia's bedroom, where she'd left her suitcase. She swapped her T-shirt for a short-sleeve, button-down top, then went into the bathroom to freshen up her hair and makeup.

When she made it back to the living room, Rosie was still in Jane's lap, and they were leaned in close, murmuring to each other. Grace's heart melted a little bit at the sight. She was *not* a romantic, but it was hard not to appreciate the way they obviously adored each other. "I'm ready when you are," Grace said.

"Ready." Rosie pressed another kiss against Jane's lips. Then she stood and ruffled Brinkley's furry head before hooking her arm through Grace's and steering her toward the door.

"Glad to leave the store early tonight?" Grace asked as they walked down the stairs.

"I am," Rosie said. "I love it there and never complain about having to work, but it's nice to have an evening off, especially when you're here. What magic did Lia work to convince you to fly home with her?"

"It wasn't Lia who convinced me," Grace told her. "Or maybe it was, in a way."

Rosie gave her a searching look. "You've lost me."

They stepped outside onto the sidewalk, and Grace inhaled the evening air, scented with car exhaust and warm asphalt. It smelled like home. She blew out her breath, gathering herself, but despite the difficult topic, she'd never had trouble talking to Rosie. "I'm here to track down my biological father."

"Oh . . . wow." Rosie gulped, stopping short in the middle of the sidewalk. "Did something happen? Did you find out who he is?"

She waved her hands in front of her face. "You'd better start at the beginning."

"Remember when I submitted my DNA to that ancestry site?"

"Vaguely," Rosie said. "It was around the time my mom died, wasn't it? Not long after we graduated from college?"

Grace nodded as she and Rosie turned the corner onto Second Avenue. "Apparently, I checked a box that let them run my DNA against other people who registered, and last week, they matched me with a woman who's probably my half sister."

"Oh my God," Rosie exclaimed. "That's huge! And you're going to meet her while you're here in New York?"

"Yes. She lives in Virginia, so I'm going to drive down. It's . . ." Grace exhaled, giving her head a shake. "It's terrifying, and I don't really know if I want to know, but it feels like maybe it's time for me to find out the truth."

Rosie wrapped an arm around her shoulders, giving her a hug that jostled them both from side to side as they walked. "I hope the truth helps you make peace with everything."

"Thanks. That's what I'm hoping for too."

"Do you want company? I could probably get Lia to cover for me and take a day off to drive down with you."

She gave Rosie a hesitant smile. "Actually, Lia offered to come. She was just waiting for me to tell you about Laurel—my half sister—before she talked to you about taking the time off. We're going to make it a little road trip so she can see the museums in DC."

Rosie's mouth fell open, and then she grinned. "I feel like my two best friends are becoming best friends without me, and maybe I should be jealous about that, but I'm not. I'm just glad you hit it off and that she'll be there with you. This isn't something to do alone, and Lia's the best."

"You'll always be my bestie. You know that." Grace bumped her shoulder against Rosie's.

"So are you and Lia just friends, or more than friends?" Rosie asked.

Grace gave her an exasperated look. "I know you're, like, the poster child for romance, but I'm not, okay? I'm not interested in any of that, and you know it."

Rosie lifted her hands with a sheepish grin. "I do, but I had to ask, and I also have to point out that you didn't exactly answer my question."

"We're just friends," Grace told her firmly, and technically it was the truth, so why did she feel like she was lying to her best friend?

CHAPTER ELEVEN

It was nine thirty by the time Lia got home from the bookstore, and she was exhausted. Thanks to jet lag, it felt like half past two in the morning. She planned to grab some leftover pizza from the fridge, check in with Grace—because she missed her after having spent so much of the past week together—and then head straight to bed.

When she opened the door to the apartment, she found Rosie, Jane, and Grace in the living room, talking. Paige and Nikki must have already gone to bed. They often had to get up early for their catering work.

"Hello, ladies," Lia said as she dropped her bag on the table by the door. Brinkley trotted over to greet her, and she bent to pet him.

"Hi," Rosie said. "I hear you decided to take us up on that offer to have Jane cover for you again when you want to take some vacation time."

"Well, I was going to *ask*," Lia said. "And Jane, please feel free to say no if you need to spend that time working on your next book."

"It's fine," Jane told her. "You and Grace have a fun road trip."

"Thank you," Lia said.

Grace looked up with a smile, and suddenly Lia wished the rest of her roommates weren't there so she and Grace could have a minute alone. She wanted to hear about her day, but maybe she also wanted to try to reclaim the closeness they'd shared in Sevenoaks. She missed that. Truth be told, she missed it a lot.

Instead, Lia walked to the kitchen and poured herself a glass of water before putting a couple of slices of pizza on a plate, which she brought with her to the living room. She sat in the chair by the window. The rest of the women were already in their pajamas, looking as tired as Lia felt. They'd all been up late last night waiting for her and Grace to arrive.

They chatted while Lia ate her pizza, and then she went down the hall to get changed for bed. She was surprised when Grace slipped into the bedroom behind her. "Hey," Lia said, feeling the smile on her lips.

"Hi." Grace looked suddenly shy, cheeks pink and eyes downcast. Her bare legs peeked out from beneath her robe, and Lia's body warmed as she remembered Grace's skimpy sleep shorts.

"How was your day?" she asked, not quite sure why Grace had come into her room but ridiculously pleased by it all the same.

"Good," Grace said. "Jane and I worked here together, and then Rosie and I went to dinner. It was nice, but I'm so tired."

Lia laughed. "Same. I was going cross-eyed the last few hours at the store."

"Night, ladies," Rosie called from the hallway, and a moment later, Lia heard Rosie's bedroom door close. She and Jane didn't usually turn in this early, but they were probably clearing the living room so that Grace could sleep.

"I emailed Laurel today," Grace said.

Lia motioned for her to sit next to her on the bed. "I was wondering if you had. Did she reply?"

Grace nodded, toying with a strand of her hair. She sat farther away than Lia would have preferred, although it was probably for the best if they were going to keep their hands to themselves. "She asked if we could meet next Friday."

"Okay. Do you still want to leave this weekend for our road trip?"

"Definitely," Grace said. "I'm sure we can find plenty of fun places to stop on our way to DC, and then we'll spend a few days there seeing museums and things. Meeting Laurel is my milestone, but having an adventurous road trip is yours."

Lia grinned, thrilled with the idea of a whole week on the road with Grace. "That sounds perfect. Let's do some research this week and plan out our journey."

Grace beamed at her, sliding closer on the bed. "It'll be fun, and it'll help to keep me from obsessing over meeting Laurel."

"A win-win," Lia said.

"Okay, well, I guess I should let you get ready for bed." Grace looked down, tugging at the sash on her robe, and it was all Lia could do not to reach out and pull her into her arms. She wanted to tell Grace to stay in her bed tonight, that she'd missed sleeping beside her last night. She wanted to surrender to the yearning to kiss her, and if the introspective look on Grace's face was any indication, she was feeling at least some of the same things.

Lia decided to land somewhere in the middle between giving in to her attraction and letting Grace walk out without doing anything at all. She scooted over and wrapped her arms around Grace, pulling her in for a hug. Grace hugged her back, arms snug around Lia as she nestled her face into the crook of Lia's neck.

Lia turned her face toward the silky depths of Grace's hair, inhaling the vanilla scent of her shampoo. Grace's heart thumped against Lia's right breast, and she knew hers was beating just as hard. This wasn't just a hug. Nothing between her and Grace was ever "just" what it was supposed to be. The connection between them ran deep, and it was intrinsically charged by their chemistry.

It seemed unlikely that they'd make it through their road trip without giving in to temptation, but that would have to be Grace's decision, and Lia wanted to be sure she'd fully thought it through before anything happened between them. Lia ought to consider herself, too, because her feelings for Grace could easily spiral into something much more significant than a road trip fling.

She stroked a hand over Grace's hair, and she sighed against Lia's neck, a sleepy, peaceful sound that made Lia want to lie back in bed—still dressed from work—and hold her all night. She had a sneaky feeling she might already be in over her head where Grace was concerned.

Grace's lips brushed against her neck, and desire tugged low in Lia's belly. Her arms tightened automatically, holding Grace closer, loving the warm, solid feel of her pressed over Lia's heart. In fact, she wasn't sure how to let her go.

After a minute, Grace made the decision for her. She sat back, releasing Lia. A strand of her hair snagged in Lia's necklace, stretching between them like a physical manifestation of their connection. Carefully, Lia disentangled her hair, and Grace straightened. Her cheeks were flushed, her expression slightly dazed.

"Good night, Lia," she murmured, and then she was gone.

The next few days felt both unbearably slow and alarmingly fast. Grace brought her laptop to the bookstore in the mornings and sipped coffee in the red chair while she worked. After lunch, she would wander through some of her favorite spots on the Upper East Side before going back to the apartment to spend the afternoon working at the kitchen table with Jane.

Evenings were sometimes chaotic, because with Grace visiting, there were six of them sharing the apartment. Grace didn't mind, since she'd always enjoyed being surrounded by friends. Jane seemed to struggle the most, often retreating to her room to get some space.

On Friday, Rosie gathered everyone to go out for drinks after work before Grace and Lia left on their road trip the following morning. They went to a bar a few blocks from the apartment, where they were met by Shanice and her new girlfriend, Riley, who both lived nearby.

Shanice was excited to meet Grace after hearing so much about her, and everyone wanted to hear about her upcoming trip with Lia. Grace was the center of attention as the group made their way into the bar, and it was overwhelming, given her anxiety about the trip.

In that moment, she wished Lia had gone to her brother's wedding alone. Then she and Grace wouldn't have met. Grace would be at home tonight. If she'd received the email from Your-Gene while she was at home, she probably would have talked herself out of contacting Laurel, and even if she'd gotten in touch, she would have done it alone.

She wouldn't be here in New York, about to embark on a road trip to meet her half sister, and maybe she *shouldn't* be here. Maybe this was all a terrible mistake.

As she settled on a barstool with her beer, she felt as restless as she had the night she'd received that email, when she'd tossed and turned in bed for hours. She wanted to enjoy this evening with Lia, Rosie, and their friends, but every time her mind spun ahead to the reason for her road trip, she started to hyperventilate.

And then there was her attraction to Lia, which had only increased during her time in New York. Surely, heading out for a weeklong trip with her was a terrible idea. Surely *everything* about this trip was a terrible idea. She gulped from her beer, hoping she didn't look as twitchy as she felt.

"Lia never remembers to post her photos online, so I'm counting on you, Grace," Rosie said as she slid onto the stool next to her. "I want to live vicariously through you on your road trip."

"I'll take pictures," Grace told her. "But maybe after Lia's back, you and Jane should take a trip of your own."

Rosie sighed, glancing at Jane, who stood nearby, talking to Shanice and Riley. "I was in crisis-management mode for so long with the store, but things are good now. Maybe I do need a vacation."

"You do," Grace agreed. "You should fly somewhere warm and sunny. You two can lie around sipping fruity drinks and being disgustingly romantic together."

Rosie grinned. "Lia's going to hate you for putting this idea in my head."

"What idea is that?" Lia asked, turning to face Rosie.

"That I should take a vacation of my own after you and Grace get back," Rosie told her.

"Why would I hate that?" Lia asked. "You should definitely take a vacation. In fact, we should both get better about scheduling time off for ourselves."

"Yeah, I guess so," Rosie said, not looking entirely convinced.

Grace suspected Rosie's idea of a vacation was hanging out in her own store . . . or maybe making out with Jane in the back room. Grace couldn't imagine being that dedicated to her job. She enjoyed her work for *Modern Style*. It was interesting, it paid well, and it allowed her the flexibility to work from anywhere. She loved her job, but it was just a job. "Vacations all around," she said, holding her beer out.

Rosie and Lia tapped their glasses against hers.

"I'll drink to that," Lia said before sipping from her beer.

Grace's gaze dropped to her throat as she swallowed, and as she yanked it back to Lia's face, she was almost certain Rosie had seen. She'd felt Rosie's eyes on her all week, scrutinizing her interactions with Lia. Rosie was suspicious, but surely her interest would fade once Grace was back in London.

Grace's hormones would return to normal once she was back in her own space. The question was, Could she ignore them until she went home? Because she felt like a horny teenager this week. She wasn't sure she'd ever been this attracted to someone without acting on it. And sleeping on the couch meant she hadn't been able to relieve her sexual frustration on her own either.

It was almost alarming to realize she could still feel this way about someone. After going so many years without wanting to have sex, she'd almost wondered if she was still capable of it. She'd wondered if she'd become so emotionally isolated that the only thing that turned her on anymore was her vibrator.

Lia turned her on more than any of the toys stashed in her bedside table in London. And she was looking at Grace right now like she could hear every thought running through her sex-starved brain. While Rosie watched. Christ.

Grace drank her beer, desperately trying to think about something other than Lia or sex.

"So what's your first stop?" Rosie asked.

"Wine," Grace blurted as she caught herself staring at Lia's breasts. God, what was the matter with her tonight?

"We're visiting the Brandywine Valley Wine Trail in Delaware," Lia clarified, saving her. "We'll sip some wine and tour the gardens, and then we're off to Annapolis for the night."

"Okay, you know what, now I'm jealous," Rosie said. "I get so caught up in the store and this city, sometimes I forget all the other things out there in the world."

"So take a vacation," Lia said. "Seriously, I'm sure Jane would love it. You two have never even left the city together, have you?"

"Um, no," Rosie admitted.

"And all I do is fly back and forth between Manhattan and the UK," Lia said. "I'm excited to go somewhere new."

"You both need to travel more," Grace told them. "The world is huge and exciting. Go see it."

"Ooh, are we talking about vacations?" Jane asked as she stepped up behind Rosie, wrapping an arm around her waist.

"Grace and Lia think we should take one," Rosie told her.

"Yes, please," Jane said, nodding.

Rosie turned to face her. "Really?"

"Hawaii," Jane said dreamily. "I've always wanted to go to Hawaii."

"Um, maybe someplace a little closer and cheaper?" Rosie said, eyes wide. "We're trying to afford our own apartment, remember?"

"Right," Jane said. "Saint Lucia, maybe?"

"Your girlfriend wants to go to the beach, Ro," Grace said. "You should take her."

Rosie beamed. "I think I will."

"We're going to the beach," Lia added, winking at Grace. "Although not a tropical one. We're spending Sunday on the waterfront in Annapolis."

"I bet we could get our toes wet if we wanted to," Grace said, and now she was picturing Lia in a bikini, which was not at all helpful.

"Keep your beaches," Shanice said as she walked over to join the conversation, holding Riley's hand. "I want to see the Rocky Mountains. God, the skiing would be amazing."

"It is," Jane told her. "My family was there for Thanksgiving last year."

"And I want to see all the cities," Riley added. "So many museums . . ." She pressed the back of her hand against her forehead.

"Shanice, you'd better watch out or Lia might steal your girlfriend," Rosie teased. "Museum nerds unite."

"Riley has good taste," Lia agreed.

"Boston for me," Paige said as she and Nikki joined them. "I just want to see Hallie. It's been ages since I've visited."

"We spent our last vacation visiting Hallie in Boston," Nikki protested. "We deserve to go somewhere on our own next time."

"Who's Hallie?" Riley asked.

"She was our roommate before her job transferred her to Boston," Paige told her. "And she's my best friend. She and I are like Rosie and Lia."

"It's true," Rosie confirmed, bumping her elbow against Lia's.

Grace turned toward the bar and took another drink of her beer. Once upon a time, it had been Rosie and Grace. She had a lot of friends, but she'd never had a *best* friend except Rosie, and she wasn't sure she wanted one. She didn't have the best track record of being friends with other queer women without falling for them, and the evidence was all around her in this bar. She chugged the rest of her beer and gestured to the bartender for another.

"Does it bother you?" Lia asked, resting her elbows on the bar beside Grace. "That our friends think of me as Rosie's best friend and not you?"

"You *are* her best friend," Grace said, a little more harshly than she'd intended.

"So are you," Lia said, watching Grace.

The lighting in the bar reflected off Lia's glasses so that Grace had a glimpse of herself, and she didn't like what she saw. She stared into the empty beer glass in front of her. "Not anymore. It's fine. I'm the one who left."

"Still," Lia said, watching Grace closely. "I'm sure it's hard."

Between her discomfort over her upcoming meeting with Laurel and the way Lia was watching her right now, Grace had a strong urge to leave, to feign a headache and just get the hell out of here. Her emotions were raw tonight, and she didn't want to talk about it. She tapped her fingertips against the bar, studiously avoiding Lia's gaze.

"Help me out here," Lia said. "What's going on in that pretty head of yours?"

Grace huffed, shaking her head. "Planning my escape if you don't change the subject." She chuckled for effect, trying to turn it into a joke, but Lia—as usual—saw right through her.

"Why don't you want to talk about your history with Rosie?" Lia asked, and then her eyes went wide. "Oh my God. When we met, you told me you'd once fallen for one of your friends. It was Rosie, wasn't it?"

Lia's stomach dropped as she took in the stricken look on Grace's face. That was really all the confirmation she needed.

"Keep your voice down," Grace hissed, glancing over her shoulder, but Rosie and the rest of their friends were still deep in a friendly argument over the best place to vacation.

"Sorry," Lia muttered.

"It was a million years ago," Grace told her quietly. "The age-old teenage lesbian cliché, falling for your best friend."

Lia's mind was reeling with this information. Did Grace still have feelings for Rosie? Suddenly, all Lia could think about was the way Rosie and Grace were always touching, hugging, sharing inside jokes that stemmed from their teens. Obviously, Rosie was in love with Jane, but Grace . . . "Rosie told me you two shared a couple of kisses, but she said there was no chemistry, so you decided to just be friends."

"I'm well aware of what she thought," Grace said, reaching for her new beer as the bartender placed it in front of her.

"So that year you lived with her . . ."

"I defined teenage angst and pining," Grace said bitterly.

"And then you left New York."

"Because I was angry with the world and I wanted a fresh start, only part of which had anything to do with Rosie," Grace said, staring into her beer.

"And now?" Lia asked.

"I couldn't possibly hold a torch that long. Jesus, Lia." Grace glared at her. "I got over her so long ago that I don't even remember what it felt like to want her."

"So she's not the reason you gave up women?" Lia asked, voicing the question that had been circling in the back of her mind for the last few minutes.

"God, no." Grace gave her a mutinous look before sliding off her barstool. "Watch my beer for me while I go to the bathroom."

Lia watched regretfully as she left. She'd pissed Grace off the night before they were embarking on their road trip together, which certainly hadn't been her intention. But it was an important question . . . wasn't it?

"Hey, you."

Lia turned to see that Shanice had hopped onto the stool Grace had vacated. "Hi, yourself," she said with a smile. "You and Riley are adorable together. I'm so glad I got to meet her tonight."

Shanice glanced at her girlfriend—who was talking to Rosie and Jane—with adoring eyes. Her braids were wound into a bun on top of her head tonight, and she wore an orange-patterned top and jeans, looking relaxed and happy. "She's great. Obviously it's still early for us, but I feel like this might be the real deal, Lia. After all my online dating, I can't believe I met her at the hospital while my nephew was being born."

"It always happens when you least expect it. Isn't that what they say?"

"It might be true," Shanice agreed.

"And how's baby Nate?" Lia asked.

"He's the absolute cutest," Shanice said as she pulled her phone out of her back pocket. She tapped the screen to show Lia a new photo of Nate. He had round cheeks and a full head of black hair, eyes wide as he stared at the camera.

"He's adorable," Lia said. "And he already looks so much bigger and more alert than the last picture I saw."

Shanice grinned as she scrolled through more photos. "He's grown a lot. God, I love him so much already."

Warmth bloomed in Lia's chest as she saw the love in Shanice's eyes for her nephew. She couldn't wait to experience that herself. "I'm going to be an auntie too."

"Oh my gosh, really?" Shanice said.

"Mm-hmm. Audrey's pregnant."

"That's wonderful. Welcome to the auntie club."

She and Shanice talked for a few more minutes before Shanice went to find Riley. Lia swept her gaze around the room, noticing that Grace was at the other end of the bar, talking to Paige and Nikki. Avoiding Lia. She hadn't even come back for her beer.

Well, fuck that. Lia picked up her beer and Grace's and walked over to her. She handed Grace her beer, receiving a wary look in return.

"It was just a question, Grace," she said. "I'm sorry if I overstepped."

Grace moved away from the rest of the group as she sipped her beer. "You're making a much bigger deal out of this than it is. I thought I was in love with Rosie when I was seventeen, but it was like . . . puppy love, you know? I did get my heart broken, but not by her."

"Oh," Lia said, absorbing Grace's words. "Who, then?"

"Her name is Carmen," Grace said, staring into her beer. "I thought she was the love of my life, and then I walked in on her having sex with another woman."

"Ouch." Lia touched Grace's hand. "I'm sorry."

She shrugged. "That, too, is ancient history."

"I've been cheated on, too, and it's awful," Lia said. "I'm sorry that happened to you, and I sincerely apologize if I offended you with my questions. I just wanted to know if there was anything sticky in your history with Rosie, because she's our mutual best friend, and as you know, my feelings for you aren't purely platonic. I wanted to understand the history so that I didn't unintentionally complicate anything."

Grace's gaze dropped to her lips, and she leaned in slightly, just enough to make Lia's pulse race. "Lia Harris, did anyone ever tell you that you talk too much?"

"As a matter of fact," Lia said, "*you* did."

CHAPTER TWELVE

"I can't believe you've never driven on the right side of the road," Grace said as she sat in the driver's seat of their rental car. "You've lived here over a decade!"

"And I've lived in Manhattan the entire time," Lia countered. "No one who lives here drives here, as you well know."

"Well, you'll get your chance this week, because I'm not doing *all* the driving on our road trip." Grace typed the address for the winery into the GPS on her phone, tapping her foot impatiently as she paired the Bluetooth with the car's radio.

"Fair enough," Lia said. "I watched a few YouTube videos to prepare me for driving on the right."

"Of course you did." Grace's lips quirked as she opened Spotify. "Driver picks the music?"

"Yes," Lia agreed.

Grace loaded an upbeat playlist, catchy pop songs that were perfect for singing along in the car. There had been a weird vibe between her and Lia since their conversation at the bar last night, an undercurrent of tension that she wasn't quite sure how to resolve. She didn't understand why Lia was so preoccupied with Grace's high school infatuation when she hadn't had romantic feelings for Rosie in too many years to count.

Meanwhile, the chemistry between her and Lia only seemed to grow with each passing day, which wasn't doing anything to smooth out the rough spots in their friendship. Knowing Lia, she'd want to talk the whole thing to death today in the car, and Grace was *so* done talking about all of it. She turned the music up a little too loud for comfortable conversation as her favorite Halsey tune began to play. Lia didn't comment, instead checking their route on the GPS on Grace's phone.

"And we're off," Grace announced as she backed the car out of its parking spot and began to wind her way out of the parking garage. They had about a three-hour drive ahead of them, which would put them at the winery around lunchtime, and she was already looking forward to it. Maybe some well-timed wine could help her and Lia get back in sync.

They were quiet as she cautiously guided them onto FDR Drive. The East River rolled by outside her window, choppy with the morning breeze. City driving was new to Grace, and she quickly realized she didn't like it. She'd first learned to drive at her grandparents' house in Albany, and later, she'd driven in Spain, but the Andalusian countryside was a world away from Manhattan's busy roads and aggressive drivers.

Her knuckles were white as she drove through the Holland Tunnel into New Jersey, although that turned out to be just as stressful. The highway had more lanes—and more vehicles—than she was comfortable with, and no one seemed content to stay in the same lane. As she settled in her seat, she realized Lia hadn't said much since they'd started driving, which was unusual. This drive was nerve racking enough without the friction between her and Lia.

Grace nudged the volume down on the radio. "Enjoying your first road trip so far?"

"Ask me again once we're farther from the city," Lia said, gesturing to the traffic outside the window.

"Yeah. This part's not great, although I'm also dreading our end destination."

"I'm sure," Lia said. "But I hope it turns out to be a good thing. Who knows, maybe you and Laurel will want to keep in touch."

"Maybe." Grace's hands tightened on the wheel. "It just feels so . . . weird that she's my half sister. Like, it doesn't feel real. Mostly, I wish I just didn't know she existed."

"Well, you don't ever have to see her again if you don't want to," Lia said. "And you don't have to meet her at all if you change your mind. Our road trip can just be a road trip."

"Thanks," Grace said, rolling her shoulders to loosen them. "But maybe don't remind me of that later, okay? I'm counting on you to convince me to go through with it."

"I can do that. Knowledge is power, right?" Lia turned her head to smile at her.

"Let's hope it's true in this case."

They drove in silence for a few minutes as she navigated through a particularly congested area on the highway. Where were all these people going on a Saturday morning? Somehow, she'd imagined a carefree drive down scenic, tree-lined roads, and maybe that would happen later, but right now, it couldn't be further from the case.

A seaport was on their left, colorful shipping crates stacked high like giant LEGOs, and the Newark airport was on their right. The highway seemed to constantly gain and drop lanes, and there were way too many cars vying for space. The roar of a jet nearly drowned out their music, and when she glanced out the window, she squealed because the airplane was *right there*. "Jesus Christ!"

Lia lurched sideways, grabbing Grace's shoulder as she burst into nervous laughter. "Oh my God. Look, the runway is right next to us."

"I don't like that," Grace said. "Nope. Nope. Nope."

The plane roared past them and settled onto the runway, which was indeed right beside the highway. Grace tried not to let herself become so distracted by it that she forgot to watch the road, because . . . traffic. Her heart pounded, and her fingers ached from gripping the wheel so tightly.

"Well, that was exciting," Lia said once they'd left the airport behind.

"You're driving after lunch," Grace told her. "And I'm going to need a lot of wine to recover from that airplane almost landing on our car."

"Deal," Lia said. "You definitely got the hard part, driving out of the city."

The next two hours passed uneventfully, although the scenery never became as scenic as Grace had hoped. They drove from city to city as they made their way through New Jersey and into Pennsylvania.

Grace's shoulders were stiff and tight by the time they finally entered the Brandywine Valley and began to follow signs to the winery. "This is more like it," she said as she drove past rolling green hills with neat rows of grapevines.

"Agreed," Lia said, looking out her window. "This is lovely."

Grace turned into the parking lot at the winery and pulled into an empty spot. Then she leaned back in her seat, flexing her hands. She blew out a breath and looked at Lia, who was watching her with a quiet smile.

"Let the fun begin," Grace said.

"I think we learned a valuable lesson today," Lia said.

"Oh yeah? What's that?"

"When we get to DC on Monday, we should park in the suburbs and ride the subway into the city."

Grace laughed. "That's an excellent idea, because as it turns out, city girls are terrible city drivers."

They got out of the car, and Grace stretched her arms over her head, wincing at the ache in her shoulders. She hadn't fully realized how tense she was from the drive until she was on her feet. She grabbed her purse, and they walked toward the winery's main building.

Lia had on a green jumpsuit that highlighted her tall, willowy frame and perfectly offset the honeyed tones of her hair, and Grace took a moment to appreciate the sight as they walked. They entered the building, which was large and open inside, with small tables scattered throughout and a bar along the far wall. Here and there, groups had gathered for a tasting. Employees in maroon shirts walked between the tables with bottles to pour.

Grace's gaze fell on a door at the back of the room. "I need to stop at the bathroom first."

"Yeah. Same," Lia said.

It had been a long car ride, and they'd both brought a coffee with them on the road. They made a pit stop in the bathroom and then headed into the tasting room.

"Are you here for a tasting?" an employee asked them.

Grace nodded. "We are."

"Excellent." He guided them to a table at the center of the room. "My name is Steve, and I'll be taking care of you today. The menu on the table shows our full wine list. You have a few options for the tasting. You can pick and choose which wines you'd like to taste or try a variety of reds, a variety of whites—whatever appeals to your palate."

He pointed to the price list on the table. "We have bottles of all our wines available for purchase, if you find something you like. There's also food available at the counter in back: cheese plates, fruit, and a few other options. We can put together a picnic if you'd like to buy a bottle of wine and have lunch on the grounds."

Lia caught Grace's eye. "Let's do that."

"Yes," Grace agreed, because a picnic in the vineyard sounded amazing, and now that Steve had mentioned food, she realized she was starving.

He talked for a few more minutes, giving them some history about the vineyard and the wines made here, and then Grace and Lia both chose the mix-and-match tasting. Lia started with a merlot, and Grace decided to try the blackberry wine, because she'd never had a berry-infused wine before.

Steve poured them each a tasting-size glass of their selection before walking over to check on the table beside them. Grace and Lia tapped their glasses together.

"To an amazing road trip," Lia said.

"Yes." Grace sipped, and *oof*, the blackberry wine was like dessert in a glass. "That's *so* sweet."

"Like it?" Lia asked as she sipped her merlot.

"Too sweet for more than a few sips, I think," Grace told her.

Steve returned and helped them make their next selection. They made their way through the menu, and Grace was already tipsy by the time they'd finished their tasting. They bought six bottles, reasoning that they'd drink them over the course of their road trip. They chose a bottle of rosé for their picnic and brought the rest of the wine to the car while the employee at the counter packed them a basket, complete with a blanket.

"Okay, now it feels like we're on vacation," Grace said as they walked out the back of the building, basket in hand.

"I could get used to this." Lia tipped her face toward the sky, a wide smile on her face.

"Let's head for that hill in back," Grace suggested, because it looked like it would have a nice view of the vineyard. As they strolled between rows of grapevines, Grace realized that this felt an awful lot like a date. The scenery was romantic as hell, as was the picnic and the bottle of wine awaiting them.

They made their way up the hill, and Lia spread their blanket over the grass. Grace sat, mindful that she had on a knee-length T-shirt dress, because despite the romantic setting, this was *not* a date. She extended her legs in front of herself, crossing her ankles as she opened the basket. Inside, she saw a variety of cheeses and crackers, grapes, mini muffins, and cookies. "Oh my God, this looks so good."

"It's perfect," Lia agreed as she reached for the paper plates the winery had provided, then handed one to Grace. The employee at the counter had already uncorked their wine and put in a plastic stopper to keep it from spilling. They poured two glasses and fixed their plates in comfortable silence.

The afternoon was warm and sunny with a gentle breeze blowing. Grace sipped her wine, then nestled the cup into the grass beside her and reached for her plate, because she could easily get drunk if she didn't put something solid in her stomach. Then again, getting drunk in the middle of this vineyard wasn't without appeal. Lia had already agreed to take over driving for the afternoon.

Grace put a cheese cube on a cracker and popped it in her mouth. The sharp, smoky flavor of the cheese hit her tongue, and she moaned, because *oh*, it was delicious.

They had finished the food and were on to their second glasses of wine by the time the alcohol really hit her.

"Are you going to be able to drive after this?" Grace asked as she lay back on the blanket, closing her eyes to soak in the afternoon sun.

"Mm, I poured my glasses smaller than yours, especially since I'm new to driving on the right," Lia said. "If we walk around the grounds for a bit before we leave, I'll be fine."

"If you say so," Grace said, because she'd gone from tipsy to drunk in record time. How much more wine had Lia poured into her glass? It *had* been pretty full, now that she thought about it. She grinned. "Being drunk on vacation is fun. We should do this more often."

"Well, we have five more bottles of wine in the car, so that shouldn't be a problem."

Lia looked down at Grace, who lay on her back on the blanket, eyes closed and a silly grin on her face. Her dark hair fanned out beneath her, glossy in the sunshine, and . . . had she always had those freckles dusting her cheeks? Lia's gaze drifted to the pastel-striped dress she wore. It ended just above her knees, revealing the smooth, tanned skin of her legs.

"Lie with me," Grace said, squinting up at her.

"Okay." That was certainly a better idea than sitting here, gazing lustfully at her. Lia stretched out on the blanket, and yeah, this was nice. The sun warmed her skin, and she pushed her glasses into her hair so she could feel it on her face too.

Grace stirred beside her, and when Lia peeked through her lashes, she saw that Grace had rolled to face her. It was a good thing the world was fuzzy without her glasses, because she definitely didn't need to see a clear image of Grace bathed in sunshine, not when she was this close, so close Lia could hear the whisper of her breath.

"Really not fair," Grace murmured.

"What's not?" Lia asked, holding her gaze.

"You," Grace said simply.

"What did I do?" Lia asked, but she was pretty sure she knew what Grace meant.

"You make me want things I shouldn't want." Grace's voice was barely above a whisper. She was drunk, Lia reminded herself, and if anything happened between them, it couldn't happen when Grace was drunk. This was a bigger decision for her than it was for Lia.

Lia reached out to brush a hand through Grace's hair, feeling that all-too-familiar jolt of longing when she touched her. "You make me want all the same things."

"It had been so long, I thought I was in the clear," Grace said. "I thought no one was going to tempt me. I'm perfectly capable of satisfying all my own needs."

"Feeling attracted to someone doesn't mean you aren't capable of satisfying your own needs," Lia said. "It just means . . . sometimes it feels good to let someone else take care of you." And she wasn't just talking about sex. Lia wanted someone to dry her tears, someone to finish her sentences, someone to send her silly texts that no one else would understand. And of course, she wanted that person to light her on fire the way Grace could with just a single look.

"Lia . . ." Grace moved closer, so that her body was pressed against Lia's side. The soft cotton of her dress was shockingly warm from the sun, and that same heat licked through Lia's veins as Grace's lips pressed against her cheek.

"Darling, you're drunk," she said, her voice gone low and husky.

"So?" Grace's arm wrapped around her waist.

"So you're not thinking clearly."

"I don't want to think clearly right now," Grace whispered, curling herself around Lia's body, and she really couldn't protest, because technically this was just a hug. No lines had been crossed, despite the arousal pulsing in her core. Grace's breath gusted against her neck, her heart thumping hard and fast against Lia's biceps. They really did make an art out of sexy hugs.

Eventually, Grace pulled back and sat up. She wrapped her arms around her knees, staring into the distance. Lia slipped her glasses into place and shrugged onto her elbows, watching her. For several long minutes, neither of them said anything. Then Grace reached for her plastic wineglass where it sat in the grass and gulped the last of her rosé.

When she turned to face Lia, she was her usual carefree self. "I promised Rosie lots of pictures," she said as she lifted her phone.

"Better take some, then, or she'll be harassing us both."

"She's already sent me three texts," Grace said as she looked at her phone.

"Oh jeez." Lia laughed, reaching for her own phone, but her only text was from Audrey.

Grace lifted her phone and took several shots of the vineyard around them, and then she spun so that it was behind her, sitting on her heels as she snapped a selfie. Her hair was windblown, her cheeks flushed from the sun, and it was all Lia could do not to ask for a copy of that selfie, because it was surely stunning.

"Get over here," Grace said. "Let's take one together."

"All right." Lia moved to sit beside her, and Grace snapped several photos.

"I'm putting them on Instagram for Rosie," Grace said. "You follow me, too, right?"

"I do," Lia told her.

Grace was quiet for a minute, lips pursed as she uploaded the photos, and then she slid her phone into her purse. She lifted their bottle of wine and tipped it back, drinking the last few swallows straight from the bottle. Then she gave Lia a slightly dazed smile. "On to the next leg of our adventure?"

CHAPTER THIRTEEN

It was past seven by the time they checked in at their hotel in Annapolis, and Grace was exhausted. A dull headache wrapped around her temples, suggesting that maybe she shouldn't have spent the afternoon guzzling wine in the sunshine, but really, she had no regrets. This was nothing a glass of water and a couple of ibuprofen couldn't fix.

"What do you want to do for dinner?" Lia asked as she sat on her bed and swiped through notifications on her phone.

Grace flopped backward on her own bed, ridiculously grateful for it after five nights on a couch. "Something simple, maybe? It's Saturday night, and I feel like most restaurants will be super busy."

"I was thinking the same thing," Lia said. "We could order room service and then go for a walk along the waterfront, if that sounds good to you."

"I love that plan," Grace said, nodding. "Do you know, I've never ordered room service before?"

"Really?" Lia asked, giving her a bemused look.

"Never. It feels extravagant, but this trip is all about trying new things, right? Let's do it."

So they ordered burgers, fries, and sodas from room service, and while they waited for their food to arrive, Grace uploaded a few more photos from their day. After they'd left the winery, they toured the nearby Winterthur Museum and Gardens, where Grace had gotten her first peek at Lia in a museum. Her nerdiness was oddly sexy.

"I'm surprised you don't work in a museum," Grace commented as she uploaded a photo she'd discreetly taken of Lia admiring a painting.

"It was my dream job when I was a girl," Lia told her.

"And as an adult?" Grace asked. "What did you want to do before you and Rosie took over the bookstore?"

"I majored in museum studies," Lia told her. "I thought I might work at one of the museums in London. The British Museum was sort of my pipe dream."

"Do you still think about it?" Grace asked. She'd never really considered what Lia had given up to work at Between the Pages, and she wondered suddenly if Rosie had.

"Not really," Lia said. "I love working with Rosie, and while she's obsessing over romance novels, I keep the store well stocked with books about art and history."

"Maybe you should put in an application with the British Museum," Grace said, telling herself her suggestion had nothing to do with Lia moving to London. "See what happens."

Lia gave her a long look, her expression uncharacteristically guarded. "Why would I do that?"

"Because it's your dream job," Grace said. "I never really had one of those. I fell into translation work almost by accident, and it turns out that I love it, but you have this dream that you shelved to help a friend, and maybe now you should chase it."

"Dreams change," Lia said with a shrug, but there was something curious in her expression, like maybe Grace had reminded her of something she'd forgotten she wanted. "And what about Rosie? We worked so hard last year to save the store."

"And you did save it," Grace said. "Between the Pages is doing great. It's Rosie's passion, her dream, but she could hire a new manager if you wanted to spread your wings."

Lia shook her head. "Well, I don't."

There was a knock at the door, and Grace stood to answer it. A hotel employee pushed a cart into their room and set two silver-covered platters on the table in the corner. She couldn't help but giggle when she looked at them, because they looked so *fancy*, when she knew they contained cheeseburgers.

They sat at the table to eat, but it wobbled dangerously when they uncovered their platters. "Let's eat in bed," she suggested, and Lia nodded enthusiastically.

"Lunch in a vineyard and dinner in bed. I quite like our vacation so far."

"All vacations should include burgers in bed," Grace agreed. She carried her plate to her bed and set it down on the white duvet. To her surprise, Lia followed. She sat facing Grace and popped the tab on her root beer. "Oh, sure," Grace teased. "You want to spill soda and ketchup in *my* bed."

"Perhaps I do," Lia said in her prim accent as she picked up a french fry and popped it in her mouth. Sometimes she sounded even more British here in America, where her accent was the outlier.

"I should try to do a few hours of work tomorrow," Grace told her as she picked up one of her own fries.

"Even though it's Sunday?"

Grace nodded. "The week will be busy, with sightseeing in DC and then meeting Laurel, so I should get ahead while I can."

"Sure," Lia agreed. "I'm happy to read for a few hours or explore on my own."

They chatted as they ate, talking about their upcoming itinerary while Grace tried not to think about the end of this journey, when she'd meet Laurel. It made her heart pound and a sick feeling grip her stomach. No, for now she only wanted to think about the fun she and Lia were going to have in the meantime.

"Look," Lia said as she finished her burger, gesturing to the duvet in front of her. "I didn't spill anything in your bed."

"Good thing," Grace said playfully as she stood. "I might have stolen yours if you did."

They cleaned up their meal and set the empty dishes in the hall, and then they walked down to the waterfront. It was almost nine now and fully dark outside, although the street was well lit, and there were plenty of people out and about.

"This will be nice tomorrow," Lia commented. "I love the ocean, and I realize that sounds silly since I live in a coastal city, but Manhattan doesn't feel that way to me. I see the East River often, but almost never the ocean."

"I know exactly what you mean," Grace said as they walked along a wooden boardwalk that ran beside the water. "We should see if we can go out on a boat tomorrow. I can't remember the last time I was on a boat."

"Yes," Lia agreed. "I bookmarked several options for scenic tours of the Chesapeake Bay when I did my trip research."

"Perfect," Grace said.

They stopped to lean against the railing, staring out across the bay. Water slapped rhythmically against the pier beneath them, and a gull cried overhead. Grace sucked in a lungful of ocean air and smiled. Their adventure was off to a good start, as long as she didn't think about how it would end . . . or whether she could ignore her attraction to Lia for the rest of the week.

She wasn't sure she could, but what would the consequences be for her if they slept together? Could she have a harmless road trip fling and get this lust out of her system before she went home, or would having sex make it that much harder to return to her single life? Maybe she'd still crave Lia even after she went home, and that was a scary thought.

Not to mention that if things between them ended messily, it might make things awkward for Rosie. Grace would never want to damage their friendship or make Rosie feel like she had to take sides.

She and Lia stood there for several minutes, each of them lost in their thoughts, before Lia's hand slid over Grace's, giving her fingers a squeeze. She turned her head, and the sight of Lia standing there, with the sea breeze feathering her hair and the streetlamp overhead glinting off her glasses, was almost more than Grace could take without kissing her. Instead, she squeezed Lia's hand in return, and then they turned together and walked back to their hotel.

The deck of the boat lurched beneath Lia's sneakers, and she gripped the railing as it bobbed over a wave. Beside her, Grace stood in jeans and a white T-shirt, her hair pulled back in a ponytail and a happy smile on her face. They'd gone straight to bed last night after their walk on the waterfront, both of them exhausted from the long day.

This morning, Lia had toured the Annapolis Maritime Museum while Grace put in a few hours of translation work, and now they were taking a sailboat tour of Chesapeake Bay. Grace lifted her phone to take a few pictures of the scenery, and then she spun to take a selfie, making good on her promise to send Rosie photos of their trip.

Lia's phone dinged as Grace tagged her in the post. "Cue an excited reply from Rosie."

"Five minutes, tops," Grace agreed as she pushed her phone into the back pocket of her jeans.

"Actually, afternoon tea is happening at the store right now, so she might not be looking at her phone," Lia said. It was strange to be here on a boat in Maryland while Rosie ran afternoon tea without her. It was their Sunday tradition, one that Lia herself had initiated. It had become extremely popular with their customers, an unofficial weekly book club where they gathered to drink tea and talk about books.

"I bet she'll check," Grace said. "She's oddly obsessed with our road trip."

"I think she's jealous," Lia said. "Maybe once I'm back, she'll actually take a vacation of her own."

"If anyone could convince her, it's Jane," Grace said.

"I bet their first vacation will be their honeymoon."

Grace turned to her with wide eyes. "Do you know something I don't?"

"No, but you haven't lived with them as long as I have. They are absolutely, disgustingly in love. I doubt it will take long."

"You might be right about that," Grace said, staring out at the choppy waves before them with a distant expression.

They lapsed into silence, but this didn't feel like the easy kind they'd shared so often recently. This silence felt vaguely uncomfortable, and Lia wasn't sure why.

"Penny for your thoughts," she said finally.

"Just enjoying the view," Grace responded, her gaze still fixed on the water, but her expression was intense, almost melancholy. She was clearly stewing on something, and Lia wanted to know what it was.

"Dreading that you might have to attend another wedding?" she guessed.

Grace looked at her then, and there was fire in her eyes. "You really think I'd dread Rosie's wedding? Because I hate weddings, or because you're still hung up on the fact that I had feelings for her a million years ago?"

"I don't know," Lia confessed. "It's ancient history for you, I guess, but not for me, since I only found out the other night. You get so prickly every time I mention Rosie. Why is that?"

Grace's eyes narrowed, and she was definitely mad now. "You're intolerable when you get fixated on something, you know that? If I'm prickly about Rosie around you, it's because you replaced me as her best friend, not because I have feelings for her. *God*, why do you make me tell you every embarrassingly stupid thing?"

"What?" Lia blinked, gripping the railing as she absorbed Grace's words. "I . . . really?"

"I was thinking about how you would be her maid of honor instead of me, so there. Now you know every petty thought in my head. Happy?" Grace's cheeks were pink, her knuckles white where she gripped the railing, and Lia felt like an asshole.

"No, I'm not happy," she said. "I'm sorry for pushing, and I'm sorry you feel that way. I didn't know." She'd assumed Rosie and Grace had mutually grown apart after Grace moved to Europe, but now she saw plainly that no one else in Grace's life compared to Rosie, while Rosie couldn't exactly say the same. Rosie had a lot of close friends, including Lia.

In fact, if Lia pictured Rosie and Jane's hypothetical wedding, she saw herself as Rosie's maid of honor as well, and she could absolutely understand why that sucked for Grace.

"If you ever tell her *any* of this, Lia, I swear to God . . ."

"Of course I wouldn't," Lia said. "And you're still incredibly import-ant to her, Grace. You must know that."

Grace was quiet, staring stubbornly into the water as a muscle clenched in her jaw, and Lia was struck again by how little she'd known about her before last week, how completely she'd misunderstood every-thing that mattered and didn't matter to her. She'd misjudged Grace entirely, and she liked the real Grace more than she could ever tell her.

"It's not stupid or petty," Lia said. "If our roles were reversed, my feelings would be hurt too."

"You don't have to say that," Grace said.

"I'm not just saying it," Lia insisted. "Friendships can be compli-cated and messy, as much as any romantic relationship, honestly."

"And I don't have those, so . . ."

"So your friends are even more important to you," Lia said, and in that moment, she might have truly understood Grace for the first time, this fiercely loyal woman who'd do anything for Rosie, despite having once harbored an unrequited teenage crush on her and later being replaced by Lia as the most important friend in Rosie's life.

The sailboat slammed into a wave, knocking them both sideways. Grace's hands slipped, and she grabbed onto Lia to catch her balance. Lia reached out to steady her, but the moment her hand touched the bare skin of Grace's arm, the tension crackling between them ignited. Heat rolled through Lia's system, and Grace let out a little groan. She pressed closer, and they crashed headlong into a kiss.

Grace kissed her with a kind of desperation that both set Lia on fire and set her on edge, because their chemistry was getting harder to ignore, but she was terrified they'd both end up burned if they gave in to it. Maybe Grace's heart was sufficiently barricaded that she could sleep with Lia this week and return to London next week unscathed, but Lia already knew it was going to hurt her when Grace left, whether or not they had sex.

Grace's hands fisted in Lia's shirt as she hauled herself against her. Lia tasted salt on her lips from the ocean breeze, and she kept one hand on the railing to keep them upright as the deck pitched beneath their feet. She pressed her free hand against the small of Grace's back, holding her close. Grace's tongue darted out to tease her, and Lia felt an answering pulse of arousal in her core.

"Grace . . ."

Grace nipped at her lower lip, hard enough to make Lia gasp. "For once in your life, Lia, just shut up and kiss me."

Well, okay then. Lia could take a hint. She slid her tongue along Grace's, drawing a whimper from her throat. Grace's hips pressed against Lia's, and Lia quit caring whether other people on the boat were watching them, not when Grace's body was fitted perfectly against hers and one of her hands had slipped beneath Lia's top to rest against the bare skin at her waist.

Another wave rocked the boat, and Grace stumbled against her. Their foreheads bumped, and a loose strand of Grace's hair blew into Lia's face, tangling in her glasses. She didn't care. The only thing that mattered was the way Grace's mouth moved against hers, the warmth of her in Lia's arms, and the arousal swamping her senses. Grace's fingernails skimmed down Lia's back, and *yes*, she liked that. She liked it a hell of a fucking lot.

She liked *Grace* a hell of a fucking lot.

A cool mist gusted over her skin, reminding her of her surroundings, and she forced herself to open her eyes. Grace was on her tiptoes, her face upturned toward Lia's, eyes closed and cheeks flushed, revealing those freckles Lia had first spotted yesterday.

Grace's eyes blinked open now that Lia had stopped kissing her, and she stared at her with a lust-drunk expression, her chest heaving. Lia was just as out of breath, and her pulse was racing. This was a problem. They were supposed to have left the kissing behind them when they left Sevenoaks.

Of course, Lia had known this might happen. She'd felt the tension between them rising, hugs that were more than hugs and emotions boiling just beneath the surface. Could they still salvage their friendship, or was it inevitable that they'd give in to temptation? And if they did, what would happen once Grace went home?

Lia knew Grace was tired of talking about it, but Lia wasn't very good at keeping her thoughts to herself. She wanted to ask Grace how she felt about this kiss and if it meant she wanted to pursue a road trip fling after all, but she could see the warning in her eyes.

Grace's lips quirked. "It's killing you not to ask me ten thousand questions about what this means, isn't it?"

Lia scoffed, extremely aware of Grace's body still pressed against hers and her fingers resting against the bare skin on Lia's back. "Killing me," she confirmed.

"Well, I don't know the answers to any of them, so you're better off not asking," Grace said before leaning in, capturing her lips for a tender kiss as they both reined themselves back in. At least Grace didn't seem angry anymore.

"Maybe we can work out the answers together," Lia suggested.

"Maybe," Grace agreed. "But not right now. This boat is a rules-free zone. Just let me hold on to you a little longer before I have to decide anything, okay?"

There was something vulnerable in her tone, and Lia nodded. She released her grip on the railing so she could wrap both arms around Grace, and for a few long seconds, they just held on to each other as they watched the Annapolis waterfront pass by. Then another wave rocked the boat, and Lia spun Grace to face the railing, standing behind her so that she could rest her hands on Grace's waist while Grace held the railing.

With her height advantage, Lia could still see the view, but right now, she was more preoccupied with the woman in her arms. She kissed the top of Grace's head, loving the way Grace's hair tickled her arms as it blew in the breeze.

They were quiet as the boat turned toward the pier. Around them, other couples stood in similar fashion, but Lia felt like she and Grace were in a little bubble at their spot on the railing, because surely no one else on this boat was feeling anything as intense as the emotional hurricane surrounding the two of them.

As they approached the dock, Grace spun to face her, tipping her face to Lia's for one more kiss . . . or maybe it was one last kiss.

"Want to watch a movie?" Grace asked as she sat on her bed. It was a little past eight, too early to go to sleep, but if they were left to their own devices in this hotel room, one of two things would happen.

Either Lia would start asking more questions, or they'd give in to temptation. And as much as Grace wanted that second option to happen, she wasn't ready for the complications that would come afterward, at least . . . not yet.

"A movie sounds great," Lia agreed. She reached for the remote control and started scrolling through their options. "Oh, look, *The Spy Who Dumped Me*. Kate McKinnon is in that."

Grace giggled as she popped the cork on a bottle of sauvignon blanc. She poured two glasses and handed one to Lia. "You say Kate McKinnon's in it, and I say Gillian Anderson's in it."

Lia's brow wrinkled adorably. "What? No, she isn't."

"Oh yes, she is," Grace said before taking a sip of her wine. "And she's extremely hot."

"I don't remember her in this movie," Lia said.

"Which means we definitely need to watch it together. Plus, it's hilarious, and I adore Kate McKinnon too. So it's a win-win."

"All right." Lia rented the movie and gestured for Grace to come sit with her.

Grace grabbed the package of oatmeal cookies she'd been snacking on and her glass of wine and sat next to Lia in bed, keeping enough space between them that she wouldn't be tempted to kiss her again . . . well, she'd try not to, anyway.

She and Lia sipped wine and laughed through the opening sequence. Once the characters arrived in Europe, Grace felt a tug of longing. America would always feel like home, but *damn*, she loved her life in London, and she couldn't wait to get back.

They were on their second glasses of wine by the time Gillian Anderson came onscreen, looking absolutely stunning as a badass MI-6 operative. "There she is," Grace said dreamily.

"That's not . . ." Lia's tone was incredulous. "Oh my God, that *is* her. But she's blonde . . . and British."

"She's not actually Agent Scully. You know that, right?" Grace teased.

"I would never have recognized her in this if you hadn't pointed her out," Lia said.

"Well, now you know."

"Mm," Lia agreed, turning her gaze back to the TV.

"I like her accent," Grace whispered, watching Lia instead of the movie.

"Is that so?" Lia's gaze settled on Grace, and the bed seemed to shrink around them.

"I'm a total sucker for a British accent." Warmth spread through Grace's veins just from looking at her, and *oh*, this was such a problem. Or not. Because really, what was the harm in one more kiss?

Apparently, her hormones made the decision for her, because the next thing she knew, she was on top of Lia, and they were kissing, and this was definitely the best decision she'd made tonight.

Lia rose up to meet her, gripping Grace's hips as she hauled her closer. This wasn't a gentle kiss. Grace's hands were in Lia's hair, and her tongue was in Lia's mouth. She kissed her until her lungs screamed for air and a fire blazed low in her belly. Lia's fingernails dug into Grace's skin, and she whimpered, throwing her head back as she sucked some much-needed oxygen into her lungs.

Her knees slid down to the mattress so she was straddling Lia's lap, and her hips automatically started moving, grinding against her. Grace was so turned on that she could probably come like this, fully clothed, without Lia even touching her.

"Grace . . . ," Lia murmured, and her grip tightened on Grace's hips, stopping her. "Wait."

CHAPTER FOURTEEN

Lia stared into the mocha depths of Grace's eyes. "We need to talk before we—"

"*God*," Grace cried, and she was gone before Lia had even realized what was happening, backing off the bed. "I don't want to talk tonight, Lia." She stalked across the room, her eyes suspiciously glossy. "I need some fresh air."

"Grace, wait . . ." Lia rose onto her knees, but Grace flung a hand out behind herself as she opened the door. It shut behind her with a solid thump, and then Lia was alone in their hotel room. Her pulse still raced from their kisses, and her mind was spinning from Grace's sudden exit. On the TV, Mila Kunis and Kate McKinnon were in the middle of a high-stakes action scene that was entirely too loud and chaotic for Lia's nerves at the moment. She shut it off.

Her first instinct was to go after Grace, but maybe she needed a few minutes by herself to calm down. Lia suspected she hadn't taken a keycard with her, so she got up, opened the door, and turned the dead bolt to prop it open for her. She went to the sink for a glass of water and then walked to the window.

"Come back and talk to me, Grace," she murmured as she looked down at the swimming pool below. Their room overlooked the back of the hotel, so there was little chance she'd see Grace.

Lia spent an anxious fifteen minutes pacing the room before the door pushed open and Grace stepped inside, looking sheepish. She walked straight to Lia and flung her arms around her, hugging her tight.

"I'm sorry," she whispered. "You're right. We *do* need to talk before we take things any further, but not tonight, okay? I think I just want to go to bed."

"Of course," Lia said. She exhaled into the depths of Grace's hair as everything inside her calmed. They held on to each other for a long minute, and Lia relished the comfort of her embrace, the way it always had the power to soothe her.

Finally, Grace pulled back. She rummaged in her suitcase for her pajamas and went into the bathroom to change. Lia changed in the bedroom the way she had at her parents' house. Grace came out of the bathroom in her skimpy pajamas, and Lia reflected on the fact that she could have brought something less revealing on this road trip after they'd stopped at her apartment. She hadn't.

"Good night," Grace said, giving her another hug, and then she climbed into bed.

Maybe it was crazy, since they constantly seemed to be at odds, but Lia felt like the bond between them was strengthening. The rest of the week should be interesting. She smiled to herself as she shut off the light.

It was late Monday afternoon by the time Grace pushed her keycard into the door of their new hotel room in downtown Washington, DC. That morning, she'd put in a few hours of translation work before they checked out of their hotel in Annapolis. They'd had lunch on the waterfront and gone for a long walk together before getting in the car to drive to DC.

They'd parked in Maryland and ridden the Metro into the city. This would be their home base for the next four nights before they drove to Virginia to meet Laurel, assuming Grace didn't panic and flee to London before she made it that far, because the very thought of meeting Laurel was almost enough to make her break into hives.

The constant sexual tension between her and Lia wasn't helping things either. Her emotions were a mess, she was so horny she could hardly stand it, and Lia wanted to talk everything to death when Grace just wanted to undress her . . . or run.

So when she led the way into their hotel room and saw the king-size bed in the middle of the room, she almost doubled over in laughter, because obviously the universe was having a laugh at her expense, so she might as well join in.

"This is the wrong room," Lia said from behind her. "I'm sure if we go back downstairs, they can swap us to a room with two beds."

Grace looked at the bed and then at Lia, so pretty in her purple jeans and gauzy white top, her hair windswept from their walk along the waterfront. And Grace was just tired. She was tired of fighting this attraction, tired of denying herself the kind of pleasure she'd forgotten she even wanted until she'd met Lia. "No," she said quietly. "I'm ready to have that talk you wanted, and then I want to share that bed with you."

Lia's eyebrows shot up her forehead. "What?"

"I can't make you any promises beyond this week, but I can't keep fighting. If you don't want to do this, then you should go downstairs and request a second room, because I can't keep sleeping in the same room as you without sleeping *with* you."

"Oh." Lia swallowed, hands clasped in front of herself. "God knows I want this as much as you do, so yes, let's talk."

Grace nodded, stepping closer. "You start."

Lia smiled. "This conversation is already so far ahead of the other times we've tried to discuss our attraction because we're calm, we're sober, and we aren't already halfway to undressing each other."

"All true," Grace agreed.

"You're sure you're ready for the ramifications of having sex after making the decision to give it up?"

"I'm sure," Grace said. "At this point, the damage is done. I was happily single before, and now I want you so much that there will be ramifications whether or not we have sex. I'm fairly confident I won't regret sleeping with you, but I know for sure I'd regret it if I didn't."

"I like the sound of that," Lia said as she moved into Grace's space, leaning in to place a kiss on her cheek. "But please promise me one thing . . . promise that we'll at least talk about our options at the end of the week before you leave."

It was a fair request, even if it made Grace tense with discomfort, because she already knew that conversation wouldn't go well. Lia would want more, and Grace couldn't give it to her. After she met Laurel, she was going to run far and fast, but Lia had been nothing but forthcoming, so surely she owed her the courtesy of one more painfully honest conversation before she left. "Oh, please, as if you'd possibly let me leave without talking this to death first."

Lia laughed, casting her eyes toward the ceiling. "You know me so well."

"And you do too," Grace said, swallowing over her suddenly dry throat. "I mean that, Lia. I can't change who I am or the reasons I don't want a relationship, but this is more than sex. You know me better than almost anyone, maybe even better than Rosie, and I hope we'll stay friends, no matter what happens."

"We will," Lia said with a confidence Grace didn't think she was capable of in any situation, let alone this one. "We will absolutely stay friends . . . if not more than that."

"I can't stay, Lia," she said quietly. "I can't promise you more than this week."

Lia reached out to tuck a strand of hair behind Grace's ear. "I know."

"And we can't let things turn ugly between us," Grace said. "For Rosie's sake."

"Agreed."

"Okay. Are we good, then?" Grace asked, surprised to realize she felt better after their talk, instead of worse.

"We're good," Lia confirmed.

"Phew," Grace said as she mimed wiping sweat from her brow. "Now let's find our wine, because I don't know about you, but I need a drink."

"Whites are in my suitcase, and the reds are in yours," Lia told her. They'd both been extra cautious with their suitcases all day, mindful of the fragile cargo in them.

"You pick," Grace said, because she'd already made the most important decision of the day, and now her brain was in chaos . . . a really hot and delicious kind of chaos.

"The whites aren't chilled yet, so . . . red?" Lia suggested.

"Sounds good to me." Grace unzipped her suitcase and pulled out a red blend they'd both enjoyed at the tasting while Lia put their bottles of white wine into the mini fridge.

Grace took the corkscrew out of her suitcase and opened the bottle with the ease of someone who'd lived in Europe since she'd been of legal drinking age, where she'd had plenty of experience with wine. She poured two glasses and handed one to Lia, who tapped it against Grace's.

"To playing it by ear," Lia said.

"And one bed," Grace added. The wine left a trail of warmth as it slid down her esophagus to her belly, mixing with the heat that already simmered there, the heat she felt every time she was with Lia. Right now, it was so hot she was about to combust. She gulped wine and stared at Lia, feeling suddenly overwhelmed. It had been *so long* since she'd done this.

"You can still change your mind, you know," Lia said, perceptive as ever.

"I know." Her voice was barely more than a whisper.

"And while we're talking, I've been tested, and I'm negative," Lia said, and of course she'd initiate a safe sex talk before their clothes came off. Grace could kiss her for it.

"Not surprisingly, I've had several checkups since the last time I was with anyone," she told Lia. "I'm good."

Lia opened her arms, and Grace stepped into them. How did she always know just what Grace needed? Lia set their wineglasses on the table and held her tight. Grace tucked her face against Lia's neck the way she'd done so many times, and all her nerves evaporated. Lia's embrace felt warm and familiar and right. And Grace wanted more. She pressed her lips against Lia's neck, loving the way Lia's breath hitched.

Grace wasn't sure she'd ever felt so exquisitely aroused from nothing but anticipation. "Lia," she whispered, lifting her head to meet her gaze. "Kiss me."

"Gladly." Lia brushed her lips against Grace's, a tender kiss that nonetheless made Grace throb with need. She couldn't decide whether she wanted to take this slow so she didn't overwhelm herself, or fast because she was already feeling fairly desperate.

Lia seemed to have decided on the former. She reached for their wineglasses, handing Grace's back to her before taking a drink herself. Grace went for a sip that ended up more of a gulp, and she was pretty sure they both saw the way her hand shook as she brought the glass to her lips. With her body pressed against Lia's, the glass of wine went down entirely too fast, adding a pleasant buzz to the lust already swimming in her veins.

Grace set her glass on the table and brought her lips to Lia's for a different kind of kiss, a kiss where she wasn't holding anything back, where she allowed herself to feel all the hot, heady things that Lia made her feel, a kiss that quickly escalated to Lia's teeth nipping at Grace's lower lip while her hands slid beneath her tank top.

"Yes," she gasped, arching her back to press herself more firmly into Lia's touch. "Please."

Lia's hands slid around to cup her over her bra, and how had she forgotten how wonderful this felt? Her nipples tightened as Lia's thumbs brushed over them, achingly sensitive to her touch. Grace reached down and yanked the tank top over her head before moving in to do some touching of her own.

She swept her hands under the loose layers of Lia's top, feeling her abs tighten beneath Grace's fingers before she slid them north to Lia's bra, which was smooth and satiny against her skin. Lia held on to her as she sat on the bed, and they tumbled onto it together. Grace lay on top of her, feeling the way Lia's chest rose and fell beneath her and the warmth where their hips met.

Grace sat up, straddling one of her thighs, because she was desperate for some friction, and she couldn't contain her groan as she rocked her hips. Lia drew her back down for a kiss. Their lips met as their hips pressed together and their hands roamed, and Grace was dying in the very best way. Her body burned with restless anticipation.

Her hair was everywhere she didn't want it to be, though, falling over her shoulders and in Lia's face, twisting between them as they moved. Grace sat back, pulling the elastic from her wrist and securing her hair into a low ponytail while Lia watched with an amused smile.

"For the record, I love your hair in my face," she said.

"Well, I don't." She looked down at Lia, whose hair spread around her like a golden halo on the pillow. Her glasses were smudged, but she hadn't taken them off. "We're wearing too many clothes."

"Is that so?" Lia cocked an eyebrow at her.

"Yep." She and Lia had already spent a lot of time in various beds, cuddling and making out, and now Grace was impatient to have her bare skin against Lia's. She reached for the button on her jeans, but

Lia beat her to it. Her fingers brushed against Grace's stomach as she popped the button, and Grace hissed out a breath at the contact.

Lia's fingers were warm against Grace's skin as she lowered the zipper. There was no graceful way to take off jeans, and Grace found herself giggling as she scooted out of hers. She had on pink seamless panties and a flesh-toned bra, nothing fancy since she hadn't exactly planned this. Lia's gaze was heated as she watched her undress.

Grace flushed, not with embarrassment but with the heady feeling that came from being looked at like she was the most beautiful woman Lia had ever seen, despite her everyday underwear and the dimples on her thighs. She didn't dislike her body, but it had been a long damn time since a woman had seen it, and who wasn't at least a little bit insecure about being seen in their underwear?

"You've been holding out on me, darling," Lia said, sliding forward to trace her fingers over the floral tattoo on Grace's hip, and *oh*, she loved when Lia called her "darling." It was so sexy and so British and just so . . . Lia.

"I have?" She shivered beneath Lia's touch.

"Tattoos are my weakness." Lia's voice had gone low and throaty.

"Oh," Grace whispered. She'd sometimes regretted that tattoo because it had no real meaning. It was just a random design chosen by an angry eighteen-year-old who hadn't had anyone in her life to tell her no, but the way Lia looked at it made her appreciate it for the first time in a while. Grace reached for her, because Lia was still fully dressed. Her fingers fumbled the button on Lia's purple jeans. "Your turn."

She helped Lia shimmy out of her jeans and lifted her top over her head, and then she took a moment to appreciate Lia in her underwear. Like Grace, she wore a flesh-toned bra, but her panties were lavender, delicate and silky and edged in white lace.

"You're so pretty," she whispered, reaching for Lia, who tugged Grace into her lap.

"So are you," she murmured as her fingers popped the clasp on Grace's bra.

She let it fall from her shoulders as she knelt with her knees on either side of Lia's hips, sliding closer. "If you love tattoos so much, why don't you have any?"

"Because I can't decide on the perfect design," Lia answered as her fingers moved to trace Grace's tattoo again. "I'm so afraid I'll change my mind later on and end up regretting it. I think I mostly love looking at them on other people."

"Interesting." Grace settled her hips against Lia's, sucking in a breath at the contact. This was so different from touching herself alone in bed. She was already in sensory overload, and they hadn't even taken off their underwear yet. "I sort of regret mine for the same reason, but . . . *God*, Lia."

Lia cupped her bare breasts with a devilish smile. She rolled Grace's nipples between her fingers, and a hot bolt of desire raced through her, fueling the fire in her belly and pulsing in her clit. She rocked her hips against Lia's, desperate for release but at the same time not ready for this to be over. Then again, they had all night, and *oh* . . . she whimpered as her need spiked.

"In a hurry?" Lia rose beneath her, flipping Grace onto her back against the duvet and stripping away her underwear almost before she'd realized what had happened.

"Yes," she whispered, not even caring how desperate she sounded because she *was* desperate, dammit. Lia's hands slid down her sides, and that simple touch was her undoing. Her eyes slid shut, and she reached blindly for Lia, pulling her flush against her body, as eager to feel Lia's skin on hers as she was to come.

This was what she'd been missing without even realizing it . . . the weight of another woman on top of her, the hot slide of her skin, the erotic press of her lips, the way it all combined to make Grace lose her mind. "Please touch me," she begged.

"My pleasure, darling," Lia murmured as her fingers slipped between Grace's thighs, finally touching her where she throbbed for her.

Yes. God, yes.

Lia rose onto her knees, and Grace grumbled in protest, yanking her back down. "I want to feel you just like this," she whispered as her hands gripped Lia's ass, bringing her closer so that their bodies pressed together from head to foot.

Lia thrust her hips against Grace's, simultaneously pushing two fingers inside her, and Grace cried out with pleasure. Her body gripped Lia's fingers, and Lia's palm rubbed against Grace's clit with each thrust of her hips. Before she'd even prepared herself, she was coming, moaning, gasping as release rushed through her.

She clutched Lia against her, panting for breath as her body tingled with the aftershocks of her orgasm. When she opened her eyes, Lia was watching her with a reverent expression, as if she'd just witnessed something wonderful instead of Grace exploding like a shaken soda the moment Lia touched her, because that had happened kind of embarrassingly fast. She hadn't even finished undressing Lia yet, let alone touched her.

"Sorry about that," she said as heat flooded her cheeks.

"What on earth are you apologizing for?" Lia asked as she slid her fingers from Grace's body, sending another shockwave of pleasure through her.

"For having the stamina of a horny teenager," she said with a bashful shrug.

"I guess that's what happens when you give up sex for five years," Lia said with laughter in her eyes. "And I for one loved every moment. In fact, I'm pretty eager to see how quickly I can make you come the second time."

"Mm," Grace mumbled as Lia's fingers circled her clit, scrambling her brain. "You first." She pushed at her, trying to reverse their positions, but Lia was undeterred.

She set her glasses on the table and swept her hair over her shoulders before dipping her head to kiss her way down the front of Grace's body. Her fingers kept moving, skimming over Grace's clit, mindful that she was still sensitive from her first orgasm while already working her toward the second. And Grace was powerless to do anything but give herself over to the pleasure of Lia's touch.

Her tongue swirled over Grace's nipple, hot and wet, maybe the best thing Grace had ever felt. Lia's fingers were still stroking her, and now she lowered her hips to rock against Grace's thigh. She could feel Lia's wetness through her underwear, and it made her impossibly more aroused. How had she ever thought she could go the rest of her life without experiencing this kind of pleasure again?

"Lia . . . ," she whispered, not even knowing what she meant to say. She was overwhelmed in the most amazing way, her body exquisitely alive, humming with pleasure.

Lia looked up at her, hair hanging messily over her shoulders. Usually, Grace found her more innocent looking without her glasses, but tonight, with her lips swollen from their kisses, her eyes glossy with desire, and her fingers between Grace's thighs, it only made her look even sexier.

As Grace watched, Lia lowered her face to place an openmouthed kiss against the tender skin between Grace's breasts before kissing her way lower, and Grace was half-gone on anticipation alone, because she'd *definitely* missed the feel of a woman's mouth on her. Nothing else compared. She could hear her own gasping breaths as Lia positioned herself between Grace's thighs.

Her legs slid over Lia's shoulders, and she resisted the urge to press her heels into Lia's back, bringing her closer. Lia's breath gusted against her sensitive flesh, and Grace gasped.

Lia pressed the flat of her tongue against Grace's clit, and she jumped as pleasure burst through her system, overwhelming her senses. Lia swirled her tongue, and Grace was pretty sure she saw stars. Her eyes slammed shut, sparks bursting behind her lids. Lia clearly knew what she was doing, licking and kissing her way over Grace's body, making her gasp and squirm and moan, because *God*, that felt amazing.

Need coiled hot and tight inside her, and just when she'd had the hazy thought that she was again going to come embarrassingly fast, Lia retreated, kissing her way along Grace's inner thigh. Her fists clenched in the duvet, and okay, this was surprisingly erotic. After a few minutes, Grace was convinced that her inner thigh was an erogenous zone she'd never known about . . . or perhaps she'd just forgotten. But she would remember now.

She was trembling with desire by the time Lia returned to her clit, licking and sucking until Grace was absolutely mindless with need. And then she was gone, kissing her way down Grace's other thigh while she shook and panted and wished this could last forever. Lia kissed and teased until Grace couldn't take it anymore, digging her heels into Lia's back to urge her on.

Lia's fingers thrust inside her as her mouth closed over Grace's clit, sucking hard, and she cried Lia's name. Her hips bucked. Lia's fingers curled inside her, and just like that, Grace broke, groaning as release ignited in her core, rolling through her system in blissful waves. She lost herself in the sensations as pleasure cleansed her of all the ugly things that sometimes overtook her brain, replacing them with an avalanche of happy-making endorphins.

When she came to her senses, she had two fistfuls of Lia's hair. Her back was arched, sweat slicked her skin, and she was breathing like she'd just run a marathon. "Wow," she whispered as Lia slid up to lie beside her.

"You're exquisite," Lia murmured as she pressed a kiss against Grace's cheek.

Grace sucked in a breath as tears filled her eyes. Her chest was bursting with so many things: satisfaction, pleasure, and an almost over-whelming rush of affection for the woman beside her. As she exhaled, a sob lodged in her throat, and then she was crying for real, tears coursing over her cheeks as she rolled toward Lia.

"Hey, are you okay?" Lia asked. "Talk to me."

"I'm really, really great," Grace gasped against her bare skin. "Just a little overwhelmed."

"I've got you," Lia said as her arms came around Grace, holding her close.

This was everything Grace wanted, and everything she feared. She'd never been very good at keeping her emotions out of sex, which was one of the reasons she'd given it up. And the things she was feeling for Lia right now made her want to run as far and fast as she could. But they also made her want to stay here in Lia's embrace forever.

And she wanted to give Lia as much pleasure as she'd given Grace. She dried her eyes and brought her lips to Lia's, intent on doing just that.

CHAPTER FIFTEEN

Lia was certain she'd never seen anything as lovely as Grace looked right now, blinking at her out of happy, tear-soaked eyes, cheeks so pink that Lia wished she was wearing her glasses so she could see those elusive freckles she'd come to adore.

She didn't need her glasses to feel the heat of Grace's gaze, though. It sizzled through her, settling into a warm ache between her thighs, one that had been building steadily since Grace made the decision to keep this room with its one bed. There was always a hum of electricity when she was around Grace, but after getting her off twice? Lia's body was a live wire, and Grace was the fuse.

And that fuse lit as Grace trailed her fingers down the front of Lia's body, exploring her dips and curves. Lia rolled toward her, meeting her for a kiss as Grace hooked a hand behind Lia's knee, hauling her closer. They kissed for a long minute, hips pressed together as Lia savored the arousal burning inside her, and then Grace popped the clasp on her bra, pulling back to help Lia slide out of it.

"Gorgeous," she murmured as she took Lia's breasts in her hands.

Lia responded by pressing forward, intoxicated by the feel of Grace's hands on her skin. Her breasts had always been sensitive, but Grace seemed to have a magic touch. Lia had a feeling Grace could touch her nose, and she would find it sexy. Maybe it was because they'd been dancing around this moment for so long, or maybe it was just Grace.

As someone who dated a lot, Lia knew a thing or two about connections. There were people she had immediate chemistry with, but often that chemistry was limited to the bedroom. Some of the best sex of her life had been with people she didn't particularly enjoy hanging out with.

And then there were the people she *did* enjoy doing things with, people who shared her love of museums, people she could talk to for hours without getting bored but that she had few sparks with once their clothes came off. In her experience, it was a lot harder to find someone who ticked both boxes, chemistry and companionship.

Grace was one of those people. She hadn't even finished undressing Lia yet, but she already knew it was going to be amazing. Hell, Lia was so turned on right now that it wouldn't take much. If Grace smiled at her, she might combust. In all likelihood, Grace would return to London at the end of the week, and Lia would have to put these feelings behind her to keep Grace as a friend. Hopefully, it wouldn't be as difficult as she was anticipating.

Grace stripped away her underwear. "I've been waiting a long time to do this," she whispered as her fingers slipped through Lia's folds. "You feel so good."

"You make me feel so good," Lia managed, swamped with pleasure.

"I've barely touched you," Grace said as her eyes locked on Lia's. She pressed forward, rocking her hips as her fingers thrust inside Lia, and it was impossibly arousing. Grace moved with all the elegance of her name, putting her whole body into the motion, and Lia never wanted it to end.

Their breasts pressed together, and their feet bumped as they sought purchase against the sheets. Lia wrapped an arm around Grace, holding on. She didn't realize she'd closed her eyes until her other senses came into sharper clarity, the vanilla scent of Grace's shampoo, the warm, damp slide of Grace's skin against hers, and the need pulsing in her core.

Grace's fingers moved in an ever-quickening rhythm, stroking inside her while her thumb circled her clit, and Lia could already feel the first tingles of her impending orgasm. Her thighs shook, and her breath hitched, and a needy whimper spilled from her lips.

"Come for me, Lia," Grace whispered, thrusting harder, and . . . well, Lia had always been good at following directions.

She clutched Grace against her as release rushed through her, silencing her thoughts for a few blissful moments. It radiated out from her core, filling her with a delicious heat.

Once her brain had rebooted, she knew one thing for sure. She and Grace were combustible together, both in and out of bed. Could they possibly find a way to make this work after their road trip was over?

Grace snuggled closer, one leg draped over Lia's while she wrapped an arm around her, and Lia reached for the elastic in Grace's hair, gently tugging it free so she could run her fingers through its soft depths now that she had the freedom to do so.

"That was amazing," Grace said quietly.

"It sure was." Lia drew a strand of Grace's hair over her shoulder, combing it with her fingers. "No regrets?"

"None," Grace answered. "Not even that we waited until now. I wasn't ready before."

"I agree."

"I feel . . . I don't know what the right word is." Grace's fingertips traced a lazy pattern on Lia's stomach, and she exhaled, resting her head against Lia's chest. "Happy," she whispered.

"Happy is a good way to feel after sex," Lia said.

"Mm," Grace agreed.

They lay together for a while, wrapped in each other's arms, relaxed and comfortable. Eventually, the air-conditioning cooled them, and Grace moved to scoot under the blankets. Lia sat up and refilled their wineglasses. As Grace reached to take her glass, Lia's gaze caught on the tattoo on her hip. On impulse, she reached for her glasses and put them on.

Grace gave her a quizzical look. "Planning to study me in bed?"

"Just that tattoo." She sipped her wine and put the glass back on the table so she could lie on her belly beside Grace and trace the tattoo with her fingers.

"It was an impulsive decision," Grace told her. "Mostly, I got it because I knew my mom would have hated it."

Lia kept her face impassive, but her heart hurt to think of young Grace rebelling against her late mother, secretly wishing her mom were there to yell at her for her decision. "You make good impulsive decisions," she said instead. "This is gorgeous."

Grace's hip was covered with rich pink blooms. Lia wasn't sure what type of flower they were, peonies or geraniums perhaps, interspersed with winding stems and green leaves. The design extended onto her thigh, and Lia thought it must have been close to peeking out from beneath Grace's sleep shorts. It was a good thing she hadn't known about it then . . .

"I don't always like it, because it reminds me of a bad time in my life, but I like the way you look at it," Grace said, watching her. "I guess it's pretty. I definitely could have picked something worse."

"How old were you?"

"I'd just turned eighteen."

Lia smiled as she rose up on her elbows to kiss her. "You could have done so much worse. Imagine if you'd gotten a tattoo of your favorite boy band?"

Grace scrunched her nose. "I'm a lesbian, remember? I would have been more likely to get a Lady Gaga lyric or something."

Lia chuckled as she pulled the sheet over their legs. "The flowers were an excellent choice."

Grace drifted awake, feeling warmer than she was accustomed to, and as her eyes blinked open, she realized she'd nestled herself against Lia as she slept. Grace's face was pressed against the back of Lia's neck, and her arm was wrapped around Lia's waist. Lia's hair mixed with her own in front of her eyes.

It had been so long since she'd had someone in her bed to cuddle. She'd wanted to snuggle with Lia since that first night they'd shared a bed at her parents' house in England, at least on some level. As soon as they got in that bed together, Grace's walls started coming down. She'd shared things with Lia that few others knew, and now she'd let her all the way in. She'd given her the power to hurt Grace in ways she'd vowed never to give anyone again.

Lia stirred, rolling to face her. "Morning."

"Morning," Grace said with a smile. Their toes bumped under the covers, and she loved being this close to Lia. Grace had lots of friends, people she hugged and danced with, so it wasn't as if she'd been starved for physical touch, but this was different.

The press of naked bodies in bed was its own form of intimacy, even when it was just a morning embrace, and Grace had always been a tactile person. She liked to be touched, and she loved the way Lia's skin felt against hers.

Their morning embrace soon turned into more as the heat that always seemed to simmer between them blazed to life. They moved together under the covers, stroking each other to release before rinsing off in a much-needed shower.

An hour later, they were seated at the restaurant downstairs for breakfast. Grace's stomach rumbled as the waitress placed a plate of pancakes in front of her. Lia had gotten an omelet with a buttered croissant and was already on her second cup of tea.

"I really want to explore museums with you, but would you mind if I stay in the room this morning to get some work done?" Grace asked her as she drizzled syrup over her pancakes.

"Not at all," Lia replied. "I don't want you to fall behind on your work, and I'm afraid I'd bore you if you went to *every* museum with me."

Grace made a face at her. "I don't think you could ever bore me, but there might be a limit to how many museums I can tour consecutively."

"I'd also like to visit some of the monuments," Lia said. "And we should take a tour of the White House if there are any openings this week."

"I'd love that, although I doubt we could get in on such short notice," Grace told her.

After breakfast, she went back to their room, set up her laptop, and got to work. She put in a solid four hours before Lia texted, asking if she wanted to meet for lunch. They messaged back and forth to make plans, and then Grace closed her laptop and locked it in the safe.

She finished getting ready and headed out to spend the rest of her day with Lia. This was the first time she'd left their hotel since they arrived in DC yesterday afternoon, and as she stepped outside, she felt a buzz of excitement to be here in the capital.

She hadn't been here since a class trip in eighth grade, a trip she'd mostly spent goofing off with her friends, not even remotely interested in history or politics. Now, she was excited to explore with Lia, and not just because she was a lot more interested in history and politics than she had been at thirteen. She always seemed to have fun with Lia, and she couldn't wait to see her geek out in as many museums as possible.

Grace slipped her sunglasses into place as she walked, taking in the imposing stone-faced buildings around her. In a way, DC reminded her of London, because so many of its buildings featured elaborately carved facades, more than any other city she'd seen in America. Everything about DC felt historic and important.

Lia had suggested they meet on the National Mall and grab something from one of the food stands there, and Grace found her easily, sitting on a bench with pigeons circling her feet. Lia bent forward, tossing something into their midst. She wore a pink-patterned sundress that belted at the waist, her hair in a loose braid over her shoulder, and Grace felt herself smiling at the sight.

Without thinking, she pulled out her phone and snapped a few quick photos of Lia feeding the pigeons. Rosie would enjoy them, because surely there wasn't any reason for Grace to want adorable photos of Lia just for herself. "I leave you alone for a few hours, and you become a pigeon lady?" she teased.

Lia turned to stick her tongue out at Grace. "I bought a granola bar earlier that tastes absolutely dreadful, but my feathered friends are enjoying it."

Grace put her hand out, and Lia passed her a piece of the granola bar. It was dry and crumbly on her palm. She knelt, extending her hand toward the pigeons.

"They aren't pets," Lia said. "They aren't going to eat out of your hand."

"Want to bet?" Grace said, glancing at her. "They're city pigeons. I used to hand-feed the ones in Central Park all the time."

Lia made a sound of disbelief.

"Shh," Grace said. She held completely still, crouched on the sidewalk beside Lia with her hand outstretched, crumbs plainly visible. A pigeon with a shiny purple head and red beady eyes stalked closer to her, head bobbing as it walked. It cocked its head to the side, eyeing her, before grabbing a bite from her palm.

"Now who's the pigeon lady?" Lia whispered.

"City animals have no fear," Grace replied quietly. She watched as another pigeon nabbed a piece of granola from her hand before dumping the rest of the crumbs on the ground. "They're used to being fed by people. We've probably ruined them for life."

"Probably," Lia agreed. "Still, that was impressive. It never would have occurred to me to even try." She stood, and Grace took a moment to appreciate the way she looked in that dress. It fell loosely to her ankles, looking light and comfortable, and yet it was also effortlessly cool.

Lia was the type of woman who turned heads with her colorful, funky clothes. She was beautiful, but she certainly didn't see herself that way, which was part of the allure. She walked like she was lost in her own thoughts, oblivious to the attention she garnered.

Grace stepped forward and gave her a kiss before she could second-guess herself. Despite Lia's tendency to overtalk everything, they hadn't laid any ground rules for whether they were friends who took advantage of sharing a bed, or if they were publicly a *thing*—dating felt too formal, since they only had this one week together. But right now, Grace wanted to take advantage of every moment, and Lia seemed to agree as she kissed Grace back enthusiastically.

When they parted, they just smiled at each other, and Grace felt light on her feet . . . *happy*. There was that word again. When she was with Lia, she just felt good.

They walked hand in hand to the nearby food stand and bought hot dogs and soda, and then they sat to people watch while they ate, Lia occasionally tossing bits of her chips to the pigeons.

"What would you like to do this afternoon?" Lia asked.

"I want to go to a museum with you," Grace told her. "The nerdier, the better. I want to see you in your element."

"Well, I toured the Museum of American History this morning," Lia told her. "That might have been the nerdiest. How do you feel about going to the National Gallery of Art?"

"Yes," Grace agreed. "I love art . . . in an abstract way. I don't know much about it, but I like to look at it."

Lia gave her an amused look. "Then let's go look at some art."

They crossed the National Mall together and approached the National Gallery building, which was as impressive as everything else here in DC, with marble steps leading up to the entrance and big white columns in front. As they walked inside, Grace was enchanted by the way Lia's demeanor changed. She became quiet, almost studious, as she examined each painting and read the plaque that described it.

"Do you know a lot about art?" Grace asked as she followed behind her, as interested in watching Lia as she was in looking at the art itself.

"Only from a layman's perspective," Lia told her. "I've never formally studied it, and I'm certainly not an artist myself. I've seen a lot of art, though, and I enjoy adding to my knowledge. I like to think about what life was like for the artist when they created it. Were they lounging around in their mansion in Victorian England? Or were they watching loved ones die of the plague? Or surviving a war? That kind of thing."

"That's very deep," Grace told her. "I mostly look for colors and designs that I like."

"That's the beauty of art," Lia said with a kind of reverence in her voice. "There's no right or wrong way to enjoy it. Whatever you're drawn to, whatever you take from it, it's all up to each person's interpretation."

"Tell me about this one," Grace said. They were standing in front of a landscape painting, a river dotted with boats with big white sails. Trees lined the shore, and behind them Grace saw a church with a tall steeple.

"The artist is Dutch," Lia told her. "It was painted in 1649, and it says here that the painting reflects the sense of pride that the Dutch felt after having recently won their independence from Spain. See the people on the riverbank? To me, it looks like they're dressed in their finest clothes. And these cows are likely symbolic of their economic prosperity. It seems like an idyllic portrayal of what was probably still a very tumultuous time in their lives."

"Okay," Grace said, looking at the painting with new eyes. "You got so much more out of that than I did. I was kind of admiring the brushstrokes on the trees. The artist gave so many layers to the texture."

"And that's every bit as valid," Lia told her. "Everyone takes something different from each work. I think that's beautiful."

They spent the next two hours wandering through the gallery together, exchanging thoughts and opinions. Grace wasn't sure she'd ever spent so much time talking about art, but she was having a good time. Eventually, they made their way outside to the sculpture garden, where they strolled along the paths as late-afternoon sunshine cast everything around them in a golden glow.

They sat on a bench next to a huge metal spider to discuss their options for dinner, eventually deciding on a steak house not too far from their hotel. They hadn't gone out to a nice dinner yet on their road trip, and Grace was looking forward to the opportunity.

In a way, this was like their first date.

CHAPTER SIXTEEN

Lia couldn't take her eyes off Grace if she tried. The restaurant they'd chosen for dinner was fancier than she'd expected. They'd been seated upstairs at a table for two by the window, looking out at the busy street below. It was quite a view, and yet, Lia couldn't concentrate on anything but the woman on the other side of the table.

Grace had changed into a simple black dress with a long silver neck-lace that shimmered in the low lighting. A candle flickered on the table between them, making shadows dance across her face, and Lia thought she was more exquisite, more interesting, more *everything* than all the art they'd seen together today. Grace was a masterpiece.

"Oh, wait, we almost forgot." Grace picked up her phone and came around the table to pose for a selfie with Lia. "Rosie will yell at me if I don't keep the pictures coming." Her vanilla scent wrapped around Lia as they smiled for the photo, and she wondered if she'd ever smell vanilla again without thinking of Grace.

Lia looked at the photo on Grace's phone. "You don't think this looks too much like a date?"

Grace's lips twisted to one side. "Do you think so? I mean, maybe . . ."

"It *is* a date," Lia said. "At least, I hope you think so too."

"I do," Grace said, giving Lia a small smile as she slipped back into her seat. "A no-strings kind of date, I guess."

"Yes. I just don't necessarily want Rosie to think it's a date," Lia said. "You and I need to sort things out on our own at the end of the week before we get Rosie involved, because as I'm sure you know, we'd never hear the end of it."

"No, you're absolutely right," Grace said.

"She was already suspicious when she saw us together in New York."

"I know." Grace's gaze fell to the tablecloth, and then she looked at Lia with a self-deprecating smile. "There was really no hiding the chemistry between us, even then."

"No," Lia agreed.

"Okay, so let's make this look less date-like." Grace glanced around the dining room, and then she took a picture of the view outside the window. "We'll just post this one."

"But send me the other one?" Lia asked, because she wanted to remember this date, no matter what happened at the end of their trip.

"Sure." Grace tapped her screen, and Lia's phone dinged with an incoming text.

"Thank you."

"No problem. So I was thinking . . . you should really apply for a job in a museum."

"What?" Lia looked up from the photo on her phone.

"You should see yourself when you're in a museum," Grace said, and the way she was looking at Lia sent a tingle down her spine, like Grace was seeing her in a way no one else ever had. "Your whole demeanor changes," Grace said. "It seems like your happy place, like the bookstore is for Rosie. I mean, don't you owe it to yourself to chase that dream?"

"I don't know," Lia said. She hadn't considered it since she'd become the manager of Between the Pages. She loved her job, and she loved working with her best friend. "Dreams change sometimes, you know? I wouldn't have foreseen myself managing a bookstore, but sometimes the best things in life happen unexpectedly."

"That's true," Grace said. "I just think it's something you should consider."

"You're right," Lia said. "It is. I don't know if I'll do it. I don't know if it's even something I still want, but there's no harm in thinking about it."

Grace's smile was brighter than the candle still flickering between them. "I'm picturing you at your desk, surrounded by sculptures or paintings or artifacts, looking all gorgeous and studious in your glasses, making everyone who comes through your office swoon for you even more than the actual art . . . phew." She fanned her face with her hand.

Warmth crept up Lia's neck. Was that how Grace saw her? For some reason, it made Lia sit a little taller in her seat. It made her want to press Grace against the nearest wall and kiss the breath out of her. And . . . it made her want to apply for a job in a museum. "You're a flatterer," she said, reaching for her wine.

"It's the truth," Grace said. "I happen to find your nerdy side extremely hot."

"Good to know." Lia lifted her glass and sipped, and the warmth of the wine only added to the heat already building inside her. This thing with Grace was like playing with fire, because Lia already liked her a hell of a lot. They were combustible together in bed. In any other situation, Lia would be certain this was the start of something wonderful, maybe the start of a whole new chapter in her life.

If only Grace weren't going back to London at the end of the week . . .

Lia hoped they might try something long distance. She was certainly open to it, at least while they got to know each other better and worked out where the future might take them. But everything she knew about Grace said she would cut all romantic ties when she left town. She'd been up front about her relationship issues, so Lia had no one to blame but herself if she did something stupid and fell for Grace over the course of their road trip.

"It doesn't have to be the British Museum, you know," Grace said. "You could find a museum job in Manhattan."

"I know, and that's probably what I would apply for . . . if I decide to apply for something." She took another sip of her wine, wondering whether she would be overstepping if she voiced the obvious. "Unless I had a reason to go to London."

Grace's shoulders visibly tensed, and her gaze fell to the wineglass in front of her. "It has to be your reason, Lia, not mine. I can't offer you anything worth crossing an ocean for."

That was exactly what Lia was afraid of. "This is a strange conversation to have after one night together, but perhaps we should—"

"No," Grace interrupted. "Please don't make me overthink this, Lia, or I'll end up getting a second hotel room after all."

Lia inhaled, and her stomach soured. She wished they weren't having this conversation in a restaurant, because she wanted to sit close to Grace, to hold her hands and look into her eyes and speak freely without an audience. She didn't like to argue in public. "If you're that unsure about being with me, then maybe a second hotel room is best."

"I don't want that," Grace said quietly, and there was a pleading note in her voice. "I'm really enjoying this, but I don't want to look ahead. Can't we just live in the moment?"

Lia nodded, then stood, gesturing for Grace to come over. She rounded the table, and Lia pulled her into her arms, hugging her as they stood somewhat awkwardly wedged between their table and the wall. "Living in the moment is hard for me. I'm a planner, but I'm really enjoying this too. I like you a lot, Grace, and I just wanted you to know that *if* we kept up a long-distance relationship after you go back to London, it's not impossible for me to move there at some point in the future."

"See, that doesn't sound at all like living in the moment," Grace murmured against her neck, her body tense beneath Lia's fingers. "And when I met you, you told me that you didn't want to live in London anymore, that New York was your home now."

"All I'm saying is that the possibility exists," Lia told her. "Don't go back to London thinking that you'd have to move to New York if you ever want to see me again."

"Stop," Grace whispered, growing even more tense in Lia's arms.

"I'm sorry," Lia said, rubbing a hand up and down Grace's back. "I'm not trying to make you uncomfortable. I'm just trying to be honest with you."

"By offering to move to London for me after we slept together once?" Grace pulled back to face her, frowning. "Because that sounds a little extreme, don't you think? Especially after I told you I don't want a relationship."

"It does when you phrase it like that," Lia said, holding on to Grace's hands. "I'm not trying to pressure you, I promise."

"It sure feels like it," Grace whispered, and to Lia's horror, tears welled in her eyes. She tugged her hands from Lia's grasp.

"I'm sorry," Lia said as a painful lump rose in her own throat. "I promise I'll do my very best to live in the moment for the rest of the week."

"I'm going back to London, Lia, and I'm going alone," Grace said quietly, eyes still glossy, arms folded tightly over her chest.

And Lia had royally fucked this up. Here they were, about to enjoy a lovely dinner, their first official date, and she'd pushed things so far that she'd pushed Grace away. Why did she self-sabotage herself this way? This wasn't the first time one of her partners had accused Lia of getting ahead of herself. She hadn't wanted to do it with Grace—*especially* not with Grace—and yet, here she was, repeating past mistakes. "I'm so sorry. Can we just forget this conversation happened? I was trying to reassure you, and instead, I've done the opposite."

Grace blew out a breath. "I promised you we'd talk before I leave at the end of the week, but I'm afraid I gave you more hope than I should have, because I can't change who I am, and I . . . I'm the last person who ought to be promising you *anything*, Lia."

"It's okay," Lia told her, determined to push aside her hurt feelings and salvage their meal. "Let's just enjoy dinner, okay?"

Grace nodded, and then she stepped forward, wrapping her arms around Lia. "I really do like you. You know that, right? I'm sorry I can't give you all the things you want."

Lia appreciated her honesty, no matter how much it hurt to hear. "All I want right now is to enjoy the rest of our road trip. We'll face next week when it arrives."

Grace swept her tongue over the chocolate chip ice cream on her cone, one hand in Lia's as they strolled past the White House, which was impressively lit under the night sky. Instead of a fancy dessert at the restaurant, they'd opted for ice cream from one of the food carts on the National Mall and a walk to clear their heads. Maybe it would cool them off, because Grace was still simmering from their predinner argument.

She wasn't mad at Lia. If anyone was to blame, it was Grace. She was the one who had overreacted when Lia offered to keep her options open after they parted ways this week. It was a perfectly reasonable offer, if only Grace's heart wasn't such an atrophied thing, and it wasn't a muscle she wanted to strengthen.

"You're awfully quiet over there," Lia said before taking a lick of her own ice cream.

"Just enjoying the view," Grace said, turning away from the White House to face Lia. She leaned forward to capture her lips, which were cold and tasted sweet like her peach cobbler ice cream.

"The flag's up," Lia said, nodding toward the White House. "I wonder if that means the president is home?"

"I don't know," Grace said, glancing at the building before returning her gaze to Lia.

"That's how it is at Buckingham Palace," Lia said. "When the flag's up, the queen is in residence."

"Cool," Grace told her. "I'll have to take a walk by once I get home."

"I saw her once," Lia said. She had a dot of ice cream on her nose, and Grace reached out to wipe it away, drawing a smile from Lia. "My family was on holiday in London, and we went to the Trooping the Colour parade and saw her go by in her carriage."

"Was little Lia starstruck by the queen?" Grace asked with a smile before taking another lick of her ice cream.

"Not really," Lia said. "I mean, I was impressed, of course, but I'm not really one to get starstruck. Rosie, on the other hand . . ."

Grace giggled. "Ask her about the time she and I saw Cate Blanchett coming out of *The Tonight Show* studios. I think I might have hearing damage from all her squealing."

Lia smiled. "That sounds about right."

"Is she like that with the authors who come into the store? She swears she's professional with them, but I've always wondered."

"She's very professional," Lia said. "Although I've seen her get a bit starstruck with some of the bigger-name authors. And of course, there was the time she met Brie . . ."

"That was wild," Grace agreed. "I was so confused trying to follow along from afar. She hated Jane because she'd evicted her, but then she found out Jane was Brie, and she still hated her, but then she loved her. I got some weird texts."

"I can only imagine," Lia said. "It was certainly entertaining to watch them go around in circles."

"Speaking of Rosie . . ." Grace pulled out her phone and took a selfie with her ice cream and the White House visible behind her. Then she stepped closer to Lia, framing both of them in the shot. Lia tipped her head to the side, licking her cone as she gazed toward the White

House while Grace laughed, and it turned out so cute she sent it to Rosie, who immediately replied with a bunch of smiley faces.

Lia's phone buzzed with an incoming text, and when Grace saw Rosie's name on the screen, she didn't look away, since they were all mutual friends at this point.

Rosie Taft:
You and Gorgeous Grace sure look cozy together ☺

"'Gorgeous Grace'?" she blurted as Lia quickly swiped the text from her screen. "What the hell is that about?"

In response, Lia took a huge bite of her ice cream and turned to face the White House.

"Lia . . ." Grace's stomach tightened uncomfortably. Why was Rosie calling her "gorgeous" in a text to Lia? It felt like some sort of inside joke that she wasn't a part of.

"She's just being her usual nosy self," Lia said finally.

"'Gorgeous Grace'?" she repeated.

Lia looked skyward, giving her head a slight shake. "I'm going to kill her for this. When I talked to Rosie on the phone after I first met you in London, she asked what I thought of you, and I . . . well, I stupidly said you were gorgeous. Not that calling you 'gorgeous' is stupid, because you *are* gorgeous." Lia was talking so fast, almost stumbling over her words, sounding completely unlike herself.

Grace could only stare, because this story had taken an unexpected turn.

"Telling Rosie you were gorgeous was stupid," Lia clarified, "because she's been calling you 'gorgeous Grace' to me ever since, insinuating that I like you and being generally, well . . . Rosie."

Grace laughed awkwardly. "Okay."

"She's trying to play matchmaker, and I guess . . . I assumed she was doing it with you too?" Lia looked at her questioningly.

"Um, no," Grace said. "I mean, she's dropped a few hints, but she's not being nearly that obvious with me. God, she really needs to chill." She flailed her hands, managing to drop her ice cream on the sidewalk in the process. "Dammit."

"Grace." Lia sounded like her usual calm, composed self again. "Rosie's always like this with me, with Shanice, with all her friends. It doesn't mean anything, and I swear, I'm not going to make a scene when you leave at the end of the week."

Grace frowned, looking at her spilled ice cream. She believed Lia. She wouldn't make a scene, but that didn't mean she wouldn't get hurt, and she would definitely want to talk everything to death. Once they got back to Manhattan, Rosie would start meddling. Grace's heart couldn't handle any of it. She just wanted to have a little fun to distract herself from her upcoming meeting with Laurel.

Actually, that wasn't true. She liked Lia a lot, so much that she wished there was a way to make this work, which was exactly why she couldn't try. Grace had a terrible track record when it came to matters of the heart. No one she loved had ever loved her back as strongly—not Rosie, and certainly not Carmen. She wasn't going to make the same mistake with Lia.

Especially not Lia, because she was Rosie's best friend, and Rosie was Grace's best friend, and that meant she and Lia were linked for life, whether they liked it or not. If they crashed and burned, they'd still have to hear about each other through Rosie, and Grace couldn't handle that kind of pain.

"Tell her 'gorgeous Grace' is going to give her hell for giving me that stupid nickname," Grace said, pointing at Lia's phone.

"I'm not telling her you saw that text!" Lia exclaimed.

"Then I will." Grace pulled out her phone and started typing.

Grace Poston:
Knock it off with the Gorgeous Grace nonsense.

Rosie Taft:

Busted! Sorry.

Grace Poston:

No, you're not . . .

Rosie Taft:

Fine, I'm not, but only because you two are SO ADORBS together.

And you *are* gorgeous btw

Grace Poston:

I'm not. We're not. And you're going to stop meddling.

Rosie Taft:

Sure, sure, my gorgeous friend.

"Ugh, she's hopeless," Grace said as she put her phone away, but she was smiling. As much as Rosie infuriated her sometimes, she couldn't really be mad, because Rosie wasn't wrong. She and Lia *did* look cute together in that photo. "Just for that, I'm not sending her any more pictures of us together."

"Oh, sure, because *that's* the way to not look suspicious," Lia countered.

"I can't win," Grace muttered.

"Here, finish my ice cream and call it a win." Lia pushed the cone into her hand. "And let me make it up to you once we get back to our hotel room."

"I like the way you think." As she took a bite of Lia's peach cobbler ice cream, she felt like she was winning after all. She chased the ice cream with Lia's lips, kissing her until she'd forgotten all the reasons she'd been upset, all the reasons she had to leave at the end of the week, all the reasons she'd closed herself off in the first place.

She'd convinced herself she didn't miss this. She'd been satisfied with her life, happy to surround herself with friends and a job she loved and an exciting new life in London. And now she wondered how she'd ever be satisfied without feeling Lia's lips on hers, the way it made everything inside her heat up and ignited the most delicious ache in her core.

Someone whistled, and when she opened her eyes, she saw a group of college-aged men and women passing by on the sidewalk. One of the men was making a rude gesture at them, and as she watched, Lia flipped him off.

Grace pressed her face against Lia's neck, smiling. She held on to her until the group had passed them, and then Lia tugged her in for another kiss.

"Come on, darling," Lia murmured against her lips. "Let's take this back to our room."

CHAPTER SEVENTEEN

"I need your help," Lia said as she and Grace strolled through the *Deep Time* exhibit at the Smithsonian National Museum of Natural History. Around them, the hall teemed with people, tour groups and families all gathered to have a peek at history.

It was Thursday afternoon, Lia and Grace's third full day in DC. They'd fallen into a routine where Lia played tourist in the mornings while Grace worked at the hotel; then they'd sightsee together in the afternoons.

"My help?" Grace gave her a curious look. She wore black jeans and a blue top, her hair in a ponytail that made her look entirely too adorable, and Lia couldn't get enough.

"I've always wanted to kiss a beautiful woman in front of a dinosaur skeleton," Lia told her, keeping her tone serious.

Grace smirked. "This is something you've actually thought about?"

"Oh yes," Lia told her. Actually, she hadn't imagined that exact scenario, but she'd always wanted to make out with someone in a museum, and since she and Grace had arrived in DC, she'd wanted it to be her.

"In that case, I'm happy to help you fulfill your wish," Grace said, her eyes sparkling playfully.

"I appreciate it."

"I think it's got to be the *T. rex*," Grace said, tugging Lia's hand as she led her toward the crown jewel of the exhibit, the towering, fossilized skeleton of the king of the dinosaurs, and Lia could kiss her for being so enthusiastic about this, for finding humor in Lia's eccentricities and picking the most perfect fossil in the damn museum for them to share a kiss in front of.

They reached the *T. rex* skeleton, and Grace stared up at it while Lia read the plaque describing where the fossils had been found and all the other pertinent information. When she looked up, Grace caught her eye and struck a pose, flexing her hands and miming her best dinosaur roar.

Lia whipped out her phone and snapped a couple of quick photos. Grace was always photogenic, but her personality really came through in photos like these, where she was being silly and carefree. Looking at her, Lia felt a tug in her chest that told her she was falling hard and fast for this woman. Grace was everything she'd ever wanted in a life partner . . . except for the part where she didn't want a partner of her own.

"Amelia Harris, get over here and kiss me." Grace puckered her lips and blew a kiss in Lia's direction.

"We definitely won't send this one to Rosie," Lia said as she held her phone at arm's length. She leaned in and pressed her lips to Grace's, snapping several photos. She wasn't sure why she wanted to document this moment, only that it felt extremely important.

She wanted to remember kissing Grace in front of the *T. rex*. She wanted to memorize every detail, although she doubted that would be a problem. Even this chaste kiss, lips pressing together as they posed for the camera, sent warmth through Lia's veins. It made her ridiculously happy at the same time as it made her yearn for things she couldn't have.

"Better be convincing," Grace murmured before parting her lips to give Lia a real kiss, the kind that left no question that they were more than friends, at least at this moment in time. Lia snapped more pictures as Grace tilted her head, kissing her deeply and thoroughly. Her hands rested on Lia's waist, drawing her closer.

Lia slipped her phone into the pocket of her skirt and wrapped her arms around Grace, wishing she could stand in front of this *T. rex* and kiss her forever, even though she knew they needed to stop. They were surrounded by people—including families with children—which meant this wasn't the place for them to make out.

Regretfully, she lifted her head, breaking their kiss. She didn't step back, though, holding Grace in her arms as she turned to look at the dinosaur. Grace rested her head against Lia's neck, a habit of hers that Lia absolutely adored. It underscored their height difference, but it also felt intimate and familiar.

They stood like that for a few minutes, looking at the skeleton as people passed around them. Finally, Grace stepped back, keeping one of her hands in Lia's as they moved on to look at the next exhibit. They made their way through the museum and out into the late-afternoon sunshine.

This was their last day in DC, and they'd decided to spend a casual evening, getting burritos from a nearby food truck and walking past the monuments they hadn't had a chance to see yet. They held hands as they walked, sharing easy conversation. Sometimes, Lia felt like she'd known Grace so much longer than two weeks, but in other ways, things between them still felt so new.

She didn't really know what Grace was like at home in her day-to-day life, or what her life had been like in Spain before her recent move to London. How many friends did she have in London, apart from Ollie? Would she tell any of them about Lia once she got home?

"It's so beautiful," Grace whispered as they stood together in front of the reflecting pool at the Lincoln Memorial. The sun had set now, casting long shadows around them. The Washington Monument glowed against the evening sky, tall and white, mirrored on the water in a rippling reflection.

Lia wrapped an arm around Grace, and she settled against her. She turned toward Lia, lifting her face to kiss her. Lia was tempted to take a photo of this, too, with the monument and the reflecting pool as their backdrop, but she wanted to keep this moment just for the two of them, and anyway, a photo probably wouldn't turn out well in this low lighting.

"We should have started this tradition sooner," Grace whispered against her lips. "Kissing our way around all the DC landmarks."

"Never too late to start," Lia said. "Although, we kissed at most of the places we've been. We just weren't documenting it."

"True." Grace went up on her tiptoes, deepening the kiss. Her tongue teased Lia's, and Lia pulled her closer, pressing their hips together, loving Grace's warmth through the layers of their clothing. They'd done a lot of kissing today, and a restlessness had been growing inside her for hours, the need to get Grace naked and satisfy her yearning for her.

"Ready to call it a night?" she asked, and Grace nodded.

"If calling it a night means doing sexy things with you in bed, then yes."

"That's exactly what I was thinking," Lia said.

"Let's go, then."

Lia turned to take one last look at the Washington Monument, watching the red light that blinked at the top. A duck paddled across the reflecting pool, making the monument's reflection swirl and ripple. It was beautiful.

They started to walk back to the hotel. On the surface, they were unhurried, stopping to enjoy the views and take a few final photos, but beneath that, a current ran between them, chemistry snapping every time their hands brushed. Tomorrow, they'd drive to Virginia to meet Laurel, and everything might change. Grace's life could be upended in a wonderful way, or it might be the opposite.

Lia had noticed moments today when Grace zoned out, her expression blank as she withdrew inside her thoughts, no doubt worrying about what tomorrow would bring. Whatever happened, Lia would be here to hold her hand and dry her tears if there were any. Maybe they'd go back to separate beds in Virginia, when Grace was preoccupied with family things, and that would be okay. Maybe it would bring them closer together, but Lia would do her best not to push. She'd made her wishes clear, and it was up to Grace to decide what happened next.

They walked through the lobby of their hotel and stepped into the elevator. Grace leaned against the wall as it climbed, and there was that distant look again. After a moment, she blinked it away, stepping purposefully into Lia's arms. If she needed a distraction tonight, Lia was happy to provide it. There was nothing to gain from Grace pacing the hotel room all night, worrying, not if Lia could help her relax.

The silver doors to the elevator slid open, and they stepped out, arms still wrapped around each other, exchanging kisses as they stumbled down the hall to their room. Lia got her keycard out, pushed it into the slot, and unlocked the door. They tumbled inside. Lia's hands were on Grace's waist, and she felt so small, so petite . . . before Lia realized what she was doing, she was lifting Grace right off her feet.

Grace yelped in surprise, and then her legs wrapped around Lia's waist, clinging to her as she brought their mouths together. Lia had been wanting to sweep Grace off her feet ever since the wedding, an uncharacteristically possessive urge. But then again, Grace had always been different for her, and now Lia couldn't remember what she'd ever found so appealing about grunge wear, not when Grace's soft, feminine body was wrapped around hers.

She carried Grace across the room, staggering slightly beneath her weight, because even though Grace was petite, Lia still wasn't accustomed to carrying a full-grown woman in her arms. She was about to lower her onto the bed when something prompted her to spin them, pressing Grace against the wall instead.

Grace whimpered as her back met the plaster, Lia's hips resting firmly between hers. She wiggled in Lia's arms, settling against her. They kissed, tongues tangling while they clung to each other, Grace's hips moving against hers.

Lia brought a hand between them and traced her index finger up the seam of Grace's jeans, teasing her. She was rewarded as Grace dropped her head against the wall behind her, letting out a shaky breath.

"Take me, Lia," she whispered. "Right here."

"My pleasure." Lia would love nothing more, although it was easier said than done with Grace wearing those tight-fitting jeans. Lia popped the button, then pushed down the zipper, and Grace gasped as Lia's fingers brushed against the front of her underwear.

She pushed her hand as far as she could reach, but she couldn't get the leverage she needed with Grace's jeans in the way. Reluctantly, she pulled back and lowered Grace's feet to the floor. Together, they rid Grace of her jeans and underwear, and then she climbed back into Lia's arms. She was still wearing her shirt, but Lia was too distracted to remove it, because Grace's bare legs were wrapped around her hips, and it was impossibly arousing.

She brought one hand between them, the other braced against the wall, letting Grace ride her fingers. It was a heady feeling, taking her against the wall like this. Lia thrust her hips against Grace, using the momentum to push her fingers deeper inside her. She loved the way Grace's inner walls tightened around her and the wetness that coated her fingers.

"Yes," Grace panted. "God, Lia . . . *yes.*"

"You're perfect," Lia murmured as she took her in, the way Grace's breasts bounced with each thrust, the flush on her skin, and her warmth as it surrounded Lia. She rubbed Grace's clit with her thumb, and Grace let out a keening cry, her hips moving faster, grinding against Lia's hand. With a soft moan, she was coming, her body clamping rhythmically around Lia's fingers. She tensed and then sagged in Lia's arms, gasping for breath.

"That was amazing," Grace whispered, dropping her forehead against Lia's shoulder. Lia's legs were starting to tire, so she spun them. Grace released her, dropping onto the bed, where she stared up at Lia with a dazed expression. A soft smile curved her lips, and she extended a hand toward Lia. "Now get down here so I can return the favor."

The clock beside the bed read 3:12 a.m., and Grace had yet to sleep. Not wanting a repeat of the night in Sevenoaks when she'd tossed and turned until she woke Lia, tonight Grace had done her best to lie still. But this was torture. Her mind spun, and her body had become so restless that she couldn't stand it any longer.

Quietly, she slipped out of bed, wrapped her robe around herself, and walked to the window. Outside, buildings gleamed beneath the darkened sky. A few cars passed by on the street below. New York wasn't the only city that never slept. Every city she'd lived in had been this way.

What would happen tomorrow when she met Laurel? Her stomach cramped just thinking about it. Would it be unforgivably rude to back out now and just go home? The urge to run was strong. Her legs twitched with it, and she paced in front of the window, wishing she weren't trapped in this hotel room.

Lia lay facing her, eyes closed and lips slightly parted in sleep. Grace watched her for a minute, remembering the way they'd kissed in front of the *T. rex* skeleton earlier, and she was surprised to feel herself smiling. They'd had a lot of fun on this road trip, and she was glad for it, *all* of it, even if it meant hurt feelings when it was time for her to leave.

She turned to face the window, resting her palms against the cool glass as she sucked in deep, slow breaths, attempting to tame the anxiety swirling inside her. She leaned forward, resting her forehead against the glass, and closed her eyes. Exhaustion pressed over her, making her body feel heavy, and yet, she was still too wired to sleep.

And suddenly, she was engulfed in warmth as Lia's body pressed against her back. "Can't sleep?"

"No," she said quietly. "Sorry. I was trying not to wake you."

"I'm a light sleeper." Lia rubbed a hand up and down her back, and Grace felt something deep inside her relax. She spun and wrapped her arms around Lia.

"Can we drive straight back to New York tomorrow?" she whispered, resting her head on Lia's shoulder.

"We certainly can, but are you sure that's what you want?"

"No," Grace admitted.

"I would never pressure you to do something you don't want to do," Lia said. "But I also don't want to see you back out of something this important just because you're scared, especially not when I'll be there to hold your hand and back you up."

"What if I don't like what I learn?" Grace asked. "What if my father's a horrible person? What if this is some kind of a setup so Laurel can blame me for whatever happened?"

"I can't promise that won't happen, but I do think it's often better to have answers—even if they aren't the ones you wanted—than to be left wondering."

Grace exhaled, her fingers clutching Lia's T-shirt. "I wish I could fast-forward to tomorrow night, so I'd have my answers and the meeting with Laurel would be over with."

"I hear you," Lia said. "But in the meantime, you need to sleep."

"I wish I could," Grace mumbled.

"Here, let's see if I can help relax you." Lia guided her toward the bed.

Grace took off her robe and lay down, so tired she felt dizzy but still just as restless and twitchy. Lia picked up her cell phone and tapped the screen a few times, and then the sound of ocean waves filled the room.

"White noise sometimes helps me," she said as she slipped into bed beside Grace. "Just close your eyes and listen to the ocean. Picture the waves sweeping along the shore to give your mind something relaxing to focus on."

"I'll try," she whispered.

Lia's hand rubbed up and down her back, which was soothing in and of itself. Grace focused on that, letting it ground her as she listened to the soothing rhythm of the ocean, and blissfully, she felt her body starting to relax. The edges of her consciousness softened, and the next thing she knew, she was blinking awake into the muted light of morning.

Her brain felt groggy and sluggish, but at least she'd gotten a few hours of solid, restful sleep. The clock read 8:32 a.m., and the room was quiet. Lia's white noise app must have shut off sometime during the night.

Speaking of Lia, Grace peeked over her shoulder to see that she was still asleep, so Grace slid quietly out of bed and went into the bathroom for a shower. A knot of anxiety twisted her stomach as she stood beneath the shower's hot spray. What was the best-case scenario today?

Did she want to learn that her biological father was happily married to Laurel's mother? Or would she rather find out that she and Laurel had both been raised without him? Maybe Grace's mother had broken up Laurel's parents' marriage, or maybe he was a player who carelessly got women pregnant and didn't stick around.

There was no best-case scenario today, because Grace didn't like any of them. And despite her reluctance to meet Laurel or her biological father, Grace also feared their possible rejection if this meeting didn't go well. She kept herself at arm's length from people for this very reason. Her heart was a delicate thing. Instead of toughening her up, each loss or heartbreak only seemed to make her more fragile. She stepped out of the shower and wrapped herself in a towel before blow-drying her hair. Then she tiptoed into the bedroom to get dressed.

"Morning," Lia said from the bed.

"Morning." Grace crossed the room to give her a quick kiss.

Lia reached out and caught her hand. "How are you feeling about things this morning?"

"Like an animal that's about to bolt," Grace told her, surprised all over again by how easy it was to tell Lia the truth. She didn't hide behind the defensive layers that she usually kept up, even with Rosie.

"Bolting's okay," Lia told her. "But if you feel like you'd regret it afterward, maybe you should let me drive to Virginia and just hand over the reins, so to speak."

Grace sucked in a deep breath and blew it out, nodding. "You'd better drive, then."

"All right. That's settled." Lia sat up and gave her another kiss before heading into the bathroom.

Grace turned her attention to her suitcase. What did someone wear to meet their long-lost half sister? Most of the clothes she'd packed had already been worn at this point, so her options were fairly slim. She located a gray-striped knit dress with a drawstring waist that was comfortable but looked nice and then put it on. As she stood in front of the mirror to do her makeup, her fingers shook, and there was a prickly ball wedged in the pit of her stomach.

The shower ran in the bathroom as she finished getting ready, adding simple jewelry and black flats. She packed everything but the toiletries she'd left in the bathroom while the tension inside her grew, constricting around her chest. If only she were back in London already . . .

Lia came out of the bathroom dressed in a blue-patterned jumpsuit. They spent a few minutes to finish packing, and then Lia said, "Shall we go downstairs for breakfast before we check out?"

Grace nodded, although she couldn't imagine eating right now. She'd regret it later if she didn't, though. Surely, she could at least choke down some toast to try to settle her stomach.

So they went downstairs, and Grace got a bagel with cream cheese and coffee while Lia ordered an omelet, fruit, and tea. She was relentlessly cheerful this morning, and Grace was so thankful for it, even if she didn't have the words to tell her.

"I've never been to Virginia," Lia told her as they wheeled their suitcases out of the hotel room an hour later.

"First time for everything." Grace handed her the car keys, thus assuring that she didn't panic and bolt.

Lia took them with a reassuring smile and led the way toward the elevator.

CHAPTER EIGHTEEN

They didn't talk much during the drive to Charlottesville. Lia was focused on her driving, navigating the busy streets from the right-hand side of the road. Beside her, Grace sat with a faraway look in her eyes. Her hands fidgeted with the strap of her purse, and her knees bounced restlessly. At least she'd had a few hours of sleep last night.

Lia had no idea what to expect once they got to Laurel's house for dinner, but she desperately hoped that this went well . . . whatever that looked like. Hopefully, Laurel had good intentions and wasn't planning to ambush Grace over whatever circumstances had led to them sharing a biological father.

If this had been Lia's meeting to plan, she'd have asked for as much information from Laurel as she could in advance so that she'd know exactly what she was walking into. But Grace being Grace, she'd said yes to Laurel's invitation to meet and then stuck her head in the sand about the whole thing. They knew absolutely nothing about Laurel, other than her name and address.

So they'd be walking in blind tonight, which Lia didn't feel great about, but Laurel was probably as nervous and unsure about this as Grace was. In all likelihood, they were both looking for answers. Still, Lia hated to be unprepared.

She exhaled in relief as their Airbnb came into sight. They'd rented a little cottage on the outskirts of town for the night, and while Lia had initially thought they might miss the amenities that came with a hotel, she was glad for it now. Something told her Grace was going to need privacy to deal with whatever needed to be dealt with later.

"This looks nice," Lia said as she turned into the driveway. Their cottage was on the edge of someone's property in what was supposed to have been the guesthouse. It was nothing much to look at, but it had everything they'd need tonight, and there was supposed to be a pond and some walking trails nearby, which might be a good way to help Grace burn off some of her nervous energy.

Grace gave her a tight smile. "Nice to be out of hotels for a night."

"Yes. We should stop by the grocery store after we're settled and pick up a few things, maybe have a light lunch here at the cabin?"

"That sounds good," Grace said.

Lia parked in the driveway, and Grace was out of the car almost before she'd shut off the engine, bustling around to get her luggage. She rolled her suitcase to the door and punched in the code they'd been given, her lips set in a firm line. Lia followed her in, and Grace went straight down the hall to the master bedroom and shut the door behind her. Lia let her go, happy to give her space if that was what she needed.

Grace wasn't used to having anyone in her life in a romantic capacity . . . or family, either, for that matter. She had friends, but that wasn't the same. Friends didn't share the kind of physical—or emotional—intimacy she and Lia had shared this week.

Lia pushed her suitcase into the living room and reached for the binder of information their host had left them, which included numbers for several local restaurants that delivered and information for nearby shopping. She sat on the sofa and checked her phone, finding a text from Rosie, asking how Grace was doing.

She debated how to answer, because although Rosie and Grace were friends, Lia still felt uncomfortable talking about her without her knowledge. The fact that Rosie had texted Lia for an update meant

Grace probably hadn't been answering her texts, though, so Lia sent back a quick response to let Rosie know they'd arrived in Virginia.

Lia messed around on her phone, locating the nearest grocery store and double-checking how long it would take them to get to Laurel's house. What was Grace doing in the bedroom? Lia wanted to make sure she was okay, but she didn't want to push when Grace obviously needed some space.

Lia was trying so hard not to overstep. When she and Shawn broke up two years ago, he'd accused her of trying to micromanage his life. He'd told her he felt stifled in their relationship, which didn't even remotely excuse his infidelity, but Lia knew she could be unintentionally overbearing at times. She didn't want to be that way with Grace.

Lia had checked her email and scrolled through all her social media accounts before the door to the bedroom opened and Grace stepped out. Her eyes were slightly red, and her face was damp. Lia's chest clenched as she imagined Grace crying discreetly in the bedroom and then washing her face and reapplying her makeup to cover it.

"Want to take a ride to the grocery store?" Lia asked rather than calling her on it.

"Sure," Grace said, and then she gave Lia a quick hug. "Thank you," she murmured against Lia's neck.

Lia squeezed her back, loving the way Grace softened in her embrace. "Anytime."

Grace was coming apart at the seams. Lia had distracted her with a trip to the grocery store, a picnic by the pond, and some amazing sex in their new bedroom, and it had worked pretty well.

Until now.

Now, they were in the car, driving to Laurel's house, and Grace hadn't been this panicked since she got the phone call about her parents' accident. Her heart pounded so hard that when she looked down, she could see it shaking the fabric of her dress. Her palms were damp, and that prickly ball was still lodged in her stomach, making her wonder how she'd even manage to eat dinner once they arrived.

"Do you want an escape plan?" Lia asked as she guided the car onto the main road that would take them across town.

"Like what?" she asked.

"Like, if you get overwhelmed and want to leave, just tug on your ear, and I'll come up with a reason to get us out of there."

"Okay. Thank you," Grace told her, almost overwhelmingly grateful for Lia's steadying presence. Grace had no idea how the evening would go, but she was pretty sure she wouldn't have made it this far without Lia by her side.

"Of course," Lia said, reaching over to squeeze her hand.

"What if he's there tonight?" Grace asked, voicing the fear that had overtaken her brain earlier today. What if she met her biological father tonight? She wasn't sure she wanted to meet him *ever*, after the chaos he'd caused, the lies and the deception, but she certainly didn't want to meet him tonight.

"If that happens, we'll deal with it," Lia said calmly. "And if it's too much, then tug your ear, and I'll get you out of there."

"You're pretty amazing, you know that?" Grace said.

Lia gave her a quick smile before returning her gaze to the road. "I don't know about amazing, but I'm calm in a crisis, and while I don't expect a crisis tonight, I'll be ready if one arises."

"I feel like I'm already having a crisis," Grace said, pressing a hand against her chest.

"Remember, DNA doesn't make a family. If tonight goes badly, you don't ever have to see her again. No guilt."

"I don't have to see her again, but I can't unknow that she exists." Grace rubbed her hands together, trying not to fidget in her seat. Right now, she wished she didn't know Laurel existed. Actually, she wished she and Laurel weren't related. She didn't want to have an adult half sister she'd never met. The whole thing was weird and uncomfortable, and she couldn't see any way that tonight would end well. Why had she agreed to this?

"However you and Laurel came to have the same biological father, none of this is your fault," Lia said. "And it's not hers either. If there's any blame to be placed, it's with your parents for allowing you to find out about each other on a DNA website."

Grace nodded, not trusting herself to speak. Oh, she already blamed her mother for all of this. Fresh anger and hurt welled in her chest. How could her mom have allowed this to happen? How *dare* she betray her family like this?

"I think this is it," Lia said as she turned onto a narrow residential street.

Grace's heart pounded against her ribs, making her head swim, and her stomach felt sour. If her throat hadn't been too dry to speak, she might have told Lia to keep driving, to run while they still could. But it would be stupid to leave now, when she was minutes away from finally getting the answers that she'd spent over a decade looking for. She'd go in and get her answers, and then she could finally put this chapter of her life behind her.

Lia pulled the car to the curb in front of a modest two-story house with periwinkle-blue siding and black shutters. The yard was neatly tended, with a green lawn and pots of pink flowers on the porch. Was Laurel older than Grace? This looked more like a family home than someplace a young single woman might live. Then again, Grace was old enough to be married and have a family of her own. Oh God, why was she here?

"Ready?" Lia asked as she shut off the car.

Grace cleared her throat. "As I'll ever be."

"Let's go get you some answers, then," Lia said.

Grace nodded. She picked up her purse and opened her door, standing on shaky legs. Her skin felt damp and clammy and . . . she really should have just done this via email.

"No matter what happens, you'll get through it," Lia said, coming around the car to take Grace's hand. "Lean on me as much as you need, okay?"

"Thank you," she whispered, swallowing over the sandpaper in her throat. "I'm glad you're here."

"I am too." Lia squeezed her hand as she led the way toward the front door.

They looked like a couple this way, Grace realized idly as she gripped Lia's hand. Maybe Grace shouldn't make such a bold statement about her sexuality tonight. Maybe she should play it safe so as not to be disappointed by the sister she didn't know. Maybe by holding Lia's hand as she approached the door, Grace was trying to pick a fight, looking for a reason to get upset and leave, because right now, her emotions were dangerously close to boiling over.

If Lia was calm in a crisis, Grace was . . . "volatile" was probably the best word to describe the way she felt right now.

Lia knocked on the door while Grace tried not to scream or cry or run. The seconds ticked by as loudly as her pulse whooshing in her ears, and then the door swung open to reveal a young blonde woman. She looked to be in her early twenties, maybe younger, her platinum hair in a high ponytail while her blue eyes darted from Lia to Grace.

"Hi," the blonde said with a cheerful smile. "I'm Laurel. Is one of you Grace?"

"I'm Grace," she said numbly. This was obviously a mistake, because there was no way she was related to the perky blonde in front of her. She stepped sideways so that her shoulder bumped against Lia's, needing to draw strength from her presence. "And this is Lia."

Laurel beamed at her. "It's so great to meet you. Strange but great, am I right?"

"Right," Grace managed. She forced a smile, but it felt weird on her face, like her muscles had forgotten what to do.

"Lovely to meet you, Laurel," Lia said smoothly.

"You too," Laurel said, gesturing for them to come inside. "Please come in. I apologize for inviting you to my moms' house tonight instead of my apartment, but there's more room here, and they wanted to meet you too."

"Oh," Grace said, swallowing as she stepped into the entrance hall. Her throat was so dry that she could barely speak. "Is it just you and your mom?" *No dad? No other siblings?*

"My moms," Laurel clarified, still smiling as she motioned Grace and Lia into the living room. "They'll be down in a minute, but they wanted to let us get to know each other a little bit first. Would you like something to drink?"

"Some water would be great," Grace said, and now her mind was spinning in an entirely different direction. *Moms.* Did that mean Laurel's parents were both women, and if so, how did her biological father fit into the picture?

"I'll have some water as well," Lia said.

"Sure. I'll be right back." Laurel walked through a doorway at the other end of the living room that Grace presumed led to the kitchen.

"She seems nice," Lia said quietly. "We're off to a good start, wouldn't you say?"

"I don't know," Grace whispered, her gaze automatically searching out the family photos on the mantel, but she couldn't see them clearly from where she stood, and going over for a closer look felt a little bit like snooping . . . or maybe she was just afraid of what she might see—a man who looked like her, a man who'd raised Laurel but not Grace.

"Relax," Lia said, leading her to the couch. She tugged at Grace's hand until she sat. "It's going to be okay. Laurel is friendly. This is a good thing."

"*Why* is she so friendly?" Grace asked. "Why isn't she demanding to know who my mom is and how any of this happened? And . . . is this even real? I mean, she doesn't look anything like me."

That was maybe the most disconcerting thing of all. Grace had always been a little jealous of her friends with siblings, not knowing what it was like to have someone who looked like her, other than her mother. She'd expected to see *something* of herself in Laurel, but the woman looked like a stranger.

"I've known plenty of siblings who look completely different, and you and Laurel are only half sisters," Lia said, calm as ever. "Maybe her friendliness is just southern hospitality, but whatever the reason, it can't be a bad thing. On the contrary, I have a good feeling about this."

While they waited for Laurel to return, Grace looked around the living room. It was painted a light gray with purple undertones, and the couch and love seat were dark gray. There was plenty of art on the walls, modern paintings with bright colors. Grace liked it . . . or she would have liked it under other circumstances.

"Here you go," Laurel said as she walked in with a glass of water in each hand. She handed them to Lia and Grace and sat on the love seat across from them. "Where did you come here from today? I was a little confused by your email. You mentioned London, and New York . . . neither of which are very close to Virginia."

Grace took a grateful drink before placing the glass on a coaster on the table in front of her. "Um, I live in London," she said, glancing at Lia. "And she lives in New York."

"But . . ." Laurel's brow furrowed. "Your accents are backward."

Lia laughed. "Yes, I grew up in the UK but live in New York now, and Grace grew up in New York but lives in London. It's a long story. We were already planning a vacation together when Grace found out about you, so we decided to add you into our road trip."

That wasn't entirely true, since their trip had come about after Grace had heard from Laurel, but she appreciated Lia's spin on it. Simplicity was best right now.

Laurel's eyes were wide. "That's . . . complicated, but I'm so glad you're here. I admit that when I submitted my DNA to Your-Gene, I was hoping I might find someone like you. My moms weren't entirely on board at first. I think they were a little afraid I felt like I'd been missing something, growing up without a dad, you know? But that's not it at all. I just figured I *must* have half siblings out there, and once I found one, well . . . I couldn't resist meeting you."

"Oh my God," Lia murmured, sitting up straight as if she'd just realized something important, and maybe she had, because Grace definitely felt like she was missing something. Nothing Laurel said made any sense. She'd known she had half siblings? How? Why?

What is going on? Grace wanted to scream. Her fingers clenched around her knees. "I'm so confused," she said instead.

"Perhaps you should start at the beginning," Lia said, looking at Laurel. "Why did you grow up without a father?"

Now Laurel looked confused, her brow bunching as she looked from Lia to Grace. "Well, my moms are lesbians, you know? They used a sperm donor to get pregnant. I assumed . . ." She looked at Grace as doubt crept into her expression. "Didn't your parents?"

CHAPTER NINETEEN

A sperm donor.

Grace's skin flushed hot, and her pulse pounded in her ears, blocking everything else out. Laurel's parents had used a sperm donor, and that meant . . . oh God, that meant Grace's parents might have too. And if they had . . .

That meant Grace had been wrong about everything.

Was the room spinning? She was spinning. Had she answered Laurel? Was she supposed to say something? Oh God. Oh God. Oh *God.* She heard a rasping sound that might have been her attempt at breathing, or maybe someone else in the room was freaking out too.

"Breathe." Lia's voice filtered in from somewhere, and there was a warm hand on Grace's back, rubbing up and down.

Tears flooded her eyes, and she blinked them back, staring at her hands as she attempted to drag air into her lungs. She wished she were anywhere but here, sitting in this stranger's living room while she learned that her parents had used a sperm donor. If that was true, if her mom hadn't cheated . . .

It meant Grace had spent thirteen years blaming her dead mother for something she hadn't done. She'd let it poison her entire life. And . . . what if she'd been wrong?

"Can you give us a minute?"

She heard Lia say those words, and she must have been talking to Laurel, because it didn't make sense for her to ask Grace to leave the room, but right now, nothing made sense. Grace's head felt like someone had just given it a hard shake, like she didn't know which end was up, like the floor had just dropped out from beneath her.

"Grace," Lia said, still rubbing her back. "I'm here." She didn't ask if Grace was all right. Obviously, she wasn't.

Right now, the urge to run was stronger than it had ever been. She couldn't get out of here fast enough. She wanted to run and keep on running. She didn't realize she was crying until she felt Lia's fingers on her cheeks, wiping away her tears.

"This isn't bad news, you know," Lia said gently. "In retrospect, it makes so much sense that I can't believe neither of us thought of the possibility."

"It might not be true," Grace said, lifting her head to look at Lia. "Maybe Your-Gene was wrong. Laurel and I don't look anything alike, and just because her parents used a sperm donor doesn't mean . . ." She ran out of breath, blinking at Lia, desperate for her to tell Grace what was happening, because Lia was the logical one, and she was thinking a lot more clearly than Grace was right now.

"DNA doesn't lie, Grace. You and Laurel are half sisters. Obviously, we don't know for sure that your parents used a sperm donor, but it would explain everything. You were so blindsided to find out your dad wasn't your biological father because your parents seemed to have the perfect, loving, happy marriage, and perhaps they really did. They just needed help getting pregnant."

"If that were true, why didn't they tell me?" she whispered.

"They probably planned to tell you when you were older, in case anything ever came up health-wise. You were only, what, seventeen when they died? They probably thought they had a lifetime to tell you. Grace, there was no deception. Your dad always knew he wasn't your biological father, and it didn't matter to him. In fact, he chose it. Like

I said before, DNA doesn't make family. They were your parents, end of story."

"But . . ." Her voice broke, and she pressed her lips together, blinking back the tears that wanted to fall. Her body shook, and she still felt oddly numb.

"It means you've been hurt and angry for a very long time about something that didn't happen," Lia said, pulling her in for a hug. "And I'm so sorry about that. I'm sure your parents would have told you sooner if they'd had any idea this would happen, but who could have possibly predicted it? They should never have died so young, and if you hadn't tried to donate blood to him that day, you never would have known."

Grace pressed her face against Lia's neck, trying to steady her breathing and regain her composure. "How do we know if this is true?"

"Well, it's the most likely explanation, now that we've met Laurel," Lia said. "You said you had never discussed this with any of your relatives, right?"

"Right," Grace said. "I couldn't bear to break my *abuela's* heart by telling her that her daughter had been unfaithful, and I felt just as awful about telling my dad's parents that we weren't actually related, so I never said anything."

"Then it's possible they know," Lia said. "They might have decided not to mention it. Why would they complicate your life by telling you that your dad wasn't your biological father? What difference did it make after he was already gone?"

Lia's words made sense, even as they turned Grace's stomach. She'd come here for answers, and she'd gotten them, but this was somehow worse than her worst-case scenario. Her mom hadn't betrayed her. Grace had betrayed herself by jumping to conclusions without getting all the facts. This was all her fault, and that was the one scenario she'd never thought to prepare herself for.

Lia cut a bite of eggplant parmesan, sneaking a glance at Grace. She'd composed herself after the initial shock of learning that her parents had likely used a sperm donor, but she was quieter than usual, and Lia knew she must still be reeling.

"How are you enjoying London?" Macy, one of Laurel's moms, asked Grace as they ate.

"I love it," Grace told her. "I grew up in Manhattan, so city living is in my blood."

"I visited last summer after I graduated from college, and I loved it too," Laurel said. She'd been nothing but sweet since they arrived, and Lia suspected Grace would have been a lot friendlier if they'd met under other circumstances.

As it was, Grace gave her a somewhat stiff smile. Maybe the Byrnes wouldn't see through her polite facade, but Lia knew Grace well enough now to know she was going through the motions. She could see the turbulence in her eyes and the tension in her shoulders. Grace was probably going to fall apart later, and Lia would do her best to be there for her when it happened.

On the surface, it was wonderful news that Grace's mother probably hadn't cheated, that her parents had chosen a sperm donor to overcome infertility. Grace's parents were the happy, devoted couple she'd believed them to be. But that perceived betrayal had had a profound impact on Grace's life in the years since their deaths. It had tainted Grace's memories of her mother, and Lia feared she was hating herself for that right now.

"How did you two meet?" Tegan—Laurel's other mom—asked, glancing from Grace to Lia.

"We share a mutual friend who introduced us," Lia told her.

"And are you an item?" Macy asked. "Or just friends? Sorry for being so forward, but as you might imagine, I just love meeting other lesbian couples, and I thought I picked up on something between you two."

Lia looked at Grace, deciding to let her answer, since she was the one who was skittish about committing to a relationship.

"Somewhere in the middle, I guess?" Grace answered, darting a nervous glance at Lia. "It's complicated."

Lia reached over to squeeze her hand beneath the table, appreciating the honesty of her response.

"Well, I hope it works out," Macy said. "And sorry for prying."

"No need to apologize," Lia told her. "I'm happy to be in the company of another sapphic couple too. It was a lovely surprise when we arrived tonight."

"To women who love women," Tegan said, lifting her glass.

They all drank to that, and laughter flowed around the table, with Laurel playfully lamenting her status as the only straight woman in the room.

"Would anyone like more wine?" Macy asked, rising to retrieve the bottle they'd opened earlier.

"No, thank you," Lia told her. She was driving tonight and also needed a clear head to help Grace work through everything she needed to process later, but she was surprised when Grace also declined a refill. She'd only had a small glass with dinner.

Macy refilled her and Tegan's glasses, and they began to clean up from the meal. They moved to sit in the living room, five women brought together under such odd circumstances. Lia hoped the meeting had been helpful for both Grace and Laurel. They talked for a little while about trivial things, all of them making an obvious attempt at keeping the conversation light, before the evening began to wind down.

"I'm so glad I got to meet you," Laurel told Grace. "I know the circumstances are weird, but I just think it's cool that a DNA site connected us. I'd love to stay in touch if you're open to that."

"I'm not opposed to it," Grace said. "Although I'm not very good at keeping in touch—just ask Lia."

"That's true," Lia said diplomatically. She was here to back Grace up, after all, but suddenly, she felt like Grace was talking about their relationship, and that hurt. She'd keep her own feelings under wraps tonight, though. Tonight was for Grace. Tomorrow, Lia would broach the topic of what would happen after their road trip ended.

"Oh, I totally understand," Laurel said. "You've got my email, so feel free to say hi if you feel like it. I'm not very active on social media, but I do have Instagram. It's mostly pictures of food and my cat, but you're welcome to give me a follow."

Grace smiled. "Sure. I'll do that. I've been posting a lot of photos of our road trip."

They exchanged information, and that seemed to provide a natural ending place for the evening. Laurel and Grace hugged, and it was all very friendly, but as they walked to the car, Grace's expression was alarmingly blank. Lia took the driver's seat while Grace sat quietly on the passenger side. She pulled out her phone as Lia started the car.

"Three texts from Rosie," Grace said. "Who's surprised?"

"No one," Lia said. "How are you feeling about everything?"

"Fine," Grace said as she tapped her screen, maybe responding to Rosie.

"Laurel seems nice." Lia started the GPS on her phone to guide them back to their Airbnb, noticing that she had a few texts from Rosie as well. She ignored them for now and set her phone in the center console before she pulled onto the road.

"Yep," Grace said.

When Lia glanced at her, Grace was staring out the window. Lia had expected her to let it all out once they were in the car, whatever emotions she'd been holding on to during dinner. Surely, she was feeling *something* about it, because Lia had seen her shock and confusion when she first found out. Grace had looked like she was about to have a nervous breakdown a few hours ago, and now she was too quiet.

"I'm here if you want to talk about anything," Lia offered.

"I don't," she said, and there was something cold in her voice, almost detached.

"Okay," Lia said, focusing on the road in front of her. Laurel's suburban neighborhood was quiet after dark, hardly any other cars on the road even though it was only nine o'clock, and Lia was glad for that, at least. She was still a novice at driving on this side of the road.

She made a few more attempts to get a conversation going, but Grace gave her one-word answers, staring stubbornly out the window. She'd completely shut down, and to Lia, that was a clear indication that Grace was *not* fine, but she knew better than to push, at least not in the car.

Ten minutes later, she pulled into the driveway of their rental cottage. Grace got out of the car and walked to the door, unlocking it for them. A light misting rain had started to fall, dampening Lia's clothes and fogging her glasses. She took them off to wipe them as she followed Grace inside. Grace went down the hall to the bedroom and shut the door behind her.

Lia didn't have a great feeling about this. She'd gone into tonight's dinner feeling cautiously hopeful, and Laurel had definitely exceeded her expectations. She was sweet and unassuming, with no ulterior motives, at least not as far as they knew. But she'd still delivered an unexpected bombshell, and now Grace had to deal with the fallout.

Lia went into the kitchen for a glass of water, hoping that Grace might let her walls down after she'd had a few minutes to herself. But when she emerged from the bedroom, she was as blank faced as she'd been for the last few hours.

"I'm going for a walk," she said as she headed for the back door.

"I'll come with you."

"I'd rather be alone," Grace said.

"Are you sure?" Lia couldn't help asking. She wanted to hug Grace, to hold her and comfort her and help her sort through her feelings.

But Grace just nodded before letting herself out the back door, closing it solidly behind her. Lia watched her go. Every instinct in her body screamed for her to go after Grace, but this was a woman who'd moved to an entirely different continent the last time she'd needed space. When the going got tough, Grace ran, and Lia didn't know how to handle that.

She debated changing into her pajamas and curling up on the sofa to read until Grace returned, but that felt more casual than she was capable of at the moment. Pacing in front of the glass doors at the rear of the cottage wasn't a good idea, either, in case Grace was near enough to see her. So she forced herself to sit on the sofa, thumbing through notifications on her phone without really seeing them.

It was wet outside. Had Grace taken an umbrella with her? And it was dark. Was the path to the pond lit at night? What if Grace slipped and fell in the dark? Lia huffed a breath. She felt helpless, and she hated that. Lia was a problem-solver. She wanted to help, even if it just meant holding Grace while she cried. Instead, she picked up her phone to distract herself.

Rosie Taft:
Grace said things went well with Laurel tonight. Phew! What a relief!

Lia Harris:
Yes. Laurel seems lovely.

Rosie Taft:
I'm so glad. I'd have to come kick Laurel's ass myself if she tried to pull anything shady.

Grace didn't say if she found out anything new about her biological dad.

Lia Harris:
I'll let her fill you in on the details herself.

Rosie Taft:
Yeah, well, you know how Grace is with details.

Lia Harris:
I do.

Rosie Taft:
You're not going to tell me. Got it. You're a good friend, Lia 😌

Lia Harris:
I try.

Rosie Taft:
I'm glad Grace has you there with her. I'm sure tonight was a lot to process. Give her a hug for me.

Lia Harris:
Will do!

Lia put her phone down, legs bouncing restlessly. She looked at the door. She'd give Grace a half hour, and then she'd go after her, because Lia couldn't stand thinking about her sitting outside in the rain by herself, especially after dark. They didn't know this town. It seemed like a safe area, but what if something happened? Logically, she knew she was overthinking this, but she couldn't seem to override the need to make sure Grace was okay.

She sat on the sofa as the minutes ticked by on the clock. Outside, it was dark and quiet. Somewhere in the distance, an owl hooted, and the sound sent a shiver down Lia's spine. She'd grown up in the countryside, but she'd lived in the city for so long now that it felt strange to be out here in a cabin in the woods.

Were there bears in Virginia? Wolves?

Okay, now she was really letting her imagination run away with her. And it was ten, which meant it was time to go after Grace. She'd just check in with her—assuming she could find her—and then, if Grace wanted her to leave, she would.

Lia went out the back door, finding that the temperature had dropped, probably due to the rain. It wasn't cold. This was June in Virginia, after all, but the air was cool and damp against her skin. Her shoes sank into the mulch on the path as she began to walk, and that misting rain enveloped her, fogging her glasses.

The sky overhead was a deep gray, gleaming from what might have been the moon behind the clouds, just bright enough for Lia to make out the looming shapes of the trees around her. She took off her glasses to wipe them, hoping they'd stay clear now that they'd adjusted to the humidity. The path wasn't lit, but light from the windows in the cabin illuminated her first steps.

The idea of walking into the woods after dark . . . well, Lia felt like the ill-fated heroine of every horror film right now, even though she knew she was being ridiculous. The owl hooted again, and she jumped, wrapping her arms around herself. A breeze rippled through the trees overhead, causing a shower of water to fall on her head.

"Grace?" she called, partly because she needed help finding her and partly because she didn't want to sneak up on her unannounced, although she wasn't exactly being stealthy as her shoes squished along the path.

There was no answer, and Lia was trying not to panic. She hated being out here in the dark while the trees pelted her with rain. What if she stepped in a hole? Or an animal came at her? The light from the cabin had receded by now, and Lia wished she'd thought to bring her phone so she could use its flashlight. Maybe she should go back for it.

Something wet and stringy wrapped around her face, and *oh God*, she'd just walked into a spiderweb. She flailed her arms, imagining a wet, angry spider crawling around in her hair. Sticky strands clung to her fingers as she swiped them over her face. Adrenaline spiked through her system, and she couldn't help it. She screamed.

"Lia?" Grace's voice reached her.

"Spiderweb!" she shrieked, and oh God, it was on her glasses too. Where was the spider? Was there more than one? Her skin crawled as if she were covered with them.

A light shone in her direction, and footsteps approached, making wet noises against the path. "Hold still," Grace said, and then she was in front of Lia, using her phone as a flashlight.

"Find the spider," Lia gasped, pulling off her glasses. "Oh my God, make sure it's not in my hair."

"I don't see anything in your hair," Grace said, shining her flashlight over Lia's head. Her fingers poked through Lia's hair while Lia wiped her glasses on her pants.

"I feel like spiders are crawling on me." She shivered, resisting the urge to claw at herself.

"Well, they're not," Grace told her firmly, giving her shoulder a squeeze.

Dammit. She'd come out here to comfort Grace, and now Grace was comforting her instead. But *spiders* . . . "Are you sure there aren't any spiders in my hair?"

"I'm sure."

Lia blinked the rain from her eyelashes and slipped her glasses into place. They were smudged and streaked, but not so dirty that she couldn't see Grace's red eyes or the wetness on her cheeks that might be rain but was probably tears. "Are you okay?" she asked, trying not to think about spiders or whatever else was lurking in the wet, dark trees around them.

Grace nodded. "I was on my way back to the house. I figured you'd come after me if I stayed out too long. Looks like I was right."

"I was worried, but then I face-planted into a spiderweb."

Grace gave her a wry smile. "That's what you get for following me into the woods."

"You're impossible," Lia huffed. She wanted to yell at Grace for leading her into the forest, and she wanted to hug her and dry her tears, and she wanted . . .

"I know," Grace whispered right before her lips crashed into Lia's.

CHAPTER TWENTY

Grace held on to Lia, hands buried in the wet depths of her hair as she lost herself in the hot pleasure of her mouth. She didn't want to think anymore. She'd tried to run from Lia's knowing eyes and endless questions, but sitting by the pond in the dark had only made the chaos in her brain even louder, and now she was soaking wet.

Kissing Lia was by far the best decision she'd made all night. She yanked Lia against her, rewarded by a gasp and Lia's hands gripping her ass. They kissed, deep and desperate, hands groping at each other's clothes.

"Grace," Lia whispered. "Let's take this inside."

Grace laughed. "Still worried about spiders?"

Lia shivered in her arms. "Hell yes, I am. In fact, let's take this into the shower, because I need to rinse off the feeling that they're crawling on me."

"Shower sex sounds perfect," Grace said. "Lead the way."

In response, Lia grasped her hand and took off at a run, half dragging Grace up the path. She giggled under her breath as she stumbled after her. Water trickled down the back of her neck and splashed against her lower legs as she ran, and before she knew it, she was truly laughing, which was such a relief after the flood of tears she'd shed by the pond.

Lia was the distraction she needed. Lia was *everything* she needed. They raced across the clearing behind the house and stumbled inside, kicking off their shoes to keep from tracking mud through the living room. Grace felt like she'd gone for a swim in her clothes, and Lia looked just as wet, her hair slicked to her skin and droplets glistening on her glasses.

Wordlessly, they rushed down the hall to the bathroom. Lia turned on the shower, and then they started stripping out of their clothes, kissing while their hands fumbled with wet fabric. Lia's jumpsuit hit the floor a moment before she yanked Grace's dress over her head. Lia's fingers brushed over the front of Grace's underwear, lighting her on fire.

Steam filled the bathroom as the shower heated, and their underwear joined their clothes on the floor. Lia set her glasses on the counter and pulled back the shower curtain, testing the water temperature before she stepped inside, tugging Grace after her.

Hot water sluiced down the front of her body, and then Lia pulled her closer, bringing their lips together as water poured over their heads. Grace swiped her hands over her face and then buried them in Lia's hair, holding her close. She kissed her until the cold fist gripping her stomach had loosened.

"Checking for spiders?" Lia murmured as Grace dragged her fingers through her hair.

"Yes," she answered with a smile, because spiders were a tangible threat Grace could check for and then move on from. The damage caused by her assumptions about her family wouldn't be nearly as easy to repair.

"Please do, because I'm still twitchy thinking about them," Lia said, spinning so that Grace could check the back of her head.

She combed her fingers through Lia's hair until she could definitively confirm that there were no spiders, then ran them over Lia's body for good measure. "All clear."

"Thank God." Lia turned to face her, sliding her hands down Grace's back as she pressed their bodies together. Hot water rained down on them, and this was without a doubt the best part of Grace's day.

Between the water and Lia's hands, she was on sensory overload, physical pleasure overwhelming her emotional pain. She captured Lia's lips, submersing herself in the heat she found there, loving the way Lia's tongue slid against hers, igniting the ache in her core.

Lia pushed a thigh between Grace's, and she gasped at the contact, her hips automatically beginning to move. She felt frenzied, desperate, out of control. She threw her head back, and the hot water rained over her breasts and down her stomach, which felt surprisingly erotic.

For once, even Lia seemed more focused on doing than talking. She kissed Grace's neck while their hips moved together, and *yes*, this was perfect. This was amazing. This was *hot*. She was on fire, inside and out, from the combination of the water and Lia's touch. This position wasn't enough to get her off, though, and she didn't think it was for Lia either.

Grace brought a hand between them, rubbing against Lia's clit. In response, Lia's hips sped, and her breath came in gasping pants against Grace's neck. And then Lia returned the favor, sliding a hand down Grace's stomach to stroke her. They moved together in a messy sort of rhythm, hips undulating while their fingers stroked and their chests heaved.

Grace's orgasm rushed through her so fiercely that it nearly took her knees out from under her. She clung to Lia, fingers moving frantically, and then Lia was coming, too, shuddering in her arms. They sagged to the floor together, legs intertwined and heads on each other's shoulders as the shower poured over them.

"Shower sex lives up to the hype," Grace said finally, once she'd caught her breath.

Lia chuckled. "I've had shower sex before, but never like this."

"We needed to blow off some steam, I guess."

"We did," Lia agreed.

"Lia . . ." But she didn't know what to say.

"I know," Lia whispered, and maybe she did. It was uncanny some-times, the way Lia seemed to understand her. "We have a lot to talk about before we drive back to New York in the morning."

And just like that, Grace felt like she was drowning under the steady downpour of the shower. When she lifted her head, water splashed onto her face and into her mouth. It was too much, this thing with Lia was too much, and everything Grace had promised to discuss with her before they went home tomorrow was definitely too much.

She sucked in a breath, spluttering as she inhaled water. She swiped a hand over her face, backing away from Lia, because she needed to get out of this shower. Lia brushed a hand through Grace's hair, smoothing it back from her face, an unexpectedly tender gesture that made Grace yearn to fling her arms around her and hold on forever.

Instead, she climbed to her feet. Lia followed, and they finished rinsing themselves before shutting off the water. They were quiet as they dried off and went into the bedroom to put on their pajamas.

When she looked at Lia, she saw the questions in her eyes, but maybe she was smart enough to know that if she asked them tonight, Grace might scream. Her nerves were already so raw that it was all she could do to keep herself together.

"Ready for bed?" Lia asked instead.

Grace shrugged, and her shoulders ached from the tension bunched in them. "I am, but I'm not. I mean, I'm exhausted but also wired."

"What if we put the TV on while we settle?" Lia suggested.

Grace gave her a grateful smile. "I'd like that."

So they curled up in bed together, watching a marathon of *Love It or List It* until Grace's eyes finally grew heavy. And when she slept, she dreamed she was drowning, Lia's fingers slipping through hers as Grace sank helplessly into a dark abyss.

Birds chirped, announcing the arrival of morning and reminding Lia that she was in a cabin in the woods with Grace. She shuddered as she remembered last night's spiderweb incident, but the scene in the shower afterward had more than made up for it. Smiling, she opened her eyes to find the other side of the bed empty.

She sat up, reaching automatically for her glasses on the nightstand, but she didn't need them to see that she was alone in the bedroom. She slid out of bed and went into the bathroom to freshen up, then padded barefoot toward the kitchen.

"Grace?" she called. There was no response, but the scent of coffee lingered in the air. Lia walked to the back door and peeked outside.

Grace sat in one of the rocking chairs on the patio, coffee mug in hand as she gazed into the woods, looking awfully intense considering the early hour. Lia walked to the kitchen and fixed herself a cup of tea before joining Grace on the patio. She looked over her shoulder at Lia with a smile, wearing her pink robe over her pajamas. Lia leaned in to give her a quick kiss before sitting beside her.

"Hard to believe our trip's over," Lia said. Today, they'd drive back to Manhattan. Tomorrow, they would attend Pride with their friends, and on Monday, Grace would fly home. They needed to discuss their relationship today, while it was just the two of them, even though Grace probably still wasn't in the best headspace after yesterday's meeting with Laurel.

"I'm not looking forward to the drive." Grace lifted her coffee mug for a sip, her gaze fixed somewhere in the woods behind the house.

"I'm not either," Lia said. Impulsively, she scooted her chair closer to Grace's so she could take her hand. "This has been a wonderful week."

"We had a lot of fun," Grace agreed.

"It was more than that," Lia said. "I like you a lot, Grace. We've shared so many amazing things together since we met, so much more than I've shared with anyone in a long time." That was an understatement. Lia was falling for her, if she hadn't already fallen, but she didn't want to overwhelm Grace by saying it too soon.

"It was wonderful," Grace said softly. "You're the first person I've shared *anything* with in years, and I'll cherish it, Lia."

Lia gave her fingers a squeeze. "We said we'd talk about it once the week was up, and I guess that's now, isn't it?"

Grace shook her head, and her bottom lip trembled. "Please don't push me, not today."

"I don't mean to push," Lia said. "I really don't."

"I told you from the beginning that I was going back to London at the end of the week." Grace set her coffee on the table, and then she stood and walked to the edge of the patio, her back to Lia.

"You also promised we'd talk about what that meant for us before you left."

"What can it possibly mean?" Grace whirled to face her, cheeks flushed, and the pain that had been visible in her eyes before had vanished behind a hard glint of anger.

"It means that I think we have something worth fighting for. Can you honestly tell me this was just sex for you?"

"Of course not," Grace said, her voice rising. "I told you I have to know someone before I'm attracted to them. It's *never* just sex for me. That's the whole problem, because I don't want a relationship. It's why I quit dating." She raked a hand through her hair. "I'm a disaster, Lia, and I'm sorry. I wish I could give you what you want, what you deserve, but I can't. I just . . . can't." Her eyes were wild, and her chest rose and fell with rapid breaths.

Lia knew the feeling. Hysteria rose inside her, constricting her lungs. "It's for me to decide what I want and what I deserve," she said, her voice hoarse. She set her mostly untouched tea on the table and crossed the patio to Grace. "All I'm asking is for you to keep the lines of communication open. I can do long distance, or casual, or whatever you want. I just don't want to say goodbye."

"And I don't know how to do anything *but* say goodbye." Grace's jaw flexed, and tears shone in her eyes. "I never should have suggested we share that bed in DC. It was selfish of me, but I just . . . you were the first person in so long who made me feel anything, and you made me feel *so much*."

Lia gave in to the need to hold her, wrapping her arms around Grace. "Is it really so hard to leave the door open to the possibility of more?"

"Yes," Grace whispered. Her chest heaved against Lia's, and when she lifted her head, tears streaked her cheeks. "It's too much for me, Lia, and I'm so sorry. I know it's the most clichéd thing in the world to say, but it's not you, it's me. It's all me."

"Please," Lia said, holding Grace tighter as if that might help her hold herself together, because right now, Lia's heart was breaking. "What part of it feels like too much? Because all I'm asking for is a chance."

"All. Of. It." Grace enunciated each word as she pressed her palms against Lia's chest, pushing herself backward out of her arms. "I told you I could only promise you a week, that I don't do relationships, and I'm sorry if you thought you'd be the magic person to change me, because you're not magic, Lia. You're pretty awesome, but you're not magic, and when you start talking things to death, it just makes me want to run as far away from you as I can."

Lia opened her mouth and closed it. Her chest seized like someone had just punched her in the diaphragm, knocking the air from her lungs. This wasn't the first time Grace had accused her of pushing too hard or talking too much. At first, she'd thought it was something Grace found endearing, but now . . . now it felt like an insult. Lia valued open, honest communication. That was just how she was wired, and she'd thought Grace of all people might appreciate that.

How ironic that a woman who translated languages for a living was so unwilling to verbalize her own feelings. Lia would have given anything right now to sit down and talk this through with her, *really* talk about all the things Grace was so desperate to avoid.

"I won't apologize for being honest with you," Lia said, wrapping her arms around herself. "Nor will I apologize for trying to talk things through instead of just running away when they get difficult."

Grace's chin went up, and her eyes flashed. "That's right. I run. It's what I do. You knew that going in."

"I guess the joke's on me, then." Lia heard the tremor in her voice, but she managed to hold back her tears. She'd been raised to keep a stiff upper lip in moments like these, and while living with her friends in New York all these years had helped her learn to open up, to cry on their shoulders when she needed to, she still had a British backbone, and right now, she didn't want Grace to see her cry.

"I'm such an asshole that I looked into changing my flight this morning," Grace said, tears coursing over her cheeks. "I didn't want to have this talk, and I didn't want to see Rosie tomorrow. She'll be so disappointed in me for hurting you. So I tried to fly back to London today. I was going to run without even saying goodbye."

"Why didn't you?" Lia asked as the bottom dropped out of her stomach all over again. If she'd woken this morning to find Grace gone . . .

"The flights today were all booked, except for a few obscenely expensive seats." Grace's face was red and splotchy, and her nose was running, and dammit, Lia just wanted to hug her.

The world seemed to have shifted beneath Lia's feet, and she couldn't seem to find her balance. She needed to sit down. Or maybe to hold on to Grace until the world had righted itself. "I wish I could be angry with you," she said instead.

"I'm angry enough at myself for the both of us," Grace responded, her voice hoarse.

"I'll leave you to it, then." And with that, Lia spun on her heel and marched back inside the house.

CHAPTER
TWENTY-ONE

A silly pop tune filled the otherwise quiet car, and while Grace's first instinct was to punch the button to shut it off, she didn't. Without music, there would be nothing but sticky silence in the car, or maybe the waves of hurt rolling off Lia from the passenger seat had a sound of their own. Maybe that was the source of the endless scream inside Grace's head.

She should have at least picked an angstier playlist for the drive, but it felt too obvious to change it now, and anyway, she needed to concentrate on the road. The drive from Virginia to Manhattan felt even more stressful than the drive down had been, maybe because her nerves were already raw and frayed, stretched tight like a rubber band about to snap.

I'm sorry.

She wanted to scream those words until her throat bled. She wanted to pull the car over to the side of the road, get out, and run . . . just run until she couldn't run anymore. And as her gaze fell on a sign for an upcoming rest area, she at least wanted to stop to stretch her legs and use the bathroom. But after three hours of them completely ignoring each other, Grace had no idea how to break the silence.

So she drove on. The GPS had routed her up Interstate 81 through Pennsylvania today, and the closer they got to New York, the heavier the traffic became. It was a Saturday afternoon, and it seemed that everyone in the tristate area was in their car.

Maybe they were on their way into the city for Pride. Grace had been looking forward to it so much a week ago, and now she would have to make an excuse not to go. She couldn't fathom celebrating anything right now, least of all being queer, right after breaking up with Lia, and she couldn't face Rosie, not yet.

Grace just wanted to be alone. And she should have stopped at that rest area, because she really had to pee. Her muscles ached from clutching the steering wheel. And she was hungry. In their angry departure from Charlottesville that morning, they hadn't packed any trip snacks.

Lia was probably similarly uncomfortable, but she didn't say a word. She just sat with her hands folded in her lap, staring resolutely out the passenger window. The absolute absurdity of the situation made Grace want to laugh. Or maybe scream. And then she just wanted to cry, because everything sucked and she hated it.

Traffic slowed to a crawl as their car approached the Lincoln Tunnel nearly six hours after they'd left Virginia. Grace white-knuckled her way through the tunnel with an empty stomach and an uncomfortably full bladder and so much anger she felt like she might shatter from the strength of it. Tunnels always made her feel trapped and claustrophobic, but today, combined with the already suffocating atmosphere in the car, she wanted to crawl out of her own skin.

And when she exited the tunnel onto Ninth Avenue, the thought of spending the rest of the afternoon at the apartment with Lia and Rosie and their roommates was just too much. There was no way.

She exhaled in relief when she finally pulled into the parking garage to return their rental car. She parked in the space for returns, resisting the urge to fidget as she waited for the attendant to come over. The tension inside the car had reached its breaking point. She couldn't bear it for another moment.

The attendant approached, and she swung her door open, lurching to her feet so quickly she smacked her head on the doorframe. *Jesus*, that hurt. Her eyes watered. Meanwhile, Lia climbed quietly out of the passenger seat, looking much more composed than Grace felt.

While the attendant checked the car for damage, Grace and Lia got their bags. One benefit of their awkward drive was that they hadn't unpacked anything—no drinks or snacks or other items of comfort.

"You were supposed to return it with a full tank of gas," the attendant, who couldn't have been much over eighteen, told her, tapping a pen against his clipboard.

Grace blinked at him. Gas. Right. She was supposed to have done that, and now it felt like a perfect metaphor for the entire trip, because she'd returned to New York with an empty tank too. She was so empty right now that she might fold in on herself. "Sorry."

He shrugged in that nonchalant way only a teenager could pull off. "We can charge your card for the gas. It's just more expensive than if you fill it yourself. Next time, you should remember to gas up."

"Right," she managed, and her throat felt dry from so many hours of silence.

"Anyway, you're all set." He gave her a form to sign, and then he got in the car and drove it down the ramp into the garage, leaving Grace and Lia alone, facing each other over their luggage.

"Uber to the apartment?" Lia said, the first words she'd spoken since they'd left Virginia.

And Grace couldn't do this. She couldn't handle another awkward moment. She was already shaking her head before she'd even decided what she was going to say. "I'm going to a hotel for the night. I can't . . . I just can't."

Lia nodded, not even looking surprised. Without another word, she lifted the handle for her suitcase and walked away. Okay. Okay. *Shit*.

Grace blinked back tears as she watched her go, suddenly realizing this might be the last time she saw her and what a stupid, awful way to say goodbye. Grace was really and truly terrible at life. She pressed a hand over her eyes, sucking in ragged breaths until she'd successfully swallowed the sob in her throat.

Now what? She pulled out her phone and opened the app for one of those budget-hotel finders, the one where you didn't know what hotel you'd booked until after you accepted the discounted rate. Grace didn't care where she slept tonight. She only cared that it had a bed. And a bathroom.

She booked a room at a hotel she'd never heard of but that—ironically—was only a few blocks from Rosie and Lia's apartment. She put the address into her Uber app, summoned her composure, and walked outside to wait for her car.

Thirty minutes later, she let herself into her hotel room. It was . . . fine. The room was small and dark and musty smelling, but it was hers. She rolled her suitcase into the center of the room and stood there for a moment, feeling like she might disintegrate into a million pieces if she let go of the handle clenched in her right fist.

The bathroom door to her right made it suddenly impossible to ignore her bladder for another moment. She rushed in to pee, and then she grabbed one of the glasses on the shelf above the sink and filled it, gulping it down without stopping. Then, with her most immediate needs addressed, she walked into the bedroom and yanked back the covers on the bed. She climbed into bed, curled up in a tight ball, and wept.

Once she started crying, it was like opening the floodgates. She'd held everything inside since breaking up with Lia this morning. And, oh God, that endless, awful car ride. She cried until some of the pressure in her chest had eased, and then she just lay in bed, too exhausted to move.

She needed food, but that was a problem she'd deal with later. In the meantime, she lay with her fingers clenched in the sheet, clutching it against her chest as if that might somehow make her feel less lonely or miserable. It didn't. What was Lia doing tonight? Grace imagined her surrounded by Rosie and the rest of her roommates as she shared all the sad details of how their vacation had ended, and it brought fresh tears to Grace's eyes.

She'd made the right decision in coming to this hotel. Feigning happiness at that apartment tonight would have been impossible. Nope. She'd desperately needed the privacy and solitude of this hotel room.

Exhaustion settled over her, and she had a strong desire to just sleep. Her stomach felt sick, though, a combination of her churning emotions and the fact that she hadn't eaten since breakfast, and that had only been a granola bar. Lia's face filled her mind, the calmly heartbreaking way she'd absorbed Grace's rejection.

Maybe somewhere deep down, she'd wanted Lia to cry, to beg her not to walk away, but of course, that wasn't Lia's style. And honestly, even if she had begged and cried, Grace couldn't have given her what she wanted—what they both wanted, at least on some level. Because Grace was miserable without her, even though the idea of a relationship was what had sent her running to this hotel room in the first place.

The worst part was that if Laurel was right about her parents using a sperm donor, then Grace had brought this all on herself. Her mother's face filled Grace's vision, ashen and lifeless as she'd been in the morgue when Grace said goodbye. She'd been so cold when Grace touched her, and that was how Grace felt now, like her heart had turned to ice.

She'd been fueled by anger for so many years, hating her mother for betraying her. At times, it had overshadowed the pain of losing her. It had tainted her happy childhood memories. And now she suspected it had all been a big misunderstanding. She might never know for sure, and that was almost as hard to accept as the fact that she might have made a mistake in the first place. Her life was an absolute mess.

The cheerful ringtone from her cell phone broke the silence, and Grace's heart lurched in her chest. Lia was calling. What would she say? Would she beg to see her? Would Grace let her? No. She couldn't do that. She shouldn't even answer the call, because she'd probably just cry and make everything even worse.

She pushed herself upright in bed, looking around for her phone. Her purse was on the floor beside her suitcase, discarded in the center of the room, where she'd left it when she'd first walked through the door. She slid to her feet so she could silence her phone, but it wasn't Lia's name on the screen. Rosie was calling, and Grace's stomach plummeted, because . . . well, maybe she'd hoped it would be Lia, no matter how stupid that was.

The call rolled through to voice mail, and Grace silenced her phone as she walked back to the bed. Rosie's name illuminated the screen again, and when it went to voice mail the second time, a text appeared.

Rosie Taft:

You'd better answer your phone, or I'm going to call every hotel in Manhattan until I find you.

Grace Poston:

Please don't.

Grace stared at her phone through tear-filled eyes. She hadn't really thought about how Rosie would react to everything. Grace had hurt Lia, and in doing so, she'd probably hurt her best friend too. Maybe she'd damaged her friendship with Rosie on top of everything else, and *God*, she'd never meant to do that. She needed to talk to Rosie, but not tonight.

Rosie Taft:

Give me one good reason why I shouldn't.

Grace Poston:

Because I need to be alone tonight.

I'm sorry.

For everything.

Rosie Taft:

Oh, Grace. I love you & please call if you need me.

But if you don't show up at Pride tomorrow, I *will* track you down.

I mean it.

Grace groaned. No, she didn't want to go to Pride. Rosie would be there. Lia would be there. All their friends would be there. Maybe it could be a chance for her to say a more civilized goodbye to Lia, but more likely, it would just be awkward and painful, and she'd exceeded her capacity for both of those things. If it pacified Rosie, though . . .

Grace Poston:

I'll be there.

Lia's finger slipped, and she blinked. Mascara burned her eye, stinging until tears sprang up, as much from her fragile emotional state as the rogue mascara. Angrily, she swiped her eye with a makeup-removal wipe, scrubbing away the offending mascara so she could try again. She didn't want to try again. She wanted to go to her bedroom, curl up in bed, and cry.

But she was going to the parade with her friends. Maybe Grace would show up. Maybe she wouldn't. Lia wasn't sure which outcome she hoped for, because in the long run, it would probably be easier if she didn't see Grace today. Best to cut ties before Grace had the power to hurt her even more deeply.

And yet, she couldn't stop herself from hoping, clinging to the possibility that she might see Grace this afternoon, if only to assure herself that Grace was okay after their awkward parting in that parking garage yesterday.

Lia tried again, successfully reapplying her eye makeup. She slipped her glasses into place and then swiped a pale-pink lipstick over her lips. She surveyed herself in the mirror. Her hair was limp today, so she'd braided it.

She wore the T-shirt Rosie had given her last year before Pride. It showed the phases of the moon in shades of pink, purple, and blue, the colors of the bisexual flag, with the words "Not a phase" below. She'd added the same colors in her eye shadow, and it shimmered from behind her glasses.

She looked forward to Pride every year. This would be the first time she attended with a broken heart, though, let alone a heart so freshly broken that it was still raw and bleeding. And she hadn't even been able to share her pain with her friends—at least, not yet. It had all been so awkward yesterday after Grace left. Lia's friends didn't know she and Grace had hooked up, let alone how it had ended.

How could she share any of it without breaking Grace's trust? Grace was so private about things, so closed off. No one but Lia and Rosie knew about her dad not being her biological father, and Lia was the only one who knew what had happened at Laurel's house. Later, she'd at least tell Rosie about their ill-fated romance, but not yet . . . in case Grace did show up today.

Rosie had already noticed that Lia was upset, though, so she probably had suspicions. Lia held back a sigh before those pesky tears returned. Hopefully her mood would rebound once the parade started.

In the living room, Rosie was buzzing around in a pink dress covered in rainbows. Jane—the more reserved of the two—wore jeans and a purple T-shirt with a rainbow over the left breast. Paige and Nikki came out of their room wearing matching shirts emblazoned with a rainbow version of the logo of Nikki's catering company.

And as she watched both couples snapping selfies while they got ready to head out, Lia felt like a fifth wheel. Surely next year, she'd have someone. God, she was so tired of being alone, and her heart ached with how much she wanted that someone to be Grace.

She wouldn't pretend to have a girlfriend again, though. If she'd learned anything from her time with Grace, it was that she should embrace herself and her life as it was. The next time she visited her family in Sevenoaks, she would stand proudly on her own. Who cared what her mother thought? That was on her, not Lia.

"Is everyone ready?" Rosie asked, herding them toward the door. "Shanice and Riley are going to meet us there. I haven't heard from Grace this morning, but I'll text her again on the way."

"I wouldn't count on seeing her," Lia said with what she hoped was a casual shrug.

"Oh, she'd better be there," Rosie said. "I don't know what happened on your trip, but she can't just leave without saying goodbye."

Lia had a feeling that leaving without saying goodbye was exactly Grace's MO, but she didn't say anything. They headed down the stairs to the street and walked to the subway. Today, the train was full of colorful people in colorful clothes on their way to the parade, and the sight gave Lia's spirits a much-needed boost.

Rosie moved to stand beside her, grasping the pole Lia had leaned against. "You'll tell me what happened soon, won't you?"

Lia nodded. "Let's see if she shows up today and take it from there, okay?"

"Okay." Rosie looped her free arm around Lia's waist, drawing her in for a hug as the subway jostled them back and forth. "I'm not used to seeing you look so sad, and I don't like it. And I really don't like that two of my favorite people have somehow made each other so unhappy."

"I don't like any of it either," Lia told her. "Believe me."

241

Rosie looked like she wanted to say more, but she held herself back, perhaps mindful of the train car full of people pressed around them. "We'll have lots of time to catch up at the store tomorrow, at any rate," she said finally.

"Yes," Lia agreed. She couldn't wait to get back to work. She'd missed the store, and even more than that, she'd missed working with Rosie.

They exited the subway as a group and walked to their usual spot along Fifth Avenue to watch the parade. Shanice and Riley were already there, wearing matching rainbow-striped feather boas, which they waved excitedly as they saw Lia's group approaching. There were many hugs and even more selfies.

Lia still felt moody and subdued, but this was Pride, so she posted a selfie of herself with her friends onto her social media. They settled in to watch the parade together, and Lia tried not to be jealous of all the couples around her, laughing and kissing and being generally happy.

As the afternoon wore on, they bought ice cream and took even more photos. Rosie kept texting Grace, but Lia thought her silence spoke volumes. She wasn't coming. She'd probably managed to get an early flight back to London. Grace was doing exactly what Lia used to tease her for—bailing at the last minute.

"Maybe you should text her, since she's ignoring me," Rosie said, nudging her elbow against Lia's.

"Nope. This is all you."

Rosie gave her an imploring look, but Lia didn't elaborate. Grace had found it so frustrating when Lia wanted to talk about everything. Ironically, she might have preferred this version of Lia who didn't want to talk about anything at all.

Riley visited the face painter and got a rainbow painted on her cheek, and Paige bought a flag that she and Nikki wrapped around their shoulders as they took selfies together. Rosie held up a copy of Jane's latest book and snapped several photos with the parade as a backdrop, which she texted to Jane so she could post them on her social media. Lia just watched, content to see her friends having a good time.

"Grace!" Rosie exclaimed, shaking Lia out of her reverie, and she spun to see Grace weaving through the crowd in their direction, wearing jeans and a green top. Her hair was pulled back in a ponytail, and sunglasses partially obscured her expression, but her lips were curved in a hesitant smile.

The sight of her was like a punch to the gut. Lia pressed a hand reflexively against her stomach as her gaze collided with Grace's. Or at least, she thought Grace was looking at her, but it was hard to be sure with those sunglasses. Lia wished her glasses had the same tint, because her emotions were probably written all over her face right now.

Rosie launched herself at Grace, wrapping her in a hug, and thank goodness for that, because it saved Lia from having to greet her. And Grace was here for Rosie, anyway, not Lia. Rosie was the one who had texted her relentlessly since yesterday, and now that Grace was here, Lia wished she hadn't come. She'd just been starting to enjoy herself, and now her fragile mood had plummeted.

"I was starting to think you weren't coming," Rosie said, giving Grace the same kind of assessing look she'd been giving Lia all day.

"Well, you did threaten to hunt me down if I didn't," Grace said, and Lia could hear the strain in her voice. Grace was hurting, too, even if it was her own fault for being too stubborn to let anyone help her when she needed it.

"I was worried about you," Rosie said. "I still am."

"I'm fine," Grace said. "I had so much translation work to catch up on after our road trip. I just needed an evening to myself."

The look Rosie gave her was so loaded that Lia almost laughed. Rosie was dying to know what had happened at dinner with Laurel, but it didn't look like Grace planned to tell her. Rosie would probably be fuming about it later. Well, that made two of them. Lia turned away, refocusing on the parade while Rosie talked to Grace behind her.

"Sorry," Jane said, coming to stand beside Lia.

"For what?" she asked.

"For whatever that's about." Jane tipped her head toward Grace.

"It's a whole mess," Lia said. "Life's complicated, isn't it?"

"So complicated," Jane agreed. "And relationships are the most complicated part."

Lia nodded, not bothering to deny it. Surely it was obvious to all her friends that she and Grace had hooked up last week. Lia would come clean about that part after Grace had gone home. The rest was her story to tell. "Well, tomorrow she'll be off to London, and that will be that."

Jane's brown eyes held nothing but empathy. "That's rough. I'm sorry."

"Thanks."

Lia managed to avoid Grace for the remainder of the parade, which wasn't very hard, because Grace seemed to be avoiding her too. The group eventually made their way to the subway and rode uptown, where they settled at one of their favorite pubs for dinner. Lia and Grace sat at opposite ends of the table.

It was almost absurd that they'd spent the afternoon together without exchanging a single word, and yet . . . here they were. They hadn't spoken since their argument on the patio yesterday morning. This wasn't like Lia, and she hated it, but what could she do? Grace didn't want to talk, and Lia wouldn't force her.

"How was your road trip?" Shanice asked while they ate, glancing from Lia to Grace. "I saw all the pictures you posted on Instagram."

"It was great," Grace said diplomatically, not looking at Lia. "We had a lot of fun and saw some really cool things. I hadn't been to DC since I was a kid."

"I haven't either," Shanice said. Since she didn't share the same apartment as Lia, she didn't know things had ended on a bad note. She only knew what she'd seen on social media.

"What was your favorite part of the trip?" Rosie asked.

"We had a really nice picnic at a winery in Maryland," Grace said, darting a quick glance at Lia. "And I got drunk, so Lia had to learn to drive on the right side of the road."

Rosie's eyebrows went up, but she didn't say anything, and neither did Lia.

"That sounds fun," Paige said.

"I got to watch Lia get all nerdy in a museum," Grace said, and Lia felt an uncomfortable heat travel up her neck. She didn't want to talk about their trip or listen to Grace talk about it. How could she sit there and rehash the highlights like this?

"Lia does love her museums," Rosie commented.

"She does," Grace agreed. "We even saw a *T. rex* skeleton."

Lia looked down at her plate as she remembered the way they'd kissed in front of that skeleton. *What the hell, Grace?*

CHAPTER TWENTY-TWO

It was past nine by the time they left the pub. Grace had faked her way through the evening, a skill she'd mastered years ago. It had taken a toll, though. She was drained. Her chest felt heavy and tight, and tears pricked insistently at her eyes. She was desperate to get back to her hotel room for a good long cry.

"Come over for a little while?" Rosie asked, stopping beside Grace on the sidewalk. "Please?"

Grace shook her head. "I need to get to bed. I have an early flight tomorrow." That was a lie, but Rosie didn't know that.

"I want to hear more about, well, everything," Rosie said, dropping her voice so her words were only for Grace. "I want to know how things went with Laurel, and all the things you and Lia aren't telling me."

"She can fill you in on all of it," Grace said, because she wanted Rosie to know, but she didn't have the strength to tell her. "Tell her she has my permission to tell you everything."

"Why don't *you* tell her?" Rosie asked, her voice laced with concern and maybe even a hint of anger. "What happened between you two? I hate all this awkwardness, Grace."

"I know. I'm so sorry. I really am." Grace was so sorry she was drowning in it. She was miserable and broken, and the only thing she knew for sure was that she couldn't fix anything with her friends before she'd fixed herself.

She glanced at Lia, who stood farther down the sidewalk, talking to Shanice and Riley. How many times over the last few weeks had Grace told Lia that she talked too much? How often had she begged her to quit asking so many questions?

Well, Lia hadn't said a single word to her all day, and somehow that was worse. This quiet version of Lia just made Grace even sadder. She missed the way Lia used to help her talk through difficult things, the way she always felt better after one of their conversations, even when she'd expected the opposite.

Maybe somewhere deep down, she'd wanted Lia to do that today, to push Grace until she broke through her walls and helped her work through this too. But Lia hadn't. And logically, Grace knew that she couldn't. No simple conversation could fix what Grace had done or convince Grace to put her heart on the line again.

"Please talk to me," Rosie implored, but it wasn't the same coming from her.

Grace shook her head. Her throat ached, and her eyes were watery. "I'm sorry, Rosie. I just . . . can't talk about it yet."

"You're so frustrating sometimes. You know that?" Rosie said. "Maybe if you talked to your best friend instead of shutting me out, you'd feel better."

Grace didn't know how to respond to that. She only knew that she was moments from losing her battle with the tears that blurred her vision and clogged her throat. Talking wasn't an option. She just needed to be alone.

Rosie reached out and touched her hand. "You know I love you no matter what, right? Whatever happened between you and Lia, it doesn't affect our friendship. And you can talk to me about it if you want."

Grace inhaled sharply as several hot tears broke free, sliding over her cheeks. She hadn't realized how much she needed to hear those words until Rosie said them, how terrified she'd been of losing Rosie too. "Thank you," she whispered.

"Oh, Grace." Rosie flung her arms around her, and Grace took the opportunity to discreetly wipe away her tears before hugging her back. "We're family at this point, okay? You're never getting rid of me, even if I do want to strangle you on occasion."

"I want to strangle me sometimes too," Grace managed, her throat painfully tight.

Rosie patted her back and then released her. "Whatever happened, it *will* get better, and I'll be here when you're ready to talk. You're sure you can't come over?"

She shook her head. "I really have to go."

"Fine, but for the record, I hate saying goodbye like this," Rosie said. "Let's video chat after you're back in London. Deal?"

Grace nodded. "Deal."

"All right." Rosie gave her a nudge in Lia's direction. "You should at least say goodbye to her, Grace. Surely you both deserve that."

Grace huffed a breath, because yes, surely they did. It had killed her yesterday when Lia walked out of that parking garage and Grace realized she might not see her again. She hadn't said a proper goodbye then, and this was her chance, no matter how badly it would hurt.

Steeling herself, she approached Lia, who turned to face her, her expression blank.

"I, um . . . I wanted to say goodbye," Grace managed, her fingers fidgeting together in front of her.

"Goodbye, Grace," Lia said, sounding painfully polite.

Grace wanted her to say something, *anything*. The Lia she'd known the last few weeks would have encouraged her to talk about why this was so difficult and made her promise to stay in touch once she was back in London. But the Lia that Grace had trampled all over yesterday didn't say anything at all.

They stared at each other for an awkward beat of silence, and then Grace turned around and walked away before Lia could see her cry.

Lia sighed as she sat on the sofa. She was drained from standing outside in the June heat most of the day, and Grace's presence hadn't helped. Avoiding her was exhausting, and honestly, the whole thing just made Lia unspeakably sad. And tired.

"Long day," Rosie said as she plopped onto the cushion beside her. Brinkley crawled in between them, tail wagging. Paige and Nikki had gone to bed already, since they had to be up early for work, and Jane was writing in her bedroom.

"Yes," Lia agreed.

"Ready to tell me more about your road trip?" Rosie asked hopefully.

"Sure." Lia unlocked her phone and handed it to Rosie. "Take yourself on a photo tour, and I'll fill in the blanks for you." She knew what Rosie would see in those photos, and she was ready for her to see it. She wanted Rosie to know about her and Grace, but she was at an uncharacteristic loss for words. She reached down to rub Brinkley's head.

"Yay," Rosie said as she opened Lia's photo roll and scrolled back to the start of the trip. "Aww, look at you two in your rental car, and here's the vineyard Grace told us about at dinner. Most of the pictures she posted on Instagram were selfies. You've got a lot more shots of the scenery."

"The scenery was worth remembering," Lia told her.

"Mm." There was a dreamy look on Rosie's face as she scrolled through the photos of their picnic. "Okay, Jane and I really need to do something like this."

"That winery would be a very romantic place to take your girl-friend," Lia agreed. "You could have them fix you a picnic and drink wine and make out with Jane in the grass."

"But you and Grace didn't do that?" Rosie asked.

Lia shook her head. "No. There was no kissing."

"Not that day, anyway," Rosie said, raising her eyebrows at Lia.

"Not that day," Lia echoed.

"Where's this?" Rosie asked, tilting the phone toward Lia to show a photo of quaint restaurants and shops along the boardwalk.

"That's the Annapolis waterfront."

"It's gorgeous," Rosie said, swiping through photos. "Oh, and here you are on a sailboat. Grace posted a picture of this too."

Lia nodded. "We went on a cruise of Chesapeake Bay."

"Wow. That looks so fun." Rosie kept tabbing. "Ah, and now you're in DC."

"My first time," Lia said. "As you might imagine, I enjoyed the museums."

"I imagine that's an understatement," Rosie said, nudging her elbow against Lia's.

Lia scoffed, relaxing against the sofa as some of the tension finally went out of her spine. It felt good to sit here in her apartment and joke around with Rosie, like she had finally returned to her real life.

"Holy shit." Rosie bounced on her cushion. "Oh my God, there are photos of you and Grace kissing!"

"And there it is," Lia said, slouching so that her head rested on Rosie's shoulder. She felt boneless with relief to finally have it out there.

"Wait a minute," Rosie said, looking at the screen more closely. "Are you kissing in front of the *T. rex* skeleton Grace was talking about at dinner?"

"Yes," Lia answered.

"Can we talk about it now, please?" Rosie implored. "You two were together?"

"Yes," Lia said quietly. "We were together, and now we're not."

"You had sex?" Rosie asked.

"We did, and we talked it all through ahead of time—you know, the ramifications for her after she'd given up dating and sex for so long."

"I would expect nothing less from you, Lia," Rosie said, lifting Brinkley out of the way so she could wrap an arm around Lia's waist. "You're the best, and I wish Grace didn't have too much emotional baggage to see it."

"Thanks." Lia swallowed over the lump in her throat, turning her face away from Rosie, because she knew her raw emotions were stamped all over it at the moment.

Rosie sighed. "I wish I didn't already know this story has a sad ending, because just *look* at you two. You're adorable together, and you look so happy. And I love you both so much. It could have been perfect." She gazed wistfully at the photo.

"We were very happy that day," Lia agreed.

"Why would she bring this up tonight?" Rosie said. "The *T. rex* skeleton?"

"Damned if I know." Lia had been wondering the same thing. "I don't think she'd try to hurt me intentionally, so my best guess is that she was feeling nostalgic. I don't think I'm the only one who developed feelings. I'm just the only one who wasn't too scared to voice them."

"Oh, Lia." Rosie pulled her in for a hug. "Did you fall for her?"

She nodded as the tears broke free, rolling over her cheeks. Her glasses fogged, so she pushed them up on her head, swiping at her eyes. "I did, and it was so stupid, because she told me from the start that she was going to leave at the end of the week."

"So that's what happened? She only wanted a road trip fling?"

"Yes, but with the added complication that the things she found out from Laurel on Friday really knocked her off balance—and no, I can't tell you what happened, because those things are private to Grace. She should tell you herself."

"She told me tonight that you had her permission to tell me everything," Rosie said. "But you're right. As much as I want to know what happened, it should come from Grace."

Lia nodded, wiping her eyes as she sucked in a breath, composing herself.

"So Grace was upset, and she panicked and ran without talking through anything with you," Rosie said. "Is that the gist of it?"

"That is precisely the gist of it," Lia confirmed. "She's running scared right now, and I hate it for her, but it's perfectly in character, isn't it?"

"It is," Rosie said sadly. "I'm so glad she had you there with her when she met Laurel. Whatever happened, I know you were her rock, because that's how you are. I'm just so sorry it ended the way it did."

Lia turned to press her face against Rosie's shoulder. "We had the most awful drive home," she whispered. "Neither of us spoke the entire time. It was excruciating. And when we got here, she just told me she was going to a hotel, and that was that."

"I'm so sorry," Rosie said. "I would kick her ass for that if I didn't know how much she'd suffered in the past to make her this way. I'm just heartbroken for both of you."

"Thanks," Lia said. "Anyway, that's the long and the short of it. The chemistry was there between us from the moment we met, and I knew deep down that it would end badly, but I guess part of me hoped for a miracle where she gave me a real chance."

"The truly sad thing is that you're perfect for each other," Rosie said. "I thought about it while you were on your trip, when I was looking at your photos, because I could see that chemistry, too, and more than that, I could see the genuine affection between you. You're so steady and up front, exactly the kind of person that would be good for her.

And she's so fun and passionate and loyal, all the things I'd want for you in a woman."

"It could have been amazing," Lia agreed. "And I hope that she and I can be friends once the hurt feelings fade. I don't want us to make anything awkward for you, and I . . . well, I can't imagine losing her from my life entirely."

"You're too good, Lia," Rosie said sadly. "You deserve all the amazing things in the world."

Lia looked down at her phone. The photo of her and Grace in front of the *T. rex* skeleton was still illuminated on the screen. It was blurry now that she'd pushed her glasses into her hair, but she remembered it in perfect clarity. And she remembered the things she and Grace had talked about that day, things that maybe she should consider even though their relationship hadn't worked out. "About that . . ."

"Yeah?" Rosie asked, giving her an inquiring look.

"Grace thinks I should apply for a job in a museum—you know, the way I had planned in college."

Rosie sat up straighter on the sofa. "Really? Wow, Lia, I . . . I had forgotten all about that." Tears welled in her eyes, and she blinked them away. "That was your dream, and then my mom got sick, and you offered to help me with the store, and here you are almost a decade later. You never got the chance to chase your dream."

"I didn't," Lia said. "And I'm not quite sure if it's still what I want. I love working with you at Between the Pages. Grace just got me thinking that maybe I should consider it, that's all."

"You should definitely consider it," Rosie agreed, grasping Lia's hand in hers. "You deserve to chase your dream, and if these last few weeks have taught me anything, it's that I *can* run the store without you. That's not to say I don't need you, because I absolutely do, and I'd happily run the store with you forever. But if this is what you want, I can hire a new manager. We'll still be best friends, even if you become a fancy museum curator or whatever. I just want you to be happy."

Lia exhaled, nodding. "I think I'll look into it, and maybe I'll apply for a few jobs, but this doesn't mean I'm leaving, so don't start looking for my replacement yet, okay?"

Rosie gave her a wry smile. "I'll need your help hiring your replacement, anyway, so don't even think of pulling a Grace and running off on me before I'm ready."

Lia scoffed. "I would never."

Rosie smiled sadly. "Of course you wouldn't. That's the difference between the two of you."

CHAPTER TWENTY-THREE

Trees passed by in an endless green blur outside the window of Grace's rental car. This drive was just as quiet as the one she'd shared with Lia two days ago, although this time it was because she was alone. A hundred miles behind her, at JFK International Airport, her flight to London was about to begin boarding.

It was absurd that she wasn't on it, when she'd spent the last few days wishing for nothing else. She'd wanted to return to London more than anything, but when it was time to pack for her flight yesterday, she froze. She'd become completely paralyzed, and that was when she realized she was running in the wrong direction. Her decision was cemented when she received an email from Tegan Byrne last night.

From: FeelTheByrne@gmail.com
To: GracePoston91@gmail.com
Subject: Nice to meet you!

Hi, Grace! I just wanted to say again how lovely it was to meet you on Friday. I think we were all blind-sided about the fact that you didn't realize we had used a sperm donor and that your parents might have too, and it didn't occur to me until later that I have some information you might like to have.

When we were choosing a donor, the agency gave us basic information about each man. We weren't able to see current photos as that's an invasion of privacy, but all the donors submitted a childhood photo. I'm attaching that to this email, in case you'd like to have it. Your donor is a music teacher who loves comics and baseball (quite varied taste, huh?). I hope this information is helpful, and please don't hesitate to get in touch if you have any other questions I might be able to answer.

Take care,
Tegan

The attached photo showed a boy, maybe eight years old, with sandy brown hair, blue eyes, and a wide, carefree smile. The truly weird thing was that he looked a lot like the man Grace had grown up knowing as her father. Maybe her parents had looked through the book of donors and chosen him for that reason. As she looked at that photo, Grace realized she had to know the truth, once and for all. So she'd called her grandparents.

And now here she was, on her way to Albany to spend a few days with her dad's parents. If anyone knew the truth, it would be them. Her dad had been close with his parents, and it was entirely possible he'd shared his fertility struggles with them . . . if that was indeed what had happened.

This might be a terrible idea. If she was wrong, if they didn't know she wasn't their biological granddaughter, it could be a disaster, which was why she hadn't told them before. But now, it felt like a risk she had to take. Her brain had been a chaotic mess ever since she'd left Laurel's house on Friday. Or maybe it was since she'd walked away from Lia. The events were tangled in her mind, and the memory of both sent her spiraling into despair.

The highway blurred before her eyes, and when she blinked, tears spilled over her cheeks. She missed Lia so much it hurt. She hated the way she'd hurt her, and she hated the way she'd hurt Rosie too. This endless nightmare about her parents had ruined enough of her life. Maybe once she knew the truth, the *whole* truth, she could begin to heal.

Because right now, she felt terrifyingly alone. She was so sad it hurt to breathe, and she didn't want to live like this anymore. She swiped at her cheeks as she drove, thankful for waterproof mascara. The GPS instructed her to get off at the next exit, and she turned onto a road that looked less familiar than it should have. Several fast-food restaurants and a gas station had popped up since the last time she'd been here.

It had been too long since she visited, so long she needed the GPS to guide her to the house her grandparents had lived in since before she was born. As she drove, the area began to look more familiar. This was the neighborhood where she'd first learned to drive. Her parents didn't drive in the city, but the summer Grace was sixteen, they'd brought her here every weekend so she could practice her driving in the suburbs.

Ten minutes later, she pulled into the driveway of her grandparents' two-story colonial. Its white paint and black shutters were just as she remembered, although the shiny SUV in the driveway was new. Memories pressed over her as she parked.

When she looked at the big oak tree in the front yard, she remembered climbing it with her dad while he told her stories about his childhood. They'd raced remote control cars down the driveway and ridden their bikes around the neighborhood. She wiped away fresh tears as she shut off her rental car.

She stood from the car as the front door opened and her grandmother stepped onto the porch. Her white hair was pulled back in a low ponytail, and even from a distance, Grace could see the wrinkles on her face. Grandma looked so much older than she had the last time Grace saw her. They had video calls often, but it wasn't the same as seeing her in person.

It was moments like these when it hit Grace that she'd never know what her parents would have looked like as they aged. In her mind, they were still in their forties, although they'd be almost sixty now. She'd never see them with wrinkles and gray hair.

"Grace," her grandma called, and her voice was the same, so familiar it made Grace's chest ache.

"Grandma." She left her suitcase in the car as she hurried to the porch and gave her grandma a hug.

She wrapped Grace in her arms, and her warm scent was as familiar as her voice. "It's so good to see you, sweetheart. So good."

"You too, Grandma. I'm so sorry I didn't visit sooner."

"Well, you live so far away." She pulled back to look at Grace, the wrinkles around her eyes deepening as she smiled at her. "We're glad you're here now. Your grandfather's in the living room. His mobility isn't so good today, so that's why he didn't come out to greet you."

Grace felt another pinch of guilt, because her grandfather had MS. On his good days, he was still able to walk unassisted, but more and more often, he'd been confined to his wheelchair. "I'll come back out for my bags after I say hi to him," she told her grandma, suddenly desperate to hug him too.

"Gracie!" he called cheerfully as she stepped through the front door. "Get in here and give your grandpa a hug."

She crossed the foyer and walked into the living room, a smile stretching her cheeks as she caught sight of him in the recliner by the window. He looked older, too, thinner than she remembered, but mostly he looked the same, so familiar she couldn't stop smiling. She leaned in for a hug.

"Aren't you a sight for sore eyes," he said, patting her back. "I couldn't believe it when Mona said you were coming to visit."

"It was sort of a last-minute trip," she told him as she straightened, moving to sit in the chair beside him.

"Is everything all right?" her grandma asked.

"Yes," she said, nodding. "Well, I have a few questions to ask you about . . . about Dad, but that's for later, after we have a chance to catch up."

Her grandmother nodded, and was Grace imagining that she saw understanding in her eyes, as if she already knew what Grace was going to ask? It was probably wishful thinking on Grace's part, to save herself from the awkwardness of the conversation.

"Of course," Grandma said. "You can ask us anything. You know that."

"Thank you," Grace told her.

She went to the car to get her suitcase and brought it upstairs to the bedroom she'd always stayed in. It still had the same purple curtains and bedspread she'd picked out when she was a little girl. There was a painting of a sailboat on the wall that she'd loved to daydream about when she was little. Now, it reminded her of Lia, of their sailboat ride in Maryland and the paintings they'd explored together at various museums.

Idly, she wondered what insights about her childhood Lia might glean from this painting. She formed a vague mental image of Lia cataloguing Grace's life like a museum exhibit, and it made her smile. Surely Lia could have helped her process what she'd learned from Laurel, if only Grace hadn't panicked and pushed her away.

With a sigh, Grace headed downstairs. She helped her grandma with dinner—pork chops with roasted carrots and turnips. They chatted about casual topics while they cooked. Grace told her about some of the recent articles she'd translated and her new apartment in London. After dinner, they gathered in the living room.

"So what brings you to New York, Gracie?" her grandpa asked as her grandmother helped him move from his wheelchair to the recliner. "Work? A pretty girl?" He chuckled at his own words, and she smiled, looking at her hands. Yeah, there was a pretty girl, but Grace wasn't here to talk about her.

"Well," she said, and all the breath seemed to leave her lungs, because there was no way to explain why she was in New York without laying it all out there, but the words were just so damn hard to say. "I came here looking for answers, actually."

"Answers to the questions you have about your father?" Grandma asked, gesturing for Grace to sit beside her on the couch.

She settled on the cushion next to her. "Yes."

"Okay," Grandma said. "Go on and ask them, and I'll do my best to answer."

Grace blinked, wishing Lia were here. She'd know what to say. She'd have helped Grace prepare for this moment and held her hand through it. Then she was thinking about how much her grandparents would like Lia, and now her brain was getting off topic. "They're hard questions, because I'm afraid I might upset you, and I don't want to do that."

Her grandma patted Grace's thigh. "Talking about him can be upsetting. I'm sure it's as hard for you as it is for us, but that doesn't mean we shouldn't try. In fact, I often find that I feel better when I talk about him instead of holding it in."

Grace drew in a breath and pushed it out. Her heart pounded, and there was a sick feeling in the pit of her stomach. "It's not just that. It's . . . oh, I'm probably making this worse by dragging it out." She sucked in another breath while her grandparents stared at her with concerned expressions. "Do you know if Mom and Dad had . . . had fertility problems when they were trying to get pregnant with me?"

"Ah," her grandmother said, giving Grace's leg another reassuring pat. "I wondered if that was what you were trying to ask, and it's something

I've often wondered whether I should broach with you, because I never knew for sure how much you knew, but yes, sweetie, they did."

Grace gulped, and her face flushed hot. "Dad wasn't . . . he wasn't my biological father. You knew that?"

"We knew," her grandma said. "Your father told us while they were undergoing fertility treatments. They used a sperm donor, but that's just a technicality, Grace. You were his daughter in every sense of the word. I don't care about genetics. You're my granddaughter."

"She said it better than I could have," her grandpa added. "We love you unconditionally, Gracie. We've never cared one bit that we aren't connected by DNA."

"Oh," she managed, but the room was spinning the way it had the night Laurel had first told her about the sperm donor. If only she'd asked these questions thirteen years ago . . .

"I didn't know if they'd told you, and it seemed kind of pointless to bring it up after they were gone," her grandma said. "I'm sorry if you felt like you couldn't ask us about it. When did you find out?"

"The night they died," she gasped as the tears broke free. "I tried to donate blood to him, but I wasn't a match."

"Oh, Grace." Her grandmother's arms came around her, holding her tight. "Oh, honey, I'm so sorry. What an awful way to find out."

"I thought she'd had an affair." She sobbed against her grandmother's shoulder. "I thought she'd betrayed all of us. That's why I never said anything." She clung to her grandmother, drowning in her emotions, because this was her fault. If she'd gotten all the facts when they died, she could have saved herself so much pain. The tears scorched her eyes, overwhelming her until she could hardly breathe.

The couch dipped, and another set of arms wrapped around her. "There, there, Gracie," her grandfather said, stroking her hair the way he'd done when she was small, and how had he gotten to the couch without his wheelchair? "There was no betrayal, only love. We all love you so much."

"Good luck." Rosie wrapped her arms around Lia, giving her a quick squeeze. "You're going to be amazing, because you *are* amazing, so you don't really need my luck, but you have it anyway. Think of it as a backup."

"Thank you," Lia told her. "I'll call you after."

"Call me the minute it's over," Rosie said. "Or before, if you need a pep talk."

"I will." Lia gave her a grateful smile. Then she gathered her bag and left through the front of the bookstore, immediately warmed by the afternoon sunshine. Today was July 1st, and Mother Nature had definitely gotten the message. By the time Lia had made it to the end of the block, she was wishing she'd remembered her sunglasses.

She headed down East Ninety-Fifth Street toward Central Park, a familiar walk, although today she wasn't headed for the park. She'd applied for a job at the Museum of Natural History last week, but she hadn't heard anything yet. It would be her dream—if she chose to switch careers—since it was one of her very favorite places in the world.

Today, she was on her way to the Guggenheim. And while she'd prefer to work with the artifacts and specimens at the history museum, she loved art too. As she walked, she imagined herself in a posh office full of paintings as she coordinated upcoming exhibits.

She'd decided to chase her college dream and see what happened. She couldn't have done this last year, or maybe even the year before. Rosie had needed her. Between the Pages had needed her. But the store was thriving in its new location. Rosie was thriving in her new relationship. And Lia . . . well, she was doing all right. Her heart was still tender, her mood still uncharacteristically maudlin. She had to find a way to get herself moving forward again, and maybe a new job would do the trick.

As she turned onto Fifth Avenue, she pasted a smile on her face, hoping it would help improve her mood. Her thoughts drifted to Grace.

How was she doing now that she was back in London? Neither Lia nor Rosie had heard from her since she left last week, and Rosie had called and texted her a *lot*. Lia gave her head a quick shake, reining her thoughts back in. The last thing she needed to think about on her way to this interview was Grace.

Instead, she pulled up the Guggenheim's website on her phone, refreshing herself on their current exhibits and the highlights of their permanent collection as she walked. Five minutes later, she stood in front of the museum's iconic spiral rotunda as butterflies flapped in her stomach. Walking here had been a mistake, though, because now she was sweaty, and her cheeks were probably flushed from the sun.

Drawing in a deep breath, she walked up the steps and into the museum. She approached the counter and informed the employee there that she had a meeting with Mr. Cameron. Then she stood staring at the art displayed in the lobby as she waited for him to come down, discreetly drying her palms against her skirt before she shook his hand. She should have called an Uber, because she hated being sweaty.

A few minutes later, a white-haired man in a crisp gray suit stepped out of a doorway to her left. He approached with a polite smile. "Ms. Harris?"

She nodded. "Yes."

"Andrew Cameron." He extended a hand, and as she shook it, she was pleased that her palms were dry. "Let me show you to my office."

She drew herself up to her full height as she followed him through the door. Here she was, interviewing for a job in a world-renowned museum. This was everything she'd dreamed about when she was younger. But as she walked down the white-walled hall, her smile was forced. Her heart wasn't in it, but hopefully she could fake her way through.

CHAPTER
TWENTY-FOUR

Grace stood in front of a brick apartment building on East Eighty-Second Street, the building she'd grown up in. Her heart beat rapidly in her chest as she walked up the front steps and entered the code she'd been given for the front door. Of all the places she'd expected to be this week, Manhattan hadn't even been on the list, let alone this particular building.

She'd spent a cathartic two weeks in Albany with her grandparents. She hadn't spent that much time with them since she was a teen, and it had been wonderful for all of them. While she was there, she'd also gotten caught up on her translation work, which she'd fallen behind on during her road trip with Lia.

Lia.

Grace didn't know how to account for the feelings that swelled inside her every time she thought of Lia. She'd never felt this way about a woman before. Even after she'd ended things with Carmen, she hadn't felt this constant ache in her chest, like she'd lost a vital part of herself when she let Lia walk away.

Like maybe Lia had walked off with Grace's heart.

Because she was starting to think she'd never actually loved Carmen, not when her feelings for Lia already seemed to run so much deeper in such a short time. Maybe that was part of the reason she was here in Manhattan, why she hadn't booked her flight back to London yet. Lia was here. And when push came to shove, Grace couldn't quite manage to walk away.

Her vision swam as she entered the elevator and punched the button to take her to the fifth floor. When Grace had gone looking for an Airbnb here in the city to spend a few days alone before she rescheduled her flight, she couldn't believe her eyes when she saw the photos for this listing.

The furniture was different, of course, but the apartment itself had hit her like a gut punch before she even saw the address. Someone had bought her childhood home and turned it into an Airbnb. And she was going to stay in it, because she was a glutton for punishment, apparently.

The elevator had been remodeled sometime in the last decade. It was shinier than she remembered and moved a lot faster. Most things around Grace seemed faster than she was these days. She felt like her feet had become mired in quicksand, slowly sucking her down, and the harder she fought against it, the deeper she sank.

With a ding, the doors slid open, and Grace stepped into the hallway. The black carpet here was the same. Finally, something familiar, and it even matched her mood. Perfect.

She pushed her suitcase down the hall and entered the code on the keypad on the door she'd opened a million times back when it took a real key. A green light flashed, and she pushed it open. She stepped into the living room, pulling the door shut behind her. She'd expected to cry as soon as she walked in, but instead she felt oddly empty, almost detached.

The walls had been painted gray, and there was a black leather couch where the blue-striped love seat used to be, the one she'd sat in to do her homework while her dad tried to cajole her into sitting at the table because it was better for her posture. The whole room was done in gray scale, as if the color had been sucked out.

She stood there for several long minutes, one hand clenched around the handle of her suitcase, unable to move. She couldn't cry. She could hardly even draw breath. This was all that remained of her childhood, this colorless shell of the place where she and her parents had shared so many happy, vibrant years.

And that felt right, somehow. She might as well have stripped the color out of this space herself. She'd tarnished her own memories, so why not this apartment too? She'd been too hurt, too afraid to ask questions, so she'd just assumed the worst. She'd wasted years hating her mother for something she hadn't done.

She'd let it poison every relationship she'd ever had, and now it was only fitting that she stood here in this soulless room while she finally came to terms with the fact that she had no one to blame but herself.

She'd brought this *all* on herself.

Lia couldn't contain her smile as she jogged down the steps of the Museum of Natural History. She was on a post-interview high as she crossed the street and entered Central Park to walk back to the store. She hadn't been sure about this potential career switch when she'd first started applying for jobs.

Mostly, she'd done it to prove to herself that she'd explored the option. She didn't want to look back someday and have regrets. She was happy at Between the Pages, but she was also comfortable there, maybe too comfortable. If nothing else came out of her time with Grace, she'd shaken Lia out of her comfort zone and inspired her to see what else was out there.

Her interview at the Guggenheim had been a bust. She hadn't been given the job, but she hadn't even wanted it after her interview. She would have been sitting in an office by herself all day. Sure, she would have been surrounded by art, but Lia was a social creature. One of the reasons she'd been so happy at Between the Pages all these years was that she got to be with Rosie all day, and she interacted with their customers, authors, and vendors.

But she'd just interviewed to manage the Museum Shop at the Museum of Natural History, and yes, it was a gift shop. She wouldn't be working with any of the actual exhibits, but she wasn't technically qualified for those jobs. She had no museum experience, but she did have eight years of experience managing a store, and the Museum Shop wasn't just any store. It was a trilevel shopping experience full of artifacts and unique gifts that truly excited her.

She'd be surrounded by people, managing a staff, and it would allow her to get a foot in the door at the Museum of Natural History. Just the thought of working there sent an exhilarating zing through her system.

Career-wise, things were looking up. Heart-wise, she was still suffering, but she would get there. She was a resilient woman. As she walked through Central Park, Lia realized she felt more like herself than she had in weeks. Maybe she should make the most of her interview-induced good mood and see if her friends wanted to go out tonight.

Once she was feeling stronger emotionally, she'd reach out to Grace. It was worrisome that no one had heard from her in three weeks. Rosie was texting and calling her daily. Once, she'd gone so far as to threaten to file a missing person report if Grace didn't respond, which had resulted in a brief "I'm fine" text, but other than that, it had been radio silence.

Lia hated that Grace was obviously hurting, but she feared that contacting Grace herself at this point would only be more painful for both of them. It might undo the tenuous progress Lia had made toward moving on, and it might be upsetting for Grace too. Rosie was a good friend, the *best*, and she'd get through to her.

And, speaking of Rosie, her name appeared on Lia's screen.

Rosie Taft:

Can't wait to hear about your interview! Hope it was amazing!

Lia Harris:

Actually, it was. I'm in the mood to celebrate. Beers later?

Rosie Taft:

Yesssss!!!!

Lia Harris:

I'm on my way back to the store now. See you in a few!

Lia pocketed her phone and turned onto the path that led to the exit at Seventy-Ninth Street. At the crosswalk, she joined the group of people waiting for the light to change so they could cross Fifth Avenue. The bright sunshine overhead further elevated Lia's mood.

"I love your blouse," the woman next to her said.

Lia smiled, glancing down at the blue-and-purple-patterned top she'd worn for her interview. It was one of her favorites. "Thank you."

They exchanged a smile, and if her heart weren't still so fragile, Lia might have tried to keep the conversation going. Instead, she glanced over her shoulder at the park, teeming with visitors. If she got the job, she could walk through Central Park like this every day. She could have lunch on a bench and people watch.

Someone screamed, and Lia looked to her right just as a black SUV jumped the curb, plunging into the pedestrians gathered at the crosswalk. A body slammed into her as people scrambled to get out of the way, and she stumbled backward. For a moment, she felt oddly detached from the situation, almost like she was watching a movie, and then the woman who'd just complimented her blouse fell, knocked down by the stampede of bodies.

Lia reached for her, but she was shoved sideways instead. Her gaze caught on the panicked eyes of the man at the wheel, and a somewhat belated rush of fear and panic flooded her, because *God*, the SUV was coming right at her.

Screams filled her ears, and she tried to run, but panicked people pushed at her from all directions. A hand smacked her face, and a body slammed into her from behind. She pitched forward, and the SUV's front bumper caught her in the chest with the force of a battering ram.

Fuck me. I can't die today. I never even got to tell Grace I love—

Lia hit the pavement in an explosion of pain. Her vision tunneled, and then it went black.

CHAPTER
TWENTY-FIVE

Grace sat at the desk in the bedroom that had once been hers, lips pursed as she translated an article about women's swimwear. Her phone dinged with an incoming text, and she sighed. Rosie had already texted three times today. First, she'd sent a selfie of herself in the bookstore, telling Grace that she missed her. Then she'd sent a photo of Brinkley, telling her that he missed her too. And finally, she'd sent her daily "Please let me know that you're okay?" text.

Grace wasn't okay, and she hated lying to her best friend. She assumed Lia had filled Rosie in on everything that happened, so there was nothing else for Grace to say. She just needed some time alone to sort herself out. That was why she hadn't gone back to London yet—or at least, she was pretty sure it was the reason.

Maybe it also had something to do with the way being in New York made her feel closer to Lia, even if she didn't know Grace was here. A few days ago, she'd lingered around the corner from Lia and Rosie's apartment just to catch a glimpse of them walking to work together, and then she'd come back to her apartment and cried.

The truth was, she seemed to miss Lia more every day, instead of less.

And she didn't want to talk to Rosie about it. Grace almost didn't pick up her phone to read the text, but Rosie didn't usually bother her again after her daily "Are you okay?" Grace felt vaguely uneasy as she slid her thumb across the screen.

Rosie Taft:

ANSWER YOUR PHONE. THIS IS AN ACTUAL EMERGENCY.

The bottom dropped out of Grace's stomach as the phone began to ring. She brought it to her ear with shaking fingers. "Rosie?"

"Grace, thank God," Rosie said in her ear, and she sounded too loud, almost frantic.

Grace's skin went hot and then cold. "What happened? Are you okay?"

"It's Lia," Rosie said, and Grace had the odd sensation that she'd been submerged underwater. Everything felt muffled, and she couldn't breathe. "Grace? Are you there?"

"I'm here," she gasped. "Tell me what happened."

"There was an accident. A car plowed into some pedestrians on Fifth Avenue. Lia . . ." Rosie's voice broke, and Grace slid out of her chair, landing hard on the floor.

"No," she whispered as ice spread through her veins. Not a car accident. Not like her parents. Not Lia. *No. No no no . . .*

"I don't want you to panic," Rosie said, sounding pretty panicked herself. "I'm on my way to the hospital now. I just . . . I thought you should know."

"How bad?" Grace managed, drawing her knees to her chest. Spots danced across her vision, and she really couldn't breathe.

"I don't know. She lost consciousness briefly at the scene, but her vitals were stable when they got her in the ambulance. Thank God she thought to put me as the emergency contact in her phone, or I might not even know . . . *God*." Rosie was rambling, and Grace just listened as tears streamed over her face and dripped from her chin. "Anyway, I

271

called her parents and Audrey and Colin. They're on their way to the airport. I'll call you when I know more, okay?"

"What hospital?" Grace asked, swiping tears from her cheeks.

"Mount Sinai, but they won't give you information over the phone. Just call me, okay? And I promise I'll call as soon as I have an update."

"I'll be right there," Grace told her, lurching to her feet on rubbery legs.

"There's no reason for you to get on a plane, Grace," Rosie said. "Let me call you back once I get to the hospital, okay?"

Grace held the phone in front of her and searched Mount Sinai Hospital. "1468 Madison Avenue? Is that the right address?"

"Yes, but—"

"I'm on my way," Grace told her. "See you in a bit."

"What?"

She heard Rosie's confused voice as she ended the call, and then she dashed frantically around the bedroom. With the phone still clenched in her hand, she grabbed her purse and ran for the door. As she waited for the elevator, she was already punching the address for the hospital into her Lyft app.

Her pulse whooshed through her ears, and she felt so nauseated she thought she might actually vomit. Not Lia. This couldn't be happening. There were so many things Grace hadn't said, things she'd been too afraid to say, things she'd been too afraid to acknowledge, even to herself.

"Please," she whispered desperately as the elevator began to sink toward the lobby. She wasn't a religious person, so she wasn't sure whom she was begging right now, but she couldn't seem to stop. *Please, please, please . . . let Lia be okay.*

Outside, dusk was falling over Manhattan. It was a deceptively balmy evening, happy people everywhere while Grace was falling apart. Her whole world had just collapsed, because without Lia . . .

She couldn't even let herself think it.

A silver Honda sedan with the Lyft logo on the dash pulled to the curb, and she got inside, vaguely aware that she must look like a mess. Then again, she'd given the driver a hospital as her destination, so hopefully that explained her frantic state. The driver gave her a polite hello but didn't say anything else before he started to drive.

Grace clutched her seat belt, because the world was spinning. Her heart thumped painfully against her ribs, and she was so cold. She couldn't seem to stop shaking. Manhattan passed by outside the window in a frustratingly slow fashion as the driver wove through rush hour traffic.

Fifteen excruciating minutes later, Grace stepped out of the car and dashed toward the emergency room on shaky legs. She burst through the doors, blinking around in momentary confusion, because there were people *everywhere*, many of them looking as terrified and upset as she felt. Some of them were bruised and bleeding. Had all of them been involved in the same accident as Lia? Rosie had said a car hit pedestrians . . .

Her stomach clenched, and she pressed a hand against it, holding in a scream.

"Grace?"

She turned to find Rosie staring at her from the other side of the room, wide eyed and pale faced. "Rosie!" She rushed toward her, registering Rosie's red-rimmed eyes a moment before Rosie flung her arms around her in a viselike hug.

"Did you teleport? How did you get here so fast?" Rosie gasped into Grace's hair. "Jane isn't even here yet, and she lives with me!"

"I was here," Grace told her. "I never left New York."

"Oh my God." Rosie's arms got even tighter around her. "I'm going to strangle you for this later, but first . . . Lia's conscious. She has a nasty gash on her forehead, some cracked ribs, and a concussion. They just took her back for an MRI."

Grace opened her mouth to respond, but only a sob came out. The shaking intensified, until it felt like even her bones were rattling together. If Rosie hadn't been holding her in a death grip, she would probably be on the floor right now.

"Oh, Grace," Rosie said, her arms loosening so she could rub a hand up and down Grace's back. "She's going to be okay."

"You don't know that," Grace gasped through her tears. "My dad regained consciousness . . . he spoke to me . . . he said he was going to be *fine*." Her throat closed up, and that was probably the only thing that held in the scream building in her chest.

"Shit," Rosie murmured, still rubbing her back. "This must be so triggering for you after your parents' accident. I didn't even think about that before I called you, and I was there with you when you got that other call. I'm so sorry."

Grace just held on to her, gasping through her tears as panic clawed inside her chest. If Rosie let go of her, she might shatter into a million broken pieces. Maybe Lia was the only thing that had been holding her together in the first place.

"Ms. Taft?" a female voice said.

Rosie slipped her arm around Grace's waist, supporting her as they turned to face the person who was speaking to them. Grace made out a nurse in yellow scrubs through her tear-soaked eyes. "Yes?" Rosie said, sounding so much more composed than Grace.

"She's back from her MRI and asking for you," the nurse said, then looked at Grace. "Only one visitor at a time."

"Grace, you go," Rosie said, giving her a gentle shove toward the nurse. "Go and see for yourself that she's okay. She *is* okay, right, Nurse Yang?"

"We're still awaiting the results of the MRI, but she's alert, and her vitals are stable." Nurse Yang looked at Grace. "Are you family?"

"Yes," Rosie answered for her. "She is."

The nurse nodded. "Amelia's an exceedingly lucky woman, all things considered. I'll take you to see her."

Grace nodded, the movement jerky as she struggled to hold herself together. She wrapped her arms around herself as she followed Nurse Yang through a set of double doors and down a hall lined with blue-curtained cubicles. The nurse stopped in front of one of them, and Grace quickly wiped the tears from her face.

Nurse Yang rapped her knuckles against a metal pole before pulling the curtain back, and there was Lia on a gurney. Her forehead was bandaged, and her shirt was soaked in blood. Grace heard a high-pitched sound, and it took her a long moment to realize it was coming from her own throat. She sobbed as she lunged for Lia, remembering at the last moment about her busted ribs. She knelt beside the bed, grasping Lia's hand and pressing a kiss against the warm skin on her wrist.

"Grace?" Lia blinked at her in confusion.

"I'm here," she whispered through her tears. "I'm so sorry, Lia."

"The doctor will be in as soon as we have the results of your MRI," the nurse said from behind them. The curtain whooshed, and she was gone.

"How?" Lia asked, squinting at her. She didn't have on her glasses. Maybe they'd been lost or damaged in the accident. The sight of her bare face only made Grace cry harder.

"I never left New York," she gasped, clinging to Lia's hand like it was her lifeline. Lia felt warm and solid and *alive* beneath her fingers, but there was so much blood . . . she could be bleeding internally, or in her brain. Sometimes people looked fine when they weren't.

"Why?" Lia asked, flipping her hand to squeeze Grace's.

"I went to see my grandparents, and then . . . I wanted to run, but . . . I think I couldn't leave you, Lia. I've been right around the corner in my old apartment. It's an Airbnb now, and I rented it." She couldn't stop talking, clutching Lia's hand as the words tumbled out. Maybe she was thinking clearly for the first time in weeks, panic slicing through the bullshit in her brain until all she could see was the truth. "I . . . I couldn't leave because I love you."

Lia gasped, her eyes wide.

"I'm so sorry I was too much of an idiot to tell you sooner," Grace sobbed. "I love you so much, Lia. I've been miserable without you, and I know I might be too late, but I needed you to know, and I . . . I'm so sorry for how I acted before."

She paused, gasping for breath, blinking at Lia through her tears. Lia held out an arm, gesturing for Grace to come closer, and she realized she was still on her knees on the floor, crouched beside the gurney. She slid into a plastic chair, leaning forward to rest her head on the pillow beside Lia's. She wrapped her fingers gently around Lia's arm, which didn't seem to be damaged. Fear for Lia's health mingled with the sheer terror that came with the words she'd just said, words she'd never expected to say again.

This was Grace's deepest fear . . . loving someone more than they loved her, the way she'd done with Rosie and Carmen. She'd closed herself off to protect her heart, run from Lia so she couldn't get hurt, but all of that felt insignificant now. Grace knew better than most that tomorrow wasn't guaranteed, and she wouldn't waste another moment hiding from the things that scared her.

"I sure as fuck hope I'm not hallucinating right now," Lia murmured.

"You're not, or maybe you are, but I'm real, and these injuries are real. Lia . . . there's so much blood . . ." Her stomach lurched as she looked at Lia's shirt.

"Head wounds bleed a lot, apparently," Lia said, gesturing to the bandage on her forehead.

"It's just a scalp wound, Gracie. I'm going to be fine." Her father smiled bravely as he leaned in to give her a kiss.

An hour later, he was gone. Grace sobbed as she held on to Lia's arm. "I can't believe this is happening."

"Come here." Lia patted the bed beside her. She tried to scoot over but grimaced, exhaling sharply as pain contorted her face. "Cracked ribs," she gasped. "You're small. Fit yourself here beside me."

"I don't want to hurt you," Grace whispered miserably, not so hysterical that she didn't realize the irony of her words, because she'd hurt Lia terribly when she shut her out and sent her away in that parking garage three weeks ago. She was also painfully aware that Lia hadn't said those three magic words back to her yet.

"You won't hurt me. I need to be sure you're real." Lia sounded so calm, while Grace was on the verge of a nervous breakdown.

She managed to perch herself on the edge of the mattress, one foot on the floor for balance because she couldn't exactly grab on to Lia to support herself. "I'm real," she whispered. "And I'm sorry, and I love you."

Tears shimmered in Lia's eyes. "Keep saying those words, just in case I'm hallucinating."

"I love you," Grace murmured, reaching a tentative hand to stroke Lia's cheek.

"I love you too," Lia said in a tremulous voice, and Grace's heart soared. "I love you so much. I wanted to tell you in Virginia, but I didn't want to overwhelm you. And when I hit the pavement earlier, I couldn't believe I might die without getting the chance to tell you."

"You can't die," Grace whispered desperately, her tears soaking Lia's pillow. "I can't lose you."

"You're not going to lose me," Lia whispered.

"I'm going to be better, Lia. I promise. The next time I get scared, I'll try to run toward you instead of away from you."

"You just did," Lia said, turning her face toward Grace's.

"What?" Her brain was in chaos, but Lia loved her, and those words had flooded her with so much happiness. Combined with her fear and panic, Grace was swimming in adrenaline. Maybe they were both hallucinating.

"Today," Lia said. "When you got scared, you ran to me instead of away."

"Oh," Grace gasped. "Yeah, I guess I did."

"In fact, if you've been here in New York this whole time, you never actually ran away."

"I don't think I *can* run away from you, Lia. I tried, but I couldn't leave."

Lia smiled, and Grace smiled back, and for a moment, all was right with the world.

"I'm so glad you're here." Lia's fingers found hers and squeezed.

Grace stared at her for a long moment. Now that she was this close to her, she could see the bruise already blooming on her cheek and the way Lia took shallow, measured breaths because of her damaged ribs. Her face was tense with pain. "I can't believe you got hit by a car. God, Lia . . ."

"It was terrifying," she admitted, exhaling shakily. "It just came over the curb and plowed into us while we were waiting to cross the street."

"I can't even imagine." Grace wanted to squeeze her tight. "You're really okay, aren't you? Did they check you for internal bleeding? Your spleen can rupture, you know, even after they've stabilized you." She'd never forget the way the machines had wailed in her father's room. His eyes closed, and the room filled with medical personnel . . .

"No internal bleeding," Lia assured her. "My spleen's fine. My ribs and my head took all the impact."

Grace gulped at the reminder that they didn't know for sure yet if Lia's brain was okay. They lay together on the bed for a while, hands clasped. Lia closed her eyes, her brow furrowed. Grace just watched her, trying to control the fear still threatening to overwhelm her. She'd give anything to trade places with Lia, to take her pain.

Finally, she heard a knock, and then the curtain slid open. Grace lifted her head to see a young Black man in a white coat. His name tag read M. Blevins.

Dr. Blevins stepped into the cubicle. "Good news," he announced as Grace hastily sat up, perching on the edge of the bed. "The MRI shows no sign of intracranial bleeding or swelling. We'll want to keep you overnight for observation, but I expect you'll be able to go home in the morning."

Grace heard herself exhale, and it was all she could do not to pull Lia into her arms, because this was the best news. She was really and truly going to be okay.

"Thank you, Doctor," Lia said, calm as ever, while Grace sat there with tears of relief coursing over her cheeks.

"Someone will be along shortly to move you up to a room," the doctor told her.

When he'd gone, Lia gave Grace's hand a squeeze. "Will you go and give Rosie the good news so she can pass it along to everyone else?"

Grace nodded, sliding off the bed. Her knees were shaky beneath her, but it was a good kind of shaky this time. "I'll be right back."

Lia narrowed her eyes at her. "You'd better be, or I'll have to get out of this bed and track you down myself."

Grace grinned through her tears as she leaned down to press a kiss to Lia's lips. "I love you."

"Love you too."

She went through the curtain and made her way back to the waiting room, feeling a bit like she was floating, like she'd come untethered from her body. She pushed through the double doors, and her gaze immediately fell on Rosie, who was now flanked by Jane, Paige, and Shanice, all of whom were staring at Grace with terrified but hopeful eyes.

She nodded, swallowing hard. "She's okay. The MRI was clear."

"Oh, thank God," Rosie said, rushing forward to pull Grace into her arms.

Relieved murmurs ran through the group, and then Paige joined their hug, followed by Jane and Shanice. Everyone was hugging and crying and laughing, and Grace stood at the center, feeling slightly delirious from all the emotion of the afternoon. She was so incredibly glad for this group of women, especially the one at the other end of the hall.

"We need to hear the full story of how you happened to be here in Manhattan, missy," Paige said in a mock-serious voice when they'd finally broken free.

"I know." Grace cleared her throat, because her voice was raspy from her tears. "I'll tell you everything, but they're about to move Lia up to a room, and I promised I'd be right back."

"I need to know one thing before you go," Rosie said, giving Grace a meaningful look. "Did you two make up?"

"I told her I love her," Grace said, nodding as fresh tears fell. "And she said it back."

The whole group broke into whoops and cheers, and there was another round of hugs.

"I'm so sorry to all of you for being such an idiot and running off the way I did," Grace murmured through the crush of arms. "I really am."

"It's okay," Rosie said. "We *all* love you, Grace. Now go be with your girl."

Later that evening, Grace lay beside Lia in her hospital bed, their hands clasped tightly. Lia had finally been pumped full of the good drugs and was resting much more comfortably. Grace felt utterly drained from the day but also calmer than she'd felt in weeks. She'd happily stay in this hospital bed with Lia forever, as long as it meant they were together.

"This is going to be complicated," Lia said, sounding very serious for someone who was high on pain medication.

"What is?" Grace asked, because everything felt pretty simple right now as far as she was concerned. She loved Lia, and Lia loved her, and Lia was going to make a full recovery. Anything else was inconsequential.

"Us living on separate continents," Lia said.

"I'm staying here in New York with you until you're recovered, and then we'll figure it out from there, okay?" Grace said. "We'll do long distance for a while. I don't know, but we'll make it work."

"I interviewed for a job today at the Museum of Natural History . . . it was really great. I could apply for a job at the British Museum, you know." There was a dreamy quality to Lia's voice that Grace attributed to the drugs.

"That would be wonderful." She leaned in for a kiss.

"Tired," Lia mumbled as her eyes slid shut.

Grace snuggled closer against her, careful not to touch any of Lia's sore spots. "You sleep. We have the rest of our lives to figure out the details."

"Mm," Lia murmured in agreement. "Details don't matter as long as I have you."

"And you do," Grace whispered. "You have me. I'm yours. Forever."

EPILOGUE

Lia pressed the last sweater into her suitcase and smoothed it down. Then she zipped the case and set it on the floor. "All packed."

"Two road trips in four months? Epic," Rosie said from where she sat beside Lia on the bed. "You're finally having the adventure you dreamed of when you first moved to New York."

"I am, and at least you and Jane have had a proper vacation now too," Lia said.

"Yeah." Rosie's expression turned dreamy. Last month, she and Jane had spent a week in Saint Lucia, and they'd come home tanned, relaxed, and more in love than ever. "You were right. Vacations are amazing."

Rosie leaned in, giving Lia a somewhat gentle hug. Her ribs were fully healed now, but her friends still tended to handle her like a porcelain doll that might break if they were rough with her. Right now, her chest felt light, excitement over her upcoming trip filling her with each breath.

She had a pink scar running along her hairline that she treated every day with a special cream to help it fade, but she wasn't worried. She'd survived being hit by an SUV, and she wore her scar like a badge of honor. By some miracle, no one had died that day, and that was really all that mattered, as far as she was concerned.

She'd had to pass on the job at the Museum Shop, though, needing the comfort and flexibility of Between the Pages while she recuperated. Grace had stayed with her for two weeks, sharing her bed and caring for her when her ribs were too sore to shower or dress on her own. When Grace finally returned to London, it was with the understanding that she and Lia would visit each other as often as possible until they sorted out the logistics of their continental divide.

And once that happened, Lia planned to start interviewing for museum jobs again. Grace had inspired her to chase her dream, and she couldn't wait to see where it led her. In the meantime, they were taking another road trip, this time heading west to Chicago.

This time, they were traveling as girlfriends without any uncomfortable truths to face along the way, only good things on the horizon. Grace's flight had landed at JFK over an hour ago, so she should be here any minute, and they'd start their drive first thing in the morning. Lia could hardly wait.

A clang echoed down the hall from the kitchen, followed by a muffled swear. Nikki and Paige were cooking chicken marsala for all the roommates tonight, and if the smell was any indication, it was going to be delicious. Even better than the food, though, when Lia sat down to dinner tonight, there would be six women at the table. Three couples. Lia was no longer the odd one out.

"Jane and I have some news to share at dinner," Rosie said, "but I wanted to tell you first, since you're my bestie and all."

"Yeah?" Lia darted a quick glance at Rosie's ring finger, which was still bare.

"Well, it's kind of bittersweet news," she said. "Jane and I are moving into our own apartment at the end of the year."

"Oh, wow." Lia blinked. She'd known this was coming. Rosie and Jane had always said they would look for their own place as soon as they could afford it, and the apartment had been crowded with five of them sharing it, but still . . . "bittersweet" was a good word for it. "That's wonderful, Rosie. I'm so happy for you."

"Thanks," Rosie said. "It's exciting. A little bit sad because we've been roommates for so long, but mostly exciting."

"Definitely exciting," Lia agreed. "And as you know, I've been thinking about moving too."

"To London?" Rosie asked.

Lia nodded. "I plan to have a conversation with Grace about it while she's here." Lia had never imagined that she'd move back to London, but the idea was growing on her, especially if it meant starting a new life there with Grace.

"I can't wait to hear how that conversation goes," Rosie said with a smile. "I guess Paige and Nikki might end up looking for their own place, too, if you and I both move out."

"It's the end of an era." Lia felt an unexpected tug of nostalgia. She, Rosie, and Paige had lived together since college. The idea of them moving on now felt so final, although in a good way. They'd all fallen in love, and what was better than that?

Rosie's eyes were misty. "I can't wait to take this next step with Jane, but I'm going to miss living with you."

"Same," Lia told her. "Where's your new place?"

"It's a little one-bedroom over on Eighty-Third. Look." Rosie pulled out her phone, tapped the screen, and then handed it to Lia.

She tabbed through photos of an apartment with dark-wood floors and big windows. "It's so charming. I can already picture Jane sitting by the window writing her next book."

Rosie laughed. "Yes. She fell in love the moment we walked inside. See that wall over there? I'm going to put in floor-to-ceiling book-shelves. Jane will finally have a place to display her books, and there will still be plenty of room for mine."

"I love it," Lia said. "I'm sad that I won't be your roommate anymore, but it's for a great reason, and we'll still see each other every day at work . . . at least for now."

"We will."

The buzzer rang, and a whole swarm of butterflies took flight in Lia's stomach, because Grace was here. She lurched to her feet so quickly that Rosie laughed.

"Someone's eager to see her girlfriend," she teased.

Lia didn't even bother to deny it as she rushed toward the door. One of her roommates had already buzzed Grace in, and now Lia could hear the occasional thump of her suitcase as she climbed the steps. She opened the door, waiting impatiently until Grace came into view. She had on a pink tunic and black leggings and was grinning at Lia as she climbed the last flight of steps. Brinkley darted between Lia's feet, scampering into the hall to greet Grace.

She sidestepped him as she bounded into Lia's arms, and then they were kissing, and any lingering indecision Lia had felt about moving to London evaporated, because Grace's arms felt like home. Lia settled her hands on Grace's waist, absorbing the press of Grace's lips on hers and the warmth of Grace's breath on her cheeks. This was where Lia was meant to be . . . forever. It didn't matter which continent she lived on as long as she was with Grace.

"Missed you so much," Grace murmured against her lips.

Lia pressed her palms against Grace's back, holding her close as Brinkley circled them, yipping his excitement. "Missed you even more."

Rosie giggled behind her, and Lia glanced over her shoulder to find all her roommates watching with delighted expressions. "Welcome back, Grace," Rosie said.

Grace smiled at Rosie before returning her gaze to Lia. "It's good to be back."

Grace rested her head against Lia's chest, snuggled beside her in bed. After dinner, Lia's roommates had all suddenly left to run errands, giving her and Grace some much-needed privacy. She traced lazy patterns over Lia's skin, content with the world.

"I added a stop to our road trip itinerary," Lia said. A pink scar stood out against the pale skin at her temple, the only visible reminder of her accident.

"Oh yeah?"

"Mm," Lia said. "A winery in Pennsylvania."

Grace grinned. "Perfect. It'll be our road trip tradition . . . visiting a winery."

"And room service burgers in bed," Lia added.

"And kissing in museums, of course."

"Yes." Lia closed her eyes, her expression dreamy as if she was imagining all the places they would visit. They lay together for a minute in comfortable silence, happy just to be together after six long weeks apart.

"Laurel emailed this morning," Grace said. "Apparently, she has a crush on one of the men in her nursing program." She'd never actually intended to stay in touch with Laurel, but she'd started commenting on Grace's Instagram posts, relentlessly friendly, and now they were emailing each other too. Grace thought of her more like a friend than a sister—at least for now—but she was glad they'd met and hoped they might see each other again sometime.

"Good for her," Lia said, sounding amused.

Grace tilted her head to meet Lia's eyes. "So . . . I have some news."

"So do I," Lia said.

"You first," Grace said, ignoring the little flutter of alarm in her belly, because while she had no idea what Lia was about to tell her, surely it wasn't bad news. Grace was trying to recondition herself not to always expect the worst, but it would take time . . . and therapy, something she'd abandoned when she left New York but had recently resumed.

"Now that Rosie and Jane have found a new apartment, it will likely be the catalyst for all of us to look for someplace new," Lia said. "I've thought about it, and I don't see any reason not to move to London . . . if you're ready to take that step."

"Really?" Warmth spread through Grace's chest. "You'd do that for me?"

"Of course I would," Lia said. "I'll apply for museum jobs there, and we can look for a flat together."

"But do you *want* to move to London?" Grace asked, because it was an important distinction. "Or are you just doing it for me?"

"I'll miss Rosie and the rest of my friends here in New York," Lia said. "And I'll miss New York itself. It feels like home in a way I never imagined I'd find in America, but I've always loved London, and I love *you*. Plus, I'd be closer to my family, so I don't mind moving there."

"Not minding it is a lot different from wanting to do it," Grace said, snuggling closer. "Now let me tell you *my* news."

"Yes, please do."

"I've decided to move to New York," Grace told her. "Unless you'd rather move to London, because I'd happily stay there, but I'm ready to come home. I want to live here with you and be near Rosie and my grandparents. I stayed away before because I was running from stupid shit that festered for a decade longer than it needed to if I would have just stayed and confronted it in the first place. My grandparents knew the truth the whole time, Lia. If I'd just asked . . ."

Lia stroked a hand through her hair. "You were doing the best you could with what you had at the time, and so were they."

Grace nodded, blinking back tears. "Anyway, they're older now, and my grandpa's health isn't the best. And while I was here with you last month, it really started to feel like home again. What do you think?"

"I think it will be perfect," Lia told her, eyes glossy. "We'll get our own place—hopefully near Rosie and Jane—and we'll be so fucking happy together."

"Oh, Lia, I can't wait," Grace said, happier than she could ever remember feeling. Everything was falling into place, like she'd received a missing puzzle piece from her past and now she could see her future with perfect clarity. She sat up and slid out of bed, easily finding two T-shirts in Lia's dresser. She'd learned her way around Lia's room when she stayed here with her after her accident. She tossed a shirt to Lia, who gave her a puzzled look. "Get up. I have a surprise for you."

"A surprise?" Lia tugged the T-shirt over her head and stood.

"Mm-hmm." Grace led the way out of her bedroom and into Rosie and Jane's room next door, where a row of boxes was stacked neatly against the back wall.

"Oh my gosh," Lia said. "Have they already started packing to move?"

Grace shook her head, grinning. "Those are *my* boxes. Rosie's been keeping them for me so I could tell you in person. I'm here to stay, Lia. I'm not going back to London."

Lia slapped a hand over her mouth, her eyes round behind her glasses.

"I moved out of my apartment. Ollie's going to move in with Raj."

"I can't believe it," Lia whispered, clutching Grace's hand in hers as she stared at the boxes. "This might be the best surprise I've ever had."

"Let's start apartment hunting as soon as we get back from our road trip."

"Definitely," Lia agreed, tugging Grace into her arms.

Grace smiled into her hair. "It used to drive Ollie crazy that I'd always say 'Honey, I'm home' when I walked into our apartment."

"I remember," Lia said.

"Well, now I can say it for real," she murmured against Lia's neck.

"Yes," Lia whispered. "I can't wait to come home to you every day for the rest of our lives."

ACKNOWLEDGMENTS

Writing books during a pandemic has been a complicated experience. It's hard to be creative when you're exhausted and anxious about what's going on in the world, but at times it's also been a welcome escape. I can't travel right now, but my characters can. They can take road trips and have adventures, and that's something that's brought me a lot of joy this year.

Thank you so much to my editor, Lauren Plude. You talked me through my hot mess of an opening chapter and helped me get Lia and Grace off to the right start. I love our edit calls, and I'm so glad for your support and enthusiasm. A huge thanks to the rest of the Montlake team for everything you do to make this process so easy.

A special thank-you to my agent, Sarah Younger. I am endlessly thankful to have you in my corner.

To all the bloggers, reviewers, and readers who've taken a chance on my books, I appreciate you so much. Your support means the world to me.

Huge thanks to my #girlswritenight crew: Annie Rains, Tif Marcelo, April Hunt, and Jeanette Escudero. What would I do without our daily chats? You ladies are always a bright spot in my day. Thanks to Annie Rains for critiquing this book and to April Hunt for answering my medical questions (all mistakes are my own!).

XOXO
Rachel

AN EXCERPT FROM
READ BETWEEN THE LINES
CHAPTER ONE

"There aren't nearly enough women in this display." Rosie Taft braced one hand against the stepladder as she reached to place yet another book whose cover featured a dashingly handsome man into the display case in the front window of Between the Pages Bookstore. She was in the process of filling the window display with a colorful array of romance novels, her absolute favorite genre.

"Not to worry. There are plenty of ladies waiting," Lia said as she handed Rosie the next book on the stack, a sunny yellow paperback with a woman holding an adorable pup on the cover. Lia was Rosie's best friend and the manager of Between the Pages.

"This is more like it," Rosie said as she tapped a finger against the illustrated dog's nose. "I *loved* this one. Did you read it yet?"

"I haven't," Lia said in her crisp British accent. "Unlike you, I actually try to have a social life when I'm not in the store."

Rosie carefully added the book to the display before flipping off her friend. "I go out plenty, and between you, Nikki, and Paige, I never get a moment alone at home either."

"You go out with friends, which is not the same as a date, and you know it."

"What's the point of wasting my time with the wrong person?" Rosie wouldn't apologize for being picky about who she dated.

"Because sometimes you have to date Ms. Wrong to find Ms. Right," Lia said.

Rosie balanced on her toes as she placed the yellow book on the shelf. "I'd date Ms. Maybe to find out if she could be Ms. Right, but not if I already know she's wrong for me."

"Or maybe you're holding out for Ms. Perfect." Lia lifted her eyebrows as she handed Rosie the next book.

Rosie's cheeks warmed as she recognized the cover, which depicted a woman in a business suit wearing killer red pumps, with the Manhattan skyline visible outside the window behind her. It was the latest lesbian romance by Brie, a notoriously reclusive author who also happened to be Rosie's favorite.

She had stumbled across one of Brie's books about three years ago and immediately fell in love with her writing. There was something so evocative about Brie's words. Rosie could lose herself in one of her books and not come up for air until she'd finished. Brie wrote heroines Rosie related to and the kind of swoon-worthy romance she wanted for herself someday. Books like Brie's had shown her what she wanted in a real-life partner, and she wouldn't settle for anything less.

She and Lia booked authors into the store for monthly signings, so she'd immediately reached out to Brie's publisher and to Brie herself through the contact form on her website, inviting her for a signing, only to receive the same response from both: Brie didn't do in-person events.

Rosie supposed it went along with Brie's enigmatic persona. Her headshot was artfully styled so that her hair obscured most of her face, and her bio contained almost no personal information. A few months ago, Rosie had replied to one of her tweets, and from there, they'd struck up an online friendship on Twitter that only increased Rosie's fascination with her.

Brie was warm and funny, and she and Rosie never seemed to run out of things to talk about. It was more than that, though. Rosie had never been one for celebrity crushes or even online dating, but when she chatted with Brie, she felt . . . smitten. Sometimes their interactions seemed flirty, or maybe it was all in Rosie's head. She was a hopeless romantic, after all. And if she ever met Brie in real life, she definitely wouldn't say no to a date.

"Go on and put Brie's book right up front," Lia said with a knowing smile. "You know you want to."

Rosie placed it in the center of the display. "It's a great book with a stunning cover. It belongs up front."

"Mm-hmm," Lia said. "When are you going to tell her who you are? She might agree to come into the store now that you two are friends."

Rosie shrugged as she adjusted a regency historical so that it didn't block the FALL IN LOVE sign at the top of the display. Paper leaves in various shades of red, orange, and yellow decorated the shelves. "We're just online friends. I don't even know her real name."

"Online friends are perfectly valid," Lia said. "I've met lots of lovely people online."

"Okay, that's true," Rosie admitted. "But as you know, she doesn't do signings. Maybe she has a good reason for staying anonymous. Besides, she probably doesn't even live here in the city. Her author bio just says New York. It's a big state."

"And right now, you're having too much fun flirting with her on Twitter," Lia teased.

"It's chatting, not flirting," Rosie deflected, tired of trying to define her relationship with Brie. She extended a hand so Lia could pass her another book. "We talk about books and TV, not specific things about our lives. She's very private. I'm afraid if I told her now, she'd think I was only chatting with her to try to get her into my store."

"Well, aren't you?"

"No. I like her as a person, and I like talking to her." Rosie placed the last book on the shelf and then hopped down from the ladder to survey her work. The display featured a diverse array of romance novels that made her heart happy. When her mom first opened Between the Pages over thirty years ago, she'd wanted to create a store that would welcome everyone and every genre, and now that she was gone, Rosie was doing her best to follow in her footsteps.

In today's ever-changing book market, she worked hard to keep Between the Pages relevant. She offered lots of in-store events and extras, including subscription boxes and gift baskets. Rosie's specialty was matching a person with their perfect book when they came into the store, and she had a loyal following who returned to be matched over and over again.

Books spoke to her on a soul-deep level. They had the power to change lives when someone saw themselves represented on the page for the first time, and nothing made her happier than helping a customer find that connection.

"You know, Brie may have already been in the store," Lia said, pushing her glasses up her nose. Today, she wore a blue-striped jumpsuit that would have looked ridiculous on Rosie but perfectly suited Lia's offbeat aesthetic.

"What do you mean?" Rosie asked as she led the way outside so they could see the display from the street. The September afternoon was cool and breezy, and the air was lightly scented with herbs and tomato sauce, courtesy of the Italian restaurant on the corner.

"Well, she lives somewhere in this state," Lia said. "And she obviously loves books. So, for all you know, she may have already visited us."

Rosie put her hands on her hips as she surveyed the window. The yellow book with the dog on the cover was slightly off center. "I don't think the chances are very high. Plus, she told me she mostly reads e-books."

"Maybe you should keep an eye on the women who come into the store, just in case," Lia said playfully. "You never know."

"I don't—Brinkley, no!" Rosie lunged for the door as her dog's little brown head appeared in the window display, knocking over several books. She rushed inside and scooped him up before he caused any more damage. "Of course you wake up the minute I step outside."

His tail swished happily as he wriggled in her arms, leaning to kiss her face.

"He's probably ready for a walk, and I could do with some fresh air myself. Want me to take him?" Lia offered as she knelt to straighten the books on the bottom shelf of the display.

"Sure, thank you." Rosie pressed her lips against the little flat spot between his eyes that just begged for kisses before setting him down.

Lia retrieved his leash from behind the counter and was clipping it to Brinkley's collar just as the bell tinkled over the front door, announcing that someone had entered the store. She mouthed, "Maybe that's her."

Rosie opened her mouth to give Lia a hard time for even putting that thought in her head, but it wasn't a woman who'd come through the door. It was the mail carrier, Brad. With a shrug, Lia slipped out the door behind him, taking Brinkley with her.

"Hi, Brad. Can I help you with something?" Rosie asked, because he usually just put her mail in the slot outside the door.

"Hey, Rosie. I've got a certified letter for you that requires a signature." He set the envelope on the counter and slid a small tablet toward her.

"Oh, okay." She signed her name on the screen and handed the device back to him.

"Have a nice day," he said.

"You too." She turned her attention to the envelope. It was from Breslin Property Development, the company that had bought this building a few months ago, and since the letter came certified, it almost certainly wasn't good news. This was probably a notice that her rent was about to double or even triple. Rosie's stomach swooped, leaving her feeling vaguely nauseous. She ripped the tab and removed a bundle of paper with a letter on top.

Breslin Property Development
132 W 21st Street
New York, NY 10001

Ms. Taft,
This letter is to inform you that the lease for 1450 Lexington Avenue, New York, NY 10128, will terminate on December 31st and will not renew. I have attached a copy of the lease agreement for your reference.

Thank you for being such a reliable tenant, and please don't hesitate to contact me if you have any questions.

Sincerely,
Jane Breslin
Property Manager

"No," Rosie whispered, blinking at the paper as if it might somehow change the words printed there. This couldn't be happening. Breslin Property Development couldn't just kick her out of the space Between the Pages had occupied since before Rosie was born. Well, of course they *could*. But why? As the letter said, she'd been a reliable tenant. She always paid her rent on time and kept her inspections up to date.

She couldn't lose the store. She'd spent her whole life here. Memories of her mother inhabited every inch. As she swept her gaze around the room, Rosie saw her mom adjusting books in the window display, sitting in the red chair in the corner reading to a group of eager children, standing beside Rosie here at the counter. Her chest constricted painfully around her heart.

There must be a way to stop this. Frantically, she began to read through the attached lease agreement, looking for something to fight.

She was deep in rental-termination clauses when the bell over the door chimed, and she looked up to see Lia and Brinkley reentering the shop.

"It's so nice outside today," Lia said as she unclipped Brinkley's leash. "I just love fall weather—reminds me of home. You should sneak out for a walk of your own."

Rosie stared at her as tears blurred her vision.

"Rosie? Are you okay?"

She held up the paper with shaking fingers. "Breslin Property Development just terminated our lease."

Jane Breslin walked down Lexington Avenue as her nine-year-old niece, Alyssa, skipped ahead of her, brown ponytail bouncing with each step. Jane had helped her sister out of a bind by picking Alyssa up from school today, but it meant she'd had to bring her niece with her to a meeting with the architect on her upcoming renovation project, which hadn't been much fun for either of them.

"Look!" Alyssa exclaimed, stopping on the sidewalk. "A bookstore. Can we go in, Auntie Jane?"

Jane shook her head. She owned every building on this block, or Breslin Property Development did, anyway. She'd mailed a lease-termination letter to Between the Pages Bookstore earlier in the week, and the last thing she wanted was to go into a store she had probably just put out of business. "We've got to meet your mom soon."

"Fine," Alyssa said with a sigh.

Something familiar snagged Jane's attention out of the corner of her eye, and she glanced at the bookstore's window display.

No freaking way.

Brie's latest release, *On the Flip Side*, was featured prominently at the center of the display. Jane gaped at the book for a moment in disbelief before standing a little taller in her stilettos because . . . wow. When she'd released her first book as Brie, she'd made the decision to stay anonymous. She could only imagine what her coworkers and clients would say if they found out she wrote sexy books, and her parents—well, okay, mostly her dad—had openly scoffed at the idea of her becoming an author, so it had seemed easier to keep her two lives separate.

After a while, she'd started to like it this way. She could be buttoned up and professional at work, helping to transform outdated buildings into something modern and beautiful. And at night, she let out her inner romantic, penning scorching-hot romance novels about women finding love, which was ironic, since she wasn't overly concerned with romance in her own life. She was incurably awkward when it came to relationships, preferring to live vicariously through her characters.

After her first book was released, she'd gone into a few local bookstores, trying to spot it on the shelves just for fun, but she'd never found it. In five years, she'd never seen her book on a shelf.

Until today.

There it was in the window of a building she was about to demolish. Clearly, the universe was having a laugh at her expense.

"Oh my gosh, there's a dog in the store," Alyssa said, cupping her hands against the glass and peering between them. "Can we *please* go in?"

"Just for a minute." Jane relented, because really, what kind of aunt—or author—would she be if she refused to let her niece go in a bookstore?

Alyssa grasped the door's handle and pulled it open. A bell chimed overhead as Jane followed her into the store, and sure enough, a little brown dog trotted over to greet them. Alyssa knelt to rub its head, and the dog's tail wagged happily.

"Welcome to Between the Pages Bookstore," the woman behind the counter said. "Let me know if there's anything I can help you with."

Jane gave her a quick smile before returning her attention to Alyssa. She didn't want to notice anything about this store, not the neatly arranged shelves of books, the cute dog currently charming her niece, or the attractive woman behind the counter with her bouncy blonde curls. She especially didn't want to notice the way the blonde's gaze slid appreciatively over Jane's suit.

"What's his name?" Alyssa asked, looking at the blonde.

"That's Brinkley," she told her.

"Is he yours?" Alyssa asked, still rubbing the dog, who was sitting in front of her now, tongue out and looking thrilled by the attention.

"He is," the woman behind the counter confirmed. "This is my store too. I'm Rosie. What's your name?"

"Alyssa." She giggled as Brinkley licked her hand.

Jane feigned interest in the nearest display of books, because *shit*, that must be Rosie Taft, and there was a good chance she'd already received a lease-termination notice with Jane's name on it. She slid her fingertips over a row of mystery titles, listening as Alyssa and Rosie talked about books.

"Do you know any stories about dogs that have a happy ending?" Alyssa asked. "Because I *hate* when the dog dies at the end of the book."

"Oh, me too," Rosie agreed, and when Jane darted a glance in her direction, she had a hand pressed dramatically against her heart. "But luckily, I know a lot of books where the dogs live happily ever after. Do you want to read something set in the real world or more of a fantasy setting?"

Alyssa twisted her lips to one side as she pondered the question. "A fantasy world."

"Okay. And do you want the dog to be the main character, or would you rather read about a girl or boy who has a pet dog?"

"The dog as the main character," Alyssa answered without hesitation.

Rosie beamed at her. "I know just the book for you."

Alyssa followed her to the opposite side of the store, with Brinkley at her side. Jane watched them go, noticing another employee on the other side of the store, stocking books. The woman glanced in Jane's direction with a polite smile.

While she waited for her niece to decide on a book, Jane browsed on her own. A case full of colorful paperbacks drew her attention to the romance section. Of course she would gravitate here. Her gaze tracked automatically to the beginning of the alphabet. There were several Brie titles on the shelf.

Jane inhaled sharply, the rush of seeing her books on a shelf for the first time tempered by an unfamiliar surge of guilt. Why did this have to be the one store that carried her books? Breslin Property Development was going to demolish the existing structures on this block to put in a new condominium complex. It wasn't personal. Just business. But that didn't make her feel any less terrible when she saw Rosie and Alyssa walking in her direction, laughing like old friends.

"Is it okay if I get three?" Alyssa asked somewhat sheepishly as she displayed an armful of books.

"Sorry about that," Rosie said. She had the cutest dimples in her cheeks when she smiled, and she seemed to smile a lot. She was also younger than Jane would have expected the owner of the shop to be, likely younger than Jane herself. "Sometimes I have too many book recommendations for my own good."

"But look at them," Alyssa said, showing Jane a book featuring a sparkly dog running toward a castle, another depicting a girl about Alyssa's age hugging a puppy, and one with a ballerina in a pink tutu twirling across the cover.

"Those do look perfect for you," Jane said, giving her niece's ponytail a playful tug. "And yes, you can get all three."

"Thank you," Alyssa said, hugging the books against her chest.

"You're welcome." Jane had mixed feelings about this particular store, but she always tried to encourage Alyssa's love of reading.

"Can I help you find anything for yourself?" Rosie asked Jane, gesturing to the shelf behind her. "If you like romance, I have plenty of suggestions."

Jane shook her head. "Not today, but thank you."

"No problem. I can ring you up if you're ready," Rosie said, leading the way toward the counter in back. Brinkley trotted behind her and curled up in a dog bed against the wall.

Alyssa placed her new books on the counter. "Is that you?" she asked, pointing to a photograph on the shelf behind the counter, showing a blonde girl about Alyssa's age with a woman who was probably her mother. It looked like it had been taken right here in the store.

"It sure is," Rosie said, glancing over her shoulder. "That's me and my mom. She owned this store before me."

Great, like Jane needed one more thing to feel guilty about. Her gaze landed on the envelope from Breslin Property Development beside the cash register, and she quickly looked away.

"Cool," Alyssa said, watching as Rosie rang up her purchases.

She scanned each of the bar codes and tucked the books into a blue paper bag with the store's logo on it. "That'll be thirty-four twelve."

Jane pulled her wallet out of her bag, but she couldn't bring herself to let Rosie see the name on her credit card, not after she'd been so sweet to Alyssa. Instead, she pulled out two twenties and handed them to her niece. "Would you like to pay for the books yourself?"

Alyssa nodded, passing the bills to Rosie.

"Thank you," Rosie said as she took them. "I don't think I've seen you in the shop before. Do you live around here?"

Jane shook her head. "I had a meeting nearby."

"And you went with your mom to her meeting?" Rosie asked Alyssa. Alyssa grinned, shaking her head. "She's my aunt."

"I'm just helping her mom out of a childcare jam this afternoon," Jane said.

"My mom and my aunt work together," Alyssa told Rosie.

"Oh, that's fun," Rosie said as she handed Jane's change to her. "Well, I'm glad you got some new books out of the deal."

"And I got to meet Brinkley," Alyssa added, walking behind the counter to pet him. His tail thumped against the dog bed.

"Well, if you're ever in the neighborhood again, stop in," Rosie said. Then she looked down at the envelope from BPD, and the sparkle in her blue eyes dulled.

"I'll do that," Jane said. "Alyssa, we need to get going or we'll be late to meet your mom."

Alyssa hurried over and picked up the bag of books. "Bye, Rosie."

"Bye, Alyssa. It was nice meeting you." Rosie waved as they headed for the door.

"She was so nice," Alyssa said as they pushed through the door onto the street.

"She was," Jane agreed, darting one last glance at her book in the window. She really wanted to take a photo, but Rosie was just on the other side of the display, and Jane didn't want to draw attention to herself.

She and Alyssa walked two blocks to the Ninety-Sixth Street subway station and boarded the 6 train, headed downtown. Twenty minutes later, they exited at Grand Central Terminal, where Jane's sister, Amy, was waiting for them. Alyssa was still talking about her new books and the nice lady in the bookstore when Jane left them.

Yes, Rosie was nice. Pretty too. Maybe she'd reopen her store in a new location after she left her current space on Lexington Ave. Actually, Jane hoped she would. She boarded another train, headed for her apartment in Greenwich Village.

While she rode, she checked the messages on her phone, hoping she might have heard from @AureliaRose113. At first, it had been weird for Jane, messaging with one of her readers, especially since she wasn't very active on social media, but she and Aurelia seemed to have a lot in common, and before she knew it, they were chatting about everything from favorite books to dating woes. Jane opened a new message and began to type.

@BrieWrites: How was your day?

@AureliaRose113: Shitty. Tell me about yours instead.

@BrieWrites: Sorry to hear that. Mine wasn't great either. Actually, I'm pretty sure I ruined someone's day, in a roundabout way. 😟

@AureliaRose113: You?! I can't imagine that.

@BrieWrites: It's complicated. I was just doing my job, but I still feel bad about how the whole thing played out.

@AureliaRose113: Aww, I'm sure the person knew that.

@BrieWrites: Thanks. That makes me feel a little better about it.

@AureliaRose113: I'm glad.

@BrieWrites: Read anything new I should add to my wish list?

@AureliaRose113: If you're in the mood for a romance, I know just the thing.

@BrieWrites: I'm *always* in the mood for romance.

Aurelia told her about a new series set in London, and by the time Jane exited the subway, she'd already downloaded the first book and read a few pages. As promised, it was delightful. Aurelia had yet to steer her wrong with a book recommendation. Jane climbed the steps to the street, wishing she'd brought flats to change into, because her feet were killing her in these heels and she still had a four-block walk ahead of her.

As she walked, her thoughts drifted to Rosie Taft. For a moment when Jane had first walked into the store, she'd been sure Rosie was checking her out, although she certainly wouldn't have been interested if she'd known Jane's name. And wasn't that just the story of her life? She never seemed to have her timing right when it came to dating.

Luckily, she was a lot better at writing romance than experiencing it. On the page, she had control of all the variables and could guarantee a happy ending for her characters. She thought of Brie's book in the display window. Did Rosie read her books? Jane had a vague memory of a bookstore owner contacting her for a signing a few years ago. Had that been Rosie?

Finally, Jane let herself into her building, grateful for her first-floor apartment so she wouldn't have to take another set of stairs in these heels. She walked straight down the hall to her bedroom to change into a T-shirt and lounge pants and then backtracked to the kitchen to pour herself a glass of wine.

She was on a tight deadline with her latest book, which meant she'd be writing until she went to bed. But first, she picked up her phone and tapped out a quick message to Aurelia.

ABOUT THE AUTHOR

Rachel Lacey is an award-winning contemporary romance author and semireformed travel junkie. She's been climbed by a monkey on a mountain in Japan, gone scuba diving on the Great Barrier Reef, and camped out overnight in New York City for a chance to be an extra in a movie. These days, the majority of her adventures take place on the pages of the books she writes. She lives in warm and sunny North Carolina with her family and a variety of rescue pets.

Rachel loves to keep in touch with her readers, who can subscribe to her e-newsletter for exclusive news and giveaways (http://subscribepage.com/rachellaceyauthor). Visit her at www.RachelLacey.com or on Facebook at www.Facebook.com/RachelLaceyAuthor, and don't forget to follow her on Twitter (@rachelslacey).